Nightfall

Peter B Hoole

10/11/16

ISBN: 0995397406

ISBN 13: 9780995397408

For Amy

Chapter One

It had been hours since his world changed. The information he'd stumbled across had sent shivers down his spine.

Paul was a solid reporter. Up until that day, the biggest story he'd covered had been the Hawkins assassination. And up until the previous night, he'd thought it would remain that way. Hell, people were still talking about Lincoln and Booth almost one hundred and fifty years after it happened. And that was in a time before the internet, before smart phones and satellites. People would be talking about the death of John Hawkins long after Paul was gone.

Or so he'd thought.

What he had just discovered was bigger than that. What he'd found out was enough to change everything.

It would certainly mean his death if he was ever discovered to be the source of the information. There were some very powerful people who would be implicated once Paul broke the story - people who would surely stop at nothing to prevent the truth from getting out.

He was scared.

Although he'd covered his tracks, Paul was no secret agent, no spy. He hadn't had training of any real significance, but when the occasion had called for it, he was able to sneak around. So he'd done what he thought was necessary.

He'd worn dark clothes. He'd made sure he kept his gaze lowered, so no security cameras caught clear vision of his face. He'd worn latex gloves, so no finger prints could be found. He'd slipped into the facility unobtrusively, and he was sure no one had seen him.

He'd been a little surprised by the lack of security, but he figured that was due to the remote location. While inside the complex, he'd managed to take a couple of photos and scan some documents.

While the photos were unnerving, what was written in the documents was beyond comprehension. He didn't dare to stay too long, and after less than ten minutes, he'd made his way back to the motel where he was staying.

Right after he returned to the motel, he sent the pictures to Darcy, in Los Angeles. It had been several hours since then, and he still hadn't heard back. With L.A. being more than half a day behind, time-wise, it would have been received by Darcy in the late afternoon. He thought he would have heard back from her by now. The fact that she had remained silent only exacerbated his nerves.

He would have left the small town earlier, but feared he would be noticed. So he'd decided to briefly lay-low in the small motel room. He planned to leave when he was certain he hadn't been followed; when he was confident he could escape without detection.

As time passed, he'd grown steadily more comfortable that nobody had noticed his movements during his stay. He figured if someone was coming for him, they would have been there by that point.

Though he found the thought unsettling, he would need to venture out to the store to grab some supplies before he hit the road. He hadn't eaten all day and now he was hungry – to the point of discomfort. The small town's main store was only a block from the motel.

As he left the motel room, he realised the surrounding area was empty. Not unusual for a small town, he'd barely sighted anyone since he had arrived. The only interactions he'd experience were with the motel owner and the store clerk.

As he walk down the road to the store, the wind swept through his thinning brown hair. Paul had always been average. Brown hair, about five-foot-nine and a hundred and seventy-five pounds, he had always seen his averageness as an advantage – always able to fit into any crowd with ease. The only problems came when he actually wanted to be noticed – with the ladies.

Now that he had this story, he knew that, if he could manage to return home and break the story, this would no longer be an issue.

When he arrived at the store, it was as he'd expected - the place was empty, with only the short, frumpy middle-aged woman standing behind the counter. Something about her made him uneasy. Though friendly enough, she seemed distracted.

"You still here?" Her thick Australian accent was still unfamiliar to him.

"Mm hmm," Paul replied, not wanting to get caught up in a conversation.

"We don't get many people staying," she continued "Can I help you find something?"

Paul, ignored her and proceeded down the neatly-stocked aisles. The woman wasn't lying about the lack of people staying in the town. All the shelves looked untouched. They were neatly stacked with the usual convenience store products – toothpaste, breakfast cereals and soaps, but it was as though the store hadn't ever been used by anyone, visitor or local.

"Don't get many visitors, do you?" Paul asked the clerk, although the answer was obvious.

"Not usually, love," she replied. "Only people we get around here are on their way somewhere else. Where you headin'?"

"Back to Sydney," Paul said.

"Oh yeah... that's right. Anyway, help yourself. Give us a shout when you're right".

The clerk left the counter and disappeared into the storeroom at the back of the store. Paul had a quick look around. While there was an abundance of items, there wasn't an abundance of choice. Paul grabbed a couple of bottles of water and a sandwich, before he approached the counter and called out to the clerk.

When she reappeared, she seemed more relaxed. "That'll be eighteen dollars sixty," she announced.

Paul was aware that country prices in Australia were high, but he still wasn't used to it. On any other day, he would have been outraged. Today, he was just happy to leave.

"Thanks," Paul said, turning to leave.

"No worries."

Paul stepped out of the store, turning to head back to the motel. As he did, he noticed a man on the corner, standing between him and his motel room. The sight of the man caused him some concern.

Not wanting to take any risks, Paul turned in the other direction, hoping to swing around the back of the store and avoid the man. As he strode away, he sensed the man was following him. Paul turned around the corner of the store, hoping the man would continue walking down the street.

He didn't.

The man turned down the same road. Paul kept walking, with more purpose in his step.

As the footsteps quickened behind him, Paul realised there was urgency in his shadow's pace. To try and lose the man, Paul continued down the street. His nerves tensed further with each step. He came to a standstill, pretending as though he was about to cross the road. When he stopped, so did the footsteps behind him.

Paul didn't know whether the man was still there, or if he'd hidden somewhere behind him. He decided against looking back, and continued down the street, hoping the next intersection would lead him back towards his motel room, and more importantly, his car.

The further he walked, the more his concern grew. When he paused, the man trailing him paused. When he walked, the footsteps could be heard distinctly coming from behind him.

The man wasn't being subtle. It was as though his purpose was to frighten Paul into making a mistake.

Of course there's someone there, Paul thought to himself. They wouldn't let him walk around knowing what he knew. What he'd discovered would change the world, and the people who were behind it would stop at nothing to avoid the information being revealed.

Considering his options, Paul began to walk steadily faster, reacting to the speed of his pursuer rather than setting the pace. Paul threw the items he'd bought into a bin, preparing to run.

Find some people. Get to where they are. Get to your car.

Paul began to run, giving it all he had. Running as fast as his jeans and sneakers would let him.

He tried to remember the details from the map of the town he'd downloaded. Never having travelled there before – in fact, he hadn't even heard of the place until a week ago – Paul only had a basic sense of where he was in relationship to the motel. And currently, he was not in a good position. Though surrounded by trees and bushland, outback towns provided very few places to hide in the streets.

Turning down another street, Paul saw an intersection and remembered it from the map. *This will get me to the car,* he thought.

He ran for the turn-off as fast as he could, his jacket now acting like a weight, seeming to hold him back. His breathing grew faster and deeper, and he couldn't hear the sound of the footsteps any longer. *Almost there,* he thought, *just keep going. I think you've lost him.*

Paul came to the intersection and made a hasty left turn.

"Oh shit", Paul muttered, breathing heavily. He'd turned directly into a dead-end; in the spot where he'd thought he would see his car, all Paul saw was a wooden fence.

Hoping he'd built up some distance between himself and his pursuer, Paul spun around to exit the blocked street.

"Don't fucking move" the other man said breathlessly.

"An American?" Paul was startled to hear the familiar accent.

The man was much bigger than him. Paul, still trying to catch his breath, scanned the street, hoping there would be another option, some way he could escape from his current predicament.

"Put up your hands", said the man. "Slowly".

Not wanting to further rile his pursuer, Paul complied with the request. Not that it really mattered. The only things Paul had on his body to protect himself with were his phone and wallet.

"Who..." Paul began, still breathless, "who are you?"

Paul wasn't certain why he asked, because he really didn't care. He already knew why the man had been sent.

Standing about six foot tall, the man towered over Paul, his presence more than enough to intimidate. His physique also implied many months, even years of training. But the thing that stood out most to Paul was his eyes.

There was a burning anger, bordering on hatred, in the man's eyes.

Paul had thought they'd send a professional, a hit-man. Someone who would chase him, catch him and kill him. But the man in front of him seemed anything but the quintessential killer. He was more... human. The emotion he displayed was of a man not used to killing. In fact, it was the one thing that gave Paul hope – hope that he may survive.

That concerned Paul even more. The man had not been chasing him because he was 'following orders'. He had been chasing him for much more personal reasons.

"How dare you?" said the man.

"What do you mean?" Paul stammered, now a bit confused.

"The plan is there," explained the man. "It has been in place since before we were born. How dare you think you can change any of it?"

Frozen, Paul could barely muster a response. "I... I... What can I say?"

"Say for what?"

"Wh... what do I have to do to stay alive?" Paul asked, the desperation apparent in his voice. He waited for a response for what seemed an eternity.

The man, his gun still firmly trained on Paul, finally responded. "We have been planning this for so long," he began, his anger now palpable, "and you dare to try and take it all away. Why? So you could get a story? So you could be famous? You would take away my daughter's life. My wife's life? Just so you can sell a fucking story?"

Paul's fear escalated. It seemed clear that these were going to be his last few moments. If only he could convince his captor to keep him alive. If only he could prove he wasn't a threat.

"I didn't get much…" Paul said, desperately, "I hardly saw anything!"

"Shut the fuck up. You've brought this on yourself."

Without warning, two dark SUV's pulled silently into the street behind the man. As they stopped, the doors opened and some people exited the vehicle.

One of the figures shone a flashlight at Paul. As the last of them exited the car, he spoke. "Well done Leon… Did you get his phone?"

"Not yet", replied Leon, as the man came over to stand next to him.

"Go get it then," ordered the man, apparently Leon's superior. His English accent was clear, his words clipped.

Leon kept his gun trained on Paul, and moved steadily towards him.

"It's in my back pocket," Paul said, slowly turning his hips to give the man access.

Leon looked back, towards the group of four men who had gathered next to his superior. Paul followed his gaze. The men had produced guns of their own. Upon seeing this, Leon put his own gun away.

"Good. Well done Leon," said the man, "Now grab the phone".

Leon took the phone from Paul's pocket, and handed it to the Englishman, who searched through the phone, poking and swiping at the screen. He obviously found what he was searching for and glanced up at Paul. "Did you send this to anyone?" he asked.

Paul got the impression the man already knew the answer, but sensed a way of escaping his current, precarious situation.

"Of course I did," Paul replied. "I needed to have some insurance"

"Ahhh, Paul…" the Englishman said, surprising Paul with the knowledge that he knew his name. "Don't get your hopes up. You will die tonight."

Ice flowed through Paul's veins. "If you let me go, I'll tell you who I sent it to…" Paul pleaded.

"Thank You Paul. A very nice gesture…" the Englishman paused, "but I think we can find Darcy on our own".

Fear was the only emotion Paul now knew. "Help Me!" Paul cried out. "Somebody please help!"

The Englishman let out a loud, booming laugh.

"Paul… just calm down. No one can hear you," he said. "Or rather, people can hear you… they just don't care."

Paul looked out into the street, and to his mounting horror, he saw the motel owner and the store clerk both standing behind the Englishman, guns drawn and pointed at Paul.

"Paul, you look confused," the Englishman began. "Do you really think you would have been here, if we didn't allow you to be? Do you really think you could have gotten this close to our plan, without us knowing? You've got it all back to front. You remember what you saw last night, yeah? Below the surface?"

Paul nodded.

"We didn't build that *below* the town… we built the town *over* that. Everything you see here. The store, the motel, the roads… even the people. It's all ours. Paul, there is nowhere to run to." The Englishman smiled, a cold smile which chilled Paul to the bone.

"Now?" Leon asked, drawing his gun again.

Paul was frozen. He knew exactly what Leon meant with that one word.

The Englishman turned to Leon, and paused, long enough for the sweat to trickle from Paul's temple and down his cheek. "Now" he said, coldly.

With that, Leon pulled the trigger. A bright flash burst forth from the muzzle of Leon's gun. A flash that would prove to be the last thing Paul ever saw.

Paul's limp body slumped to the ground, blood spraying across the wall behind him. The bullet had hit him, straight between the eyes.

For a brief moment, the gathered men stood and stared at Paul's fallen body.

"Well done, Leon," the Englishman said. "That was a perfect take-down, start to finish."

Leon beamed, having spent a lot of time training and waiting for his moment.

"You were patient, precise and most importantly, you didn't hesitate when it mattered."

"Thank you, sir."

"No *thank you* is required Leon. You took a big step tonight."

"Sir... does that mean we're in? My family and I?"

The Englishman paused for a moment and turned to the others. "You three," he announced, pointing to Paul's body. "Clean that up".

They moved in to do as they were told and the Englishman turned his attention back to Leon. "Not quite... there is one more thing I need you to do..."

"Anything!" Leon exclaimed.

"Leon," the Englishman began "Have you ever been to Los Angeles?"

Chapter Two

Trudging through the dense bush had always been difficult. It was a track Emmett had walked so many times, it had become second nature, but that didn't make it any easier. He could remember each turn, each shrub. He knew how many steps were between his car and the peak – two hundred and twenty-five - the distance to the ideal location.

And though he'd practised with a similar object, the package he now carried seemed much more cumbersome than what he'd prepared for. The discomfort didn't concern him, because he was about to prove his worth.

"You're changing the world now." Emmett reminded himself of his mentor's words. *"What you now know about where the world has been, and where it is, and where it will be… you are part of it. Once your task is complete, you will have guaranteed your place in the future."*

Emmett reached the opening between the trees. He stood and gazed down upon the view he'd seen so many times before. It was a view he had etched in his memory.

"I don't know when we will need you." He remembered the words from his last encounter. *"But we need you to be ready. When the call comes, you will need to take action."*

Pierre, Emmett's mentor, had told him everything he needed to know. Where to set up and what to bring. Most importantly, Pierre had taught Emmett how to *use* the equipment.

Emmett gently lowered the package onto the ground, next to where he had marked the hole dug on a previous visit. Kneeling, he brushed away the dirt and loose branches he'd placed over the wooden cover.

The flimsy piece of balsa wood came away easily, exposing the hole. Only about a foot and a half deep, the hole measured just over five feet in length and two feet in width.

He removed the blanket he'd wrapped around the package, and carefully placed it into the hole.

It fitted perfectly.

Emmett's body relaxed. His job was mostly done.

Now, all he had to do was wait.

He hoped he wouldn't have to wait long.

After placing the balsa over the box, Emmett spread the dirt and leaves back where they'd been.

After Emmett restored the camouflage, he stood and took one last look at the view. The large building opposite was relatively quiet, save for a few workers. There was little to no noise emanating from the building. No people were evident, and if it had not been for the workers in front, Emmett may have assumed the building was vacant. It appeared just as it always did at this time in the morning.

Emmett paused and considered his impending actions. There would be many lives affected by his activities, both in the long and short term. Indeed, many lives would be lost. The guilt of affecting so many lives did, at times, strain his conscience.

But Emmett was committed to the cause.

He was committed to the plan.

How could I not be, Emmett thought as he smiled.

He had turned to walk away, when his phone vibrated in his pocket. He answered the throw-away cell.

"Pierre?"

"Emmett," his mentor said. "How did you go? Did you get it?"

"Yes, I did"

"Is it in place?"

"Yes"

"And you've timed yourself? How long does it take?"

"It can be completed in twenty minutes."

"Really? That quick?" Pierre asked, seemingly impressed by Emmett's efficiency.

"I have practised," Emmett replied, smiling again.

"Excellent! Well, it won't be long now."

"Has the time been set?"

"Indeed it has. I will notify you soon." Pierre paused briefly before he spoke again, and Emmett thought he was making an effort to sound sincere. "Emmett?"

"Yes?"

"Well done." With that, Pierre disconnected the call.

Emmett hadn't expected praise. When Pierre had brought Emmett into the plan, he hadn't proven to be the father figure Emmett had expected. Instead, he'd been a harsh teacher, who had, on more than one occasion, publicly and painfully belittled Emmett in front of others.

While Emmett had always been imposing figure. Standing at six feet, he had always towered over his classmates. Everything he tried, he was the best at. Despite this, Pierre always seemed to find a way to make Emmett feel as though his achievements meant nothing.

But all that seemed so long ago.

Emmett turned to once again look at the view.

A loud noise filled the air, and Emmett steered his gaze away from the airport terminal.

From the north, a plane was coming in to land.

Emmett held his hands close to his eyes and formed them into an imaginary telescope.

Again, the secret smile crept across his face.

A target that big should be easy to shoot down.

Chapter Three

Darcy woke with a start. The loud shrill of the alarm emitted by her cell-phone was enough to force her awake. She struggled for a moment, because she hadn't slept well. Her thoughts had dwelled on the email she'd received the previous day. Paul hadn't given her much information.

> **Hi Darc,**
> **Still Down Under**
> **Keep these safe.**
> **I'll be back in a couple of days.**
> **Trust me… this is huge.**
> **P**

Darcy had to send a reply from her phone, asking Paul what she was looking at, as when she'd opened the files, all she'd seen were pixelated images. The only exception had been the last file, which opened on a blank screen.

Paul had always been competitive, but Darcy had thought he trusted her. Why he couldn't have sent a bit more information with the pictures, Darcy didn't know. She didn't even know why he was in Australia.

She had thought about it all night. Even the presence of Caleb, her long term partner, the previous night hadn't been enough to distract her.

After getting a nudge from Caleb, she turned off the alarm. She reached her arms perpendicular to the bed, and spread them wide, as if she was creating a half snow angel above the bed. On the down sweep, she managed to nudge Caleb back.

"Humph," Caleb grunted, as her firm touch roused him.

"Come on, time to move, soldier," Darcy said

"Hmmm… couple more minutes…" Caleb groaned as he rolled over.

"Couple more minutes?" Darcy exclaimed, now wide awake. "I thought you Army guys were made of sterner stuff?"

"Hmmm…" Caleb grumbled. "Marines, you mean?"

"Okay then, Marine boy. Up and at 'em" Darcy chuckled.

With a groan, Caleb sat up on the side of the bed and picked up his watch. It was 6:00am. *Why the hell am I getting up this early?* Caleb thought to himself.

For the most part, Caleb had had a great time since enlisting in the Marines, but the last couple of months had been trying. Starting as a grunt, straight from the enlistment office, Caleb had flourished under the regime and philosophy of the Corps. This reflected in his work, and it didn't take too long before he was recognized among the elite. He had established himself as one of the best fighters, marksmen and leaders the Corps had seen. His range of missions varied, with Caleb being one of the first Marines on the ground in Africa, and his work during the conflicts in the Middle East had been seen by his superiors as outstanding. And those were the engagements he *could* discuss.

After his first few years, Caleb had attained the rank of Captain and been tasked with forming his own team.

Caleb had sourced the best of the best. There were five team members at the start, but eventually that grew, with the success of missions in Beijing, Pyongyang, Havana and even more friendly places such as London, Berlin, Sydney and Wellington. Eventually, Caleb had more than a two dozen team members situated across multiple locations.

The nature of their work wasn't what Caleb had initially expected it to be. Most of the time, they were charged with getting into a building, finding some information – sometimes stealing equipment – and then returning with the information to their direct supervisor.

'Aggressive hacking' was how Caleb had come to refer to it. That's not to say the work wasn't dangerous. On all but one occasion, the mission had called for lives to be taken, and there were also lives lost. While

Caleb lamented the loss of life, he was still a solider, and he accepted the truth that sometimes, soldiers die.

For the first few years of their missions, Caleb and his team answered to Michael Dunleavy, the then Chief-of-Staff to the President. Caleb was initially honoured by the job. He had been a long-time admirer of the President, and had always seen the leader of the country as a revered position.

After a time though, Caleb had become increasingly concerned about the missions they were being asked to perform. At first, they were simple, and it was easy to interpret why they had been considered necessary. "Go to Beijing, and bring back the information," Caleb was told.

He understood that.

China, while not officially an enemy combatant, still held many secrets the United States needed to know.

But Britain, Australia, Germany – and others – they were supposed to be trusted allies. Why was he being asked to go there and steal information? Wasn't it breaking some treaty or something?

Over time, as happens with all administrations, Dunleavy left the oval office, citing stress and burn-out. For several weeks, Caleb and his team had received no further instructions. While not unusual, the fact was that the only person Caleb had ever received orders from in the past, was no longer in the job. Caleb had assumed that he would be contacted by the next person to take on the role, in due course.

After a time, he'd started receiving his orders straight from the top – directly from President Hawkins. In fact, it was Caleb who Hawkins was on the phone to, when he'd been abruptly cut-off. The reason for Hawkins' call was never apparent to Caleb. The only part he remembered was when the President referred to "The Source". That was all the information he had received, and for the past few months, Caleb not been able to figure out why it was so important.

Later that evening, news broke of Hawkins' assassination.

After that call, Caleb hadn't received any orders. Not from the new President. Not from his Chief-of-Staff. Not even from his old commanding officer.

For some unknown reason, Caleb and his team had been cut-off, and now he needed answers.

As he rolled out of bed, he contemplated his next move.

It's been long enough, Caleb thought of the months that had passed, *time to figure it out*.

"You okay babe?" asked Darcy.

"Sure..." Caleb replied easily, wanting to assuage the worry he could hear in her voice. "It's just... work."

Caleb hadn't told Darcy much about the details of his work. He told himself it was because he wasn't allowed to tell her. But deep down, he knew it was for his own self-preservation. If Darcy knew half the things he'd done, half the number of people he'd killed, Caleb worried how Darcy would view him.

The thought of possibly losing Darcy was more than he could bear. He would do anything for her, even if that meant keeping things from her.

"I know just the thing," Darcy said with a wink.

"Oh really?" said Caleb, winking back. The memories of their previous night of love-making wasn't far from his mind.

"Wait right here," Darcy ordered as she left the bed, "I'll be right back."

She left the room, and Caleb leaned back against the bedhead, wondering what she was up to. When she reappeared, a couple of minutes later, she was carrying a blueberry muffin in one hand, her laptop in the other.

"Oh baby, you know me too well," Caleb said, offering her a bright smile.

"Anything for you, babe," Darcy said, her wink even more playful than before.

She handed the muffin to Caleb, and settled back on the bed.

Darcy opened up the laptop while Caleb enjoyed the muffin. When she looked down, her hair fell down over her eyes and Caleb suppressed the urge to push it back for her. When the screen fired up, he noticed it was open on an email Darcy had received and he swallowed a mouthful of the muffin, staring at the screen.

"Babe..." Caleb said, straightening up to get a better view of the screen, "where did that come from?"

"Ummm..." Darcy began, studying the screen, "Paul sent it yesterday."

Caleb put down the muffin and took the laptop from Darcy, despite her protests. He looked at the description on the last attachment. "Paul? Why would Paul send this to you?" Caleb asked.

Darcy shrugged. "No idea... he sometimes sends me stuff as a back-up, in case his computer gets fried."

"Did he tell you what it's about?"

"Nope. All the information I got is in there. That's all he sent."

"Darc... this is important!" Caleb snapped.

Darcy's eyes widened. "Okay, Caleb... I get it... What's so important?"

"I'm not sure yet... but... do you know what that is?" Caleb pointed to the last attachment.

"No idea. It didn't do anything when I opened it... just showed me a blank screen"

"Shit," Caleb said.

"What? What is it?" Darcy asked, sounding anxious.

Caleb paused, and took a deep breath, feeling the adrenalin beginning to pound beneath his skin. "Darcy... that's a tracking program..."

Chapter Four

The tall, strongly built man walked down the corridor. As he passed the hundreds of people who were coming and going, Leon suffered his first tinge of remorse.

While his role in the plan was minor; more-or-less tying up loose ends and acting as back-up, Leon knew he was making his contribution. And that contribution was not a positive one for these people.

He steadily made his way towards his destination, not wanting to draw any attention.

He remembered his training, particularly the reasons he was chosen by the Englishman. He was, in the Englishman's words, *normal*. As far as the description went, Leon had to agree.

Prior to his first encounter with the Englishman, Leon had worked as an orderly at Miami General. He had always had ambitions of improving his social standing, and when he'd enrolled in college, he became the first of his family to do so. He even planned on doing some post-graduate studies after he finished, possibly in marine biology or something similar.

Then, at just nineteen, in the infancy of his degree, he'd met Josie.

Josie had quickly become the love of his life. They were inseparable and after a brief courtship, they married. This was against the advice of pretty much everyone, including his family.

Still at college, Leon continued to do well, achieving excellent scores in most classes and his plans remained firmly on track, despite the slight detour of adding a wife to his path.

Then, towards the end of his freshman year, Josie fell pregnant with their first son, Aaron. Leon's son was born in the December of that year, his daughter Lilly following the year after. Though he only had a year and a half left to obtain his degree, Leon had few choices left. He asked his family for help, but after their objections to his marriage, he wasn't surprised when they refused to give him any financial help.

With a wife and two young children to support, Leon was down to his only viable choice. He left college and took up work, wherever he could find it. He eventually ended up employed as an orderly, a job he despised, but none-the-less appreciated for the steady pay check it provided. After all, work wasn't easy to find, especially for an unqualified college dropout.

For several months, Leon toiled in his work, hating every moment of the menial occupation. Over time, he started to come to terms with his lot.

Then, he met the Englishman. He was approached at work, and offered a free meal and Leon couldn't see the harm in accepting.

It was over that dinner when the Englishman offered Leon an opportunity. An opportunity that would not only change his life, but would ensure his family would flourish well into the future.

It was an opportunity Leon simply couldn't refuse.

After accepting, Leon began devoting much of his time and energy to the wishes of the Englishman. It was during this time when Leon came to realise and appreciate the true nature of the work required of him.

Last night was the first time he'd been set a task that didn't require direct supervision. The Englishman had made all the decisions previously, and pulled the trigger if required.

The night before was the first time Leon had done it himself.

It was the first time Leon had killed a man. He was surprised he hadn't felt any remorse.

Perhaps it was his conditioning. Perhaps it was the thought of setting up a viable future for his family.

Perhaps it was his rage at the journalist, who had dared to threaten that future.

Or, perhaps it was just his nature, but Leon had been surprised by just how easy it had been to pull the trigger.

He pondered this as he walked to the departure gate, approaching the security inspection.

Remember your training, Leon thought.

Leon slowed his breathing, deliberately returning his elevated heart-beat to normal.

He thought about his family, and the future they would have. The prospect calmed him. He even managed a smile when he handed his bag and laptop to the bored, middle-aged blonde who was responsible for placing items on the belt.

His carry bag disappeared into the X-Ray machine, and Leon walked through the security scanner, knowing there was nothing in his bag or on his body which would cause the security officials to stop him.

His last remaining concern was the final sweep. He hoped the bomb he'd handled recently hadn't left any residue on his skin or clothing. Leon picked up his bag from the rollers – it had passed through the X-Ray without any issues – and proceeded towards the waiting security officers. To his relief, he simply walked past them, unhindered.

One more step, he thought.

Needing only to clear the customs line, Leon readied his passport. He opened it, repeating the contents to himself, one more time.

The only part of the document that Leon recognised as true, was the photo. According to the small book, Leon was a Canadian resident, from Maple Ridge, British Columbia. He had been born on July ninth, 1981. *Do I really look that old?* He thought.

His name, according to his documentation, was Frederick Jerome Crenshaw. As he was leaving the country, it would be easier to pass through the security area, as the officials would ask fewer questions.

He arrived at the desk and managed to conjure up a smile.

Now all he had to do was wait.

After finding his gate and a place to sit, Leon reached into his pocket and pulled out his phone.

He dialled the only number stored in the memory of the phone.

"Leon?" The Englishman answered on the first ring.

"Yes," Leon replied.

"Are you through?"

"Of course." Leon smiled, the confidence he'd experienced after yesterday's task returning.

"Good. We have the location and have made the drop-box. You'll need to get it done fast. Check your email. All the details are there. Use the cipher from the London office. Call me when you arrive, okay?"

"Yes, sir."

"Good luck, Leon. Remember… you get this done, and your family's future is assured."

Leon smiled at the last comment, "I won't let you down, sir."

"I know you won't".

With that, the Englishman hung up.

Buoyed by the conversation, Leon turned off his phone, opened his laptop and settled it the table he had sat down at.

Using a mobile broadband stick, he opened his email account – a private website that had firewalls in place. The only email he had was from the same name all his emails came from on this account – Molyneux Industries. There was no text in the body of the email, just an attachment. The attachment appeared to be a normal JPEG, but Leon knew this was a disguise. He opened the attachment, and a pop-up asked for the Entry Code. He entered the cipher from London, as the Englishman had told him.

The attachment expanded into three documents.

The first was a map of greater Los Angeles. There were two points indicated. The first marked by a star, indicating the target location. The second marked by a circle, indicating the drop-box.

The second document was a set a building schematics, no doubt those for the target location. It had an apartment on the second floor highlighted.

Leon opened the third document and what he saw surprised him. The image of the woman was beautiful, reminding him briefly of Josie.

This girl was different to his wife though, with much shorter brunette hair, which barely covered her ears.

The other feature t stood out were her eyes. Although a beautiful shade of green, it was the kindness in them that stood out. Leon suspected the woman could easily have been a model or an actress, destined for a future of parading down catwalks or shining on the big screen.

Leon knew, however, that this wasn't the case. This woman had no future – she was his target. She was the only thing standing between his family and their future.

She must die, he thought.

Leon glanced at the words printed at the bottom of the picture.

"Priority Target", the sentence began.

He read her name.

"Darcy Chamberlain."

◆ ◆ ◆

The Englishman sat silent after he hung up the phone. He had worked with Leon for the past few years. For all that time, he'd kept some vital aspects of the plan from him. It would have been a mistake to provide Leon with all of its major aspects. However, he did need to share some information.

Leon knew what was happening under Haven, the town where they'd disposed of the reporter the previous night. And he also knew the basics of the overall plan.

What the Englishman was contemplating now, was the next step to take with Leon. He had no doubt Leon would complete his task. He had confidence the female reporter would be dead within the next twenty-four hours.

Unfortunately for Leon, the Englishman was now contemplating whether he would be of benefit to the plan in the long-term. After it all came to fruition, would Leon and his family help, or hinder the cause?

It was a question the Englishman had been mulling over for several months. He was receiving pressure from the Council, to ensure his final group was ready in time. How much time he had left, he didn't know. All the Englishman knew, was that he had to be sure Leon was a capable and appropriate choice for the next phase.

Last night, Leon had performed well, and the Englishman's confidence in him had grown.

The Englishman had been monitoring Leon's progress the previous day, and, despite Leon's mistake of forgetting the jamming signal, the Englishman was able to scramble the images the reporter sent to his contact. He'd also managed to hack Darcy Chamberlain's email account and attach a further file, one that when activated, would send them a GPS tracking signal.

With this, the Englishman had located Darcy Chamberlain, and using his contact in the FBI, had gathered all the information available on their subject.

Leon had done well with the execution last night, but not nearly well enough in protecting the overall plan.

So now – so close to beginning Phase Two, the Englishman had to make a decision.

He pulled his cell phone from his jacket pocket, and chose the number he'd dialled many times previously.

The phone rang only once, and a familiar voice answered.

"William?" asked the Canadian voice.

"Hello Pierre," William responded. "How are things faring in Zone Three?"

"Things are progressing well. We've got an asset in place to take out the plane. Hopefully, we'll have the go-ahead on that soon. How are things in 'One'? Still keeping it all safe?"

"Indeed we are. I just need your help with something."

"Of course," replied Pierre. "Anything for the cause."

William smiled. His old friend had never let him down before. They were bound by something that withstood any and all outside pressure. They were bound by their faith in the plan. They would both be beneficiaries of the outcome, assured by the Council. And with Phase Two so close, they would both do anything necessary to see it through.

"I have a new target for you Pierre…" William began, "one of ours."

"Okay," said Pierre, not surprised to hear their numbers were being cut down so close to Phase Two. "What are the details?"

"I'll send you a photograph. He's could be hard to take out, so whoever you send needs to be good."

"I've got just the guy."

"Good. The target will be arriving at LAX in about twenty hours…"

Chapter Five

"What do you mean, tracking?" Darcy asked, her eyes firmly focused on the final attachment.

"I've seen this before..." Caleb began, "It was in Berlin. We were sent on a mission to retrieve some documents and equipment. Nothing all that interesting, really. Standard stuff. A couple of loose files and some hardware..."

Darcy knew everything about Caleb, except anything related to his work. And for the most part, it didn't bother her. Such was her relationship with him, she knew he could always be counted on when she needed him.

Darcy knew Caleb was originally from Sacramento and he came from a large, working class family. She knew that he'd always worked hard at school and done well as a result. She knew he had a determination to help people, which was why he'd joined the Marine Corps straight out of high school.

Caleb could have gone to college, even the Naval Academy in Annapolis. But instead, he'd chosen to enlist, and work his way up the hard way.

It was one of the many things that attracted her to him.

In fact, there was very little Darcy didn't love about Caleb. He was kind, sweet and considerate. Caleb made sure that whenever he was in town, Darcy knew she was his first priority. His smile was her favourite thing, and his physical features were a special bonus.

Standing over six feet, Caleb had the chiselled physique and bone structure that reflected his dedication to his work. He was the strongest person she'd ever met, and she always felt protected in his presence.

It was only Caleb's work that kept them separated in any way, shape or form.

While on occasion, Darcy did have to travel for work, it was usually only for a few days.

In contrast, Caleb would be gone for weeks at a time. Whenever he returned, he always seemed a bit jaded. After a time, Darcy had accepted that this was her lot. She loved Caleb, and that meant loving everything about him, even when his work took him away from her.

She had always hoped he would one day open up to her about what his job entailed with the marines, and hearing him speak now, she thought perhaps that day had come.

"As part of our brief," Caleb said, drawing her back from her thoughts, "I examined the laptop before we left the building. I'd been given a picture of the icon I was supposed to search for. I opened up the laptop and saw that icon. It was a target tracker."

"Wait... you just opened the laptop, everything was open? Surely something like that would have had a security code, or a password, or something?" Darcy asked.

"I'm sure it did..." Caleb replied, "and it would have been unopened, if we hadn't surprised them, but..." Caleb paused. Never before had he spoken to Darcy about killing a man. He knew she suspected it was part of his work he did when he was away for months at a time, but now, if he admitted to it, it would become part of their lives.

"But... what?" Darcy pressed.

Caleb took a breath. "As part of the mission, we had been ordered to ensure no one would know we'd been there. And if they did, we needed to ensure they didn't remember us. That means, basically, that the people inside the building needed to be—"

Darcy interrupted, realising what he was alluding to. "Caleb... you had to kill them, didn't you?" she asked bluntly.

"Yeah. It was our only option," Caleb admitted, knowing he was crossing a threshold, and he couldn't step back once he did. Caleb waited for a response.

"Oh… okay. Why didn't you just tell me the truth?" she asked cautiously.

"I didn't want to freak you out," Caleb admitted, feeling relieved to finally be honest with her.

"Caleb… I had already figured out what you must do when you go away. No-one, especially soldiers, gets called away for weeks – weeks without contact – unless they're doing something important, or dangerous. Or on a secret operation or something. I thought it must be part of what you do."

Caleb watched her cautiously for a reaction. "And… you're okay with that?"

Darcy nodded. "Are you?" she asked in return.

Caleb hadn't been expecting that question, but he was stoic in his response. He'd admitted the worst, there wasn't much point in keeping anything secret now. "It is the worst of what we do, but sometimes it is necessary."

Darcy raised a sympathetic smile, relieved to hear that Caleb didn't enjoy all the aspects of what he did.

"Anyway, I saw the program…" Caleb began, resuming their conversation, "and noticed it was a tracker. When I opened it up, there was a world map, and it had about half a dozen or so places highlighted on the screen. The dots were scattered throughout. Places like Brazil, Canada, Australia…"

"You said it was a tracking program?"

"Yes… I did"

"Should I be worried, Caleb? After all, I did open it."

"I'm not sure babe." Caleb frowned. He got up from the bed, walked to the window and opened the blinds slightly, just enough so that he could check outside, to see if there was anything out of place.

As Darcy had only received the email a few hours earlier, Caleb was reasonably sure there hadn't been enough time for anyone to organise a succinct plan for a hit. But it had him worried. This sort of tracking device – he had no doubt, whoever had planted it, intended to come after Darcy for some reason, but he didn't want to freak her out too much. Given that Paul had sent the email from the other side of the world, Caleb hoped that meant he had some time to figure out what to do next.

As Caleb peered out at the view of the outside street, the morning sunshine created a yellow hue across the roof of the bodega opposite. Towards the east, there were a couple of the locals going about their business, a postal worker was delivering mail and a dog was barking. To the west, a few more locals were starting their days.

Nothing seemed out of the ordinary.

"I can't see anything..." Caleb said over his shoulder. "We should probably get out of here anyway, just in case."

"In case what, Caleb?" Darcy asked curiously.

"I'm not sure, Darc. All I know is that I've only ever seen that program once, and I was ordered to capture it. Before we did, I was briefed on what it was and why it was dangerous..."

Darcy knew Caleb was holding back the details of who had given him the orders and who was leading who to places. She trusted him, so she knew he would tell her anything she needed to know, when the time was right.

She was drawn back to the present by the sound of Caleb's voice. "...so I know we're in a situation we can't predict. Not yet, anyway."

"Okay... so what do we do?" Darcy asked.

"First of all, we need to get dressed. Wear something you can move around in easily. Grab some spare clothes, and make sure you take something warm with you."

"Where are we going?" asked Darcy, and he could hear the building anxiety in her voice.

Caleb put his hands on her shoulders, offered her a reassuring smile. "It's okay, babe... I'll figure it out." He brushed his lips over hers, kissing her. "We should just get away from here for now. Once we're somewhere safe, we can regroup, figure out what's going on.

Darcy did as she was told, grabbing a pair of loose jeans and pulling them on, before slipping her feet into sturdy walking shoes. She donned a singlet and slipped a baseball cap over her hair.

"Ready?" Caleb asked, as he finished dressing.

"Ready enough," she responded, reaching for the laptop. She never went anywhere without it, but Caleb knew taking it with them would be a mistake.

"No, leave that here for now..." he instructed. "Remember, if they are tracking you, they're tracking your laptop. They already know where that is."

"Oh, right. Okay," she responded, putting the laptop back on the bed.

Caleb grabbed his car keys, snatched up the bags he and Darcy had hurriedly packed, and they left the apartment.

◆ ◆ ◆

The vibrating phone shook the table, creating enough noise to waken the young man. Swiftly coming to alertness, Matthew snatched up the phone before it fell off the nightstand.

"Matthew?" Pierre announced.

"Pierre?" Matthew replied, surprised by the early morning phone call. "Is it time?"

"No, no. Not yet. I have another task for you, though. One that requires your immediate attention."

Matthew stifled a yawn. "What is it?"

"I need you to leave now, and get on the next plane to Los Angeles."

"Okay..." Matthew frowned, wondering what had happened that would need his attention so early in the morning.

"When you arrive, I will provide you with more information."

"How should I prepare?" asked Matthew, still confused by the remnants of sleep.

"Ensure you have enough equipment for an overnight stay," Pierre ordered. "Flights to and from L.A. have already been arranged. Hopefully, you will be in and out of Los Angeles in less than twenty-four hours. Coordinates for the drop will be sent once you land... Do you have any questions?"

"Any indication on the job?"

"Yeah... it's a standard take-down. Just one person."

Matthew instantly grew more alert. While he'd practiced this kind of task many times, he'd always had Pierre by his side on previous missions.

"Okay..." Matthew responded, annoyed to hear doubt in his own voice. "You're sure I'm ready?"

"Of course I am," Pierre said confidently. "I trained you, after all."

"Okay. Who's the target?"

"His name is Leon... He's a Zone One asset."

"Really?" Matthew asked, unsure why he was being asked to kill one of their own.

"Indeed, Matthew. The time of Phase Two is drawing near. We need to ensure the people we take through are worthy."

"I can assume that this... Leon... is not?" Matthew questioned cautiously.

"You can indeed. We were asked to take him down by the Englishman, so you can be assured it is necessary."

Matthew had only ever met the Englishman once. It was on the last day he and Emmett had seen each other. "Indeed," replied Matthew.

"Good..." Pierre said, "Call me when you land."

"Will do."

"Oh... and Matthew..."

"Yes Pierre"

"You can do this."

Chapter Six

After driving in random directions for more than an hour, Caleb was satisfied they hadn't been followed. He'd stopped the car on a couple of occasions, first to fill up with gas, and the second time to pretend they were posting a letter.

On both occasions, as he had when they first left Darcy's apartment, Caleb made a mental note of the people and cars in the area. At each location, there had been no matches, nothing to suggest they were being tailed or watched.

"Are we okay?" a nervous-sounding Darcy asked when he slipped back into the car.

"Looks that way," replied Caleb.

"Where are we headed?" she asked.

Though the majority of the drive had been spent focusing on his surroundings, Caleb had been formulating a plan. He knew they needed more information. "How much trust do you have in your boss?" Caleb asked.

Darcy was surprised by the question, and uncertain how to answer. She had a professional relationship with her editor, Marcus Freeman. To say she trusted him would be an overstatement. She'd heard rumours about how he'd landed the position of editor-in-chief at the L.A. Examiner, the city's second largest newspaper. When President Hawkins had been assassinated, the editor's position at the Examiner had been vacant. According to some of Darcy's co-workers, the London-born Freeman was not the only person available at the time to take the position. From what she'd heard, many corners had been cut, ruthlessly, to ensure the transition was quick and done in a hurry. As such, Darcy was unable to trust him completely. "I don't really know him that well..." replied Darcy.

"Well," Caleb began, continuing to observe the cars and people around them, "we need more information. Do you know anything else about what Paul was working on?"

"Not at all. I told you, Paul was a competitive ass. We were competing for the same jobs, the same stories. We were both employed on incentive-based contracts, which meant that we were paid based on the amount of hits our stories got on the internet. Consequently, we tend to be secretive about new stories we can get an exclusive on. It was always difficult to say what Paul was thinking or doing."

"Would he have told your boss? Freeman, is it?"

Darcy nodded.

"Would he have told Freeman about why he was in Australia?" Caleb asked, taking a turn which would take them in a southerly direction.

"He would have. I might not know him all that well, but I'm certain Freeman wouldn't have signed off on Paul's expenses without knowing the details. He's usually hassling us about budgets and assignments."

"Have you heard anything else from Paul yet?"

Darcy pulled out her phone and opened her email program. She shook her head.

Caleb turned left onto West First Street. "Darc, we need more information. Can you think of anyone else, besides this Freeman, who might know what Paul was doing?"

"I don't think so. Sorry, babe" replied Darcy.

Caleb thought for a moment or two, weighing up their options. "Okay then... Give your boss a call and tell him you're on your way"

Being a Saturday, she wasn't sure her boss would be in the office. Darcy called him on his cell, just in case.

"Yes, Ms. Chamberlain?" Freeman answered almost immediately. "What can I do for you?"

"Mr Freeman, are you in your office?" Darcy asked.

"News doesn't stop on the weekends, Ms Chamberlain," he said condescendingly.

"I need to see you."

"Come on in, then…"

Caleb held up two fingers on his left hand.

"We'll be there in two minutes."

"We?" Freeman asked, sounding suspicious.

"I'll explain when we get there."

"Very well. See you then."

Caleb soon pulled up outside The Examiners offices. The two-storey building blended in perfectly with the surrounding office spaces and city apartment blocks.

As they exited the car, Caleb once again scanned their surroundings. It was logical to suspect that the trackers, whoever they were, could be waiting at Darcy's workplace.

Once Caleb established the area was clear, he and Darcy made their way into the building, and entered the quiet lobby area, before making their way to the elevator.

"You okay?" Caleb asked, aware of Darcy's increasing nervousness.

"Yeah… I'm fine," Darcy replied, "I just want to know what's going on."

"Before we go up, tell me about Freeman," Caleb prompted.

"Not much to tell really, he started around the time the President was shot. He comes from England. Cambridge-educated. Always has time for the staff, but will kick your ass if he needs to…" Darcy's voice trailed off, and she twisted her fingers together nervously after she punched the 'up' button for a second time.

"Go on…" Caleb prompted.

"Nothing else. He's published pretty much everything I've submitted. Not that all of it was good, I think he figures that the more content we have, the more hits we'll get, and the more advertising—"

"So he's driven by money?" asked Caleb, trying to get a read on Freeman's agenda.

"I guess. I know his bonus depends on the hits and advertising sales. But that's the same for everyone. As I said though, he only came on board just after the President was shot, so…"

"I know babe. But, I think he can help us figure this out."

Caleb was satisfied with what Darcy had told him, and it had become obvious she didn't have any *major* reasons not to trust Freeman.

At the first floor, the doors opened to Darcy's work area. Caleb saw a seemingly endless sea of cubicles in front of them. It reminded Caleb of how much he enjoyed his own work and the freedom of movement it entailed. He couldn't imagine himself sitting in one of these cubicles for hours at a time.

There were six other people in the vast room, most of them tapping away feverishly at their keyboards, while one talked on the phone.

"Do you know all these people, Darc?" Caleb asked, not willing to let his guard down.

"Yeah," she replied, as they walked towards Freeman's office.

The office space was typical of corporate America. There were at least twenty rows of cubicles, each containing a desk, a keyboard and a computer monitor. There were mountains of paper on some, and barely a sticky-note on others.

In the middle of the room, was the print and copy station. Towards the east end of the vast room was a kitchen, and towards the west were three offices, with the titles of the occupants noted on each door.

As Caleb and Darcy made their way towards the offices, the titles grew clearer. On the right was the office of the Sports Editor, the left the News Editor. The middle office, with double doors at least twice the size of the others, had 'Marcus Freeman, Editor-In Chief' emblazoned across the glass wall. One of the doors stood open.

Not wanting to startle her boss, Darcy knocked lightly on the door-frame.

"Sorry... Mr. Freeman?" she said.

The rather average-looking man motioned for Darcy to enter.

"Yes, yes, Ms. Chamberlain, come in" Freeman said, seemingly annoyed by the interruption.

Darcy stepped into the office, closely followed by Caleb.

Freeman looked up from his screen, and rose from his seat, as though affronted by this intrusion on his space.

"Ms. Chamberlain," he began, "this is not a public area. Your friend will have to wait in the lobby."

Darcy signalled for him to sit down. "I'd rather Caleb stayed for now... once you hear what I've got, I'm—"

"Caleb?" Freeman scrutinized him carefully. "Caleb Jackson?"

Darcy and Caleb were both surprised. Darcy had never mentioned Caleb to her boss before, and wondered how he could possibly know him. "How do you know Caleb's surname?" Darcy asked.

"Not such a poor reporter, am I, Chamberlain?" Freeman said, coming around the side of his desk with his hand held out towards Caleb. "I didn't get to where I am, just because of who I know. Captain Jackson's reputation precedes him – it's a pleasure to meet you."

Caleb eyed Freeman curiously. Just how much did the man know? He gave him a curt nod as he briefly shook hands.

Freeman motioned for them to sit down. "Rest assured, Captain, your biggest secrets are still intact... not for lack of trying, though."

"Mr. Freeman, why have you been investigating Caleb?" Darcy asked, bristling at what she suspected was an intrusion into her life.

"What do I owe the pleasure of your visit to, Ms. Chamberlain?" Freeman asked, completely ignoring her question.

"Last night I received an email from Paul. Paul Jenkins." She glanced across into Caleb's eyes, clearly wondering how much she was supposed to admit to Freeman. Caleb gave her an almost imperceptible shake of his head. Not that he even needed to – Darcy knew him so well she knew his intent as soon as she looked at him.

Caleb wanted information from Freeman, not the other way around.

"Anyway... it was a bit strange. I mean, there were some pictures and..." she finished lamely, "and... some text"

"Hmmm... What sort of pictures?" asked Freeman

"Not sure... they were heavily pixelated."

"And there was nothing else?"

"Well, he mentioned he was in Australia, and he would be back soon..."

"Go on" said Freeman, as if he knew there was more.

Darcy twisted her fingers together in her lap. "Well… he said that he was onto something big."

"Hmmm," Freeman began, a small smile creeping across his face. "The plot thickens."

"What plot?" Darcy asked "Do you know why Paul was in Australia?"

"Now that question I can answer," said Freeman, turning his attention to Caleb. "He was there because of you, Captain Jackson."

◆ ◆ ◆

Helen swung her feet to the side of the makeshift cot.

The motion sensors detected her movement, and turned the lights on in the laboratory. The brightness of the almost completely white laboratory shocked Helen awake.

For the third day in a row, she had slept where she worked. Knowing how critical the timing was on the project, she'd made sure she was never too far away from where she could be most effective. As soon as her part was complete, Phase Two could commence.

This had been the fourth trial in as many months, with the results improving on each occasion. Ever since the Council had made the announcement during the previous year, that Phase Two was swiftly becoming necessary, Helen and her team had been working around the clock.

She tied her long blonde hair back into a tight ponytail and put on her glasses. Rising to her feet, Helen was startled by the phone when it nearly vibrated off the injection chair she'd placed it on earlier. Luckily, she caught it in time. Glancing at the screen, her heart skipped a beat. It was the call she'd been waiting for.

She pressed the 'Accept' button. "Did it work?"

"Indeed, it did" came the reply.

"The tests went okay?"

"Better than okay. A one hundred percent survival rate."

"One hundred percent?" she repeated, a smile spreading across her face.

"You've done it, Doctor."

"Excellent!" Helen exclaimed. Now she could turn her attention toward planning the next step. "When would you like me to start?" she asked.

The caller paused for a split-second. "As soon as you are ready, Doctor."

Helen took a moment to think. She and her team knew exactly what was required for the task, they'd been planning for months. "We can start in an hour or so."

"Good. I'll send word out to our off-site operatives, to start returning."

"That's fine."

With that, the caller hung up.

Helen stood up and began pacing around the room. She was so excited that it was all about to happen, she found she needed to use a minute to focus. *"Okay... what needs to be done?"* she asked herself.

Taking a deep breath, Helen began her preparations. She grabbed the red scrubs she'd thrown on the end of the cot when she'd lain down to rest and put them on. Next, she put on her sneakers. Once dressed, Helen stood up and walked around the room, ensuring all the equipment was there, making mental notes as she went.

Database... check.

Delivery pods... check.

Tourniquets... check.

Radio... check.

X-Ray... check.

Anti-nausea... check.

Everything was prepared and in the room.

Almost everything.

Helen picked up her phone and dialled a number.

"Mmmm hmmm..." Helen's weary assistant answered.

"Jane..." Helen began.

"What is it, Doctor?" Jane replied, and Helen could hear the sleepiness disappear from her voice when she realized who was calling.

"Jane… come to the lab," Helen said, pausing for effect. "It's time."

◆ ◆ ◆

Darcy sat in shocked silence.

"Did you just say I was the reason Paul was in Australia?" Caleb asked sharply.

"Indeed I did, lad," Freeman replied, sounding smug.

"I don't understand. I barely know the guy," Caleb protested. "I only ever met him a couple of times, at social events with Darcy."

"What do you know of Paul?" Freeman questioned.

"Very little. We didn't have much in common to be honest. And he seemed a bit…" Caleb paused.

"No, please," Freeman said, "go on."

Caleb shrugged. "I guess I just didn't trust him."

"What makes you say that?"

"I don't know. Maybe it was because whenever I was with Darcy, and Paul was there… I just thought he was… paying too much attention to what I was doing."

"Really?" Darcy questioned. "I didn't notice"

"I just thought he was jealous or something… as if he had a thing for Darc."

Freeman studied the two people in front of him, but Darcy grew impatient with his silence.

"Mr. Freeman…" she began, "where is Paul? And why was he interested in Caleb?"

Freeman seemed slightly affronted by her directness. "As I'm sure you will appreciate Ms. Chamberlain; I can't tell you much. But I'll tell you what I can." Freeman began with an infuriating pause before taking a sip of his coffee. "A few days after I began here, Paul came to me about a story he'd been working on. A story about you, Captain Jackson."

Caleb leant in, wanting to make sure he got every detail. The fact that he was somehow involved in this situation only made him more edgy about what might be going on.

"Or rather, it started being about you. You see, Paul's a very good journalist. Like a bloodhound. Once he gets a sniff of something, he doesn't let anything get in his way. While I'm not sure of the reasons why he started looking into you, Captain – whether they were personal or professional – it would seem his research led him down a particular path. Without giving away too much, he knew you were a Marine, and that you became something... more. That you'd become involved in something more... important." Freeman paused and took another sip of the coffee, much to Caleb's annoyance.. "It became apparent, Captain," he continued, "that you were involved in what the media would dub 'Black Ops'. You were doing things that were not officially sanctioned by the powers-that-be in Washington. Would that be correct?"

"What makes you think that?" Caleb asked cautiously.

Freeman spun around in his chair and opened the top drawer of a filing cabinet behind him. He pulled out a beige-coloured manila folder, the only notation on the front being 'Jackson'.

"Holy shit! You have a file of him?" Darcy asked, now visibly angry. "What is going on?"

"Relax, Ms. Chamberlain," Freeman said, opening the file.

The first page was standard. A copy of Caleb's basic information, beginning from the day he joined the Marines, listing his first Commanding Officer and other basic records.

The next sheet contained a brief memorandum. It stated that Caleb was being transferred to a different division.

"Where's the rest?" Darcy asked, curious to see what other information Freeman and Paul had collected.

"This is it, Ms. Chamberlain. These are the only two pages we could find about your boyfriend. Naturally, Paul's curiosity was piqued."

Caleb knew why there was no more information. It was standard practice that an officer's name be removed from any and all communication and documentation. Caleb and his team were off-the-grid, and their missions couldn't be permitted to be traced back, either to the government or the military.

Darcy read the short file intently before she turned to Caleb. "Can you tell us anything?"

Caleb met her gaze, squeezing her leg, he tried to reassure her with his eyes. He wanted to tell her more, but not with Freeman in the room.

Caleb changed the subject. "None of this explains why Paul was in Australia."

"Indeed it doesn't" Freeman agreed. "All Paul said, was that it was connected to the work he was doing on the 'Black-Ops' thing. In fact, I was hoping you could shed some light on it. Can I ask, both of you, what made you come here today? Has Paul found something important?"

"I'm not sure", began Darcy. "You know everything we do"

Darcy wasn't sure she believed what she'd just said, in fact, she was certain that Caleb knew more than he had told her or Freeman. But she knew Caleb wasn't going to open up in front of Freeman.

"Thank you for your time," Darcy said, getting to her feet, wanting to leave as soon as possible.

Caleb stood up.

"Are you sure you can't tell me anything more?" Freeman asked, giving one last attempt at gathering information for the story.

Darcy shook her head. "If you hear from Paul, just let me know. I'm a bit worried about him." Darcy admitted.

"Very well... good day" Freeman said cordially.

"Thanks" said Caleb.

Out of listening range of Freeman's office, Darcy opened her mouth to question Caleb as soon as they got in the elevator. Caleb put up his hand to silence her. He didn't want to talk in front of others, especially people who shared and revealed information for a living. "Babe... just wait 'til we get to the car, okay?" Caleb urged.

Darcy nodded, even though she was bursting with questions.

When they left the building, Caleb glanced around, again making mental notes and comparing who and what he saw now, to what he'd seen when they'd arrived. Only a few minor changes, but none of the cars were similar from their previous stops.

They left the building, got in Caleb's car, and drove away.

"Okay, Caleb… time to tell me something," Darcy began, before the car had travelled more than ten yards.

"Okay…" Caleb stated, "Just give me a second…" He began typing a location into his GPS system, setting it to run before he glanced across at Darcy. "I hope you've packed enough for the night, we're going for a drive"

"Where to?"

"Have you ever been to Phoenix?"

Darcy was confused. "Not for a while. What's in Phoenix?" she asked.

"Not what - Who," Caleb said in response.

"Okay, then…" Darcy replied, annoyed by Caleb's obtuseness. "*Who* is in Phoenix?"

"Mike Dunleavy."

Darcy was taken back. "Oh shit. You mean the former Chief-of-Staff?"

"One and the same."

"How can he help?"

"I'll tell you on the way, babe. Get comfortable. We've got a drive ahead of us."

Chapter Seven

It had been less than eight hours since he had buried the package.

Emmett had spent the night and day doing what he usually did – sitting in his apartment, watching television. The only time he ventured out was to buy some food – usually some vile take-out from the local Chinese place.

It had been his existence since he was moved to Seattle. He had become friends with his television and the four walls of his living room. He was not permitted to contact anyone, search for anyone or perform any task unless instructed.

It wasn't a sacrifice for him. In fact, as he had been told by Pierre at his last face-to-face encounter, if he should complete his assigned tasks, he would guarantee his place in the community. His place alongside his present and future family. That reward was greater than any sacrifice he could make.

The phone rang, and Emmett answered. He was relieved the call had finally come.

"Pierre?" he asked

"Yes, Emmett," Pierre replied.

"Is it time?"

"Yes it is. Be in position before dawn. Ensure your phone is on."

"Do we know which flight yet?"

"Yes. I will tell you the details soon."

"Okay. I'll be there."

"Good. I will call you. Now Emmett…"

"Yes?"

"In two hours, start the last bit of *chatter*."

"Yes, sir"

"Good luck"

With that, Pierre ended the call.

Emmett began his preparations.

As a part of his duties, Emmett was charged with some of the misdirection. Every once in a while, Emmett would receive a thumb-drive in the mail. On each drive would be an audio file or email text. He would then send the communications to phone numbers and email addresses provided by Pierre.

Each email and phone call would leave clues.

The details of the conversations would lead those paying attention to believe there was an imminent attack planned on America. The conversations would act like bread crumbs.

Bread crumbs that would lead the listeners wherever Pierre led them.

Now he had received the call, it was up to Emmett to lay the last of the clues.

Only Emmett, Pierre and some select members of the Council knew the real reason the plane was to be shot down.

The plan to take down the plane wasn't to cause terror to Americans. It was much simpler than that. The plane's destruction was merely a distraction.

Emmett truly believed the actions he would be taking in the next few hours would not only improve his own life, but the lives of everyone who deserved it.

With that thought, Emmett prepared for the last step in his mission. He laid out the clothes he would wear to finish the job that had been started months ago – a dark hoodie, dark jeans and black shoes.

Once prepared, he lay on the bed, and ran through the journey in his mind.

He replayed the walk up the hill, and the successful targeting of the plane.

Confident about what he needed to do, and secure in the knowledge that he was doing the right thing, Emmett fell asleep.

♦ ♦ ♦

Caleb and Darcy had begun their long journey to Phoenix. Making their way east on the I10, Darcy's mind filled with an endless number of questions. Accompanying the questions was a growing sense of fear. Fear that she might not really know the man she was with, the man she'd known since high-school. The man she had always trusted… and loved.

Her mind raced with a variety of emotions, and all the while she fought to appear calm in front of Caleb.

As they drove, Caleb kept a sharp eye on his surroundings. The further they drove, the more he relaxed. There was no sign of any cars behind them that could be tailing him.

Fortunately, the highway was relatively quiet, with more cars travelling toward the sun and fun of California, rather that the heat and desert of Arizona. It made it much easier for Caleb to keep track of the other cars on the road.

When he was completely satisfied they were safe, he turned to Darcy, summoning all the compassion he could. "Go on, Darc…" he stated, "ask me."

Darcy remained silent for a minute, which stretched out to two. She didn't know where to start, she had so many questions. Why was there no information in Caleb's file? Why did he never talk about his work? How did he know the former Chief-of-Staff of the United States? Why was Paul so interested in what Caleb was doing?

"Well…" she began slowly, "I'll ask, if you can promise me one thing."

"What's that babe?" Caleb replied trying to keep his voice light.

"Can you promise me that, whatever I ask, you will tell the truth?"

It was Caleb's turn to pause. He didn't really expect the question. For the time he had known Darcy, he had never lied to her. Why did she think he would start now? The only thing he could think was that, since she had seen his vacant file, she now saw him as a government ghost. He feared she may see him as a stranger.

Caleb turned back to Darcy and saw the look in her eye.

It was then he knew that the time was right.

Caleb knew then that Darcy was the only person he *could* trust, and the only person he *could* talk to about his work.

He knew he could only give her one answer.

"I will never lie to you babe…" he said, his emotions getting the better of him.

"Well… Ok then…" Darcy continued, surprised by his emotional answer, "I don't know where to start…"

"How about I start it for you?" Caleb asked.

"Ok…" said Darcy, happy that Caleb had decided to open up.

"Well, I'll start with the file…"

Darcy listened intently.

"It's pretty much standard operating procedure for most operations the government would classify as… covert. I was approached by my CO and asked if I wanted to do more for the country. While I had been on some pretty tough assignments, I was basically a grunt. I would follow orders, do my job and come home"

"Yeah, I remembered that. It was nice. We had a good little routine going' there for a while…"

"I know. It was good. And to be honest, it was what made the next decision I made so difficult. About five years ago, as I said, my CO asked me to do more. But I needed more information. So he gave me some. He gave me a number to call. That number led me to a meeting…"

Darcy continued to pay close attention.

"That meeting was with Dunleavy." Caleb explained

"Wait…" Darcy said, "five years ago?"

"Yeah."

"He was just ending his time in the CIA… about to take the reins in DC."

"That's right babe. That's why it didn't seem weird. I'd heard it happened all the time – where Marines, SEALs and Delta's would meet with top level intelligence. It basically meant that what you were about to do was important… or borderline illegal."

"Illegal?"

"Well… not illegal… just… not *completely* legal. It meant that if we were caught, they wouldn't admit to it, and we'd be hung out."

"Wow…"

"Yeah… 'Wow' was right. It was the kind of job that everyone aspired to. To put your ass on the line and make a real difference to the world. To make a difference to the lives of Americans. I tell ya babe, I was excited. I mean, don't get me wrong, part of me was scared…"

"Scared… you? Big Marine-boy like you?"

"Of course babe. Shit, we were going into hotspots where intelligence was a bit sketchy, asked to do things that no-one else would… or even could. Each mission meant I could die. I was scared."

Caleb paused, and made sure Darcy knew that he meant what he was about to say next.

"I was scared because I had something to lose. Something that meant the world to me. I was scared I would never see you again"

Darcy was speechless. She knew he cared about her, and he knew he loved her. She had no idea he that she meant so much to him though.

"Good news though…" Caleb continued, "I didn't die."

Caleb put his thumb up and produced a big grin.

Darcy couldn't help but giggle.

"Anyway, for about four years, the same pattern continued. Dunleavy would call, and we'd go on a mission. We went places all over the world. We had an amazing success rate. We were the best. We were his *go-to* team."

Then Caleb paused.

"I take that back. While we did what was expected, at least from a mission success to failure ratio, I can't say all the missions were a success. We lost more than a dozen soldiers over the time I was in charge. Good men, and a couple of good women."

Darcy put her hand on his shoulder. Her touch soothed him.

"They meant a lot to you?" she asked.

"They were good people…"

Caleb refocused, and continued, "After four years, as you know, Hawkins got re-elected, and Dunleavy moved on. I never found out why. Just assumed it was the ways things worked. But still, in the last six month of missions, they changed…"

"How?"

"Well… it started that we were going to the normal places you'd expect. China, North Korea, Pakistan… But then we started getting sent to, I don't know, we started doing missions in…in. Let's just say, they were supposed to be friendly countries."

"Friendly countries still have secrets babe…" Darcy said.

Caleb was caught off-guard by her candour.

"Yeah, I guess… still, it just felt… I don't know… off."

"Did you ever talk to Dunleavy about it?"

"Didn't get a chance. He quit as Chief-of-Staff and I haven't spoken to him since."

"Wait, but you said that was twelve months ago…"

"That's right."

"But, you've been on missions since…"

"I was just getting to that babe…." Caleb continued, "Anyway, I didn't hear anything for a while, then one day I get a call… from Hawkins"

"The President?"

"Yeah… he told me that he was taking over from Mr Dun…"

"Wait. Are you telling me the President was assigning you missions?"

"Yeah… Just like Dunleavy."

"Caleb, don't you get it? The President was breaking all kinds of laws doing that. Yeah sure, he's the Commander-in-Chief. Doesn't mean he can have his own private unit to do his work."

"I'm not sure babe. It's kind of the point of covert. We get told where to go, and we go there."

"So, what happened?" Darcy began.

Before Caleb could answer, Darcy was struck by a realisation, "Shit, was he killed because of this? The President?"

"I'm not sure babe, that's why we're going to Dunleavy. I reckon that Paul, while researching me, stumbled onto something that took him down to Australia. Whatever it was, I'm hoping that Dunleavy might be able to help us out."

"Shit, I hope so babe. Sounds like we are in deep. No wonder there might be someone after us." Darcy was openly panicking.

"If they can get to the President, what hope do we have?" she continued.

"Babe…" it was now Caleb's turn to do the calming, "Babe, it's gonna be ok. We've got a plan, and we're not in LA. There's no-one following us. It's gonna be ok."

"Really?" Darcy asked, not sure if she could believe him

"Really." Caleb exclaimed, trying to sound calm.

They drove in silence for a few miles as Caleb gave Darcy the time to let it all sink in.

After a short time, Caleb decided Darcy needed to know the important part.

"Darcy, there's one more thing…"

He proceeded to tell Darcy about the conversation he had with the President. He told her about the Source.

"The Source?" she asked.

"Yeah, that's what he said… 'Find the Source'."

"Was that it?" Darcy asked, somewhat calmed by her curiosity.

"No idea, but it's important" Cal replied.

"So, what do we know about the Source? After all, if Hawkins felt the need to tell you about it, with his last thought, it *must* be important."

"I agree, but nothing really comes into my mind about it. I've tried to think back to the missions, but I can't remember anything even close to it."

Darcy paused for thought.

"Maybe the Source is in Australia?" she said, trying to be logical.

"Maybe… I'm hoping Dunleavy knows." Caleb replied.

Darcy looked out the window, in deep thought about what to do next. She couldn't come up with anything.

"Well..." she said, "Better step on it Marine Boy. We've gotta get to Phoenix"

Chapter Eight

Helen had once again begun pacing around the room. The more steps she took, the more frustrated she got. Earlier, she had received some great news, news which meant the plan could move forward.

Even though she had only waited for an hour, she was growing impatient.

"Where are they?" she asked Jane, as though her assistant would know the answer.

Jane shrugged, equally unaware of the reasons for the delay. "Can't we just get started?" she asked. "Why don't we could just do ourselves—"

"Don't be ridiculous!" Helen snapped, affronted that Jane had even dared to suggest it. "You know *He* is first. He will always be first. It was He, after all, who gave us this gift. Who gave us this chance—" Helen stopped abruptly, thinking she'd heard the door. She was disappointed when the door remained closed. "He gave us our future," she continued.

"I know. I know," Jane said, realising her mistake.

Helen returned to pacing the laboratory.

In time, the double-glass doors slid open, and a tall, distinguished gentleman walked in. "Doctor… Nurse…" the man greeted the two women, "It is a great day for us all."

The grandeur of the moment, and the man himself, wasn't lost on the two women.

"Indeed it is, Sir," Helen agreed

Two more people entered the room.

The first two stood near to the man and the device. Others began forming a queue at the doorway, an older woman in the front. Everyone, aside from Helen and Jane, was dressed in hospital gowns.

"Please, have a seat." Helen said as she motioned to the injecting chair, "This shouldn't take too long…"

The man stood six feet tall, his salt and pepper hair neatly cut and styled. His strong jaw and piercing eyes added to his physical presence.

As instructed, he sat in the chair. He had been waiting a long time for this moment, and his heart was filled with joy to think that it was all starting to come to fruition.

No longer would he have to tolerate the seemingly endless injections. With the serum perfected, he could now stop with all that, and begin the next part of his journey.

As the man took his seat, he glanced at the other people in the room.

"Zachary, John – this is it," he announced to the two men in the room, unable to contain a pleased smile.

"Indeed, James. Good luck." Zachary replied. He turned to Helen, and shared a familiar smile. His pride regarding her was palpable.

The two men then both smiled back at James. They had been with him for the entire journey, and were relieved it was finally moving forward again.

"Doctor…" James announced, "You may begin."

Helen stepped forward, Jane standing eagerly by her side. "Please sit back and relax, sir," Helen said, as she began preparing the machine. Between them, the two women moved the machine into position.

Approximately five feet in length and two feet wide, the injecting machine was created from composite steel. Helen and Jane's reflections clearly visible in the machine as they began to prepare for their first patient.. A large steel plate, about three feet wide by five long, hung directly above James and in the middle of the steel plate, the adjustable injectors were loaded with the serum by the two women.

The device had been designed so the injectors could be adjusted to the height and width of each individual patient, ensuring the injections were focused on the key areas – femoral veins, and, on either sides of the neck – the jugulars.

The injections had to be both precise and perfectly timed, as the serum needed to enter the blood stream at its most vital points. This was an essential part to the procedure because the patient's blood needed to mesh with the serum virtually instantaneously.

Significant failures had occurred in the past, during both animal and human testing. Helen had grown increasingly frustrated as they'd continued to suffer failures with the single injection procedure they'd originally used. While the serum had still work without the use of the device, it was not nearly as effective as the four-point injection.

Realizing that all the injections needed to occur simultaneously, Helen had worked to perfect the delivery system, resulting in the machine now standing over the top of her first patient. She patted James's arm reassuringly as she moved the lower part of his gown to expose his upper, inner thigh.

Once again she adjusted the machine, lowering the device to within millimetres of James's skin, ensuring each injector was lined up precisely.

When she was confident everything was perfectly arranged, she spoke to Jane, who was stationed at a terminal three feet away from the patient. "We're ready, Jane. Please begin the procedure."

Jane nodded, and pressed a series of buttons to begin the insertion process. The needles lowered slowly into James's skin, teasing the minutest drops of blood from his veins. Jane paused, nodding to Helen to confirm that she was ready.

Helen checked the insertion points, ensuring the needles were correctly placed in each of James's veins. Satisfied, she motioned to Jane to continue. "Please proceed."

Jane typed swiftly on the keyboard, carefully starting the injection sequence, and as everyone watched, the cloudy, viscous liquid was plunged into James's body.

"How's it looking, sweetheart?" asked Zach. He sounded a little nervous, knowing that his long-time friend was the first person of importance to undergo the refined procedure.

"It's looking perfect," Helen replied. She ignored the hushed gasp which came from the onlookers, as James lost consciousness. "Remove the injectors, please, Jane."

Jane pressed another series of buttons. The device withdrew the needles, and slowly lifted the injection system up and away from the patient.

The room lapsed into a tense silence as the machine itself shut down, and everyone waited, hardly daring to breathe.

After a minute or so, James remained unconscious, and John spoke up, his portly figure barely covered by the gown he wore. "Is he okay?"

"This is normal. The blood is adjusting to its new form—" Helen began to explain, watching James avidly, but she abruptly stopped speaking, and a tiny smile appeared on her lips when she noticed the changes beginning in her patient.

James's hair began to change colour, the grey morphing and darkening as it returned to its original dark brown pigment. The wrinkles on his face started to disappear, the lines smoothing out as his overall muscle tone improved, and skin on the back of his hands tightened, smoothing out, the liver spots disappearing to leave his hands blemish free.

The entire process took about thirty seconds, and before them, the old man had grown young again.

Not just young, but strong, fit and healthy.

In unison, Helen, Jane, Zach and John gasped, amazed by just how quickly their leader had been rejuvenated by the injections. They had seen similar results before, but never quite so fast nor effective.

It was as though James had lost thirty years from his life.

James's eyes slowly began to open, fluttering as he adjusted to the light in the room.

"How do you feel?' Helen asked.

"A little tired," James began, before he reached up to touch his face anxiously. "Did it work?"

"Yes." Helen whispered her response, her emotions beginning to get the better of her. She had worked towards this result for so long, to see the end result like this – it was better than she could ever have imagined. After so many trials, so many heartaches and failures, her leader's dreams would be realised. Her family's dreams would be realised. Her whole community's dreams would be realised.

James sat up in the chair, and caught his reflection in the metal plate as the machine continued to slowly rise higher above him.

For a moment he stared, his expression stunned, until he broke out into a broad grin and began to chuckle loudly. "Ha ha ha…" he laughed, "Helen, oh my God, you did it!"

"We all did," Helen responded, motioning to Jane who was smiling brightly.

"Yes, yes, yes. Well done, to both of you!" James continued to study his reflection, angling his head first one way, then the other. He grew serious. "Now Helen, I need you to tell me something…"

"Yes?" replied Helen, a note of concern in her voice.

"Is it permanent?"

Helen grinned. "Yes, it is."

Relief sparked in James's eyes and he smiled. "Good, excellent. Now the next question. Nightfall? Does it survive the virus?"

Helen nodded. "Yes. All the signs point to it being resistant, sir, which is why it took so long. We've been able to make the Source permanent for some time. But, with Nightfall? That was a bit trickier."

"How sure are you?" James questioned sharply.

"One hundred percent, sir. We trialled it with five outsiders last night. The virus had no impact, once the serum was injected."

"Five outsiders? And no deaths?" James queried.

"None."

"Excellent. I trust the outsiders were dealt with?"

"Indeed they have, sir. The serum might save them from most external threats, but a well-placed bullet will always do the trick" Helen said, a casual smile spreading over her face.

"Well done!" her now youthful leader praised, "and to you, Jane," he added smiling at Helen's assistant.

"Thank you, sir."

The news of the leader's success had begun to trickle down the line of waiting people. The talk was enthusiastic, and James knew the excitement throughout the community would continue to grow. James turned his attention to Zach and John. "Alright, you two are next..." he said. Zack and John both moved forward, eager to take their turn and have their youth and vitality restored and James turned his attention to the first person waiting in the bigger queue. "Sarah, you and the first group can come in," he announced to the elderly woman standing at the front of the queue.

Sarah smiled and nodded, motioning for the group standing behind her to come in.

As the people began to file into the room, Zach took his place in the chair James had just vacated.

"Helen, you can continue," James announced proudly.

"Thank you, sir," Helen said. She motioned to Jane, and the two began their work, preparing Zach for his injections.

"How long will it take for everyone to be treated?" James questioned. He ran a hand across his face again, obviously pleased at the tightness and smoothness of his skin.

"It should all be done in the next few days," Helen reassured him.

"Good... continue, please."

James turned and strode across to the table holding the terminal Jane had worked on. Next to the terminal was a phone, and he lifted the handset.

James pressed the speaker button, "Attention," he began. "I have good news for everyone. The serum has worked and is completely successful." He paused, waiting for the news to sink in around the colony and heard a loud cheer coming from outside in the hallway. As the news spread, the noise from outside grew louder and he knew the entire colony was rejoicing.

"Now," he continued as the noise quietened, "you all know your instructions. You will be given a time for your procedure. Please be patient as you wait. You all have your jobs to do." Again he paused, and total silence overwhelmed the colony. "Phase Two... has now officially begun!"

James smiled when an even louder cheer erupted around the colony.

Chapter Nine

Caleb and Darcy had been driving for hours, and Darcy had used the time to contemplate over what Caleb had told her.

Caleb saw it as a positive that she hadn't asked him to turn around, or asked him to drop her on the side of the road. He was relieved to know that Darcy was with him, regardless of what he'd kept from her in the past.

"Caleb… I've been thinking," Darcy announced some time later.

"I assumed as much," Caleb said, once again lightening the mood. He offered Darcy a grin. "Anything in particular?"

"Not really… and well, yeah," Darcy replied, fidgeting in her seat.

Caleb glanced across at her. "Well babe, you're in now; ask me anything you want."

"Okay." Darcy paused, considering how to word her question. "Caleb, I just want you to know, that, I… I…"

"Go on Darc," Caleb prompted. "There's nothing you can't ask."

"I guess I want to know…" She straightened in her seat, took a deep breath. "No, I *need* to know."

"Yes?"

"What do you feel when you kill someone?" The words came out in a rush, as if she had to say it in a hurry before she lost courage.

Caleb considered his response for a minute. He hadn't been expecting her to be so blunt. It wasn't an easy answer to admit, but it was one that he needed to word precisely.

"I guess… nothing" he replied. "I mean, when I first started, it was difficult. Contrary to what people say, the Marines are not all about fighting and killing and blowing stuff up. A lot of it, at least when we were doing our work, was planning… and travel. Tons of boring-ass travel. So, when I was away each time, we would spend most of it either planning our entry into the building, or wherever we were headed... or travelling. I mean, it wasn't like we could just catch the next commercial flight out of LAX. If we did our planning right, then we didn't have to kill anyone. But, sometimes Darc... it was unavoidable."

"So... you don't feel anything?" Darcy sounded incredulous.

"Let me finish, babe," Caleb responded. "I learned to turn off my emotions, but that's a bit of an exaggeration. Of course I feel something. I guess it's a combination of guilt and remorse and... I dunno, I guess I feel uncomfortable with what I have to do. But it didn't happen when I actually killed someone. The guilt happened afterwards. And you know what? It never goes away".

Darcy sounded perplexed when she spoke again. "But, I've never even noticed it. I mean, you never acted depressed—"

"Babe... I never was depressed. I guilty, yeah, but I don't get depressed over the decisions I've made. One of the first CO's I had, the one who really showed me what being a true Marine would be, he taught me something I've never forgotten. Yeah, the killing is shit, and if I can avoid ever doing it again, I will. But he taught me that I needed something, how did he say it, he said I needed to find 'light, when there was darkness'. I had no idea what he was talking about at the time. But after I came back from Iraq, and you were there, and I knew exactly what he was talking about. I knew that day, that *you* were my light, and whenever I felt guilt about what I'd had to do... I just thought of you. About the time I get to spend with you. And that, babe, has been more than enough to get me through the tough times."

It was a shame they were driving, Darcy thought as she stared lovingly at Caleb, watching him as he drove.

All the doubts she'd had, any of the negative feeling she'd experienced over what Caleb did... they had all seemed to disappear with his honest response to her question. She'd made the right decision. Not only to get in the car with him and drive to Arizona - it was more than that.

She knew that all the lonely nights she had experienced while he'd been serving overseas, or on secretive missions, when all she could think about was being with him – he had been thinking the same.

"So, Dunleavy…" she began

"Yeah… Dunleavy" Caleb replied.

"How do you know he's even in Phoenix?" Darcy questioned.

"Well… the honest answer is that I don't. Not one hundred percent. But, I'm sure you've probably heard, he's taken a job in the Arizona Governor's Office."

Darcy was surprised by Caleb's response. "He has? Nope, I didn't know that."

"Well, I'm guessing he's got a place there, so, with any luck, we'll be able to make contact him."

"Why don't you just call him?" Darcy asked curiously. It was the way she'd usually resolve a question – pick up the phone, make a call, get an answer. She wondered why Caleb hadn't considered calling Dunleavy, make sure he was even in Phoenix, before they'd started this road trip.

"Babe, from what I can tell, this is the last thing we should be discussing on the phone. Besides, going to Arizona solves two problems. One, we get to possibly meet with Dunleavy, and two, it means we're not in LA."

"You really believe someone is coming after us?"

"Like I said earlier, Darc, I'm not sure. But I'd rather be somewhere other than where your laptop is. At least we've given ourselves a head start."

"Shit Caleb… are we in a lot of trouble?"

"Babe… if we are, I'm promising you, I'm not gonna let anything happen to you. Remember, this is what I do for a living," Caleb said, offering her an encouraging smile.

◆ ◆ ◆

"Shit… what the fuck are they gonna do in Phoenix?" Pierre asked loudly down the phone line. Then it occurred to him. "Wait, that's where Dunleavy is, isn't it?"

"Dunleavy? Yeah, I think so." William replied, his London accent filled with condescension.

"Fuck! Alright, Will, I'll do what I can," Pierre said, angrily. He was annoyed that he needed to clean up a mess that William and his people had created. Even though they were friends, Pierre didn't have time for incompetence. In his mind, there were far more important things he needed to attend to – helping Emmett not the least of them.

"Has your man arrived in LA yet?" William asked

"He should be touching down in a few hours," Pierre replied

"Is it our plane?"

"No, he had to go commercial."

"Dammit Pierre, it's not like Phase Two is about to start," William said, sounding disappointed Pierre had taken such a risk.

"Relax, Will. All our Kites are transporting our people back to the colonies. There was no other option. You can trust me though. I'll sort it."

"Pierre, I don't need to remind you of the mission's importance, do I? You've done well with the diversion, but we need to make sure there's no-one looking our way for the next few days."

"I know, I know. Just leave it with me."

"Okay."

William hung up, leaving a seething Pierre on the other side of the world.

Pierre and Will had always gotten along – you could even call them friends. He knew the stakes, but he didn't like to be spoken to like a recalcitrant child.

What did William expect? Pierre thought. He was the one who was tracking Darcy's phone…

◆ ◆ ◆

The day was drawing to a close, and the sun was starting to set. They had been on the road for several hours.

"Now it's your turn," Caleb said, turning to Darcy.

"Okay," she responded slowly. Caleb remained silent, watching her expectantly, and Darcy huffed out a breath. "You're gonna have to give me a clue..." exclaimed Darcy.

"Fair enough..." replied Caleb, "I need you to call someone. Someone that can locate Dunleavy. Someone you trust. If you can trust them, so do I."

"Okay. And...?"

"We need to know exactly where Dunleavy is. Is he at the Governor's office, or is he at his home? And we need an address."

"Okay, let me have think," Darcy said, running through the list of contacts she normally used for such a task.

She had two criteria to meet. She needed someone who could definitely get the information, and quickly, which usually meant bending a law or two. And she also needed someone who was absolutely trustworthy.

She thought hard, because the two criteria seemed mutually exclusive.

Making a decision, Darcy called Chuck, 'her favourite nerd' as she had dubbed him in the past.

The phone only rang once before it was answered. "Darcy!" Chuck said excitedly.

"How's my favourite geek goin', Chucky?" Darcy said, trying to keep the mood light.

"Great, just great, Darc. Haven't heard from you for a while. I thought you'd forgotten about me?"

"Now Chucky, how could I forget you? You're one of my favourites."

"Ha-ha, Darcy," Chuck laughed. "I've missed you. You still with that meat-headed Marine of yours?"

"Yeah, Chucky. I'm with him right now, actually."

Darcy sensed the change of tone in Chuck's voice. "Oh shit. I'm not on speaker phone, am I?" While he had often helped her, Darcy knew Chuck was quite fragile, and any wrong word could put him on edge.

"Of course not, Chucky," she said in as much of a big sister voice as she could manage. At times, that's exactly how Darcy had to treat him. While he was the best hacker Darcy knew, she also had to temper him.

"Phew... anyway..." Chuck began, his caution lifting, "I guess you're not calling to ask me on a date?"

"Well, not yet Chucky," she giggled. While she didn't share his feelings, she was still able to use them to her advantage.

"Actually, I need you to find someone for me..."

"Ahhh, that's easy Darc. Who do you need?"

"Ummm... I can trust you? Right Chucky?"

"Of course you can," Chucky replied, sounding somewhat offended, "You're my girl."

Chuck's flirtations, while harmless, were never well executed. All Darcy could do was laugh it off.

"Thanks Chucky," she replied, "Now, I'm gonna give you a name, and then I need you to find him."

"Okie dokie. What do you mean, find him?"

"I mean 'Where is he right now'."

"Like... right now, as in, 'Where does he live'?"

Darcy shook her head, speaking slowly. "No, Chucky. I need to know his exact location. Right now."

"Ahhh, well, that's not as easy..."

"But doable?" Darcy pressed.

"Absolutely. What's the name?"

Darcy paused. She pondered over whether giving Chuck the name was the right choice to make. Was she certain she could trust him?

Darcy thought about her and Caleb's circumstances – the events of the past twenty-four hours, and realised she had no choice. "Michael Dunleavy."

"Shit, Darcy," Chuck said, his voice full of concern. "What have you got yourself into?"

"It's okay, Chucky." Darcy smiled at Chuck's concern. "No need to worry, I'll tell you a bit more when I can."

"Okay, Darc. I trust you… I think. Just hang on a sec."

Chuck opened his own tracking program. After dropping out of the Massachusetts Institute of Technology – according to Chuck, they were just holding him back – he'd spent the majority of his time in his apartment, developing new ways to get information from people. And, at times, he would sell that information to the right people.

He was a classic nerd, and a very clever one. Despite his high intelligence, when it came to other people, Chuck was often found wanting. He was most comfortable at home, in front of his computer.

The only person, apart from his family, that he had ever developed a connection with was Darcy. They had met by accident; Darcy was doing a piece on email spam, and the people who perpetuate it. As she looked further into the story, one name continued to crop up – Chuck's.

Rather than expose Chuck in her newspaper, Darcy decided to become his ally. Or rather, she allowed him to become hers.

After a time, they had developed a close bond, and Darcy knew she would never let him down, despite his less-than-legitimate past.

"Okay… do you have his phone number?" Chuck questioned.

Darcy turned to Caleb, and held her hand over the mouthpiece. "Do we have Dunleavy's phone number?" she asked.

"I've only ever called a number I *thought* was his…" Caleb admitted.

"Sorry Ch…" Darcy began.

"It's okay, Darc… I've got it." Chuck said, having located Dunleavy's private number through his own program.

Darcy grinned. Once Chuck had his eyes on a prize, he didn't let anything stop him.

"I take it Marine-Boy is there?" Chuck questioned.

"Yeah, he is."

"Okay, listen closely. Get him to dial this number '555 480 4527'."

Darcy repeated the number to Caleb as Chuck read it out.

"Now," Chuck continued, "it's very important you don't let Dunleavy answer the phone!"

"Why? I thought that's how we track him?" Darcy responded.

"That's what the movies *want* you to think. Trust me, he doesn't need to answer. Just get Marine-Boy to dial. Once he hears the ringtone, get him to hang-up."

"Okay." Darcy repeated the instructions to Caleb. Caleb stared at her, seeming a little concerned they might scare Dunleavy off.

Darcy nodded, trying to reassure him it would be okay.

Caleb dialled the number as instructed, waited to hear the ring, and then immediately hung-up.

Darcy waited on the phone, impatient to hear what Chuck had to say.

"Good... it didn't quite connect."

"Have you got a location?"

"Patience, petal... it'll happen," Chuck said in a soothing tone. "You can't rush these things." Darcy heard Chuck tapping away at his keyboard, before he spoke again. "Hope you like pubs?"

"You've found him?"

"I told you, Darc... anything for you."

"Great. That's fantastic, where is he?"

"He's in Phoenix, so you've got a bit of a drive."

Darcy smiled into the phone. "Not really. We're already here."

"Shit, Darc, you must have it hard for this guy," Chuck said casually, before he quickly backpedalled. "Shit, sorry Darc," he blathered.

Darcy could hear the regret in Chuck's voice, and knew he hadn't intended to insult her. While Chuck seemed taken with her, she knew that he enjoyed the relationship they shared. "That's okay, Chucky. I know you didn't mean it." Darcy felt the need to hurry things up. "Where is this pub?"

"West Monroe Street, nice place called Connor O'Sullivan's... Geez, very imaginative these Irish guys."

"Thanks Chucky. I really appreciate it."

"Anytime, Darc"

With a final goodbye, Darcy hung up and then typed the address into the GPS. "We need to turn right in about a hundred yards," she said, reading the directions.

"So we've found him?" Caleb questioned. "In Phoenix?" Caleb sounded surprised by how easy it had been.

"Yep, he's at a pub."

Caleb began to drive, taking the first right as Darcy had directed. "It's been a long time since I've seen or even spoken with Dunleavy. Hopefully, he'll be able to give us some answers."

Chapter Ten

The drive to the small Irish pub took less than five minutes – Caleb gave the building the once over when they arrived, noticing the green awnings typical of any Irish pub. Typical anywhere but Ireland.

Caleb pulled into one of the angled parking bays across the street from the pub. With the back of the car facing the pub, surveillance of the building wouldn't be easy; he would need to rely on the mirrors, and Darcy.

Of course, it also meant Dunleavy wouldn't be able to spot them, and they could safely sit and wait without disruption. Additionally, while Caleb had not chosen his car specifically for surveillance purposes, the midnight blue Ford Edge blended in well with their surroundings.

Noticing the parking meters on the side of the road, Caleb asked Darcy to jump out and feed some coins into the machine. The last thing they needed was to have some bored parking inspector drawing attention to them.

With daylight fading, Caleb was having some difficulty assessing the building. While the alfresco area at the front of the pub was reasonably well lit, he couldn't see his former contact. The only people present at the front of the pub were two young women, both brunettes in their early to mid-twenties. One was dressed in a pink dress, the other in black.

"No sign of him." Caleb said when Darcy got back in the car. He glanced at his watch. The day had passed quickly, it was nearly six o'clock.

"Hopefully we don't have to wait too long…" Darcy said.

Caleb glanced away from the building for a moment, to offer up some reassurance. "It's okay, babe… if it takes more than an hour, I'll go in and find him," Caleb replied.

Darcy remained silent. Caleb knew she must be frustrated – with her only alternative to follow Caleb's lead at this point. He was the one with experience in this sort of situation. He knew Darcy had been involved in a couple of stakeouts before, but that was more along the lines of waiting for people who *knew* they were being waited for – politicians, celebrities, sports stars and the like.

Caleb was hoping they weren't going to wait for too long. It had been a long, tiring day, and constantly keeping an eye on his surroundings had created a tension in Caleb's shoulders that he couldn't shift.

And he was worried about what they'd discover when he confronted Dunleavy. Ever since his Marine missions had shifted focus, Caleb had grown increasingly concerned by Dunleavy's actions, or more the lack of action.

As they waited, the crowd enjoying an evening at Connor O'Sullivan's began to steadily grow. Being a Saturday night, the two girls who'd been sitting at the front were soon joined by three more, plus a couple at the adjoining table, and a steady stream of people, of various ages, were streaming in and out of the pub.

"Shit…" Darcy said. "How will we be able to spot him among all those people?"

Caleb didn't share Darcy's trepidation. The extra people only meant that Caleb had to sharpen his alertness to a higher level, something he was used to doing in his work. He stared, almost unblinking, into the rear-view mirror.

"It shouldn't be much longer. I doubt a man like Dunleavy wants to be where so many people are…" Caleb said, hopefully.

"Should I go in?" Darcy asked, "I mean, he doesn't know me."

Caleb noticed their target in the mirror.

"No need," Caleb said, inclining his head. "There he is."

A stocky, balding man walked out of the front door of the pub, almost stumbling.

Darcy turned in her seat to get a better view. Sure enough, there was Dunleavy, dressed in jeans, an untucked button down blue shirt, and some neat black shoes. "Wow, Chucky really came through."

"Yeah, he did. I might even let that 'meat-headed Marine boy' comment go," Caleb said, a wry smile on his face. When Darcy looked surprised, he grinned. "Babe... you really need to turn down the volume on your speaker."

Darcy chuckled. "Fair enough," she retorted.

Dunleavy began making his way east on Monroe as Caleb kept a watchful eye on him. "Okay, as you said, he probably doesn't know you. You get out, and follow him." Caleb instructed.

"Where will you be?"

"I'll follow you. I'll stay back far enough so that, even if Dunleavy is being cautious, he'll only see you, and won't even notice me."

"And that works does it?" Darcy asked.

"Only if you don't know what you're looking for..."

Darcy paused a little, Caleb maintaining a view of Dunleavy.

"So, what then... I mean, we do *need* to talk to him."

"When he stops at a place where we can safely talk to him, I'll over take you and make contact. Sound good?"

"Is there a choice?" Darcy asked with a smile and a wink.

Caleb chuckled, "Not really."

"Ok then...." Darcy said as she exited the car.

She moved towards the road, waited for a single silver sedan to pass, and began after Dunleavy.

The crowd around the pub was picking up, with the numbers more than double what they had been when they'd first parked. Caleb kept an eye on Darcy, who had slipped on a navy hooded-jacket to accompany her jeans and sneakers. As she walked, Darcy lifted her white cap, lightly brushed her hair back into place, and replaced the cap.

Caleb focused on the white baseball cap. From his training, he knew that if he tried to make sense of all the things going on around him, he would lose her. So he focused on the hat.

When Darcy was about a hundred feet away, Caleb exited the car and quickly crossed the road. He managed to manoeuvre gracefully through the crowd – or at least as gracefully as a six foot three, two-hundred-and-forty-pound Marine could. He followed the road, crossing over Central Avenue to East Monroe, keeping Darcy about a hundred feet in front of him. From his vantage point, he couldn't see Dunleavy, but knew Darcy would signal if she lost him.

Darcy crossed over North First Street, and abruptly, her white cap stopped moving.

Uncertain of why she had stopped, Caleb decided to do the same, maintaining the distance. Perhaps she'd lost him, or perhaps she had been seen? Caleb couldn't tell what the circumstances were.

After about five seconds, Darcy's white cap began to move again, slower than before. She took another four or five steps, the white cap turned to the right… and stepped into a large building.

Shit! Caleb thought, taking off at a run towards where Darcy had left the street.

As he approached the building, Caleb's mind raced. Confusion, fear and guilt, all rolled into one. It was the same feeling of dread he'd experienced, before the first shit-storm he'd dealt with in Iraq. At least then though, he knew the situation he was entering.

When he caught up to where Darcy had disappeared, a large grey structure greeted the Marine. While the façade made it plain what the structure was, Caleb knew this only complicated matters. The parking structure, with its simplistic design, had too many dark shadows, too many places for Dunleavy to hide and surprise his followers.

Just these thoughts were enough to make Caleb consider more caution in his approach. Unfortunately, the same could not be said for Darcy, as it had become apparent she had walked straight in.

Caleb, dismissing any remaining caution he felt, ran into the structure. He tried to remain as calm as he could, but it had been several moments since he had lost track of Darcy's white cap, and panic was starting to set in.

As he ran, Caleb made a quick scan of his surrounds. As he suspected, there were far too many places Dunleavy could conceal himself.

He began his search of the area, and turned around one of the large concrete pylons. As he turned the corner, he saw the white cap.

He was relieved when he saw Darcy. To his surprise, Dunleavy was with her. He was talking to her, as though trying to calm her down.

After a few moments, Dunleavy turned and saw Caleb. Dunleavy smiled, and motioned for Caleb to join them.

Caleb did as he requested. As he didn't know the situation, Caleb thought it best to play along.

Caleb walked over to where Darcy and Dunleavy were standing.

"Jackson," Dunleavy said, raising his hand to shake Caleb's.

Judging by the tone of Dunleavy's voice, Caleb realised he was neither surprised, nor upset by the unplanned meeting.

"Sir?" Caleb said, unable to hide his confusion.

"Jackson, I'm surprised it took you so long," Dunleavy began, "but I tell ya – it's about fucking time!"

"Why's that, sir?" Caleb asked, more confused than ever.

"Jackson. Everything we've been working for. Everything we've done…" Dunleavy's voice trailed off and he stared at Caleb, his eyes willing him to understand.

Caleb still didn't get it. He shrugged. "Yes?"

"You know the how they say 'the shit's about to hit the fan'?" Dunleavy asked.

Caleb nodded.

"We're about to get a whole new definition for it."

Chapter Eleven

Throwing off his initial shock, Caleb walked with Darcy and Dunleavy towards the centre of the structure, with Dunleavy taking the lead. By Caleb's judgement, there were maybe twenty cars on the lowest floor of the structure. The lighting was dim, but there was enough to see where they were going. The sun hadn't completely set, still providing limited additional light. That was, until they reached their destination.

Dunleavy's Black Chrysler 300C, while stylish, stood out in what was essentially a public parking lot. Dunleavy opened his mouth to talk again, but Caleb stopped him, holding up one hand while he did a quick check of the immediate area of the parking lot. While there was no indication they'd been followed throughout the day, and Darcy's laptop was safely stashed back in LA, Caleb still felt the need to be vigilant.

"You done?" Dunleavy asked, sounding offended that Caleb had even looked.

"Yeah, just about. Would you open your car, sir?" Caleb asked in a loud whisper.

"What the fuck are you talking about, Jackson?" Dunleavy responded, making no attempt to muffle his voice

"Sir— I— I haven't…" Caleb stumbled over his words, but took a deep breath and centred himself. "With all due respect. I haven't heard from you close to half a year, and you expect me to trust you?"

"Okay, okay, Caleb. Calm down," Dunleavy said, pushing the keyless entry button to his car.

"Caleb, it's okay. He's got no reason to deceive us," Darcy said, trying to calm her boyfriend down.

Caleb wasn't convinced. "Darcy, with respect, we don't know that. All we know is that he seems to have been expecting us…" Caleb replied.

"Okay kids, let me interject," Dunleavy said. "I'm guessing something happened, causing you to come to Phoenix. Something was obviously a catalyst for getting you off your ass, Jackson?"

"And?" Caleb responded testily.

"Well… let me tell you this. If I wanted you dead… you'd be dead. Caleb… Can I call you Caleb? Oh fuck it! Caleb it is."

Caleb crossed his arms over his chest. "Whatever you say… Mike."

Dunleavy grinned. "Ha! Fair enough… Anyway, Caleb. You know the reach I have. I can have anyone taken care of if I need to. You know that. But I haven't."

Caleb and Darcy glanced at each other, starting to come around to Dunleavy's thinking.

He continued, not really wanting a response, "Anyway, as you've probably seen Caleb… we're a bit exposed here. I mean, we're safe for now, but who knows if it will be the same in ten minutes?"

"So…"

"So… get in the car. Fuck it, you can even drive, Caleb, if that'll make you feel any better."

Dunleavy threw the keys to Caleb, who almost fumbled them.

"Good hands," Darcy quipped.

"Babe… not the time," Caleb said, abruptly.

"Okay then, get in," Dunleavy said. "We can talk and drive."

The trio entered the car. Caleb settled into the driver's seat, Darcy directly behind him. Dunleavy walked around the front of the car, and got into the passenger seat.

Caleb started the engine and turned to check on Darcy. "You comfortable back there?" he asked.

"So…" Caleb asked, turning to Dunleavy. "Where to?"

"This is your show, Caleb," Dunleavy responded. "Up to you."

Caleb steered out of the parking bay, and exited the lot. He drove towards First Street and Caleb turned left.

"So, Caleb," Dunleavy began, "I'm sure you've got some questions to ask me?"

Caleb considered the offer. Though part of him was reluctant, he de-cided to go for the biggest question he had. "You know I was the last per-son President Hawkins spoke to, right? He was probably on the phone to me when he was assassinated."

"No, I didn't," Dunleavy said, and Caleb could hear the surprise in his response. "There was a rumour he was in the midst of a phone call, but nothing was ever substantiated. Whoever shot him did the job, they took all the evidence from the room with them. Hawkins' phone, his wallet, even his fucking Broncos pass were missing when the body was discovered."

"So, you don't know who shot him?"

"I have my suspicions, but nothing concrete. My contacts at the FBI, CIA, NSA, even the fucking Washington PD didn't know jack about it. They guessed it was the work of a new splinter Al-Qaeda cell, but that's what they blame everything on nowadays. But still, that told me everything I needed to know. You see, for a while we've been following a *group*."

"Terrorists?"

"Not really. Though you'd think they were, based on the shit they've done. But no, they have other motivations. When it boils down to it, Caleb, terrorists are simple to understand – their motives anyway. That doesn't mean to say they're easy to catch. No... it's their *motives* which are al-ways clear. For fuck's sake, every time they do anything, they broadcast it on fucking Al Jazeera, or even on fucking You-Tube. No, these guys, this group we were after, they were different."

Caleb was growing impatient for answers. "What do you mean *different*?"

"While terrorists live up to their title – creating terror – these guys, it was as if they just did whatever they did to... please themselves. I don't know why, really."

"What are you saying? They're just anarchists?"

Dunleavy shook his head, drumming his thumb against the window-sill. "Not anarchists, Jackson. There was a pattern to what they did. After a time, it became clear there was something else going on. I'm certain they had a plan. Something big—"

"What was it? Do we know what their end game is?"

"No. Or at least, I never found out. These guys had people concealed everywhere. They have their own people in the CIA, NSA, FBI – and yeah – even the fucking WPD. Shit, it wouldn't have surprised me to discover they had people in every freakin' city in the United States."

Caleb whistled. "Really? It was that advanced?"

"Yeah... but we caught a break. Remember that mission in Beijing?"

"Vaguely. It was a simple *aggressive hack*. From memory, we didn't come up against much resistance."

"Yeah, that was because the group hadn't quite got their hands on China yet. No one can really, the place is a vault. Anyway, I'm getting side-tracked. The info you brought back—" Dunleavy paused, turning back to glance at Darcy. "I'm not sure I can speak openly in front of her, Caleb," Dunleavy admitted. "A reporter?"

"I'm assuming you're going to share some pretty critical information with me, right?" Caleb responded. "And it's going to breach all kinds of laws?"

"Sort of," Dunleavy replied.

Caleb grinned. "Anything you tell me, I'm gonna tell her later, so you might as well save me the effort of repeating it."

Darcy smiled at the notion.

"Okay," Dunleavy continued, after a moment where he scrutinised Darcy carefully. "Where were we? Right – the China mission. Anyway, what we discovered was that while the group didn't have an active member in China, they were using the place as a routing station."

"Routing station?" Caleb questioned blankly.

"Yeah... you know. Basically, a message would get sent from one place, and it would go through five or six, maybe even dozens of different computer terminals. Each terminal sends the message to the next point. At first, we couldn't break the encryption they were using. But eventually, we got through it. While we couldn't tell where the information came from initially, we were able to discover where it went."

"And where's that?"

Dunleavy inhaled a deep breath. "DC."

Caleb took his eyes from the road for a moment and stared at the former Chief-of-Staff. "Shit. Who was it?"

"Some low level piece of shit in the WPD. This guy was nuts. We located him and with a bit of pressure, eventually got him to talk."

"Okay, back up a little. Who is 'we'?"

"You know how I said we didn't know who to trust? I wasn't kidding. We really didn't. I only had a small team that I trusted enough to be involved in investigating this stuff. There was me, and a couple of nerds I recruited from MIT. Fucking losers, all of 'em, but they could definitely work a computer. I had one other guy, who was a former Marine. He was one hard mother, but he followed orders without question. You were my go-to guy when I needed a team of operatives. He was the guy I used when a team would have been too many."

"Okay. So what information did you get?"

Dunleavy shrugged. "Once again, not much. From what I could discover, the group we were after, well, they didn't give out much information. They weren't terrorists, that much we confirmed. This was in spite of the type of acts they were undertaking, but they learned some important tactics from the real terrorist groups. Basically, everyone in their organisation seems to be on a need-to-know basis. They've shared their information very sparingly."

"So what did you get from the WPD guy?"

"We really only found out how he was recruited."

When Dunleavy lapsed into silence again, Caleb stared at him. "And how was he recruited?"

"Caleb – I hate to tell you this, but this group were recruiting their people in exactly the same way I recruited you."

"And? How was that?"

Dunleavy paused, seeming to contemplate, once again, whether he should share the information with Caleb and Darcy.

Caleb had been driving random streets during their discussion, taking turns randomly to ensure they weren't followed. He probably would have enjoyed the serenity of the drive, if it hadn't been for the conversation he found himself embroiled in.

They were approaching an empty Walmart parking lot, and Dunleavy pointed toward it. "Caleb, you should probably pull over for this."

Agitated by Dunleavy's serious tone, Caleb turned left into the empty lot. He reverse-parked the car up against a wall, ensuring he had a decent view of the road and the rest of the lot. Once stopped, Caleb turned off the engine and braced himself for whatever Dunleavy was going to say.

Dunleavy sighed. "Caleb, I should probably start from the beginning."

Chapter Twelve

Pierre pulled over to the side of the road. He opened the car door, surveying the house opposite his position. He'd tracked the call to this address, and made his way over as soon as he could.

He was about to cross the street when his phone rang. He answered it swiftly, trying to avoid announcing his presence to anyone.

"William?" Pierre began, sounding very agitated, "William, I'm about to sort out *your* mess, and I don't need interruptions."

"Good" said a voice Pierre wasn't expecting.

"Sorry sir, I was expecting it to be William," Pierre said, struggling to deal with the shock of hearing this particular voice.

"Yes, I imagine you did," James stated. "I hear we have a problem."

"No problem sir. Just a wrinkle that needs to be ironed out," Pierre replied, nervous to think that James had felt the need to intervene. It was something he'd never done before. No matter the mission, nor the target, James had always kept a distance.

That distance had created a comfortable boundary. While Pierre trusted James, he also knew of his reputation for ruthlessness. Only a few select people knew about this reputation, and those who knew, also knew it was imperative not to lose James's trust.

Pierre also figured, with the implementation of Phase Two so close, his leader would be on edge.

"Okay," James said, "Pierre, I'm sure you've got a solution, and will ensure its successful outcome."

"Of course, sir. I haven't let you down before, have I?"

"No, you haven't. But this is different, Pierre. This is the most important task you have. Is Emmett in place?"

"Yes, he is."

"We've been tracking the movements of the intelligence agencies. It's a bit quiet. Will Emmett be putting out the recordings?"

"Yes, sir" Pierre glanced at his watch. "More information should be sent out in the next few hours."

"Good. And Matthew?"

"He's in LA. He's following William's man."

"Good."

"Sir, I assure you the reporter won't be a problem for us."

"I hope so, Pierre. For all our sakes," James warned, and then promptly hung up.

Something about James's tone during the conversation disturbed Pierre. In his long relationship with the man, it was the first time Pierre had heard him sound so.... *nervous*. Everything was on the line, and Pierre knew the plan *might* fail if he didn't do his job.

The trick was to lure the reporter and her boyfriend back to LA, where Leon could carry out his task, and Matthew could complete his. Pierre had thought about going to Phoenix and finishing the job himself, but it would expose him, and create too big a risk.

He worried the plan might be exposed. He didn't know Phoenix and he had no contacts there.

Pierre pondered on this as he moved towards the house. More of a cottage than a home, the target's house was quaint, reminding him of scenes he'd seen on a postcard.

Pierre knew exactly what he needed to do once he got into the house. It was something he had done so often now, he felt nothing.

After all, these people were going to die eventually, anyway.

Pierre walked up the steps and onto the patio. The patio itself was made of wood, obviously in need of a recoat of lacquer. Various bushes and shrubs hung around the vicinity, in no real discernible pattern.

He knocked on the door, and took a moment to focus himself for the task.

After about twenty seconds, Pierre heard the door unlocking. Being a relatively quiet neighbourhood, the occupant obviously felt safe enough to open the door without checking on who might be waiting on the other side.

It would be the last mistake they made.

As the door opened, Pierre raised the Glock he'd concealed in the back of his jeans. The suppressor pointed at the sixty-something year old woman who had opened the door, no more than an inch from her forehead. There was fear in her eyes, something that would have distracted Pierre in his younger days. Not now.

He pulled the trigger, and the woman slumped to the floor.

Pierre quickly stepped inside the house and closed the door quietly behind him.

His gun still drawn, he surveyed the small house quickly but came across no other occupants. He began a closer inspection.

He had tracked the call to this house, and he knew the person he was looking for should definitely be here. He decided to check the basement.

◆ ◆ ◆

The parking lot was almost completely silent. Save the cars driving past, and the light breeze occasionally shuffling leaves across the road, there wasn't a sound to be heard.

Caleb was suffering a fresh bout of nerves. Dunleavy had been so open on the car trip so far. Why had he suddenly asked Caleb to stop? What was the information he thought Caleb should hear when he *wasn't* driving? Caleb struggled to think straight and focus, such were the shifting thoughts in his head.

Dunleavy also remained quiet. Caleb could tell from his expression that he was searching for the right words to explain whatever he was about to say, but Caleb grew impatient. "Okay then," he said, trying to prompt Dunleavy into speaking.

"Alright," Dunleavy began, "do you remember your junior year in high school?"

Junior year in high school? Caleb thought to himself. He couldn't begin to imagine what Dunleavy was alluding to.

"Not really," Caleb said, "it's been a while."

"During junior year, everyone was given a basic IQ test. It was around the time when Congress was pushing for better educational standards. The best way to do that was to compile a baseline of where students were at. Congress figured using those students in senior year would be too difficult to compile accurate results, what with the SAT's and all. It was decided that something should be done to target those in their junior year, to create a more accurate result."

"Okay," said Caleb slowly, still unable to see where Dunleavy was leading.

"At the time, I'd been in the CIA for about ten years, and the recruitment pool was languishing. Remember, this was the late nineties. The cold war was well and truly over, and 9/11 had yet to happen. In order to locate viable new recruits, we organised with Congress to add our own section to the tests. A *personality* test of sorts. Basically, it told us what type of person you were, and whether you were predisposed to serving in the CIA. The questions would appear completely normal to any outsider, but would give the CIA very clear indications of how people could be useful, in the future. All the results were sent back to the Department of Education, and we made sure we had a guy in the department, one who would sort through and flag anyone who might be of interest to the CIA. Simple profiling, really"

"What happened?" Caleb asked, sceptical about what Dunleavy was telling them.

"Almost one hundred percent of the people we assessed were not of interest to us. We discarded their information, shredded their results. We had no interest in them for any future planning. Sorry, Ms Chamberlain."

"No need to apologise, I reckon I'm probably one of the lucky ones," Darcy responded, sounding relieved.

"So what happened to the others? The ones you *were* interested in?" Caleb prompted.

"We followed you all for a year or so, learning as much as we could – backgrounds, lifestyles, propensity for violence – in doing so, we were able to cut it down to a few dozen persons of interest."

"And I was on that list?" Caleb asked.

"Indeed," explained Dunleavy, "and you definitely remained a person of interest to us."

"Why? I came from a loving family, a decent home. Shit, you know Darcy. The people we hung around with were fine—"

"Agreed. But remember, the purpose of the tests was to ascertain who would be most suitable to work for us."

"So what's your point?" Caleb said. "This is hardly ground-breaking information. There have been rumours around for years about the Government testing people and profiling them for their own uses."

"I know. That's what makes it so easy… morally speaking. Our logic was, if people think you're fucking them over, you may as well make use of it."

Darcy huffed her disgust in the background, and Dunleavy momentarily lost track of his thoughts before he continued.

"Anyway," Dunleavy said. "Let me continue. Caleb, the reason I asked you to pull over is because… after those tests, we followed your life very closely."

"And?" Caleb snapped.

"I'm not sure you understand Caleb. Your results were of such interest to the CIA that we followed you closely enough to learn everything about you. We knew where you ate, what your grades were at school, your girlfriend. We even had access to all your medical records."

Caleb shook his head, as the implications began to filter into his mind. "Shit."

Dunleavy tapped his fingers against the windowsill. "Indeed, Caleb. We took your right to privacy and wiped our ass with it."

"Why are you telling me this?"

Dunleavy took a moment to think before he responded. "Basically, if my gut instincts regarding what's coming is anywhere close to right, then

I need to be upfront with you. We're gonna need more than Darcy's smile to stop this thing."

"Can't you be more specific?" Caleb asked.

"Fine. You need to know this for two reasons. One, I've seen your handy work in the field, and I'd rather you hear it from me, now, than you hear it from somewhere else. If that was to happen, there's no doubt you would be none too happy with me. Honesty Caleb... the good news, for us at least, was that you decided to become a Marine. It was easier for us to keep track of you that way."

"And what's the second reason?"

"After 9/11, a process began where we talked to other national intelligence agencies, both foreign and domestic. We showed them how we recruited, and trained our people. In turn they showed us the same. We were all trying to be better communicators to make sure 9/11 would never happen again."

Caleb listened intently, still trying to figure out what the hell Dunleavy was alluding to.

"Anyway, remember that guy we brought in? The cop?" Dunleavy continued. "He was recruited in the same manner. But rather than looking for the positives, the group, as he claims, were looking for the negatives. The down-trodden, the easily malleable. The people who, given a good enough incentive, would do anything for them."

"So, they used our technique against us?"

"Absolutely. Not just us though."

"Who else?"

"That's the million-dollar question Caleb."

"What exactly do we know?" Caleb asked.

"Some... but not much really. I could never seem to get much information. Each mission you went on answered a question, but asked even more. The plan, whatever it is, is big. Too big for just us to take down."

"Let me ask you, Mike – did the President know what you were doing?"

"Not at first, but over time, he got suspicious. I knew I had to tell him. Like I said, the group seemed to have influence everywhere. Over time, I began to feed the President information."

"So, why did it stop? Why did you leave?"

"Fucking politics."

"Sir?"

"He didn't approve of some of the missions we were doing. I was only following where each mission led, though. I knew the path we had to go down, so I sent you on the missions, regardless of where they led."

"What do you mean '*Where they led?*'" asked Caleb. "How did we even get started?"

Dunleavy was silent for a moment.

"Before we met, I started receiving emails. At first, they were merely information, suggesting I look at a certain bank account, or monitor a certain facility. I was able to verify the information provided as accurate. After time, the emails stated directing me to take action. After time, the actions we took, they led us on our *own* path."

"Who was sending the emails?"

"To this day I don't know. Someone with a pretty in-depth knowledge of the groups plans. I tried to back-trace the emails, but they bounced around so many IP's that it was impossible to ascertain their origin. Eventually, the missions became the priority, and I always figured that once the end-game of the group was discovered, and stopped, then I'd be able to find out who was on the other end."

Caleb contemplated the situation, "So what happened? Why did you leave? Why Did Hawkins take control?"

"After the London mission, Hawkins took over." Dunleavy shrugged, "And I was out."

"Why though?"

"The President realised we were doing missions in *friendly* nations, and asked me to step aside. He said I was unable to make the correct decisions and make proper use of your team."

"So, you left?"

"Yes, and no. I still kept my ear to the ground. Remember I told you about my other operative? I was able to get him a job in the White House. He kept me appraised of the situation. He passed on what he could."

"So far, it doesn't sound like much," Caleb pointed out.

"Granted, it's not. There is more, but let me ask you something first."

Dunleavy had been upfront; and now it seemed it was Caleb's turn to do the same. "What would you like to know?"

"Why do you think the President called *you*? You know, before the end?" Dunleavy asked.

"I've been asking myself that same thing, ever since it happened. I haven't been able to come up with anything. He told me to 'Find the Source'. Do you know what that means?"

Dunleavy frowned.

"The Source? Are you sure that's what he said?"

"Yeah. Trust me, I've replayed that conversation a million times in my head."

"Never heard of it. Did it come up in any of your missions?"

"Nope, not that I know of."

"Another fucking mystery then!" Dunleavy growled. "Can I ask you something else? Why did you come to me? I mean, what was the catalyst for you to come to Phoenix. You could have tried so many times before now. My whereabouts was never a secret."

Caleb explained the email Darcy had received, and their suspicion that Dunleavy would know more about it, having been sent the information from the Berlin mission.

"The Tracker?" Dunleavy asked. "Shit, I sent the info off to the *nerds*. The ones in DC. They came back with, well, fuck-all, really. They knew it was advanced, and was something they'd never seen before. It basically turned any device which opened the program into some kind of homing-beacon – one they could track from a central location. You say you've seen the program?"

"Yeah, it was on my computer," Darcy spoke up, obviously tired of being left out of the conversation.

"Okay then. We'll have to call them," Dunleavy said.

"Call who?" Caleb asked.

"The nerds… in DC."

"Actually, Caleb and I have our own nerd," Darcy announced.

"She's right," Caleb agreed. "How do you think we knew you were at the pub?"

"Can you trust him?" asked Dunleavy.

"About as much as we trust anyone right now," Darcy replied. "Should I call him, Caleb?"

Caleb pondered. It was true that Chuck had found Dunleavy. But, Dunleavy's men knew the situation, and had worked with the tracking program before.

"Mike, can you call your guys instead? I don't think we can take the chance of going back to LA."

"Okay, I'll give it a try." Dunleavy dialled his phone. Caleb waited impatiently for him to say something, anything.

Dunleavy spoke into the handset. "Hi, is Doug there? Tell him it's Mike."

Dunleavy continued the conversation – asking about Doug and what Caleb could only assume was his offsider, Timothy. After a brief exchange, Dunleavy hung up the phone. A worried look had settled over his eyes.

"Well?" Caleb demanded. "What did they say?"

"Two weeks ago, Doug and Tim were on their way to work – and they were in a car accident."

"Both of them?"

"Yeah," Dunleavy said, rubbing his temples worriedly. "They're both dead."

Chapter Thirteen

The only thing that surprised Caleb was that he wasn't surprised. He had a suspicion the bodies might start piling up. "Wait… did they drive to work together?" he asked.

"No. They didn't even live close to each other, and, they were both employed at different offices when they weren't working for me," replied Dunleavy.

Caleb let a low whistle slip between his lips. "One car accident… maybe. But two, on the same day? To two of the guys who are in the loop regarding what we know…"

"Agreed. It's bullshit."

"What about the person who answered the phone?"

"Doug's mother. She seemed very distraught, understandably."

"I guess they're chalking it up to coincidence."

"Indeed. But, like I said, this group we're up against, they seem to have a knack for doing just that. They give out just enough information to point toward the solution they want you to see." Dunleavy turned to Darcy. "Darcy, do you trust this… what's his name?"

"Chuck," Darcy supplied.

"This Chuck…" Dunleavy began, before he stopped, arching an eyebrow.

"Yes, we can trust him." Replied Darcy, anticipating Dunleavy's question.

Dunleavy exchanged a look with Caleb, as though trying to gauge his response.

"Like Darcy said, we can trust him about as much as anyone right now. Shit Mike, I'm still trying to trust *you*."

"Fair enough," Dunleavy replied.

"Darc, call Chucky. See what he can tell you over the phone." asked Caleb.

Darcy dialled the number. It took a little longer than the usual one ring, but eventually her nerd friend picked up the phone.

"Hi Darcy," Chuck said when he answered.

"Hey Chucky," Darcy began. "Thanks for your help before—"

"Oh... you found Dunleavy?"

"Of course, I mean, we only managed it with your *brilliant* help," Darcy said, trying to keep the usual flirty tone going.

"Good," Chuck replied, sounding decidedly less flirtatious than normal. "What can I do for you?"

"Everything okay, Chucky?" Darcy questioned carefully.

"Of— Of course it is," Chuck replied.

"You don't sound it. Are you sure you're okay?"

"Yeah, of course." Chucky replied guardedly. He paused, and let out a deep sigh. "I guess I'm just... shit, Darc, I'm nervous, that's all. I just tracked down the former Chief-of-Staff..." He stopped for a moment, before his next words came out in a rush. "That's max level crossing-the-line shit..."

"Ahhh, fair enough," Darcy replied, relaxing with the knowledge that Chuck had a decent reason for his trepidation. "Anyway, I hate to ask, but I need your help again."

"Of course you do."

Darcy frowned. "Chucky, are you mad at me?"

"No, of course not. It's just... well... um... what can I do for you?"

"If I showed you a computer program, could you tell me about it?"

She didn't miss the interest in Chucky's response. "What kind of program?"

"We think it's a tracker or something. I just need to know where it came from, who might have created it."

"Ah..." Chuck paused, considering the question. "Um... is it on a computer, or a phone?"

"Laptop."

"No problem. I just need to see the file."

"Ok. I'll forward the email."

"No, that won't work... I need to see the laptop"

"Really? Can't I just send it to you? I don't know... Isn't an email attachment the same regardless?"

Chuck again paused and stumbled over his response.

"I don't really have the ability to figure it out, without the machine... I'll explain, Darc. I just need the laptop. If it is a tracker, I can get a lot more information directly from the machine it's tracking. Can you get a hold of it?"

"I guess," Darcy began doubtfully. "Just hang on a sec." Darcy placed her hand over the speaker of her phone, leant forward, and whispered to Caleb. "Can we go back to LA? Chuck says he needs to see the laptop."

"Why?" Caleb asked.

"Chuck says he can understand the program better if he can access the laptop itself. He was pretty adamant."

"Well... is there another choice?"

"I don't think so."

Caleb released his breath in a noisy whoosh. "I guess we're going back to LA then."

Darcy uncovered the phone receiver, and spoke with Chuck. "Okay, we'll be there in the morning."

"The morning? Ahhh... are you still in Phoenix?" Chuck asked.

"Um... maybe..." Darcy didn't lie. All the time Caleb had been driving around, Darcy had been so focused on the conversation that she'd lost track of where they were.

"Oh... ok... Well I guess I'll see you in the morning." Chuck said.

"See you then Chuck... Sweet dreams..." Darcy responded.

"Darcy... wait..." Chuck added as Darcy was about to hang-up

"What's up?"

"Um... there's just a bit of heat on at the moment, so I'm gonna have to go offline. I'll call you in the morning ok, and we'll organise a time ok?"

"Okay. Chuck, are you sure everything's ok?"

"Yeah... of course. I'll just be offline until the morning though..."

"Alright Chucky. See you in the morning"

"Night, Darc."

With that, the phone call ended.

"So..." Caleb asked. "I guess we're going back to LA then."

"Yeah." Darcy said.

Caleb turned to Dunleavy.

"We can drop you off somewhere." Caleb said

"No fucking way, Caleb," Dunleavy replied, "I'm coming with you. I've waited a long time for answers. I think it's time we figured out exactly what was going on."

"Okay, then," Caleb said. "Buckle up and get comfortable."

Caleb started the engine, and moved the car out of the vacant parking lot. He drove his way back to the I40, and they began their journey back to where they started that morning.

◆ ◆ ◆

Chuck disconnected the call, placing the phone on the table before he glanced over at the man who'd been monitoring. "How... how was that?" Chuck asked. He could feel the beads of sweat, trickling down his back and wondered if this man would be satisfied with what he'd done.

"That was fine," Pierre began. He glanced down at his phone, opened the tracking program, and saw the dot which indicated Darcy was heading back to LA.

"It worked..." Pierre said with a smile, "They're coming home."

"Good," Chuck replied, clearly relieved to learn that he'd managed to convince Darcy to come home. "Does that mean I can go? Can I see my Mom now?"

"Yes, Charles. Yes, it does."

Chuck smiled, his relief visible in his expression.

His smile quickly vanished when Pierre drew his gun, aimed and pulled the trigger in one smooth move. The bright flash of the suppressed gunshot was the last thing Chuck would ever see. His large, pimple-ridden face was thrown backwards by the impact, his skull exploding and blood spraying across the *Firefly* poster behind him.

Pierre admired his handiwork "You'll be seeing her right now," he said to the lifeless body in the chair in front of him.

Chapter Fourteen

Pierre admired his handiwork. It had been a while since he'd had to get his hands so dirty. But, as time was critical to the next part of the plan, he felt he had little choice. The fact that the kill was so easy was of little surprise to him. He'd killed many people for the cause, and over time, it grew easier with every new victim.

He was comforted by his belief in his work, and that ultimately, once he'd claimed his place in the future, he would be able to further justify every life he'd taken.

Besides, according to the plan, one death would be miniscule compared to the scale of what the plan was about to achieve.

He took one last look at Chuck's hefty, lifeless frame, and made his way up and out of the basement.

As he approached the front door, he saw day had turned into night. Being suburbia, it was easy for Pierre to slip out of the house and not be noticed. Not that he really cared much at that point. Whether he was seen or not was irrelevant.

He walked back to his car, the light breeze ruffling his sand coloured hair. He opened the door, entered the driver's seat, and sat for a few minutes while he contemplated the situation.

While his exterior seemed relaxed, Pierre's mind was moving fast as he addressed the multiple scenarios in his head.

His earlier conversation with James had spooked him.

After thinking for several minutes, Pierre decided to play it safe. He would make contact with his young protégés and check their progress. Once established, he would then decide his next move.

His first call was to Emmett.

The phone only rang once.

"Pierre?" the young man asked.

"Yes Emmett," Pierre replied, his soft, serene tone effectively masking his emotions, "just calling to check in. How's the progress?"

"Um… yeah… it's all going well sir. I've organised the emails and files. I was planning to send everything to the usual places soon."

"Good… good" said Pierre, relaxing slightly. "I just wanted to check in, Emmett. We are so close to the end; I can taste it."

"How close sir?" Emmett asked, his voice pleading for information, his isolation starting to affect him.

"Emmett…" he began, trying to reassure his young student, "Once the plane is down, I will tell you where the nearest colony is. Then you can join them and take your place."

The news surprised Emmett.

"Really? Wow," Emmett replied, unable to contain his enthusiasm, "and my parents will be there? Like you promised…"

At this point in time, Pierre decided honesty was *not* the best policy.

"Indeed," he responded, trying to keep any hint of deception from his voice. "They're waiting for you there."

"Excellent… was there anything else?"

"No, Emmett, you're doing well. Just make sure you send the files out. It's the most crucial part of your mission."

"Will do, sir, will do"

"Good. I'll speak to you in a few hours."

Pierre disconnected the call. He experienced little remorse in having to deceive Emmett, and was unsure how he would take the news of his parent's demise. Though it had been a necessary task, Pierre had taken no pleasure in murdering Emmett's mother and father.

If only they hadn't asked so many questions, Pierre thought, *they'd still be alive.*

"Such is life," Pierre said aloud, using the words to inspire himself to continue.

His second phone call went to Matthew. Once again, the phone only rang once.

"Pierre?" Matthew answered, sounding happy to hear from his mentor.

"Matthew, I'm just checking in."

"Everything's fine, sir. I got here about an hour ago, but the target hasn't arrived yet.

"That's fine," Pierre said reassuringly, "Do you have a good view of the apartment?"

"Yes sir."

"Will you have him covered?"

"Sir, there's no chance he's getting out of there alive."

"Good Matthew. Excellent."

"Easiest task I've had so far," Matthew quipped, and Pierre suspected he was trying to impress his mentor.

"Well done." Pierre paused, considering his next move. "I don't need to tell you how critical the mission is, Matthew. Settle in, as the target will be there soon. It might be some time before he completes his task. I'll come and join you soon."

Pierre heard the surprise in Matthew's voice. "Really? Okay," he replied.

"Don't worry Matthew, it's not a comment on your abilities. I trust you, and I know you will do exactly what you need to do."

"Okay."

"I just need to be onsite in case your target fucks up. From what I've heard, he may just do that. It's imperative *he* completes his mission too."

"Okay then."

"So, tell me where you are, exactly." Pierre listened intently as Matthew gave him the address. Just before Pierre hung up, he reassured Matthew once again. "Don't worry. Your place in the colony, and the future, will be assured once this task is complete. On that, you have my word."

♦ ♦ ♦

"Gentlemen, this is where we part ways."

The three men stood inside a hangar. It was a vast open space, almost the length of an aircraft carrier. Standing so close to one another was the only way to communicate without losing the sound in the echoes.

James looked at his two life-long friends. They momentarily stood silent, contemplating how far they'd come since that first endeavour, so many years ago.

"We're nearly there," Zach said. "We're so close, I can taste it."

"Indeed," replied James, his face beaming at the thought.

The silent joy lingered for a moment, and was broken by the first pilot.

"Sirs; we're ready for you," the young female pilot announced.

Zach and John shook each other's hand, then turned to James. As was the case with their leader, both men had reverted to their much younger selves.

"Reminds me of when we first arrived," James said. "How young we were, and how excited we were."

The three men savoured the moment, each experiencing a sense of satisfaction to know their plan had come so far.

"Good luck lads," James announced. While he enjoyed reminiscing, there was still much work to be done. The sight of his friends, returned to their former youthful looks, was almost enough to bring a tear to James's eyes. Before his emotions could get the better of him, he ushered them away. "Go on, off with you both then" he said.

With one last smile and nod, the two men turned away, approaching two identical jets parked about two hundred feet away. Both were sleek in design and looked magnificent as the below ground lights reflected from them. As the men approached, they were each greeted by their pilot, who ushered them to their planes, each bound for a separate destination. Zach would be travelling to London, John's flight would soon be bound for Berlin.

As he moved away, Zach turned around and jogged back towards James.

"Now James, make sure you look after Helen for me." Zach said.

"I'll treat her as though she were my own." James replied

"Are you sure I can't convince you that we need her in London?" Zach asked already knowing the answer.

"I'm sure Zach," James replied, half smiling at his friend. "Trust me, she'll be fine here."

"Okay then," Zach said. "See you in the next life."

He jogged back to the plane, up the stairs and into the main cabin.

The stairs of Zach's plane lifted. As the door was closed, James contemplated how far they'd come, and how close they were to the next part of the journey. The journey which had started so long ago.

As he stood and pondered their achievements, a young female technician approached him. "Sorry sir, you're going to need to step into the control room. It's about to get very hot in here," she said.

Following her instructions, James walked with her towards a room on the side of the hangar. She opened the door for him, and he walked through. The technician followed closely behind, her shoulder-length, brunette hair tied back in a ponytail and protruding through the hole at the back of her cap. When she sat down, she looked towards James. "Take a seat, sir." she said as she motioned for James to sit in the chair beside her.

"No thank you, I'd prefer to stand," he replied

James studied the touch-screen panels and monitors. While he had been the mastermind of the plan, and inspiration to all who followed him, of late James had little to do with the day-to-day workings of the facility. One of his greatest traits was the ability to harness the skills of those around him.

"You've done well to create such efficiency." James complimented the technician, "Talk me through what you've been able to do."

"As you've always told us, sir, efficiency is the key." Replied the technician, flattered that James would show such a keen interest, "I designed most of it, and the pilots had input into the jets and the runway. They've been able to modify the jets to avoid radar – stealth additions, no transponders, et cetera. Also, we held a number of discussions with the London and Berlin colonies, as well as some of the others. They're all doing the same thing at their ends."

"Well done," James commented, genuinely impressed with the work, "It's certainly much better than the farm we've been using."

Up until a few weeks earlier, the planes were required to land at a farm located about five miles from where they were. While they had never had any issues in the past – their government infiltrations had seen to that – all ground operations were now underground, assisting with their clandestine operation.

"Yes sir, thank you, sir," said the woman. "I must admit, it wasn't easy. Took a while to get it all sorted out to function correctly. It's not easy to launch a plane from underground. All the necessary modifications have been made."

"And the workers, what has happened to them?"

"After they completed the work on the runway, and the hangar, they were sent back to their holding areas."

"Oh," James said, "I thought how they were to be dealt with was made clear?"

"Oh, you mean..." The technician replied. "Of course. They will be. I didn't want to *complete* the task until I knew we definitely didn't need them anymore."

"And when will you know?"

"The next day or so. Once these planes take off, we'll have finally confirmed the system, the hangar and the runway are all sound."

"Wait," James began, a little concerned about the planes carrying his friends. "Is there still some doubt?"

She shook her head, lifting her chin confidently. "No Sir, I'm sure it will all work according to our computed outcomes. And all the other runs have been successful."

"Good," he said,

"I'd bet my life on it working to your satisfaction, Sir"

James admired her confidence. He'd instructed his people to ensure the brightest and the best were recruited. He was glad to discover it was apparently the case. "Let's get this show on the road, then," he said.

"Yes, sir." The woman pressed a series of buttons, and the hangar grew dark, with only the lights delineating the two runways creating any visibility.

"Opening the hatch," she announced into the headset, communicating with the pilots.

She pressed a further series of buttons. When she'd finished the sequence, a large metal door slowly began to open at the far end of the hangar. From his viewpoint, James watched with great interest...

"Ladies... start your engines," the technician said with enthusiasm chuckle.

As James turned his attention back to the two planes, he saw them preparing to take off. "Tilting the floor," the technician said into the headset, typing feverishly at the touchscreen in front of her.

The large floor began to move, one end slowly rising higher with every passing second, reaching towards the large opening created by the receding hatch.

Once the ramp was in place, the controller stopped typing and turned her attention to him momentarily. "Just one more thing sir..."

"Yes?"

She smiled at him as she spoke into the headset. "Pilots – See you in the next life," she announced.

James returned her smile.

Over the speaker, the two pilots, almost in unison, repeated the same phrase. "Roger, Control. See you in the next life."

"Ready, sir?" the technician asked.

James nodded.

The controller pushed one final button, and the planes both exploded into motion, flung forward by the slingshot attached to the under-nose of each of the planes. They were hurtled down the runway, and up the ramp.

Within a second, both planes had left the hangar and flown off into the distance. Within thirty seconds, they were no more than tiny dots in the sky.

"Well done," James said, as her turned and shook her hand.

"Thank you, sir?" she replied, "Is there anything else you need?"

"One more thing...." James contemplated his next move. "Get those workers back here, and get them to do a final check of the systems. The mechanics of the ramp. Everything. Once that's done, pick two of them. Those will stay with us to look after the ongoing maintenance and up-keep. They can also train anyone else to do the work."

"And the rest sir?"

"Well..." James paused as though to add drama to his words. "We can't take them all with us..."

The woman understood.

"Just don't make a mess" said James.

"Yes sir."

James left the control room, and walked out of the hangar. His friends were on their way, and soon their colonies would have the serum.

Phase Two was well and truly underway.

Chapter Fifteen

It had been a long flight, and Leon was glad when it ended. He'd experienced very little trouble getting through customs.. While he was happy with the ease of his entry, there was part of him that was bewildered.

He was there to kill a person, having just killed another just twenty-four hours ago.

Leaving customs behind Leon walked straight towards the long-term storage lockers in the terminal –where the email had revealed the equipment would be located.

It had been placed in the locker more than twelve months ago, a proven tactic to avoid detection. If police or federal investigators had shown any interest in watching the locker, they'd be in for a long wait, as it was protocol that no 'drop' location was accessed for at least six months.

Leon took the package from the locker. It had been wrapped in a white, non-descript cardboard box. Without examining the contents, he slipped the package into his bag, and walked out of the terminal. No one in the vicinity was any the wiser.

Following his training and instructions, Leon caught a cab, and requested it take him to a location approximately half a mile from the target destination. After a short walk, Leon found a quiet café. He found an empty seat, and opened his laptop, reassessing his mission.

He studied the apartment he was targeting, and closely examined the photo again.

Before proceeding, Leon sat back in his seat, and examined his surroundings. The thought of being back in the U.S., after being away in Australia for so long was an almost surreal experience. He had always wanted to come home, and the sights and smells and people were somewhat familiar to him. At the same time, they were also strange.

His time with William had changed him. No longer was he a struggling orderly. Now, he was part of something greater, and as he looked at the people around him, he knew his life had changed irrevocably. He knew he was important, and that his meaningless life was far behind him.

He considered his situation briefly, and then reminded himself of exactly why he was there.

Needing some privacy to open the package, Leon walked casually through the café to the restrooms. The small, dingy room held only two cubicles. Choosing the one furthest from the entry, Leon entered the cubicle, and shut the door, twisting the lock. Satisfied that he would not be disturbed, Leon settled on the closed toilet lid and opened the package he'd collected at the airport. The shoebox contents were not unexpected – it held a CZ 75 9mm pistol, the weapon of choice among the colony members and its agents. The weapon was first designed in the Czech Republic in the mid-seventies. From there, different variations have been made, but overall more than one million CZ 75's had been produced. The serial number of this particular handset had been filed off. Given this, and the gun would be virtually untraceable.

The exact reason the colony chose to use it.

Leon assessed the weapon. The chamber was clear, and the clip full. Due to the fact that the weapon had been in storage for potentially twelve months or more, Leon ensured he carefully cleaned the gun. Once satisfied, Leon put the pieces back in place, loaded the clip, and loaded a round into the chamber.

Ready to proceed, he left the restroom, exited the café, and strolled down the street towards the apartment block.

As he got closer, Leon remembered to make sure he wasn't seen for the last one hundred yards or so.

From what William had told him, his target was a reporter, but he knew little about her. He kept a wary eye on the apartment block, watching for people leaving or entering.

Seeing no one around, he was confident enough to proceed.

Leon strode towards the side of the apartment block and swiftly turned down the side of the building, searching for the entry point he'd noted from the plans – a downpipe, located next to the bathroom window of the apartment.

Leon had received training in maintaining strength and upper body mobility, so he had no trouble climbing the downpipe, up to the bathroom window. Gripping the pipe with one hand, he leaned to the side in order to push the window open. It had been a long shot, and he wasn't surprised to discover the window was locked. He glanced down, ensuring the alleyway he was in remained empty. The fact that it was out of view of the street, gave him the advantage of privacy.

Using the butt of the gun, he tapped on the bottom left corner of the window. The impact made an initial crack in the glass, just enough to weaken the surface. He tucked the gun back into his jeans, and using the heel of his gloved hand, repeatedly punched at the window. After about a few hits, the bottom corner of the window gave way, and an opening the size of a volleyball appeared. Fortunately, the window latch was on the left side of the window, and Leon was able to easily open it.

After some careful manoeuvring, Leon swung his legs to the sill, and hoisted himself through. He did a quick sweep of the apartment, and found nobody was home. The bed hadn't been made, and there were cupboards still standing ajar as though the target had left in a hurry.

Doing a second sweep, Leon confirmed he was in the right apartment, as numerous photographs displayed throughout the apartment showed the target with a man.

The other man was large, almost as large as Leon, but he doubted the guy would be a threat.. Leon had undertaken a lot of training to get him to the point he was at currently – he was confident he could handle the targets male friend.

Leon made an assessment of the apartment, and found the perfect spot to wait for the target's return. There were two couches in the main living area, separated by a small gap. The gap was large enough for Leon to hide. He crouched down, lay flat on his stomach and faced the door. *They never look down*, he thought.

Now, all he had to do was wait. He was a patient man; he was prepared to wait for as long as it took. Shortly after he'd positioned himself, his phone rang and a glance at the screen confirmed it was William.

"Yes?" said Leon

"Leon," William's voice was vibrant. "How are things?"

Leon adjusted his position incrementally. "Okay."

"Good. Are you in position?"

"Yeah, just arrived. I'm in the apartment."

"Excellent. I'm sure you're wondering where your target is?"

"Indeed, sir."

"No need to fret. They'll be arriving in a few hours. They're on their way back from Arizona."

"Okay," replied Leon, glad to have a timeline.

"You've done well, Leon. You have followed your training well. Otherwise, you would have been picked up breaking and entering by now."

"Of course, sir. I remembered what you taught me."

"Good, now just—"

"Sir, if I may," Leon interrupted.

"Yes, Leon?" William replied, and he sounded annoyed by the interruption.

"Can I speak to Josie?" Leon asked quietly, expecting his request to be rejected.

"Of course," William said. "I'll put you on speaker. Go ahead."

"Josie?"

"We're here, honey" Josie replied, unable to contain the joy in her voice. "We miss you."

"Yeah, we miss you, Daddy," said Leon's daughter, Lilly.

"Yeah guys. I miss you all. I love you all very much."

"We love you too, honey. When will you be back?" Josie said.

"Soon, baby, soon. There's just one thing I gotta take care of first."

"Hurry up, won't you? I'm just about to be processed." Josie paused. "Baby, I'll see you in the next life."

William smiled at her and the kids.

"See you in the next life, baby," Leon said, holding back tears.

William came back on the line. "Now Leon, I will contact you when the target is near…"

"Okay sir. I'll hold my position here."

"Good… and well done." William disconnected the call.

Leon was chuffed. He hadn't spoken to his family in several weeks, as he had been on assignment for William, but the conversation he'd just had with his family renewed his desire to succeed in his mission.

He put the phone back in his pocket, settled back onto his stomach and focused on the door, just in case.

◆　◆　◆

William turned to Josie, Lilly and Aaron once he'd disconnected the call. With a smile, he motioned to a man, who had been waiting just outside his office, to enter the room.

"Now Josie," William began. "I want you to go with this man. It's time for you to receive the serum."

"Thank you, sir…. Thank you for everything."

"Don't thank me… thank your husband when he returns."

"I… I… will" Josie said.

She turned to the kids, and they walked to the door. As they left the room, the man accompanying them paused, and turned back to William.

William looked the man in the eye, and inclined his head.

The man held up his index finger, signalling 'one'.

William shook his head, and signalled with his thumb, index and middle finger – three.

The guard knew what this meant. He turned back to follow the family, and closed the door behind him.

The next thing William heard would have sent shivers up anyone else's spine.

Bang! Bang! Bang!

William smiled.

Three less things to worry about, he thought.

Chapter Sixteen

The drive was drawing to a close.

It had been conducted in several hours of virtual silence. Darcy had opted to sleep in the back. Caleb and Dunleavy were sitting in the front seats, both used to going for long periods without sleep.

They were now less than two miles from the apartment and the laptop, and Caleb could feel his adrenaline flowing through his bloodstream, as he prepared himself for what they faced. Caleb still couldn't understand why Chuck needed the device, as he'd thought the program operated in exactly the same manner, regardless of the machine used to access it.

He bit his bottom lip thoughtfully, his tension level increasing, the closer they got to the apartment. Darcy trusted Chuck, and Caleb trusted Darcy, so he thought he had no option other than to play along with this plan, even though his gut instincts suggested it was a mistake to return to Los Angeles.

It would be on his terms, however. Based on his past experiences, Caleb knew he could still control the situation. He was determined to protect Darcy no matter what potential obstacles faced them.

Caleb turned to Dunleavy, and motioned for him to wake up their other passenger.

At Caleb's behest, Dunleavy turned, reached into the back seat and gently shook Darcy's knee.

Darcy slowly woke up from her nap and sat up, stretching.

"You okay, babe?" Caleb asked over his shoulder.

"Hmm... yeah..." Darcy mumbled.

"We're nearly there."

Darcy sounded surprised when she responded. "Really? That was fast."

"Not really, you've been out of it for a while." Caleb responded with a smirk.

Darcy's eyes widened. "Oh, okay. Wow, I must have been really tired."

Caleb drove into a parking lot, about a half-mile from Darcy's apartment, stopping the car and turning off the engine. "Okay, here's where we part ways," he announced.

"Wait... what?" asked Darcy, her eyes widening.

"Babe, there are people tracking the laptop. I'm not going to let you get anywhere near it, not until I know it's safe. I'll go and get it, and take it to Chuck myself."

"Caleb... if you think there is any way I'm not going with you..."

"Darcy," Caleb said, his voice steady and firm. "I am not putting your life in danger."

"Caleb," Darcy replied, and Caleb knew she was trying to sound calm and composed, "my life is already in danger. I only feel safe when I'm with you. I don't know who I can trust... no offense Mike."

"None taken," replied Dunleavy.

Caleb considered the situation. It had several unknowns, and he wondered if he could guarantee Darcy's safety if she stayed with him.

Until he knew the entire situation, and who exactly was after him, he knew he couldn't be sure.

But she did have a point. He would worry if she wasn't with him, and he didn't completely trust Dunleavy, even though Dunleavy had given him no real reason *not* to trust him at this point in time.

Caleb assessed his options, and decided to opt for the lesser of the two dangers. "Alright. I give in. But, I want you to stay here for now. I'll go to the apartment and get the laptop. Dunleavy... you stay with her, at all times. Get it? You don't let her out of your sight."

Dunleavy nodded his agreement and Caleb glanced back at Darcy.

Darcy nodded, reluctantly.

Caleb left the car, walking from the carpark and out to the road leading to Darcy's apartment. Before he turned the corner, he looked back at her, and smiled reassuringly.

Darcy returned the smile, although hers was a little more tentative.

If it was to be Caleb's last image of her, he was glad it would be her smiling. The thought comforted him, and Caleb began jogging toward the apartment.

"You've got a good one there," said Dunleavy, watching his former charge jog away. "He's never failed me before, and I can't see him doing it now. Not when he's fighting for you."

"I know," Darcy replied.

"I don't think you do. In all the research we did, all the profiling – the one trait that always stood out with Caleb, the one element of his character which seemed to always stand out was fidelity. No matter what choices he made, he was completely loyal to that choice. Probably why he joined the Marines. Sempre Fi—"

"I know that, Mike," Darcy said tersely.

"I realise you do," Dunleavy responded. "But I thought you should know, there's more to him—"

"You think you know him?" Darcy snapped, "You think you know him because he answered a quiz in a certain way, or because of the way he carried out these *missions* you sent him on? You think you know him, because you think all your mind games and manipulations were perfect. Well, you know what? You don't know shit about him, Mr. Dunleavy. Caleb is the *best* person I have ever met. I *know* him better than any of your tests, any of your psychological games ever could!"

Dunleavy was taken aback by her anger, not used to being spoken to in such a way. He'd always been treated with respect; to have this little spitfire shouting him down was quite a shock.

"Have you ever seen him when he's not about to go on a mission?" Darcy asked, not waiting for a response. "No, you haven't. You don't know the real Caleb. I've seen him do acts of kindness for people, the things that no one else does. He's the kind of guy who stood up for the bullied kids at school. The kind of guy who gave up his spot in the Varsity football team, to the kid whose parents had just been killed. He's the guy who, no matter the situation, always does the good and right thing. He is everything the rest of us aren't. That's who he is, and you're lucky you had him working for you!"

Darcy lapsed into silence, her arms crossed over her chest, her annoyance evident. Dunleavy had no doubt that she knew Caleb better than anyone else ever could, and obviously, she wasn't going to let anyone tell her otherwise. He admired her spunk. "My apologies, Ms. Chamberlain."

She remained silent for almost a full minute before she spoke. "Okay, then." There was another long pause before Darcy continued. "Just don't you dare think you know him better than I do. You've only seen him at his worst. I've seen him at his best."

With that, they both fell silent, waiting for Caleb to return.

◆ ◆ ◆

Leon's eyes were drooping. He'd been waiting in the apartment for hours, and the conversation with his family seemed so long ago. Leon was happy to know that regardless of how the situation turned out, his wife and children would prosper into the future. It would all be worth it, to know that he'd secured their safety.

He was startled by a vibration from his pocket and he hurried to retrieve the phone, seeing William's name on the caller ID he answered the call.

"Leon," William said, without waiting for Leon to speak. "The car is parked about a mile away. Be prepared. It appears they might suspect something."

"It's okay, I'll get them as soon as they walk in. I'm in position and they won't know what hit them."

"Just don't fuck this up."

"I won't, sir."

"Stay alert. The target will be there any minute."

"Yes sir."

"Good luck," William said and disconnected the call.

The adrenaline pumped through Leon's body, his alertness heightened, and he worked to block all external thoughts from his mind.

His family.

The plan.

Everything.

His focus was on the door and the taking down of anyone who entered.

Seconds turned into minutes. Lying on his stomach between the couches, Leon pointed the pistol towards the door. He struggled to block all the sounds coming from outside the apartment.

The passing cars caused several distractions. The lights rebounded from the wall, and made the door seem like it opened. The sound of the engines prevented Leon from hearing anything unusual in the vacant apartment.

After several minutes, a motorcycle went past outside. The engine was loud, and the lights brightened the room.

Blinking from the sudden flash of brightness, he felt a huge blow on the back of his head,.

Chapter Seventeen

Caleb had approached the building cautiously, working his way around from the front to the side, where he noticed the broken bathroom window. He entered the apartment exactly the same way Leon had, keeping his movements completely silent. Once he'd entered the bathroom, he considered the apartment and how an assassin would plan his attack.

He was dealing with a trained professional, someone who'd made an effort to hide how he entered the building. Considering this, and the apartment layout, Caleb reasoned that whoever was here would have wanted a good view of the door, and hidden themselves – probably at floor level.

The space between the couches, he thought.

Caleb cautiously made his way through the apartment, hugging the walls, only moving when a vehicle passed in the street below, to mask his movements as much as possible.

He reached the couch, and moved into position, keeping his eye on the assassin. His target was lying on his belly between the couches, his gaze fixed on the apartment door.

Caleb waited, completely still, his slowing breath controlling his heart-rate. He waited for his moment, for another vehicle to pass. It didn't take long before a motorcycle roared down the street, passing the apartment in a blur of sound and light.

Caleb made his move.

He swung down and struck the gunman hard on the back of the head, causing him to reactively fire. A bullet shot from the barrel, embedding itself in the wall beside the door. Due to the apparent shock, the gun fell from his hands.

Startled into action, the gunman sprang to his feet, turning to face his opponent. Caleb leapt at him, getting the man into a bear-hug, trying to keep his opponent as confused as possible while he tried to gain the upper hand. The man was a bit bigger than Caleb, but no more so than he had dealt with in the past.

The gunman pushed himself away with a loud roar of anger, causing Caleb to lose his balance and step back towards one of the couches.

Struggling to regain his balance, Caleb was attacked by the gunman, who landed a series of blows. One caught Caleb's jaw, another one his ribcage and he suffered a glancing blow to his sternum.

Caleb quickly realized that while the man was not the best fighter, he'd obviously had *some* training. Countering the man's continued attack with defensive parries, Caleb found his own punches being blocked and struggled to penetrate the man's defences.

Rethinking his plan, Caleb adjusted his stance into an attack posture, placing his weight on his back leg, and delivered a roundhouse kick to the assassin's sternum.

The impact of the kick was enough to shatter the man's ribcage, and the force sent him stumbling backwards, until he fell through the coffee table in the middle of the lounge, shattering the glass top.

The man cried out in pain and Caleb suspected some of the glass had embedded itself in his back. Not wanting to kill the man – information was more important – Caleb backed away.

To Caleb's surprise, after a moment or two, the man stumbled back up onto his feet, although he was hunched over in pain.

As Caleb watched, the man reached over his shoulder, and removed a large piece of glass that protruded from his upper back. The man shuddered, and Caleb could only imagine the intense pain he'd experience from such an act.

The assassin wavered a little on his feet, blood flowing freely, staining his shirt. He eyed Caleb carefully under the limited light filtering in from outside, and his eyes narrowed. "You!" Once again, he tried to attack, but his movements were completely restricted by the wound in his back and the damage to his ribs from Caleb's kick.

Caleb was easily able to get out of the way and when the assassin attempted a punch, he lurched forward, falling onto the floor.

When he remained motionless, Caleb moved closer, turning on a lamp to get a better look at the man who'd been determined to kill him and Darcy.

The man's back was completely covered in blood. Caleb took a closer look, but with so much blood, he couldn't distinguish exactly where the wound was. The blood was still flowing freely from the man's back, and Caleb reasoned that the shard of glass must have nicked an artery. With the amount of blood flow, Caleb realised the man only had minutes to live, at most.

Caleb flipped the man over, and told him the situation. He told the man he was sure to die.

The man smiled.

"Who are you?" Caleb demanded, taken aback by the leering smile on the man's lips.

"It... it doesn't matter," the man replied. "You will be dead, soon enough."

"No, *you're* the one who's going to die," Caleb said, determined to get some answers. "Tell me who you are. Why did you want to kill Darcy?"

"The plan..." the man said, struggling to breath.

His next words surprised Caleb.

"My family's life... my family. They will live. That... that's all that matters."

Caleb grabbed the man's shirt, shaking him. "Tell me who you are?" Caleb begged the man.

The man shook his head weakly, his words coming out between gasps for breath. Caleb leaned in closer, and heard the man whispered something.

A moment later, the life left the man's eyes.

Caleb stood up and stared down at the man. He still didn't know who he was, but his last words had the desired effect.

"See you in the next life".

Chapter Eighteen

Matthew and Pierre ran across the road, and entered through the front of the building. They'd been alerted by the gunshot, and weren't willing to risk the possibility that Leon might slip away.

Pierre had joined Matthew approximately thirty minutes before the gunshot.

Everything was in place. Emmett had sent out the files and emails, Matthew had positioned himself in a great vantage point, and Leon had just shot the reporter.

The only thing now was to ensure that Leon was eliminated. Pierre was confident that between the two of them, they could easily account for one of William's men. While he trusted and respected William, Pierre had always believed he was the better mentor, and his trainees were better equipped to deal with most situations. After all, *he* had never asked a neighbouring Zone to take care of *his* problems, as William had done earlier.

Once the task was complete, and Leon was eliminated, both Pierre and Matthew could return to the colony, and receive their duties for Phase Two. He also knew they would receive the serum.

The pair entered the building through the lobby. Dressed in nondescript clothes, wearing baseball caps and with their jacket hoods pulled low over their faces, they were sure that even if they were seen, they couldn't be identified.

Within two minutes of hearing the gunshot, Pierre and Matthew were closing in on the apartment door. As they approached, Pierre held up his hand – ordering Matthew to slow down. Matthew obeyed and Pierre slowly approached the door, his gun aimed in case Leon appeared unexpectedly.

Pierre gave Matthew a hand signal, ordering him to wait on the far side of the doorframe and wait for Pierre's mark. When they were both in place, Pierre silently counted down on his fingers.

Three... two... one... go.

Matthew crashed through the door.

He scanned the room, and saw the signs of a struggle. It was immediately apparent the kill hadn't gone as smoothly as they'd hoped. Matthew walked through the room, and discovered a body on the couch. He stood his ground, and whispered softly, but loud enough that Pierre would hear.

"*Aider requis*" said Matthew, informing his Canadian master that help was required.

Dammit, thought Pierre. He did not anticipate any issues. However, just to play it safe, took out his phone, and sent a quick text to Emmett – the details of the flight he was to target.

After confirming the text had been sent, Pierre replaced his phone, and entered the room.

He crept inside, surveyed the scene quickly, and seeing what Matthew had discovered, ordered him to maintain position while he checked out the rest of the apartment.

Pierre, his pistol still drawn, moved slowly towards the body on the couch. It was instantly apparent it wasn't the female reporter. The strong, masculine frame gave that away. "*Merde*!" he exclaimed.

"What is it?" Matthew asked.

"Fuck. You stay here," Pierre said, "I'll check out the rest of the place."

"Okay. But... what happened sir?"

"It's the Asset.."

Matthew immediately tensed up. If Leon had even a small portion of the training that he had received, he was a force to be reckoned with. But, that wasn't what concerned Matthew. At that point he was more worried about the person who'd killed him. It couldn't have been the reporter.

Pierre raised his weapon when he felt a slight breeze coming from the bathroom. He shifted his weight to his front foot, and slowly walked in that direction. Matthew kept lookout in the living area, while paying heed to any possible threat to Pierre.

Pierre continued to move slowly, stepping on the glass that had shattered from the coffee table. He kept the gun focused on the bathroom area, hoping the assailant was still there. The person had managed to kill Leon, and that was bad enough, but the fact the assailant might have escaped as well would be unforgivable, and it would place their plan in serious jeopardy.

Pierre, for the first time since he came into the group, was genuinely concerned.

As Pierre entered the small bathroom, he quickly covered all visible areas with his gun. The shower, the cabinet, the closet.

Nothing.

He walked over to the open window, hoping to catch a glimpse of the assailant. He stuck his head out the window and once again saw… nothing.

Damn it, he thought, working out all the variables that were now coming into the equation.

Suddenly, the door slammed shut behind him. Pierre spun around, in his heart hoping it was just the breeze.

Caleb took one swing at Pierre, knocking him backwards, the punch connecting squarely with his jaw. Pierre fell back against the sink.

Pierre was dazed, but used the momentum from his fall to bounce off the sink and kick out at Caleb.

Caleb knew that such tactics were useless. The bathroom was quite small, and only close fighting tactics would assist him. Caleb was physically taller and stronger than Pierre, and had an age advantage of ten or so years. Coupled with the surprise of the attack, Caleb was easily in the dominant position. He absorbed Pierre's kick, and reached out, grabbing his opponent by the shoulders.

He lowered the man's head, as though intending to double him over. When he had lowered his head far enough, Caleb lifted his knee and drove it into the man's face, shattering his nose, and sending teeth flying down his throat.

Blood was streaming from the intruder's head and face, thus blinding him. The knee had also caused a concussion, which meant Canadian was off balance.

"Sir?" Matthew called out from the living room.

Pierre tried to cry out, but he choked slightly on the blood that was engulfing his throat. Before he could say anything meaningful, Caleb placed his hand over his mouth, preventing any sound. Pierre was on his knees, and the Marine was crouching at eye level to him.

"Why are you trying to kill Darcy?" he asked. He slightly loosened his grip over Pierre's mouth.

Pierre paused, trying to buy time for Matthew to come storming in.

"Fuck you!" he spat out.

Caleb had overheard the two men talking, and he knew he was talking to the superior in the relationship. He realised he was wasting his time, and decided to end the conversation. He stood up, and hit Pierre on the temple with the butt of his newly acquired CZ-75.

Pierre slumped to the floor, unconscious, but alive. Caleb knew when it was necessary to kill a man, and when it was not. He immobilized Pierre so he was no longer an immediate threat.

He stood, and stepped towards the bathroom door. He knew the younger man in the living room was probably still scanning the room. He would have to be fast, and hoped the speed would be enough to get to him.

He opened the door, and a hail of gunshots flew towards him. As they flew, Caleb dropped to the floor, and crawled out of the room, hiding behind the couch adjacent and waiting for the shots to finish. Once they did, he waited for shots to come towards the couch.

They did not. Matthew had not seen Caleb crawl out of the room, being more focused on the door opening. Matthew called out for Pierre.

When no answer came, Matthew stepped towards the door, keeping his gun focused on the opening. He stood at the threshold of the bathroom and looked inside. He saw his leader, slumped unconscious on the floor.

After several seconds, Pierre opened his eyes and spoke. "BEHIND YOU!!!" he whispered loudly, with all the meagre energy he could muster.

It was then Matthew realised his mistake. He spun around, but not fast enough. Caleb had got the young apprentice in a choke hold, slowly cutting of the circulation to his brain.

Matthew dropped his gun and struggled - proving to be more resilient that Caleb had hoped.

The pair wrestled. Caleb tried to tighten his grip, and Matthew flailed his legs, knocking photos and other knick-knacks of the mantle that ran adjacent to the bathroom door. Matthew used the wall, and threw himself back into Caleb, causing them both to fall to the floor. Caleb released his grip, and Matthew broke free.

As Caleb tried to stand up, Pierre emerged from the bathroom. He screamed at Caleb as he rushed towards him.

Caleb was still crouched, when he saw Pierre running towards him. As Pierre approached, Caleb turned to face him.

As Pierre closed in, in one fluid movement Caleb extended his arm, with his palm flat and facing to the roof. Using his legs for power, Caleb drove his full two hundred and forty pound frame into the movement. As the movement's force reached its apex, the heel of Caleb's hand connected with the underside of Pierre's jaw, crushing the mandible bones on each side.

The force of the blow caused Pierre's skull to snap back and crush his C1 and C2 vertebrae, instantly crushing his spinal cord. The blow also caused Pierre's instantly dead body to rise a foot in the air. When his body crashed back down, Pierre bounced before settling in its final resting place.

◆ ◆ ◆

Matthew, having just witnessed the violent death of his mentor, could not take his eyes away from the corpse. After the thud, a few silent moments passed.

Caleb stood and walked over to Pierre's body. He picked up Pierre's gun and pointed it at Matthew. This attracted the young man's attention. The death of his mentor was no longer his immediate concern. He now feared for his own life.

Sensing the young man's fear, Caleb tried to calm him down. He had seen too many people, friendly or not, become completely irrational and unpredictable when confronted with fear. "What's your name?" he asked, in as calm a voice as he could muster.

"Matt... Matthew," he replied.

"Well, Matthew. I assume that was your boss?"

Matthew nodded.

"If you do as you're told, you will be fine... okay?"

Matthew nodded again.

"Good."

Caleb sensed it was time to leave the apartment. He told Matthew stand, keeping his hands on his head.

Matthew complied, still compelled by fear.

Caleb patted him down. He found a phone, which he placed in his own pocket. He kept the gun trained on Matthew, ensuring that his back was never towards the young man. He moved over to Pierre, patting down the dead man, in the same manner as he had with Matthew moments earlier. There was no ID, just a cell-phone, which Caleb also put in his pocket.

Caleb walked over to Leon's body. He hadn't had an opportunity to search the first man, as he'd been interrupted by the second set of killers. Once again, he patted down the assailant, only to find no identification, only a cell phone.

"Now... you stay right there." Caleb said, after he had all three men's phones.

Caleb pulled out his own phone and dialled Darcy.

"Babe," she said, having waited anxiously for an update, "are you okay?"

"I'm fine."

"Did you get it?"

"Hang on..." Caleb remembered the laptop. "Where is it?"

"On the bed, remember?"

"Oh yeah, hang on." Caleb kept Darcy on the phone, and motioned for Matthew to move to the bedroom making sure he was never out of his sight.

"Grab the computer," he ordered Matthew.

Darcy overheard the conversation. "Who are you talking to?" she asked.

"I'll explain it all soon."

Matthew grabbed the laptop.

"Now bring it out and place it on the couch"

Caleb returned back to his conversation with Darcy. "Drive over here now and meet me out the front in one minute."

"Alright, is everything okay?"

"I'll explain when I see you. It's not safe to talk on the phone."

"Okay, we're on the way."

"One minute"

"Okay."

"And Darc? We're gonna have company." Caleb hung up. With the gun still aimed at Matthew, he ordered him to turn around and place his hands on his head.

Caleb grabbed the only wire he could find – a phone charger. He walked across to Matthew pulling Matthews's hands behind his back. He tied them together securely. Caleb retrieved the laptop, knowing they needed to deliver it to Chuck, and guided Matthew out of the apartment.

"Where are we going?" Matthew asked.

"That's what you're going to tell me," Caleb replied.

Chapter Nineteen

Darcy watched anxiously as she drove towards the apartment, relieved when she saw Caleb appear from beneath the awning of the building. He was accompanied by a young man - who couldn't have been more than twenty years old. The young man was about six feet and strongly built. She noticed his hands were tied behind his back as Caleb led him to the car.

The car stopped, and Dunleavy got out, quickly opening the back door. Caleb shoved the young man into the back seat. Caleb slipped in beside him, and pointed the gun at the young man.

Once Dunleavy got back into the front seat, Caleb spoke. "Drive."

"Where?" Darcy asked, pulling away from the sidewalk.

"Just drive for now, I need to think for a few minutes," Caleb said tiredly

As Darcy drove, Dunleavy turned to better assess their prisoner. "Who the fuck is this?" he asked casually.

"I have no idea," replied Caleb, "but he was there to kill us."

"Act— Actually…" Matthew began, "We weren't there to kill you."

"You've got a weird way of showing it," Caleb replied.

"Okay, my boss did try to stop you, but only because you were in the way."

Caleb shifted the gun to aim at Matthew's knee, and leaned in closer, to reinforce his message. "I'm going to ask you some questions" he began, "and if I think for one second that you're lying to me… you saw what I did to your boss"

Matthew swallowed heavily. "Okay, okay." he said, a hint of panic in his voice.

"First, what's your name? There was no ID on either you or your friends." Caleb knew the young man's name already, having just asked him while they were in the apartment. He only asked again for one main reason, to make sure the kid gave the same answer twice. Failure to do so would indicate he could be deceptive, even under strain.

"Matthew," he replied.

"Okay, Matthew," Caleb said, trying to build familiarity, "why *were* you in the apartment?"

"The guy. The guy that was dead. The guy on the couch."

"Yes?"

"I was sent to take him out."

"Him? Why him?"

"I'm not sure. I was just told to take him out," Matthew said, staring at the gun pointing at his knee, "Probably because he was no longer required —" He stopped abruptly.

Caleb noticed the pause. "Now Matthew, when I say 'don't lie to me', I should also add 'Don't hold anything back'." Caleb took Pierre's phone from his pocket and flipped through the contacts. All he saw were a series of alpha-numeric indicators. All starting with the letter Z, the numbers appeared in sequence. "Z-1-1, Z-1-2" etcetera, right down to Z-15-3. His most recent call had been from Z-1-1, and his most recent to Z-3-14. Frowning, Caleb scrolled through the text messages. All appeared to have been deleted but one and it had been sent to the last number called; Z-3-14. "What does this mean?" Caleb asked Matthew and showed him the screen.

"I don't… I really don't know" Matthew replied, sounding as confused as Caleb about the message.

"What does it say?" asked Dunleavy, who'd been paying close attention to the conversation.

"All it says is," Caleb read the message aloud, *"E. Landing at 0700. Good luck. P"*

Caleb directed his next words to his prisoner. "What was your boss' name, Matthew?"

"Pierre," the young man said.

"So obviously, Pierre sent the message. Now, who is E?" Caleb demanded.

"I don't know," Matthew said.

Caleb saw the deception in Matthew's eyes, and placed the gun more firmly against Matthew's knee. "Now, Matthew, you remember what I said about lying, don't you?" Caleb began to put pressure on the trigger.

"Caleb! Wait!" Darcy shrieked from the front seat.

"What? What is it Darc?" Caleb asked, surprised Darcy had interrupted the conversation.

"Caleb, just, just wait a minute," Darcy said, as she pulled over to the side of the vacant road. She stopped the car and turned to face Caleb. "You don't need to do that."

"Darcy, sometimes a message needs to be sent."

"No, not like this," she said swivelling. "Can't you hear it?"

"Hear what?"

"The fear. The fear in his voice"

Caleb frowned. "What do you mean?"

"Caleb... I've spoken to so many people. I've heard so many speeches. I've *heard* so many emotions. This guy... this *kid* is scared."

"Of course he's scared, babe... that's how I want him to be!" Caleb said, frustrated with the interruption.

"Caleb, the only time he's shown any *real* fear is when he said his boss' name. He knows he's betrayed him. Isn't that right, Matthew?"

Matthew didn't respond.

Now that Darcy had pointed it out, Caleb saw it too. He knew there was no threat he could make to cause Matthew to tell the truth. Perhaps a softer approach would be required.

"You're right." Caleb said tucking the gun into the back of his jeans.

"For fuck's sake, Jackson, at least keep the gun on him!" Dunleavy demanded.

"Nah, let's give the kid a chance. Matthew, I know you're scared, but we need some answers..."

Pierre's phone began to ring.

Caleb pulled it back out of his pocket, discovering the display showed 'Z-1-4', "Who would be calling Pierre now?" Caleb asked

"I... I don't know." Matthew replied, sounding just as surprised as Caleb.

The phone rang again.

And again.

Caleb was still deciding what to do. Should he answer it? Or leave it?

The questions was answered for him, as the phone abruptly stopped ringing.

◆ ◆ ◆

Shit, William thought. In all the time he'd worked with Pierre, regardless of the situation, he had *never* let his phone ring more than twice. And he certainly wouldn't have on this occasion, especially with so much happening. Since they'd last spoken, William knew James had spoken with Pierre, but he had no idea what had happened in the interim.

With Pierre's apparent inability to answer the phone, William took the appropriate precautions, following procedure. He opened his phone again, and input the shutdown code. Each phone in the organisation was identical. It was manufactured by Molyneux Industries, and could only contact other members of the organisation. There was no Sim card, and there was no phone company involved. The phone calls and messages bounced off satellites – satellites that were owned by the group. Operating on a rotating frequency made the phones, and the conversations, untraceable.

In fact, the only way to contact another member of the group was via these phones. There were no emails, no faxes, no Instant Messaging. All had been deemed as too insecure.

In this case, when Pierre's phone wasn't answered in two rings, or even three in emergencies, then connection to the offending phone needed to be severed. The shutdown code William entered connected immediately to Pierre's phone, sending a programmed algorithm to the phone, causing the system to shut down. The shutdown would also spark a chemical reaction in the battery, and the phone would self-destruct, acid from the battery destroying the interior workings.

Some of the members of the colony believed the protocol to be extreme, and it had caused significant hurdles in the past, particularly for field operatives. On this occasion however, William felt the instigation of the protocol to be vital. He only hoped, that if the phone had been compromised, whoever had it hadn't had enough time to retrieve any information from the device.

While the possibility made him nervous, it paled in comparison to his next task – alerting James to the situation.

Chapter Twenty

Caleb contemplated the phone call, and wondered if he'd made a mistake in not answering it.

"Who was it?" asked Dunleavy.

"I don't know," Caleb replied. "Caller ID said Z-1-4"

"What is that, some kind of code?" Dunleavy asked Matthew.

Matthew remained silent.

Caleb checked the phone again. When he reopened it, the screen was dead. No matter which buttons he pressed, he couldn't get it operational. "Shit, the phone's dead," Caleb said. "Darcy, we haven't got a choice now – we need to get some information from him."

Darcy turned in her seat to look at the young man. "Now, Matthew," she began, "I've never been in this kind of situation before. I don't really know how it works. But, I'm guessing - and I'm sure you're thinking the same thing - I'm guessing that if you don't give us the information we need, then we don't need you anymore."

Matthew, glanced up, and saw the sincerity in Darcy's eyes.

"I'm sure you can understand that?" Darcy continued.

Matthew nodded, resigned to the situation.

"Just tell us what we need to know."

"I… I can't. There's… there too much at stake."

"What's at stake, Matthew? I don't even know why someone tried to kill me?"

"You?" Matthew asked, seemingly surprised.

"I'll fill you in on what I know, Matthew…" Darcy began. She told Matthew everything. The email, the reporter in Australia, the tracking device. Everything about why she thought she was being targeted.

"That's it?" Matthew asked, stunned.

"Yes... That's it. So, please help us. I don't want to die."

Matthew lapsed into silence, staring out the window.

"Don't think for too long," Caleb warned, interrupting Matthew's thoughts, "We can't wait forever. Someone was sent to kill us, and they failed. If your group is as powerful as I think they are, they'll send someone else. I'm not going to wait around for them." Caleb paused, allowing time for his words to sink in. "I'm going to give you a minute. Once that minute's up, you're going to do one of two things. One; you'll tell me who 'E' is... or two; you'll prove that you're of no use to us. It's up to you."

Matthew remained stubbornly silent.

"Fifty seconds left," Caleb said, counting down the seconds on his watch.

Matthew looked up at Darcy, his eyes pleading with her to help.

"I... I can't help you. Caleb is right... we can't risk it," she said

"Forty seconds."

Matthew remained silent, still staring at Darcy.

"Thirty seconds..."

Still Matthew remained silent.

"Twenty..."

Suddenly, Matthew spoke. "Emmett. His name is Emmett."

Darcy was relieved he'd spoken. She didn't want Caleb to kill anyone, unless he had to. "Thank you Matthew" she said.

"Yes, thank you Matthew," Caleb added. "Can you explain the rest of the message?"

"No, no, I can't. But I can tell you where he is."

"Okay, that'll be a start."

"He's in Seattle."

Caleb glanced over at Darcy. "Darcy, we need to get moving now".

She started the car, and pulled out onto the street.

♦　♦　♦

Emmett had received the text message and he checked all the flights that were inbound to Seattle International. There was only one due at 0700, a Pacifica flight arriving from Beijing. As instructed, he'd distributed the files Pierre had sent him. In the files were details, coded as before, that would lead investigators to believe there was a terrorist plot to take down a flight that had left China and been scheduled to land in the United States. This would, if protocols were followed, lead to an all-out attack on the terrorists by both governments. Hundreds of lives would be lost during the attack, but it would serve its purpose.

The attack would provide a sufficient distraction for the governments of the world, and thus allow the plan to proceed uninterrupted.

Emmett began his preparations. He collected up his identification papers – false of course – his wallet, and all the cash he had. He placed them in the metal garbage bin in his rented apartment, before standing on the bed, and unplugging the smoke alarm. Taking a match, he set fire to his belongings, ensuring no-one would be able to trace him. Then he grabbed his phone, and left the apartment for the last time.

Emmett walked out to his car, and drove toward his destination. While the journey was the same, this time he felt very differently about it. He knew he was about to kill more than two hundred people and make a real difference to the world.

Any feelings of guilt Emmett experienced were fleeting. He knew the deaths of the passengers on the plane were part of a greater plan, a plan that was going to help the whole world.

After the short drive, he came to a stop at the base of the hill and began to walk, enjoying the fact he was not required to carry the package this time. After counting out three hundred steps, he left the path, and made his way through the shrubs, to the clearing he'd prepared and fumbled in the darkness, searching for the piece of balsa wood he'd recently buried. It was time to open the package.

Emmett lifted the balsa wood, and placed it to one side. He knelt down and lifted the package out of the ground, thinking it was lighter than he'd remembered, but he didn't complain.

Carefully he opened the packaging, to reveal a MANPADS (Man Portable Air Defence System) – a man operated rocket launcher. Developed in the 1940's, MANPAD's were now a staple of air defence, easy to aim, and easy to fire. Almost anybody could be trained to use one with minimal time involved. The unit was designed to fire using a laser-guided system. *Point and click,* was how Pierre had described it.

He removed the launcher and the missile from the box, and inserting the missile into the barrel, Emmett followed the start-up procedure. He aimed the weapon in the direction he wished to fire, visualizing a target in sight. Satisfied he was ready, Emmett placed the launcher on the ground and settled next to it, and patiently waited.

Chapter Twenty-One

Darcy drove along the highway, en route to Chuck's house. As she drove, Caleb tried to formulate a plan. He knew they were still being tracked, after all, they now had the laptop.

Unfortunately, his planning was out of focus, as he tried to pull all the pieces together. He knew this *Emmett* guy, if that was really his name, was in Seattle. And he knew that Emmett had been sent a text message by someone called *Pierre,* and that message told him that something would be landing at seven in the morning. It was obviously a prelude to something more, but what that might be, he didn't have a clue.

Something told him that whatever it was, it was going to be bad, and they needed to do anything they could to stop it.

But Seattle was at least sixteen hours away, and before they could deal with that problem, they needed to stop-off at Chuck's house with the laptop.

Also weighing on his mind, was what to do with Matthew. They couldn't very well talk about their own plans in front of him. But they needed him. They needed someone who knew the inner machinations of the people they were fighting. While Dunleavy seemed to have some insight, Caleb knew Matthew was their best resource.

"Pull over here, Darc," Caleb said to Darcy, when he saw an all-night diner up ahead. It was as good a place as any to reflect on the situation and try and get a handle on his errant thoughts.

When the car pulled to a stop, Caleb handed Pierre's gun to Dunleavy. "Mike, you stay here, keep Matthew company. Darcy, come with me. I need to figure out our next move."

Dunleavy nodded in acknowledgement. "Bring me a coffee, I think I'm gonna need it."

"Sure. We won't be long," Caleb said.

Darcy and Caleb made their way across the nearly-empty parking lot. The lot itself was dark, and the only other vehicle parked was a small blue truck. Caleb couldn't make out the model, but took note of the licence number. It wasn't one he could recall from their earlier travels.

He and Darcy entered the diner and Caleb took a moment to survey their surroundings.

The diner itself had a retro feel about it. Caleb assumed this was not out of any specific design plan, merely the fact that the aged décor hadn't been updated for some time. They sat together in one of the booths, Caleb picked the one furthest from the door, with a wall behind it. The only other customer in the diner was an older man, hunched over his coffee and pie, reading a magazine. It was well into the early hours of the morning, so the limited people inside was to be expected.

Caleb sat with his back against the wall, so he could survey the diner's interior. From his vantage point, he could see anyone coming in or out, the other customer, and the solitary waitress, who was making her way over to their table.

"Coffee?" Caleb asked a clearly weary Darcy.

"Sounds good" she replied.

"What can I getcha?" the middle aged waitress asked.

"Just two coffees please," Caleb asked

"Two coffees," the waitress said as she wrote down the order. "Anythin' else?"

"No, thanks. We won't be staying long."

"Two coffees, then. Comin' up"

The waitress walked back behind the counter. She returned with two barely-clean coffee cups, and two jugs of coffee.

"Decaf?"

"Not for me," Darcy said

"Me neither," said Caleb.

The waitress poured the drinks, and returned to her position behind the counter.

When he was sure they wouldn't be overheard, Caleb began to speak. "Darc…" he began.

"You're wondering what to do next, aren't you?" Darcy asked. "Do we go to Chuck's, or do we go to Seattle to try and figure out what that text was about."

Caleb was pleasantly surprised. He knew Darcy knew him very well, but she could apparently read his mind, too.

"Yeah, I am," he replied.

"What do your instincts tell you?"

He lifted an eyebrow. "My instincts?"

"Yeah… I mean, they seem to have been working for you so far. Not just today, from what you and Mike have said, you've been in some pretty shitty situations. Situations that would have been worse than this one. And guess what, you're still here. Just on that basis alone, you have to admit, your instincts work."

"It's different this time" Caleb admitted.

"Why?"

Caleb frowned. "You're asking why?"

"Yeah, why? Someone's trying to kill you, and you've got an objective. I think if you just treat it like that—" Darcy started to explain.

"That's not why it's different," Caleb interrupted, taking a sip of his coffee.

"So what's different this time?" she demanded.

"All the other times, I had my guys around me. *With* me. I trusted all of them with my life, and they trusted me. Even before that, we worked the plan together before we headed out into these shitholes. Dunleavy and Hawkins, they gave us the missions, they told us the objectives. But, after that, we pretty much had free rein on how the mission would be carried out."

"So," said Darcy, "let's call your guys."

He shook his head. "I can't. There are enough people in danger already."

"Caleb, you've just finished telling me you trusted them and they trust you. What would you do if they called you?"

"I'd probably do anything I could to help them."

"There you go," Darcy said, offering him a reassuring smile.

He smiled back, but shook his head. "That's not the only reason this mission's different."

Darcy crossed her arms. "What else?"

"On the other missions, *your* life wasn't in danger."

She shook her head firmly. "You need to forget about that, not let it be part of the equation. This is too important, and you're probably thinking the same thing I am."

"Oh yeah, what's that?" Caleb teased, proud of Darcy's bravery.

"I'm thinking that whatever this Emmett is going to do, it's going to be bad. And by bad, I mean *President-Hawkins-getting-shot* bad."

Caleb nodded, and sipped his coffee, "Yeah. I think you're right."

"That, Caleb, that needs to be the priority right now. We need to do what we can to stop him."

Caleb thought over Darcy's words. She was right, of course – they needed to get to Seattle, and fast.

"We can't drive and get there in time," Darcy added. "Do you know any pilots?"

After a moment's reflection, Caleb smiled. "I do."

◆ ◆ ◆

Dunleavy shifted in his seat, trying to get a better view of the couple. They were still sitting in the diner, seated towards the back. "Got yourself into some deep shit here, son, haven't you?" he said.

Matthew stared blankly out the window his expression morose.

"Well, unless you can figure out a way of helping us out, I'm pretty sure you are going to die."

Still, Matthew looked out into the darkness.

"I mean, that's gotta suck. How would you be able to take the serum then?"

The question shook Matthew into reacting. He looked straight at Dunleavy, wondering who this man was, and how he knew about the serum.

"Oh yeah… I know all about that stuff," Dunleavy said, pausing for dramatic effect, "Crazy thing, that serum. The ability to stave off any disease on the planet, and it gives you back your youth… Shit, with that stuff, you could live… I don't know, probably forever."

"How…" Matthew began, then swallowed heavily before he continued. "How do you know about this?"

"Ahhh, I don't think you need to know that son. Suffice to say, we know a lot more about your group than you probably do."

"Shit," Matthew mumbled under his breath. "And them, they know about it too?" He nodded his head towards where Darcy and Caleb were visible, talking together in the diner.

"Them? They know what I want them to know. They're serving a purpose right now." Dunleavy paused to let the message sink in. "So if you want to have the opportunity to access the serum, I suggest you help us out."

"I'll do anything…"

"Yeah, I bet you will."

Dunleavy lowered the gun. "Now Matthew, I can help you get the serum," he said, "but you need to do what I ask."

"Okay" Matthew said cautiously. "Anything."

"Good" Dunleavy pulled his phone out of his pocket and dialled. He didn't really care if Matthew could hear, he assumed the young man would be dead soon enough.

The phone rang twice before it connected. "Who is this?" replied a harsh voice on the other end.

"Dunleavy"

"Bullshit."

"Jacob, it's really me."

"Prove it."

"Okay... Remember Bogota, Jacob?"

"What about it?"

"Remember how I pulled your nuts out of the fire? How you'd be dead, if my team didn't get you out?"

"Shit! What are doing? You shouldn't be calling me!"

"Jacob, you know me. I wouldn't be doing this unless I had to."

"What's the problem?"

"What's your current location?" Dunleavy queried.

"DC."

"DC? Still?"

"Yeah, I had some cleaning up to do. Had to lay-low."

"Okay, well get your ass to Seattle, ASAP. I need your help with something."

"I'll be there by asap."

"Good. See you then."

As he hung up the phone, Dunleavy saw Caleb and Darcy making their way out of the diner. As they approached the car, Dunleavy raised the weapon to take aim on Matthew. "Now remember, you gotta make them feel like you're helping them. Caleb... well, Caleb's a walking bullshit detector. So make sure whatever info you give him is legit, otherwise..." Dunleavy pretended to pull the trigger.

Caleb opened the back door. "Hand me the laptop," he said to Matthew.

Tucking the computer under one arm, he took it to the side of the parking lot where a dumpster leaned against the wall of the diner. He located an empty pizza box in amongst the dumpster's contents, and placed the laptop inside. Then he placed the pizza box behind the dumpster. He returned to the car, and motioned to Darcy. "Give me your phone babe."

"My phone?"

"I'm guessing they're also tracking your phone, so we need to leave everything here. Anything they *could* use to track us."

"But, why my phone?"

"We need to make sure they can't find us. You have email on your phone, and the tracker is in the email. It's probably how they knew we had arrived at your apartment. We just need to get rid of it."

Without further argument, Darcy gave Caleb her phone.

He walked back to the dumpster, and placed Darcy's phone into it.

He returned to the car, and slipped into the back seat beside Matthew.

'So, I take it you have a plan?" Dunleavy queried.

"Yep. Darcy and I came up with something."

"Care to fill me in?"

"Not yet. But I can tell you this, we're going on a plane ride."

"Where to?" Darcy asked.

"North."

Darcy started the car, and pulled out of the parking lot. "What direction?" she asked.

"Long Beach for now. I'll let you know more when we get there," replied Caleb

"We're obviously not flying commercial, then?" asked Dunleavy.

"No, Mr. Dunleavy. No, we're not."

Chapter Twenty-Two

They drove south on Lakewood Boulevard, barely passing any other traffic. Being four in the morning, this wasn't unexpected. As they approached a golf course on the left, Caleb told Darcy to turn right into the airport complex.

Taking the long way around, they pulled over to the Gulfstream depot, near the south side of Daughtery Field. "Pull over here babe," Caleb said to Darcy.

Caleb sat in silence. It had been half an hour since Caleb made the call, giving his teammates just enough time to prepare.

"What are we waiting for, Caleb?" Dunleavy asked.

As he spoke, Caleb sighted the person who they had been waiting for. They'd emerged from the bushes, and were making their way towards the car.

The three of them approached the car. From their walk, Caleb was able to discern each of them, having known them all for so long.

Caleb had called Murphy – full name Lieutenant Charlene Murphy - known as Murph for short. She was arguably the best pilot in the corps – which was why Caleb had selected her for his team. Even without a plane, she was one of the most lethal fighters in his group. Not that you'd know it to look at her. Standing a touch over five feet seven inches, Murphy had a seemingly slight frame. But what she lacked in strength, she more than made up for in speed and agility. Coupled with these skills, Murphy was also the smartest person Caleb knew, able to figure out just about anything she laid her eyes on.

Caleb stepped out of the car. As the trio approached, he recognised the others; faces he was happy to see in the circumstances. "Murphy! Casey! Walker!" exclaimed Caleb. "Boy, am I glad to see you."

They jogged up, and stood in front of their commanding officer, offering him a respectful salute. "As ordered, sir." said Murphy.

Casey pulled a fake pout. "Sir, I'm hurt you didn't call. I've been waiting by the phone, just pining to hear your voice." Darryl Casey was, judging by his physique, a stock standard Marine. Strong and tall, Casey was the kind of guy you wanted with you in a fight. The main thing that separated him was his attitude. Never short of a quip, Casey managed to make the team laugh at many inappropriate moments. That was one of the main reasons Caleb chose him. While an excellent soldier, his humour and personality revealed a deeply compassionate, human side. A side that could be used as a moral compass for the rest of the team.

"Why Sergeant, did you miss me?" Caleb replied.

"Every day, sir. Every day." Casey said with a bright smile.

The third member was Declan Walker. A shorter and slighter version of Caleb, Walker was arguably the second best pilot Caleb had known. A great mechanic as well, Walker had spent much of his time as Murphy's apprentice, trying his best to learn what he could. Walker was not as tall as Caleb and Casey, but the youngest member of their squad was more than handy in a fight.

But it was not his fighting skills that would be called on for this mission.

"Murphy said you needed a ride, sir?" Walker interrupted.

"Yeah… need to get up to Seattle, pronto."

"Seattle, sir? May I ask why?" Murphy asked.

"I'll explain on the plane

"Will be tricky to land though, Sir" said Murphy, "Major airport and all."

"You're right Lieutenant. Did you bring the 'chutes?"

It then became clear to the people listening as to how they would be disembarking the plane.

"I can see some of you are nervous," Caleb said, referring to Darcy and Dunleavy in particular, "But we can't think about that now. It's time sensitive, so we need to get going."

Caleb tried to change the thought processes of his companions.

"I assume one of these is ours, Murphy?" Caleb asked, pointing to a row of jets near the runway.

"Ummm, sort of sir," replied Murphy.

"What do you mean 'sort-of'?

"Let's just say we're going to borrow one."

Caleb shrugged, he had little choice other than to trust his team at this moment in time.

The others began to exit the car, and Caleb began introductions. "This is Darcy…"

"THE Darcy?" asked Murphy.

"Yep," Darcy said, happy to discover Caleb must have spoken about her during his times away, "that'd be me"

As Dunleavy moved toward the group, Caleb was about to introduce him, when Casey interrupted in a hushed aside. "Holy shit, sir. What is *Dunleavy* doing here?"

"Like I said, Sergeant, I'll explain later."

"I thought you said we had three additional, sir?" asked Murphy, glancing from Dunleavy and Darcy and back to Caleb.

"Indeed we do," Caleb replied. He made his way around to the other side of the car and opened the door. "Out!" he ordered.

Matthew did as Caleb ordered, struggling to exit the vehicle, with his hands still bound behind his back. Caleb grabbed him under his arm, and helped lift him out of the seat.

"Sir?" Murphy questioned, her eyes widening at the sight of the bound man.

"I can guarantee you, Lieutenant, it will all makes sense, in time. Where's the plane?"

Murphy motioned the group to follow her, and she led the way, followed by Darcy, then Dunleavy. Caleb escorted Matthew, still holding his left arm. Casey held the rear.

They headed south, and approached a fence which couldn't have been more than five feet high.

As Casey climbed over the fence, Caleb turned to Matthew. "Now... I'm gonna untie you. That doesn't mean we trust you, okay?" Caleb said.

Matthew nodded.

"If I think there is a possibility you might run, or try to hurt us – I will kill you."

Again Matthew nodded. He had no intention of running. After his conversation with Dunleavy, he now saw the old man as his only option. He had to stay with the group.

"Okay then," Caleb said, as he made his way around the back of the young man. "You got him, Sergeant?"

"Already on it, Cap," replied the ever-vigilant Casey.

Caleb released the cable which had been holding Matthew's hands behind his back. Enjoying the regained use of his arms, Matthew placed two hands about shoulder-width apart on the fence, quickly hoisting himself up and over.

Caleb followed, placing the gun in the small of his back and in one fluid motion, he placed his hands on the fence, and propelled himself over. Such was his strength; he was able to catapult himself about two yards from the fence-line.

"Geez, Cap, no need to show off," Casey said, "you're making me look bad!"

With Casey keeping a watchful eye on Matthew, Caleb made his way to the front of the group. Collectively, they made their way south to the main hangar. Once there, they shimmied along the northern side of the hangar, and turned south. One hundred and fifty feet ahead, they came across the main holding area for aircraft.

Sleek in design, the jets were the vessel of choice for the rich and famous, the type of people Los Angeles had an abundance of. In a town where image was everything, the Gulfstream certainly helped cement the facade.

"Okay Murphy, which one is *sort-of* ours," Caleb asked.

Murphy surveyed the jets, strands of her mousy-brown hair catching the light where it protruded from the back of her black cap.

"I can't see it just yet; it might be on the other side."

"Okay then, which way?"

"Follow me."

Murphy led the way across the open tarmac area. As they headed south-west, with the other section of the hangar on their right, Caleb heard a noise. It wasn't loud, but it was enough that Caleb could detect it and consider it worth investigating.

"Murphy, cover right," he said quietly.

Without hesitation, Murphy led the group towards the side of the hangar, ensuring they weren't out in the open. When everyone was lined up, their backs to the wall, Caleb moved.

He switched positions with Murphy, and led the group down the side of the external hangar wall. The noise he'd heard grew louder. Caleb drew his weapon, just in case.

Footsteps.

Judging by the stride and weight of the steps, Caleb recognized they weren't being pursued by anyone. It was more than likely a security guard, doing his rounds – a rather chubby guard at that. A take down would be relatively easy.

The footsteps drew closer.

Caleb put the weapon away; his intention was to subdue the guard, rather than eliminate.

The footsteps were just about upon them when Caleb lifted his arms into position. The only possible complication he could see, balanced on whether the guard would turn left, directly into the path of the six trespassers, or whether he would continue in a straight path. Either way, Caleb was prepared to adapt.

The guard came into view, and turned left. Startled by the sight of six trespassers, he reached for his radio. It was all to no avail. Before he could put his hand on the radio at his waist, Caleb had moved behind him. He placed one arm across the front of the man's neck, and the other across the back. As the chubby guard struggled, his cheeks began to puff out, his arms and legs flailing.

"Just relax and you'll get through this" Caleb whispered in his ear, trying to soothe the man.

Within three seconds, the guard stopped fighting. After five, he began losing consciousness, as the blood supply was cut off from his brain. Ten seconds, the guard's body slumped, and Caleb carefully placed him on the ground. "Okay, let's move," he said to the group. "Darcy, grab the guard's radio."

Darcy grabbed the guard's radio. She was stunned to think she'd adapted so easily to the sight of her boyfriend subduing a stranger, but she was very glad he hadn't killed him.

Murphy moved to the front of the group, taking the lead. As they turned a corner and headed west, Murphy saw the plane she'd selected, "There it is…" she told the group, "About two hundred yards."

The plane was sleek in design.

First produced in 2009, The Gulfstream G280 was near top of the line as far as business and private jets go. Having a range of about thirty-six hundred miles, the jet would have no trouble making the journey north to Seattle. With a cruising speed around five hundred miles per hour, they would be able to make it to Seattle in plenty of time.

Murphy approached the plane, with the others following closely behind. She typed in a code on the panel connected to the left hand side of the door. After she pressed 'enter', the door opened, and the stairs lowered into place.

"Okay then, everyone on board," Caleb ordered.

Darcy went up the stairs first, followed by Dunleavy, Matthew, Walker and Casey. Murphy ducked under the plane, removing the chocks from the wheels.

"How did you know about this, Murph?" Caleb asked when she returned to the stairs.

"I know the guy who owns it. He owes me one," she replied.

"Do I even wanna know what that means?"

"Girl's gotta keep herself busy during downtime," she smiled.

Caleb ushered her onto the plane, following closely behind.

Murphy turned left as she entered, taking her position in the cockpit. Walker had already sat down in the Co-Pilot seat.

Caleb turned right. The ten seats were made of soft white leather. Darcy had settled in the front seat, Dunleavy directly behind her. Casey had taken a seat next to Matthew, ensuring he had a window view. Caleb was pleased to see there was little or no space between them, Casey ensuring Matthew knew he was being constantly watched.

"Okay, everyone, buckle up," said Murphy from the cockpit. "It might be a little bumpy, but I'm guessing we're a bit time-poor." She quickly ran through the start-up procedure, missing many of the hundred or so pre-flight checks. The engine came to life, and the plane began to move.

Caleb was still standing when the plane jolted into action. He fell into a vacant chair.

"C'mon, Cap, pay attention!" Casey shouted good-naturedly from his chair.

The plane continued to move forward, briskly taxiing around the runway. After another minute or so, the plane came to a gentle halt. "Okay everyone," Murphy said. "We're doing this without any lights on the runway, so my best advice is to tuck your head between your knees, as you may need to kiss your ass good-bye."

"Hang on a sec, Lieutenant," Caleb said.

Darcy stared at him, lifting a questioning eyebrow.

"Darc, hand me the radio," Caleb said.

Darcy silently handed it over, watching as Caleb pushed one of the buttons. "Attention. If anyone can hear me, please be aware that one of your guys is unconscious. He's lying by the south west corner of the main Gulfstream hanger. He's okay, but he might require some help. Over." Caleb removed the battery from the radio, and disconnected the handset.

He dropped the handset into the seat pocket and met Darcy's eyes. Caleb held her gaze, offering her a reassuring smile. "We'll be fine," he said.

"I know," Darcy replied.

The plane started moving off and sped up, reaching take-off speed. The plane slowly lifted off the tarmac, and as they began to gain altitude, Murphy changed their heading to north.

They were on their way to Seattle.

◆ ◆ ◆

"Can you please repeat that?" an angry James said, wanting to ensure he'd heard correctly.

"Um, yes, sir. I think we've been compromised," William repeated. "I can't get in touch with Pierre and I've instituted the required protocols."

James's anger grew. "What happened?" he asked.

"I don't know, sir."

"What do you mean, you don't know? I thought you had this reporter thing under control?"

"Sir, all I can tell you is Pierre always answers his phone, and about an hour ago, when I called, he failed to pick up the call."

"So, the reporter? Is she still out there?"

"I don't know, sir."

"You'd better bloody find out, William! If word gets out about what we're doing, if the government, *any* government pays any attention to us this week, well, I don't think I need to tell you about the consequences."

"No, sir, you don't. I do have a plan, though."

"What is it?"

"We'll have to reactivate *him*, sir."

James hadn't been anticipating this. He paused for a few seconds, as he considered the proposal. William was right. The agent had proven useful in the past.

"Okay. Just don't promise him anything. We do not want animals like that as part of Phase Two. Don't you agree?"

"Agreed, sir. I'll make the call."

"Alright. Off you go then"

With that, William turned to leave James's office walking toward the door. As he approached the threshold, he turned back to James. "Sir, I was just wondering," William began sheepishly.

"What is it, William?" James snapped, annoyed over any further interruption to his day.

"I was due to get the serum earlier, but didn't receive it. I was just wondering when my turn would come?"

"I rescheduled you. After the incident with the reporter, I thought it best to keep you focused on that task. No reflection on you, of course..." James said, his voice filled with condescension.

"Oh." William couldn't keep the disappointment from his voice.

"Don't worry. When the female reporter is nullified, I'll ensure you're rewarded appropriately."

"Yes, sir, thank you, sir," William said, and he left the room.

James stood for a few minutes, staring out the window. It was William's quick thinking that had saved him on this occasion. Had he not thought of suggesting the agent in time, he might not have been receiving the serum at all. That was the punishment for failure, James mused. It wasn't death, nor was it banishment.

The greatest punishment any of the colonists could receive was exclusion from receiving the serum, which would mean exclusion from Phase Two. Every colonist's dream was to be part of the future, and William couldn't imagine the torment that some of the former colonists had to endure. Being ignorant was one thing, but having to deal with full knowledge of the plan, and then not being completely part of it... that would be agony.

William tried to banish the thought from his mind. He had worked almost his entire adult life to get to where he was, and he wasn't about to let a pesky reporter get in his way. He took out his phone, and dialled a number he hadn't used in months.

The agent he was calling could best be described with only two words – brutally effective.

Any mission requested of him, he succeeded in completing. His last mission had been the most decisive - the death of the American

President. The agent had completed that mission with both effectiveness and efficiency.

However, such was the nature of the mission; the colony had needed to distance themselves from him. Once the mission was complete, they ordered him into hiding, and they hadn't contacted him since.

As an additional measure to distance themselves from the assassination, the colony had leaked information about a new terror cell – the New Light group. The measure had worked.

It worked so well in fact, that Pierre and Emmett had been leaking further information regarding New Light to various governments for months – the Americans, Chinese, British, Germans and even to smaller nations, such as Australia and Japan.

As the colony also had people embedded in most countries' intelligence divisions, the material and information was sure to be seen and read by the appropriate people.

Over time, all the intelligence agencies had been able to talk about was New Light, and the threat it posed to world security.

While William dialled the number, he glanced at his watch. Judging by the time, he was certain Emmett would have released the latest information about New Light, and the Chinese and Americans would be in full alert mode, making it easy for the agent to come out of hiding. The phone rang but once before it was picked up.

"Where the fuck have you been?" the angry voice came clearly down the line.

"Nice to speak to you, too," replied William.

"What do you expect? I did the job for you, and then, nothing!"

"I'm talking to you now, so just listen," William stated coldly.

"Fine. I take it I get my serum soon though? Been a fair bit of chatter about New Light, so I'm guessing Phase Two's about to start."

"Indeed. As soon as the Zone Three colony has the serum, we'll let you know the location."

"Fine. So, what do you want?"

"I need your help."

"My help? Lord William *Z-1-4* needs my help?" The sarcasm was thick in his voice.

"Indeed. I need you to talk to Dunleavy."

"Dunleavy?" replied the voice, his tone changing significantly. "Why now?"

"We have a problem. A reporter who may have some information about the colony, about Phase Two. And last I heard, she was on her way to see him."

"And?"

"I need you to make contact. Find out what they spoke about."

"I have some good news for you, William."

"What's that, Agent?"

"I spoke with Dunleavy no more than an hour ago. I'm meeting him tomorrow at noon."

"Well done, Jacob! Did he say anything else?"

"No, nothing."

"Okay then, here's what I need you to do…"

Chapter Twenty-Three

Such was the tension on the plane, even the luxurious white leather was beginning to irritate Caleb. After ten minutes in the air, Caleb stood up and paced the cabin. He couldn't help but think of what had happened throughout the day. It was time to fill in his team on the situation. "Dunleavy, can you watch Matthew?" he said.

"Yeah, no problem," Mike agreed.

He stood up and followed Caleb to the back of the plane.

"Come with me, we need to talk," Caleb requested Casey. Casey stood up, and Dunleavy took his place, settling in beside their prisoner.

Together Caleb and Casey walked back towards the front of the plane and entered the cockpit. As he walked past her, Caleb motioned for Darcy to follow.

She declined his offer, finding the seats much more amiable than her partner.

Caleb and Casey entered the small cockpit crouching so Murphy and Walker could comfortably hear them.

"Can you all hear me ok?" Caleb asked

They all gave the thumbs-up.

"Alright, I'll start at the beginning…" Caleb recounted the events of the day, the mysterious email from Darcy's colleague and the meeting with her boss. The drive back from Phoenix when Dunleavy spoke about Caleb's recruitment, and their missions. The encounter with the strange men at Darcy's apartment, and lastly, the text message sent to 'E' in Seattle. He gave them a moment for the information to sink in.

"I've only got one question, Cap?" Casey began.

"What's that, Casey?" asked Caleb.

"Why did it take you so long to call us?"

"Yeah, you're probably right," Caleb replied, "but guys, there's one more thing I think you need to know."

"Okay, sir. What is it?" asked Murphy.

"The night the President was shot… I spoke to him. In fact, I think I was on the phone with him at the exact moment when he was shot."

"Holy shit, sir" exclaimed Casey.

"What did he say?" asked a cautious Murphy

"Something about the 'Source'," Caleb replied.

"The Source?" Casey replied.

"Yeah, I don't suppose you guys have heard of anything like that?"

"No, not me," Casey replied.

Murphy was more reluctant to respond.

"Murph… anything ring a bell?" Caleb asked.

Murphy remained quiet for a few seconds. "Nothing comes to mind." she said.

"Well… can you think?"

Murphy lapsed into silence again.

"Lieutenant?" Caleb prodded.

"I just remember some vague references from our missions."

"Like what?"

"Nothing really. Like I said, it's a bit vague."

"So… what do you *know* about the Source?" asked Caleb.

"Like I said sir, I'm not sure." Murphy replied as she glanced up at the console. "Good news is, we're less than an hour out of Seattle."

Caleb looked at his watch, confirming it was about five thirty in the morning. With luck, they would get to the terminal by about half-past-six, giving them some time to discover where Emmett would be.

"Time, I think, to have another chat with our young guest," Caleb said.

Chapter Twenty-Four

Caleb made his way out of the cockpit, Casey following closely behind. As he walked past Darcy, he beckoned for her to follow. Caleb settled into the seat in front of Matthew, spinning it around so could face him.

"Now Matthew," Caleb said, "What can you tell me about Emmett and his mission?"

Matthew glanced around at the others, looking anxious.

As he panned across the group, his gaze eventually landed on Dunleavy. As he made eye contact with the former Chief-of-Staff, Matthew decided to give them any information he could. If he could help Caleb, that might in turn assist Dunleavy, and if Dunleavy was helped, then logically – at least in Matthew's mind – it would help him receive the serum. "I can't tell you anything about his mission, they didn't tell me anything. But I can tell you some stuff about Emmett."

"That would be a very good start."

"About, I don't know, maybe twelve months ago, Emmett and I were recruited."

"Recruited? By who?" Darcy asked.

"By Pierre. I didn't know his name at the time. All he told me was to meet him at the local YMCA. There, he told me that I was chosen, that 'they' had been watching me for some time, and he asked me if I wanted to be part of something special."

"Who are they?" Casey demanded.

"To be honest, I still don't really know. Pierre called them 'The Colonials'."

"Okay, we'll get back to them later. Go on. What happened next with Emmett?" asked Caleb, trying to focus on the more immediate task.

"We all met in a park in North Carolina, there we were given an ulti-matum. Basically, we could go off with Pierre and learn more, or we could leave. All but one of us – there were nine of us to start with – all but one of us went with him."

Caleb and Darcy glanced at each other. "Matthew… just hold up. Why did you go with him? How did you know where you were going?" asked Darcy.

"Ma'am, you know I'm really not sure. All I know is that, I was, I dunno, just looking for something important to be a part of. You know that feeling?"

"I certainly do," said Caleb. *But I joined the Marines instead of a cult,* he thought.

"So anyway, we were driven to a warehouse where we went through heaps of training. Most of it was theory, learning things. Stuff about physics, chemistry, and biology. We were tested on stuff all the time. After a while, some of the other guys were taken away—"

"What happened to them?" asked Darcy

"I'm not sure, ma'am. I never saw them again. I guess they went home."

Caleb wasn't so sure that was the outcome, but he could not focus on that.

"So, obviously you and Emmett made it through."

"Yeah, eventually it was just me and him. We were pretty much separated from then on. I was trained in hand-to-hand combat, sniper rifles. You know, just… army stuff."

"And Emmett?"

"He… he was training with rockets. Specifically, MANPADs." the young man continued.

Caleb's calm expression was swiftly replaced with one of deep concern.

Darcy was unsure of what Matthew was talking about.

She turned to Caleb, and saw the look on his face. She scanned the rest of the group. Casey and Dunleavy also had similar expressions to Caleb.

"Caleb, what's a MANPAD?" Darcy asked.

"A MANPAD is a Man Portable Air Defence System. In civilian terms, it's a rocket launcher. You know, the one's you put on your shoulder—"

Understanding dawned. "Holy shit, Caleb, is he gonna..." Darcy's voice trailed off as she lifted a hand to her mouth.

"Yeah, babe – in about two hours, Emmett's gonna shoot down a plane."

◆ ◆ ◆

A myriad of thoughts were passing through Emmett's mind as he waited. They were the same thoughts he'd been dwelling on since he'd first received his mission parameters. While he was honoured to be carrying out the task, he was equally burdened by its lofty ambitions.

By now, various governments were probably going crazy searching through all the variables to the messages he'd sent. They were probably wondering where and when a plane would be shot down. Emmett had even fed them specific details about where they could find members of the New Light cell. The thought made him smile.

His smile intensified when he remembered his reward. His place in the colony, in the plan, in Phase Two – it was all about to come to pass. And he couldn't wait.

He looked at his watch. There was less than an two hours remaining.

Chapter Twenty-Five

Caleb got to his feet. Knowing there was a plane about to be shot down, there was a greater sense of urgency to their actions.

From a positive viewpoint, it did provide them with some mission parameters. Where Caleb felt as if he'd been chasing his tail for the past twenty hours, now it seemed he had something tangible to work with. "Casey, come with me," he ordered. "Mike, you keep watching Matthew. Darcy, try to get more information out of him."

"Like what?" asked Darcy.

"I don't know... anything that could help," Caleb muttered as he strode towards the front of the plane, Casey close closely behind. Taking a seat at the front, Caleb began planning. "Casey, do you have your tablet with you?" he asked.

"Of course." Casey reached over to the seat where he'd first been sitting, and grabbed the large backpack he'd brought on board with him. "You know I'm always prepared." Casey pulled the tablet out of his pack.

"Good," Caleb began, "there's something I need to cover first though, Sergeant."

"Yeah, what's that Cap?"

Caleb glanced towards the cockpit. "You and Murphy?"

The words caused Casey some obvious discomfort. While Caleb didn't have a rule in place regarding relationships between officers, it was never advisable. Especially in such a tight team as the one Caleb had formed. Any relationship could compromise each mission, causing some members to act for personal reasons rather than for the good of the team.

"Don't worry sir..." Casey said, "We won't compromise the mission."

Caleb tried to calm him down. "Casey... Darryl" Caleb said, adding familiarity to the conversation, "I'm just glad you two have finally got together. Shit, you've been tip-toeing around it long enough."

"Not really, sir," Casey replied.

"What do you mean?"

"Well... we've been together nearly a year and a—"

"Half right? Eighteen months?"

Casey looked dumbfounded. How did Caleb know?

"It was right after the London mission right? I noticed a change in both of you then."

"Shit Cap, I'm sorry..." Casey began

"Darryl, it's ok. I know you would have told me if you thought you were compromised. But I never saw any of that. I just wanted to confirm it with you, to make sure it's all out in the open, okay. I mean..." Caleb turned his head and glanced back at Darcy. She was quietly chatting with a relaxed-looking Matthew. "We've all got a personal stake in this," he said when he turned back.

"Yes, sir, we do."

"Okay then, get on the tablet, pull up a map of Seattle – we need to get a plan together."

Casey opened a mapping program on his tablet, and pulled up an aerial shot of Seattle.

As they began their planning, Dunleavy wandered over to them. He sat down next to Caleb.

"So, what's the plan guys? How can I help?" he asked.

Caleb looked at Casey, and they shared the same look.

"Mike. I think we need to stick to protocol as much as possible on this one. I mean, this is our area of expertise, and we don't need—" Caleb began.

Dunleavy looked offended. "Still don't trust me, Jackson?"

Caleb made direct eye contact with Dunleavy, not wanting to cause any confusion. "That's not it at, sir. You ask me if I trust you," Caleb began, "in this entire world, especially after everything that's happened recently, there are very few people I trust. One of them is sitting down the back of the plane with the guy who was sent to kill her, trying to help him to help himself. Three of the others I trust, well… there's one in front of me…" Caleb pointed towards Casey. "And there's another two flying this plane. I don't distrust you – I just need a lot more from you before I let you in on our planning."

Dunleavy looked annoyed. "Okay then, I get it," Dunleavy said, trying not to cause any reason to annoy the soldiers, "I understand the *lack of trust*. Just remember though, I was CIA before I was in politics. I can help you."

"I know sir. Believe me, I will let you know the part you can play," Caleb said. "I'd just like to keep the specifics *in-house* for now."

"Okay" Dunleavy said. "You know where to find me."

"Thank you, sir."

Dunleavy turned, but stopped short. "Jackson, let me just make a phone call."

Caleb narrowed his eyes, watching Dunleavy with something akin to suspicion. "Why, sir?"

"Look, we don't have much information at the moment. Frankly, all we've got is the word of some kid who seems to have gotten himself caught up in something he didn't expect."

"What are you suggesting?"

"I still know a guy. He has his ear to the ground. I can ask him if he's heard anything."

Caleb considered Dunleavy's offer looking to Casey for some advice.

"Couldn't hurt, sir. Might I suggest he make the call on speaker phone, though, to ensure there's no confusion?" Casey suggested.

"Of course," Dunleavy replied.

Caleb inhaled heavily before he spoke. "Okay then, call your guy," Caleb said.

Dunleavy pulled out his phone, and dialled a number, pressing a button to switch the call to speaker. "He may not be awake…" Dunleavy warned as the phone rang, but even as he spoke, the connection was picked up.

"Dunleavy? What the fuck?"

"Nice to speak to you too, Carl. Didn't wake you, did I?" Dunleavy said, offering Caleb a wry grin.

"Matter of fact, you did," Carl replied, an obvious lie. Judging by the man's voice, he'd been awake for some time.

"Bullshit, Carl," Dunleavy said. "Listen, I need to ask you something."

"Shit Mike, I don't have time for this."

"Carl – you owe me, okay. I need to know something?"

Carl huffed out an impatient breath. "Fine. What is it?"

"Is there any chatter this morning? Anything about an imminent strike?"

Carl lapsed into silence.

"Carl?" Dunleavy prompted.

"How did you know?" Carl asked, clearly stunned.

"I keep my ear to the ground. What's the chatter?"

"Shit Mike; I really shouldn't be talking about this."

"Carl – don't forget I still have the photos. Pretty sure your wife and kids would rather not learn about the whore in Brasilia. Or the one in Naples, or the one in—"

"Okay, okay! Jesus, Mike! Fuck!" Carl paused, presumably considering his options. "Okay. What do you want to know?" he asked

"The details? Have you heard about anything imminent?"

Carl again lapsed into silence.

"I can send the photos via email or regular mail, Carl. Up to you."

"Fine! We're hearing a lot of talk from New Light. They've been building up to something for a while. From what we can tell, they're planning to hit something in the northern United States. Probably New York"

"Hit? What do you mean hit?"

"The chatter points at a plane, but we're really not sure."

"Shit… well, I'm thinking it's gonna be Seattle."

"Seattle, why do you say that? Shit Mike, what the fuck have you been up to?"

"Nothing really, just keeping my ear to the ground."

"Nothing we have indicates the north west. All our guys are being mobilised to New York. The place is in locked down, so—"

"Do me a favour, Carl…"

"Fuck you and your favours, Mike. I'm done."

"Just send someone to Seattle. Anyone. Can't hurt, can it?"

"Fine. I'll send local SWAT. Can you let me know where?"

"Just get them to lock down SEATAC."

"Fine."

"Thanks, Carl."

"Mike – do NOT call me again. I'm done with this. Either send me those pictures, or send them on. You do not own me!"

"Carl, if this pans out, I'll burn the pictures. You have my word."

The call disconnected and Casey and Caleb looked at each other. It was almost confirmation, and it looked like they might be getting some help.

"Thanks for that Sir," Caleb said to Dunleavy. "He's not your greatest fan, is he? Remind me never to get on your bad side, okay."

"Yeah, that would be a good idea," replied Dunleavy with no real emotion.

"Sir, he spoke about New Light. Is that the group that took out the President?" asked Casey.

"Yeah, that's what the intelligence said," Dunleavy replied.

"You don't sound confident, sir."

"No, I'm not. While I do get the occasional intel, I don't get nearly enough to be certain of anything. Still…" Dunleavy paused.

"Go on, sir," Caleb requested.

"Boys, I don't know about you," said Dunleavy, "but if I was planning a terrorist attack, I'm pretty sure I wouldn't leave any bread crumbs about when and where it was going to happen."

Caleb and Casey exchanged a long glance. "It makes sense, Cap," Casey said.

Caleb nodded in agreement. Should they have been heading toward New York? Should they have been chasing New Light? Caleb wasn't sure. All the agencies seemed to think their concerns about Seattle was incorrect. Still, Caleb doubted the intelligence agencies had ever heard of Matthew, let alone Emmett and the MANPAD training.

"What should we do, Cap?" Casey asked.

Caleb decided to do what Darcy said in the diner, and follow his instincts. "We stay the course, Sergeant. We go to Seattle."

Casey nodded in agreement.

"Thanks for the intel, Mike, but we'll take it from here," Caleb said to Dunleavy.

"Fair enough" he replied. "Let me know if you need anything else."

Dunleavy returned to the back of the plane, and Caleb watched as he took the seat next to Matthew, listening to the conversation between Matthew and Darcy. Caleb turned his attention back to Casey's tablet. "Alright then," Caleb said.

"Sir, while Mr. 'Former-CIA' was sticking his above-average nose into our business, I've pulled up a map of the city. Now, the airport is here," Casey pointed to Seattle-Tacoma (SEATAC) International Airport.

"No other major airports?" asked Caleb

"Nothing major, sir. King County's nearby, but being a Sunday it will be too quiet there. I can't imagine there would be any other priority targets, at least none that you could take out with a MANPAD."

"Okay then. Sounds like a good enough basket to put all our eggs into."

"Sir?"

"Let's face it, Sergeant, we don't have a lot of information to go on right now. We need to pick a place, and just hope we get lucky."

The pair examined the map closely. As with every mission, the planning they performed was based largely on trying to assess the state-of-mind, motivations and predilections of their target. In this instance, the only information they had, the only person they had to base their decisions on, was Matthew.

What they knew of Matthew led Caleb to believe Emmett was a young man who'd been led astray. He had been led astray with the promise of… something. What that *something* was, Caleb did not know. That would be information they would need to seek out later.

"Sir, I think," began Casey, studying the map intently. "if it was me, and I was working with a MANPAD with the intention of taking out a flight, I think I would position myself somewhere around here." Casey pointed to a large parkland area, just east of the 509.

"Agreed," Caleb concurred.

The area was roughly five hundred feet wide – plenty of space for a person to hide, and it would provide a great view of the planes as they took off and landed.

"Quite a large area to cover Sergeant, any chance of narrowing it down?"

"Give me a chance, sir, I know I'm brilliant, but at this time of morning my brilliance is somewhat dampened," Casey muttered, his eyes flicking over the map as he studied the various options.

"Okay." Caleb turned his attention to the cockpit. "How long have we got, Murphy?"

Murphy checked the GPS. "About twenty minutes, sir," she shouted back.

"Sergeant?" Caleb turned his attention back to Casey.

"Yes, sir, I'll have an option for you in time."

"Good. I'm gonna prep." Caleb stepped into the cockpit. "Did you bring my gear?" he asked.

"Yes sir, in my pack," Murphy replied, motioning towards the bag tucked in behind her seat.

Caleb opened the all-purpose survival pack. Amid the various devices and technology, he came across a spare set of clothes.

Murphy was second-in-command, his *go-to* officer. While he held the same level of trust in her as he did the entire team, Caleb always respected her decisions. In fact, after only their first mission together, he'd recommended her promotion to Lieutenant.

After that, he'd always made sure he had spare equipment he could leave with her, and she did the same with him. She was always his first call whenever they received a mission, from Dunleavy or the President.

"Thanks Murphy," Caleb said, as he left the cockpit.

He entered the main cabin, and began to change. Removing his shirt, he heard a voice.

"Caleb, we need to talk," Darcy said.

He removed his shirt, and exposed his cut and defined physique. He looked up, and caught Darcy staring. She had always been happy with his body and looks, but she knew that eventually, they would fade, and she would still love the man beneath.

While she began by admiring her boyfriend's physique, Darcy's attention was quickly drawn to the scars. There were numerous healed knife wounds, and one or two bullet wounds on his body.

Having never been part of any of the missions, nor having met anyone that Caleb had worked with, Darcy had no real concept of where the scars came from. Now that she was getting an insight into Caleb's work, she looked at the scars differently.

The pain he must have been through was inconceivable to her, and the fact he bore it with such silent bravery was something she admired.

And it made her love him even more.

Still shirtless, Caleb removed his denim jeans having lost all sense of modesty in front of the other passengers. Still, with his girlfriend, a member of his team, and two other men in the cabin, there was no real need for modesty.

"What is it babe?" he asked, as he swiftly removed his clothing and pulled on the gear Murphy had supplied.

"It's about Matthew, he's a really messed-up kid, Caleb. It's almost as if he's been brainwashed, but it wasn't done without his agreement and knowledge."

Caleb stopped buttoning his shirt and stared at her. "What do you mean?"

"It's as if he *wanted* it. It seems as if he knew he was being manipulated, but he just didn't care. Some of the things he's told me–"

"Yeah… some people are like that."

"I think I've figured out why he was chosen," Darcy continued.

"Why's that?" asked Caleb.

"You remember how Mike said that during high school there was a lot of testing done … the psychological stuff?"

"Yeah."

"I think while you and some others were chosen because of your strength, faithfulness, and intelligence and that's why you were selected to be followed," she continued, "I think Matthew, and maybe Emmett, were chosen because they were the types who, while strong, athletic and capable, were ultimately very susceptible to suggestion."

"Suggestion?"

"Yeah. I first noticed it with Matthew in the car. When he was given the choice between living and dying, he grew quiet. But when he was coerced into thinking there was a way he could live, then he paid attention."

"Bit thin, babe, don't you think? I'm sure you might be right, but—"

"Caleb, trust me on this one. You heard Mike in the car, he was sure the group that Matthew is working for are using the same techniques. They couldn't recruit you, or someone like you. Your sense of right and wrong is too strong. What they needed, especially for expendable people, like I'm sure both Matthew and Emmett are, was for them to be… malleable. They need them to do exactly what they're told and not ask any questions."

"Okay, then, let's go with your theory," said Caleb. "The group would need to dangle a pretty big carrot in front of them to get them to comply. They would need a real incentive."

"Agreed, and Matthew told me what that was."

Caleb was impressed. He knew Darcy was a good reporter. In fact, the only person she couldn't get information out of was Caleb, but that was more out of a lack of trying, than her extracting ability. "What did he say?"

"This is where it gets interesting," Darcy paused, searching for the best way to describe it. "He told me they were told they would be part of something called 'Phase Two'."

"Phase Two? What's that?"

"To be honest, I don't think even Matthew knows all the details. What he does know, is that once the missions were carried out – the missions given to him and Emmett –they were going to be given a location to travel to in Zone Three – which is North America. And at that location, they would be advised of their role in Phase Two."

"Well done, Darcy. We can certainly use that."

"I think he's still holding on to something, and I think he was about to tell me, but then Dunleavy came back, and he stopped being as open."

"Fair enough. The kids trusts you, and not even I trust Dunleavy completely."

"Really, why's that?"

"I've got a bad feeling about him. You have to remember, he just disappeared, off the radar, without a word. I wish I knew why."

"Didn't he say it's because Hawkins said he was losing focus?"

"Yeah, that's what he said," Caleb agreed. "But that was the first thing he said that he wasn't being entirely truthful about. I just didn't want to say anything about it until I knew for sure."

Darcy paused to think. She'd noticed *something* odd about Dunleavy, but she'd brushed it off as being her inherent distrust of *all* politicians. "Leave it with me, babe," Darcy said. "If Dunleavy is holding anything back, I'll find out what it is."

Caleb smiled, glad Darcy was finding her feet in his world.

"I know you will, babe," he replied.

◆ ◆ ◆

"And you took care of it, right?" James had just received an unexpected phone call. He hadn't heard from Robert in more than a week, not since his last scheduled check-in.

"Not me personally, but the deed was done," replied Robert.

"Good, because from what I can tell," replied James, "there have been too many mistakes in Zone Three in the past twenty-four hours."

"And in Zone One, if I'm not mistaken, Why did you let the reporter get any information away anyway, James? Especially this close to Phase Two?" asked Robert, James's counterpart in Zone Three.

Had any other member of the colony spoken to James in that manner, if anyone else had questioned his decisions, they would have been suitably dealt with. However, Robert was not just a normal colonist. He'd been placed in charge of Zone Three, arguably one of the more key strategic zones in the colony. Over the past years, many of the threats that had surfaced to the group was that came directly from Zone Three. Not the least of these was the potential outing of the colonies by none other than the President of the United States.

Spanning Canada and the United States, the effected population of that zone would be in excess of five hundred million. While the other Zones covered more than five billion, the external reach of those zones was limited.

Zone Three was easily the biggest threat, and that was the main reason the 'New Light' terror cell had been created, and the main reason the attack was going to be perpetrated in Zone Three. If they thought they were under attack, they would be too distracted to pay much heed to the Colonials.

In fact, so crucial was the Zone, that James had put one of his most trusted men in charge.

"I have my reasons for letting the reporter go," replied James, now seeing that his need for information had potentially threatened the plan. "I wanted to know who the reporter had discussed his visit with. That's why we allowed him to send out the information. The information was always safe, and the tracker was put into the email. Once it was opened, we knew where it went, so we sent people to take care of the problem before it spread."

"Okay then. Not the way I would have dealt—"

"Just be quiet, Robert. I don't need your petulance now. I just need to know if the problem been taken care of?"

"Yes, of course it has. As soon as we traced the call we were able to kill… what was his name?" Robert addressed another person in the room. The person replied, his answer too mumbled for James to decipher.

"His name was Carl. Carl Johnson. A lifer in the CIA, but obviously Dunleavy has something on him, otherwise he wouldn't have spoken out. But, not taking any *risks*…" Robert paused as he let his jibe sink in, "Not taking any risks, our guy in the CIA took out Johnson, and also relayed the details of Dunleavy's whereabouts."

"And? Where is he?"

Robert cleared his throat. "He's on his way to Seattle"

James was shocked. "Seattle. Does he know about Emmett? Does he know about the plan? Dammit, Robert!"

"Hey, James. This is not my fault. If you'd only killed the reporter when he arrived at Haven, we wouldn't be in this mess!"

"Need I remind you who you are talking to?"

"No, sir, no, you do not."

"Good. Now, this business with Dunleavy. Can it be solved?"

"I've already sent my Alpha Team. They'll be dressed as SWAT officers, so Dunleavy will think they're there to help. But when they find him, they'll take him and his associates out."

"And you trust this… what did you call them? 'Alpha Team'?"

"They're my best people, sir. They'll get the job done."

"I certainly hope they do, Robert, for all our sakes."

"Agreed." Robert was about to hang up, but delayed. "One last thing James. Is the shipment still on schedule?"

"Indeed it is, Robert. Once John is done in Berlin, he will on-send the required amount to your location."

"Good, because I'd hate this all to be for nothing."
"I know; we've worked too hard on this."
"Right you are, Governor. Right you are."

Chapter Twenty-Six

"OK Cap, we're on approach", yelled Murphy from the cockpit.

The next part of the plan made Caleb nervous. He knew that he, Murphy and Casey could handle it, and Walker was more than capable of fulfilling his part. What he wasn't so sure about were the other three.

He had tried to think of an alternative option, but none had been forthcoming.

Murphy had ensured there were at least four parachutes on the plane – one for herself, Casey and Caleb. Plus the additional 'chute would allow Walker to jump if needed. She had also brought additional harnesses, to ensure the others could tandem jump with the trained members of the group.

Darcy, Dunleavy and Matthew were sitting in the rear of the cabin. Caleb walked over, carrying three harnesses.

"Need you to put these on…" he said.

The three expressions could not have been more different. Dunleavy was one of shock, Darcy of caution. Matthew's face didn't change, as though he' jumped before.

"Shit…" Dunleavy said, "I hate jumping out of fucking planes."

"Well, we can't really land can we?" Caleb said as he handed them over.

Dunleavy shrugged, "I guess she's going with you?" he asked Caleb, motioning to Darcy.

Caleb began putting on his parachute. "Actually no…" he replied, "You're with me…"

Darcy looked surprised, "Why can't I go with you?" she asked as she struggled with her harness.

"You'll be fine with Murphy... she done this a ton of times. Dunleavy's with me"

They each struggled to place the harnesses on their bodies. Murphy had made her way from the cockpit, leaving Walker behind.

Murphy began assisting Darcy with her harness, and Casey did the same with Matthew.

The timing of their jump was imperative, and there was very little room for error. They needed to land at a very specific point within SEATAC.

Dunleavy's apparent trepidation was only going to hinder their scheduling, so Caleb became more forceful. As he pulled Dunleavy towards him, he spun him around, positioning Dunleavy with his back facing him. Caleb pulled him close, and attached his harness to Dunleavy's.

Normally, protocol would dictate they should do several checks of their equipment. As they were approaching their landing zone, only the most basic of checks could be made.

Caleb did, however, cast a quick eye over to Murphy, who was hooking up Darcy to her pack, just to ensure it was as safe as could be.

"Looking ok there Murphy," he said, satisfied Darcy would be ok.

"Yes sir," Murphy replied.

"Walker..." Caleb shouted to the Sergeant, now sitting in the pilot's chair, "How are we going? Have we reached altitude?"

Walker responded, "Yes sir. Cruising now at about ten-thousand feet... You'll have about thirty seconds of freefall, and then you'll need to pull it."

Caleb briefed the team. He then motioned for Murphy and Casey – who had Matthew firmly attached – to start moving towards the door.

As they approached, Murphy removed the fail-safes from the door. She would have done it sooner, but knowing what she did about the plane, it would have been redundant to try open the door sooner. The airflow outside the cabin was enough to ensure the door would be kept closed. However, as they had reached a jumpable altitude, the air pressure inside the cabin was now at a point the door could be opened.

"Everybody okay?" Caleb asked, even though a negative response would not have stopped the jump.

Everyone nodded.

Caleb motioned to Murphy, "Everyone grab onto something." Murphy said, knowing that a sudden decompression of the cabin would pull everything near the door straight out. Caleb confirmed everyone was a secure as practicable, and motioned again for Murphy to open the door.

As Murphy opened the door, a loud whoosh sprung the door immediately open, the force of the passing wind enough to completely open the exit.

Such was the noise in the cabin, Caleb could only gesture his orders to Murphy and Casey. Their respective passengers were no longer dictating their own movements, having swung their legs up and arms crossed over their chests. Caleb felt the weight of Dunleavy pulling him down. But it was no more than he could handle, knowing the weight would be for a short time.

Caleb watched as Murphy and Darcy jumped from the plane, impressed with how well she was handling the situation.

They were followed closely by Casey and Matthew. As the pair disappeared out the door, Caleb and Dunleavy moved towards the rushing air.

Before Dunleavy could issue any further protest, Caleb jumped. As he jumped, the sound of the rushing air was deafening. It was not his first jump, so Caleb knew what to expect.

After about thirty seconds, Caleb rationalised they'd made it to around five thousand feet, the safe altitude to pull the cord. Caleb pulled the ripcord, releasing the parachute. After a jerk which sent him and Dunleavy perpendicular to the ground, they began a slower descent.

After the initial shock of the movement, Caleb was able to refocus and assess his surroundings.

In the distance, Caleb could make out the other two parachutes. A sense of relief washed over him, knowing it had gone according to plan.

Now more able to keep maintain his focus, Caleb quickly identified the predetermined Landing Zone – a section towards the north of the airport runways. The area was far enough away from the terminal so as to avoid detection, but also close enough to the anticipated area they figured Emmett would be waiting.

After around four minutes of slow descent, Caleb and Dunleavy touched down. He quickly pulled the 'chute in, unhooked a clearly breathless Dunleavy, and made his way to where the others were waiting.

Caleb quickly unhooked from Dunleavy, resolute in his composure. As he gained his footing, he made his way to side of the building.

As he walked, he grabbed the hi-definition, night vision binoculars Murphy had brought along.

Shimmying down the side of the building, Caleb tried to get a view of the far side of the airport, the park where Casey had determined the best vantage point for an assault.

Caleb scanned the tree line.

About seven hundred yards away, the park was blocked off by a fence. There was no vantage point above the height of the fence. As Caleb scanned south, the fence line disappeared, exposing several open areas that had a good sightline to the runway.

He switched the view to heat vision, hoping to spot even the slightest hint of body heat.

After doing another sweep of half the view of the park, Caleb was about to switch to night vision, when a familiar shape appeared. A small yellow, red and orange circle appeared, about fifteen hundred or so yards from their current position.

Now joined at the side of the building by Casey, Caleb gave his Sergeant the coordinates, and Casey double-checked the map.

While he was doing this, Caleb surveyed the rest of the park again, but saw nothing.

"Sir," Casey said as he showed the tablet to Caleb, "There it is..."

It was one of the potential spots he had marked out earlier.

"That's gotta be him. Right?" asked Casey.

"It's either him, or a hobo's about to get a hell of a fright," Caleb replied. The pair made their way back to the Landing Zone, now with a more precise target.

Casey began preparing the equipment, with Murphy assisting. "Okay everyone, listen up." Caleb said.

Darcy and Dunleavy stood up, awaiting instructions. Both were somewhat shaken by the jump, but were ok overall.

Matthew also stood, but only after being pulled up by Dunleavy.

"Ok… Darcy, you're gonna stay here with Murphy…" Caleb said.

Darcy tried to interject.

"Darc…" he continued, "she needs some back-up in case someone comes along. She's my second in charge, so I trust her."

Darcy didn't speak, preferring to keep her objections until she had time alone with Caleb.

"Dunleavy, Matthew, you're coming with us."

Dunleavy smiled, happy to be included.

"So… do I get a better gun?" he asked, only having the gun Caleb had handed him earlier.

"Sergeant…" Caleb said to Casey.

Casey stopped his preparation, and handed Dunleavy a side-arm, the same one he had earlier.

"Fine," Dunleavy said, his disappointment apparent.

Matthew stepped forward, "So what about me then? Do I get one too?"

Caleb shook his head.

"Please to meet you. My name's Darryl, and I'm better than any personal firearm you could ever need. While I don't come with all the perks of being able to shoot unsuspecting people in the back, I will ensure that you're safe," Casey announced with a smile, before adding, "for now anyway."

Matthew forced a smile.

"Okay then," Caleb announced. "Let's get going. Once we're in Position One, we'll go through the plan," he said, referring to the place the team had chosen as their initial rally point. As the majority of the lead up to any mission was the travel, they always named their arrival destination Position One. Dunleavy was well aware of this protocol.

"And just how far is that, Captain?" he asked.

"Only about twelve hundred yards or so. Piece of cake," Caleb replied.

"Shit," Dunleavy cursed. While he'd been athletic and fit during his time with the CIA, the life of the Chief-of-Staff didn't require any such physical requirements.

Suffice to say, Dunleavy had let himself go a bit. Added to the fact he was on the wrong side of sixty, and he'd just fallen from the sky, the twelve hundred yards was going to prove a bit more problematic than he'd hoped.

"Okay then, let's go," Caleb said, pulling his pack onto his back, and grabbing his weapon of choice, an M4A1 Carbine. While it was a fully automatic rifle, it could be switched to semi-automatic if required.

When Caleb turned to leave, Darcy grabbed his arm.

"Babe," she said quietly.

Caleb turned and met her eyes. They commanded him to stay - an order he couldn't refuse. Not today. "The rest of you file out – give us a minute," he said. "You too, Murphy".

With a nod of agreement, Murphy joined the others.

"Darcy," Caleb began, "I know what you're going to ask, but the answer is no."

Darcy shook her head. "You said back in LA. You said you wouldn't leave me again."

"I'm not, babe, I just, well,"

"Well what, Caleb?" she asked, irritated by his decision.

"This could get complicated. And Casey, Mike and I... we've had the training we need to get through this. You're a civilian."

"I can help—"

"I know you can. But I need you to do some stuff here, help Murphy with some things while we're gone," Caleb said. He turned to look down the steps. "Murphy!" he called out.

Murphy left the conversation she was having with Casey, "Yes, sir," she said.

"You have a few things to do while we're gone."

"Yes, sir"

Caleb paused, ensuring he had their full attention. "One. Prep for a quick exit. I know we don't have much time, but we'll need to move quickly once we're done. Maybe see if you can find us a car…"

"Right, sir."

"Good. Now, second," Caleb said, handing his back-up sidearm to Darcy. "The next time we get in a fight, Darcy's coming along. So make sure she knows how to use this," Caleb handed Murphy the pistol, "and teach her anything else you can. Just the basics for now, but get through as much as you can." He didn't miss Darcy's grateful smile when she realized he was going to help her be a part of his team.

"Yes, sir, not sure how much I can get through, but we'll give it a try."

"I know, Murphy, that's why I've left her with you. Make sure you look after her, okay?"

"Sir, yes Sir."

Caleb looked back at his girlfriend. Before every mission, he was always acutely aware that he may never see her again. Consequently, he'd developed a superstitious pattern, making sure he did the same thing each time, hoping that by keeping to the routine, he'd get to come back home to his girl.

This time was no different. He let his weapon hang off its strap, and dangle towards the ground. He looked deeply into Darcy's eyes, placing his hands on either side of her face. After several seconds of telling her with the emotion in his eyes, he whispered the words to her. "I love you. And I will come back." For some reason unknown to him, he added some extra words this time. "You are my light when there's darkness, Darcy," he whispered.

The moment Caleb finished talking, Darcy wrapped her arms around his strong shoulders and leant in, burying a deep, passionate kiss against his lips. She knew, as well as he did, that there was a chance they may never see each other again.

The kiss was a perfect moment between them. It was as though both their worlds would be forever illuminated. A moment when, despite all that had happened and despite all that was bound to occur, they would always have. It was a moment that was over all too quickly.

"Sir, if I may?" Murphy began.

Before she could continue, Caleb grinned and replied, "Permission granted, Lieutenant."

With that, Murphy bounded over to the others and threw herself at Casey. The two shared a deep kiss, with Casey wrapping his arms around Murphy as though he'd never let her go.

When Murphy pulled back, she gave Casey a final hug, and then came back, looking a trifle sheepish. "Sorry about that, sir," Murphy said when she reached Caleb and Darcy's side.

"Not a problem, Marine. Had to be done," Caleb replied with a smile.

"Yes, sir."

"Okay then," Caleb said, "see you both soon."

"Good luck," Darcy said.

"You too," Caleb replied. "Look after her, Murph"

"Yes, sir. Will do"

Caleb smiled at the pair, and then walked down the stairs. He broke into a jog almost immediately. As he moved past the other three, he ordered them to follow.

Dunleavy look up position directly behind Caleb, already struggling to keep pace. In the third position was Matthew, obviously fit, as the jog didn't seem to disturb him at all.

At the rear, Casey kept a close eye on both of them, watching for any false moves.

Chapter Twenty-Seven

The group stayed tight, keeping a steady pace. As planned, Caleb led them west across the runways. The sun was breaking over the horizon, which added a further complication to the plan. Caleb couldn't risk being seen as they approached.

The airport terminal was presumably a potential secondary target for Emmett, and with the early morning travellers making their way to the airport, the number of dead could exceed those threatened if he shot down the plane.

Still about a mile away from their target, Caleb decided that every precaution needed to be taken. He figured that, just as he had ensured all precautions had been taken, so would Emmett, having been trained for this one and only mission.

The quartet continued to jog across the tarmac at a brisk speed. Dunleavy was proving a significant hindrance to their progress, but Caleb had to admit, the guy was trying to keep up.

With this in mind, Caleb doubled back slightly, so he was running by the side of the portly sexagenarian. With words of encouragement, Caleb urged him to move faster. It wouldn't be long until they were fully exposed by the impending sunlight. Dunleavy did what he could, to pick up the pace and within a couple of minutes the group reached the edges of the parkland. Fortunately, the parkland was more forest-like than open plain. While it would slow their progress, it would provide ideal cover.

When Casey was doing the initial calculations, he'd acted on the assumption that the intended target, Emmett, would choose a location based on cover and ease of access.

The location needed to be of such design that he could hide himself and any equipment for an extended period of time, potentially even camp there for weeks. It needed to provide cover so that, until the last moment, people wouldn't be able to notice him. There was always the risk that people would, but only if they knew where to look *and* what they were looking for.

The second aspect of Casey's considerations had been ease of access. With practise, and constant repetition, the location could be accessed relatively easily. However, to the untrained person, the site would be difficult to access quickly.

For those two reasons, Casey had made three sites along the tree-line a priority. One towards the south west corner of the airport. With ease of access from the 509, it would only take moments for Emmett to get there. However, with the southern location, there was only about one hundred yards between the location and the highway. The risk of early exposure, or someone accidently stumbling on the area was too great.

The second location he'd considered was towards the north of the airport, the location they were running toward at that moment. It was more isolated from the road, and would provide a better chance of going undetected. The flaw with the site was that right at the last moment, Emmett would have to run up a sharp incline with the MANPAD and take his shot. This would leave him out in the open, and exposed, for several minutes, putting the plan at serious risk.

The last position was the location Emmett had apparently chosen; the one that Casey had said he would have chosen himself. It was, of the three potential locations, the hardest to access. Situated almost in the centre of the runways, and just north of the radar towers, the location was roughly four to five hundred yards from the highway. The place offered plenty of cover from the trees. The only real drawback, was that once the rocket was fired, it would take time for Emmett to get out and back to the highway to make his getaway.

They made it to the rally point – a place located about thirty yards in from the start of the tree line. Surrounded by a natural barrier of trees, the quartet was able to relax and compose themselves for a couple of minutes.

Dunleavy was clearly out of breath, and welcomed the short interlude.

"Sergeant, can you go through the next steps for our guests?" Caleb asked Casey.

"Yes, sir," Casey replied, pulling the tablet from his backpack. Matthew and Dunleavy stood to either side of Casey, looking at the tablet over his shoulder.

"Okay," Casey began his explanation, referring to the map as required. "This is where we are. I'm going to take a more direct route, down the east side of the tree line. I'll stay at least twenty yards in from the trees at all times. I'll travel for about seven hundred yards, passing the tower on the east, and work our way through to here." Casey pointed at an area about thirty yards short of where Emmett was thought to be. "Once we get there, I'll hold until we get word from the Captain. Matthew, Dunleavy, you'll go with Cap. You'll all travel south, but on the west side of the trees. Passing the tower on the west, you'll make your way to a position about thirty yards south of the target location."

"Once we arrive, I'll radio Sergeant Casey," Caleb began, his part of the plan now to be explained. "We'll then move in on the target area from north and south. While that leaves the east unguarded, it will be to the target's 'six'... sorry, it will be behind him. With the element of surprise on our side, we should be fine." Caleb said the words, but he didn't believe them. There was no telling how or what Emmett might do once he is approached. But there was no benefit in telling that to either Matthew or Dunleavy.

"Now, once we're there, we have to act fast. If Emmett won't surrender," Caleb said, now presenting Matthew with a harsh truth. "He'll have to be stopped – I'm not going to let him kill anyone."

Matthew nodded towards Caleb.

"Get ready to move," Caleb said to the group.

He pressed his finger against his earwig, activating his radio.

"Murph, can you hear me, over?"

After about five seconds, the Lieutenant responded. "Loud and clear sir, over."

"We've reached Position One, and we're about to move out. Radio silence from here on, over," Caleb said.

The last thing they needed was for radio chatter to alert the suspect.

"Yes, sir. Over and out."

Caleb disengaged the radio. "I make it 0635, meaning we have just under twenty-five minutes to get to our secondary locations. Let's go," Caleb said, as he turned towards the west.

"Wait a goddam second!" said Dunleavy, in a harsh whisper.

Caleb turned back. "What is it?" he said, annoyed with the interruption.

"Am I the only one here that doesn't trust this guy?" Dunleavy said, pointing at Matthew, "Why the fuck is he coming with us?"

Caleb looked at Matthew, who seemed surprisingly shocked by Dunleavy's declaration.

"Dunleavy," Caleb began to explain. "Where would you rather he be? With us, or back at the with the others??"

"Shit, if it were my call, he'd be buried next to Long Beach Airport," Dunleavy spat.

Matthew grew paler at the thought.

"I'm not a murderer, Mike!" Caleb said to Dunleavy, his tone changing as his frustration grew. Now, he was genuinely angry. "I will not kill someone who doesn't pose a threat to me. While *he* is from the enemy, I won't kill him just for the sake of it. I won't kill him just to make my job easier. Every life is important Dunleavy. Every single one, and I won't take his from him."

"You can't seriously trust him," Dunleavy replied, taken aback by the verbal barrage that was forthcoming.

"I don't, not yet. That's why he's with us, and not back at the plane with Darcy."

Caleb turned to Matthew, who was visibly more relaxed now he had a *protector* in Caleb.

"Matthew," Caleb said, "I have to warn you. Do not mistake my compassion for weakness. Do not give me a reason to kill you. Your life is important, but I will take it if I have to. Do you understand?"

"Yes sir, thank-you" Matthew replied.

"Don't thank me yet," said Caleb, "Dunleavy. Your other task is to keep an eye on Matthew. We can't risk him calling out to Emmett. If he looks like he's going to do something that we wouldn't want, you'll need to take him out."

"Fine." Dunleavy replied, as he looked at Matthew.

Casey glanced over at Caleb, waiting for his command. He lifted an eyebrow, as if he was reminding Caleb that they were running out of time.

Caleb nodded. It was all the direction Casey needed as he slapped Dunleavy on the shoulder and they started on their way.

Caleb moved along his route, and Matthew followed. After fifteen steps or so, Caleb spoke. "Okay," he said, "you take the lead, and listen to the directions I give you, very carefully."

He still didn't trust him… not one bit.

♦ ♦ ♦

"Where are they now?" Darcy asked.

"They've just made it to their first position," she replied. "We won't hear from them until it's done."

Darcy nodded pensively, trying not to let her concern get the better of her. While she knew that Caleb had plenty of experience, she was still aware of the possibility that mistakes could be made. Plus, he was with Matthew, a man she certainly didn't trust.

"Don't worry, Darc. They'll be fine," Murphy said.

"I know, I know," Darcy replied.

"The Cap is… well, the Cap. He'll have it all under control. Trust me, we've been in worse situations than this." She grinned wryly. "Not that we've ever tried to stop a rocket launch on American soil before, but we've had plenty of delicate situations that he's got us through okay, you know—"

"Yeah, I've just gotta keep telling myself that."

"Anyway, back to it then." The two women had been waiting at the start location, practising some basic self-defence as Caleb had requested.

Murphy had already shown Darcy the basic use of a hand-gun. The loading and unloading of the weapon, making sure the safety is off, not placing your finger on the trigger unless you were preparing to fire. It was basic stuff, but, as Darcy had fired at a shooting range before – a *special* date from Caleb – she basically knew what to expect.

They'd just begun going over basic self-defence strategies – which point to aim for that would cause quick, intense pain – when Caleb had radioed.

They'd also covered breaking basic holds. After several scenarios, Murphy motioned for Darcy to stand opposite her.

Murphy pulled a knife from her belt. Darcy could see it was a small blade, no larger than a paring knife. "So, we've know you can fire a gun. And you can do some basic self-defence. That's great. But, this," Murphy handed the knife to Darcy, "This will save your life one day. Consider it a gift." Murphy moved around to stand behind Darcy. "Now, put the knife in your pocket"

Darcy complied.

Murphy reached forward and placed one arm lightly around Darcy's neck. "Now, your natural inclination will be to struggle, try to pull my arm away. But let me tell you a little trick. What you do is, with your right hand, reach up and pull on my arm. Putting your right arm up, and pulling down again will fulfil your attacker's belief that you're struggling, and they'll think they have control."

Darcy moved her right arm up, and pretended to struggle. To add authenticity to the training, Murphy tightened her grip.

"With your left arm, grab the knife."

Darcy complied.

"Now, slam it into the attacker's thigh, and twist."

Darcy pretended to do the action. Once complete, Murphy released Darcy. She spun around so they were facing each other. "But Darcy, there's only so much we can practise, especially in such a short period of time. It'll be different in real life. It's much faster and there will be things that happen that you can't anticipate." Murphy noticed the somewhat forlorn expression on Darcy's face. "But the good news is that when you're in a fight, your reflexes are sharper, and with adrenalin, you become stronger. Caleb wouldn't have let you stay with me if he didn't think you could handle it. Why do you think he took Dunleavy?" Darcy thought on the question. "Because, Dunleavy, he was CIA. He's trained for stuff like this."

"Nope. He took Dunleavy because he didn't trust him to do a good job back here. He trusts me, he trusts you. Being left to fend for yourself, it's basically the highest compliment the Captain can give."

Darcy smiled at the notion. As she did, she caught movement from the corner of her eye - A large, black SUV was driving towards them.

It came into view sharply, and pulled to a stop even before Darcy could recognise what was happening. About half a dozen people exited, fanning out, their rifles in an attack posture.

Dressed similarly to Caleb, Casey and Murphy, they walked and behaved like soldiers moving swiftly and in unison.

Reaching a spot about twenty feet from the women, they moved their guns to a stand-down position, ready to be lifted if required. A seventh person exited the vehicle, and strode directly towards them, "Where's Dunleavy?"

Darcy turned her attention to Murphy. The lieutenant seemed remarkably calm.

"Who are they?" Darcy asked.

"Don't know. They move like SWAT, though," Murphy replied.

"How can you tell?"

"You spend enough time around different agencies – SEALs, Delta's, local PD, and you become aware of the differences. We used to train with some SWAT guys in LA, and these guys are behaving just like 'em"

"SWAT? Why would they be here?"

"Dunleavy call a guy. I didn't think they'd be here so fast though."

The woman shouted again.

"Dunleavy!" she said, more forcefully, looking around the area, presumably as she thought he was hiding.

Darcy looked to Murphy for guidance. "Dunleavy's gone." replied Murphy

"Who are you?" the woman demanded.

"Mr. Dunleavy has gone off to do something. Take a leak, I think." Murphy replied, ignoring the question.

"Where? Where did he go?"

"Look lady, I'm just an assistant. He doesn't tell me much."

The woman turned to the SWAT team, and motioned for them to raise their guns. "Come here" she said, "You don't seem surprised to see us?"

"Why should we be," Murphy replied as she walked towards the group, "Dunleavy asked you to come…"

When Murphy was a yard or so away from the team, one of the SWAT members moved forward swiftly, and forcefully grabbed her by the arm.

"You're not the SWAT team we ordered, are you?" Murphy asked, already knowing the answer.

The leader silently walked towards Darcy, ignoring Murphy's question. As she stepped closer, a look of recognition appeared on her face.

"Look at the pair of you," the leader said. "If you're assistants, then I'm Mickey Mouse. The woman smiled at Darcy. "Hello, Ms. Chamberlain. So glad I've found you." Her sunglasses and the black cap sitting low over her eyes hid the rest of her joy at finding the runaway.

She turned to two of the officers behind her. "You two, move in on the asset's position," she ordered. "Provide protection and ensure the mission is carried out."

The pair turned and ran towards the tree-line, following the same path Caleb and the others had jogged earlier.

Darcy exchanged a glance with Murphy. With the woman's words, it was obvious that these were not SWAT members, and she and Murphy were in a lot of trouble. Figuring she had nothing to lose, Darcy pulled the pistol from her back, and pointed it at the leader.

The woman held her hands up in front of her. "Now, Ms. Chamberlain. We've been sent to take you with us," she began. "It's up to you whether that happens with you being dead, or alive."

Darcy considered her options. She could pull the trigger, and hope she killed the leader. Though what effect this would have on the other shooters was unknown.

Just as she was about to lower the gun, Murphy made the decision for her. The Lieutenant grabbed the arm of her captor, and flipped him to the ground. The man crashed onto his back and his weapon flew through the air.

Murphy grabbed at the gun, snatching it up in one hand and rolling to her left.

Bullets flew through the air in Murphy's direction, but she was agile enough to keep moving, rolling quickly between shots. Such was her speed, that their assailants couldn't track her movements effectively.

Murphy rolled to a stop, with the gun pointed at her first target. She fired a quick succession of bullets, adjusting her sights between each shot. So effective was her shooting that she took down all but one of the armed men. One received a bullet through the neck, one got shot in the chest. The last was hit in the head with such force that his cap was blown clear off his now partially-missing skull.

As soon as Murphy made her first movement, Darcy knew the play.

She pulled the trigger and the bullet flew in the direction of the group's leader. She was agile though, and moved to the left, just enough that the bullet merely winged her. Though, it was enough to knock her off her feet.

Once Darcy had fired the shot, she looked over at the man Murphy had struggled free from. He was groaning, but still moving. As she watched, he reached towards his sidearm, pulling it out. He pointed it directly at Murphy, who had just finished the third of her kills.

Darcy pointed the gun straight at him, and pulled the trigger. The bullet flew through the air, hitting the man's jugular. Blood exploded from the back of his neck, and he was dead before he hit the ground.

Within seconds, all four of the five team members were dead, and the last lay wounded on the ground. Darcy moved quickly to the wounded woman, standing over her, with the pistol pointing straight at her face.

"Well done, Darcy," Murphy called, "hold her there."

The lieutenant stood up, fighting against the pain in her shoulder. She hadn't managed to escape the gunfight completely unscathed, one bullet had clipped her shoulder on the way through. She hurried over to join Darcy, and they both looked down at the fallen woman. The woman, who had initially been so confident and in control, was a different person altogether now - her fear almost palpable.

"You're hurt," Darcy said, noticing Murphy's wound.

"It's just a scratch," Murphy replied reassuringly.

Murphy returned her attention to the woman on the ground. All head wounds seemed to bleed profusely and this one was no different, even with the scratch the woman had endured, blood was seeping out onto the tarmac.

"So," Murphy said to the woman. "What are we going to do with you?"

The woman offered no reply, apart from for the gritted teeth she had.

Murphy looked towards the SUV, "Good… now we don't have to steal a car" she said with a smile.

Chapter Twenty-Eight

Navigating the trees and terrain had proved more difficult than anticipated. Although it had taken the majority of the allotted time, Caleb, Dunleavy and Matthew had arrived at their predetermined location.

Caleb glanced at his watch.

0655.

In a few minutes, a plane was going to land.

Their timing needed to be precise. If they attacked Emmett too early, he might fire the rocket into the terminal. If they attacked too late, the plane would get shot down.

It was a precarious position to be in, a situation unlike anything Caleb had faced before. They came to a stop about twenty yards from the clearing. Caleb turned on his radio and spoke quietly. "Sergeant. We're in position. What's your location? Over," Caleb said, hoping Casey had not been delayed. When no response came, Caleb repeated to message.

Still no response.

A couple more moments passed, and Caleb began to worry as Casey's deadline to reach his position was passed. Again, Caleb repeated the message, and still there was no response.

If something had happened to Casey, Caleb knew he would need to continue with the plan. It was too important, and too many lives were at stake, to change their course of action now. The needs of the many outweighed the needs of one Sergeant and his companion.

Caleb decided he could wait no more. "Follow me," he whispered to Dunleavy and Matthew.

"Is he here yet?" asked Dunleavy.

Caleb shook his head, repeated his instructions to Dunleavy, and they slowly crept towards the area. In the middle of the clearing, Caleb spotted a young man. He looked much younger than Caleb had anticipated. Emmett wouldn't have looked out of place at a high-school, and Caleb imagined he would never have been suspected of undertaking a terrorist plot. Indeed, that was probably a determining factor in his recruitment.

Emmett was standing motionless in the clearing, the MANPAD on his shoulder, facing the runways.

"You two stay here," Caleb ordered, "Dunleavy, keep a close eye on him."

Caleb checked his watch. 0658. It was time to move.

◆ ◆ ◆

The moment had finally arrived. Over the past four hours, Emmett had centred on the joy he would feel when he completed his mission, although there were still some minor, lingering doubts.

Once he caught sight of his target however, all the doubts vanished.

The plane came into sight, and he thought it seemed almost peaceful as it seemed to glide downwards towards the runway. The time was 0659, and it was the only plane approaching the airport.

Emmett could hear the words of his teacher, from the last face-to-face meeting they'd had, and he remembered how he'd vowed he wouldn't let Pierre down. Now, with the moment imminent, he concentrated on that thought.

He peered through the sight of the MANPAD, confirming the plane was in clear sight. He pressed the targeting button, and heard the beep which confirmed the plane was locked in. Cautiously, carefully, he adjusted his finger, reaching towards the trigger.

Suddenly, Emmett was tackled from behind. The sharp pain he experienced in his back shook the MANPAD from his shoulder, and the weapon fell away to the ground.

Emmett tried to turn over, but found himself buried under an enormous man's frame.

"Don't struggle, Emmett" the man warned.

"What the hell? Who are you?" Emmett asked, surprised the man knew his name.

"I'm a friend, stopping you from making a terrible mistake."

Anger rose in Emmet's chest and he struggled more determinedly. "A friend? You've ruined everything! Why didn't you let me finish the mission! I was so close!"

"It's okay, kid, listen, we've brought someone you know," the man continued as they struggled.

A loud thud came from the place Dunleavy and Matthew were waiting.

Caleb turned to look for clues as to the cause. But what he saw was more frightful.

To Caleb's horror, Matthew had walked over to the MANPAD and picked it up. He then stood as Emmett had, facing the airport... facing the plane.

"Matthew! Noooo!" Caleb pleaded.

"Yes, Matthew! Do it…. For the next life!" shouted Emmett

"Nooo!" Caleb screamed.

But it was too late. As the rocket flew out of the MANPAD a bullet collided with the back of Matthew's head.

Matthew's head exploded, the bullet entering through the cerebellum and out through the parietal lobe.

Casey had arrived, but it was too late.

After a second of wavering on the spot, Matthew's almost-headless body slumped to the floor, never to move again.

Caleb stared skyward, following the trajectory of the rocket. Time seemed to slow down as he watched, aghast, as the rocket collided with the side of the airplane. The back of the fuselage was vaporised in an instant, metal and debris flying towards the airport terminal as it hit the ground. With directional control gone, the plane veered to the left, spreading the remainder of the destroyed aircraft across the tarmac. The plane's momentum carried the burning shell across the tarmac. Such was the impact of the rocket that no one could have survived.

Caleb rolled off of Emmett, and knelt on the ground, his mission a failure.

He watched the scene at the airport in disbelief, dazed by the thought of so many lives being extinguished in a split-second.

Casey ran over, followed closely by Dunleavy. Casey pulled Emmett's hands behind his back and secured them with some cable ties. "Cap, we've gotta move!" he yelled to Caleb.

Caleb mentally shook himself back, stood up and tried to regain his focus. He took one more look at the wreckage, burning like a beacon at the end of the runway. Emergencies workers were scrambling to their vehicles, ready to make their way towards the destroyed plane.

"What happened?" Caleb asked Dunleavy.

Dunleavy seemed to be in shock, no doubt partly due to the concussion he'd received after being knocked by Matthew. He could only mutter some words, but Caleb could barely make them out.

Knowing there was little time to waste, Caleb attempted to regain his composure.

"Sergeant," Caleb said. "Secure the prisoner."

Casey grabbed hold of Emmett's hands from behind, "Done, sir."

"It'll be some time before they get their heads around what just happened. We've gotta move. We gotta go," Caleb exclaimed. Caleb began to run towards the runways. There was no point in hiding in the trees now. They had to get moving as quick as possible.

He stepped towards his dropped weapon, but was stopped by a bullet rushing past his head.

Caleb spun around to see what looked like a two members of a SWAT team approaching. Caleb held up his hands, remembering Dunleavy had organised for the local Seattle PD SWAT to assist. "We're friendlies!"

The SWAT officers approached, without saying a word.

"Holy shit Cap, they don't seem too friendly to me," said Casey.

Casey quickly grabbed his gun. But, for the second time in as many minutes, he was too late.

The men opened fire, hitting Caleb in the chest, the bullet impacting his bullet-proof vest. The impact knocked him over and he fell onto his back. The same fate befell Casey, who had moved up next to Caleb in the build-up.

Casey looked over at Caleb, and said "Told ya," with a cheeky smile.

Stunned by the impact of the bullets, all they could do was watch. The two "SWAT" team members hurried up to where Emmett stood. They both fired from almost point-blank range. Both shots hit Emmett square in the chest. Emmett wasn't as fortunate as Casey and Caleb, for he was not wearing a vest.

He had no protection from the blasts. His struggling heart pumped blood through the wounds, and out onto his chest - the last of Pierre's protégés now dead.

The two gunmen then turned their attention to the fallen marines, both of them writhing from the impact of the earlier shots.

Casey looked over at Caleb.

"Dammit, Cap, I'm in trouble," he said, "I promised Murph I'd do the dishes tonight."

Caleb could only muster a light laugh. As the gunmen approached, his only thoughts were of Darcy. The times they'd had together. The laughs they'd shared. He suspected it was all about to come to an end. It was then when a thought struck him.

Where was Dunleavy?

Bang! Bang!

Caleb closed his eyes, prepared to absorb the pain he was sure would be coming. The act was unnecessary.

♦ ♦ ♦

Dunleavy had waited in the trees, cautious about the approaching soldiers. From there, he'd had the perfect view of everything. There had been an opportunity to intervene, just before Emmett was shot. However,

Dunleavy decided to wait it out. Better to let them kill the young man, as he would more than likely have been a problem later had he survived.

After watching Emmett die, the men moved back over to *his* marines. Now *they* could still be useful to Dunleavy.

When he saw his opportunity, Dunleavy made his move. He moved with speed he hadn't used since his field agent days, and put a bullet in the base of each gunman's skull. Though messy, it was certainly efficient.

"Captain," he said, leaning over to shake Caleb's shoulder, "get the fuck up – we don't have much time."

It took plenty of effort, but Caleb and Casey obliged, the sting of the bullets in their vests still prevalent. "Follow me," Caleb said, reasserting his control of the situation.

The trio started to run across the tarmac, a journey that would be much quicker than their initial trek. This was due to the straight line of travel rather than the roundabout way they had previously needed to use.

As they made their way, Caleb assessed the situation.

Caleb hoped Murphy had found a car to use, otherwise they were in real trouble.

While the getaway was an issue, Caleb was sure he would find a resolution. Another concern was their next move. With Matthew and Emmett both dead, and the SWAT team that had been sent obviously placed there by the people they were chasing, it was difficult to know what to do next.

As they ran across the tarmac, Caleb continued to assess their options.

What he didn't know, was that there was already an escape option awaiting them.

Chapter Twenty-Nine

The journey back to where Murphy and Darcy waited took a fraction of the time of the away journey. They used the panic at the airport as cover, the wreckage at the southern end of the runway was still burning fiercely, despite the efforts of the arriving emergency vehicles.

The trio ran as fast as they could, with Caleb and Casey no longer seeing the need to keep an eye on Dunleavy. If he'd really wanted to betray them, he could have remained hidden, and let them be shot by the as-yet unknown gunmen.

However, he had saved their lives. While the time for gratitude would come, they needed to get themselves and the rest of the team to safety.

Running as fast as they could, they made it across the tarmac and behind the building in less than five minutes. As they turned the corner of the building, Caleb gave a signal to his Sergeant to stop.

Casey did as he was requested, putting his arm out to ensure a breathless Dunleavy did the same. Caleb raised his weapon and pointed it at the SUV, which was parked near where they had left the women. All kinds of thoughts, mainly negative, were going through his mind. His guilt over the plane exploding was being over-run by the fear for Darcy.

As he looked closer, he saw several bodies of what looked like SWAT team members strewn across the ground.

He realised a gun fight had occurred.

He turned on his radio and whispered, hoping the Lieutenant would answer.

"Murphy? Do you read, over?" Caleb whispered into the headset's microphone. He took a few more steps toward the SUV, seeing no signs of movement. "Lieutenant... do you read, over?" he asked again, his stress level increasing.

After a few more steps, a voice came through on the radio.

"Charlene can't hear you, but I'm here Caleb... um... over," Darcy said.

"Darcy? Thank God," Caleb replied. "Where's Murphy?"

"She's um," Darcy began hesitantly. "Probably best if you see for yourself."

Caleb rounded the building, past the bodies and SUV's.

Casey and Dunleavy were right behind him, as though sensing his urgency.

Continuing around the building, he saw what Darcy was referring to. Murphy had her gun squarely pointed at a new guest.

"Who the fuck is this?" asked Dunleavy.

Murphy heard the question, but made time to make eye contact with Casey before responding. She smiled at him, a smile he reciprocated. "Absolutely no idea." Murphy eventually replied, "She hasn't said a word since we took out her men."

"Men??" Caleb said, looking alarmingly at Darcy.

"Was no problem, sir. Piece of cake. We took them out. Darcy did what she had to do."

"Are you okay, babe?" Caleb asked his paramour.

She nodded back to him. While her nod said she was ok, Caleb knew her well enough to know when she was lying.

The firefight had hurt Darcy, and sent her mind spinning. Coupled with the exploding plane and the fear for her boyfriend's safety, Darcy had just had arguably the worst twenty minutes of her life.

It was taking all her strength not to completely freak out.

Caleb went over and hugged her, knowing that his touch would have no real influence. As he held her, she began to relax. Not a rainfall of tears that would be expected. No, Darcy was stronger than that. Tears welled in her eyes, a combination of relief and fear. Emotions she had experienced before, but not to the level she was feeling at that moment.

She was in a dark place, and Caleb remembered the first time he had been in a similar place. While the eventual proximity to his paramour helped, it took much longer until he was able to sleep again. All he could do was be there for her, to help her through it as much as he could.

"Sir," Casey said quietly, "we need to get going. Others will arrive on site, and we won't have a chance."

Caleb's head was spinning, and he struggled to regain his composure. But, being the seasoned veteran, he was eventually able to compartmentalise what he was feeling, and, once again, he took the lead.

Still holding Darcy, he spoke first to Murphy. "Can we use the SUV? Was there keys in it?"

"Yes sir. After I got this secured," she replied, referring to the captured woman, "Darcy did a quick check of the car."

Darcy pushed away, also trying to flip the switch back into focus. "Yeah, I've got the keys. There's plenty of equipment in the car. Various weapons, and the car seems fully tricked out."

Caleb looked at her. "Well done," he told her. "Okay then. Dunleavy, you take over from Murphy."

Dunleavy moved into position, and pulled out his firearm. He pointed it at the prisoner.

"If she moves… you have my permission to take her out," Caleb continued. "Casey, Murphy. The three of us will load up the SUV"

"Yes, sir," they replied, almost in unison.

"Darcy, pass me the keys." Darcy complied. "Now, you and Mike secure the prisoner," Caleb said. "She comes with us. Matthew won't be joining us again."

"What happened out there?" asked Murphy, a tablet and her other equipment in her arms.

"We'll debrief in the car. We'll be leaving in two minutes. Let's move, people."

Without further instruction, the group went about their tasks. Once the prisoner was secured, Darcy and Dunleavy walked her into the rear of the SUV. Designed to carry eight passengers – driver, passenger, then two rows of three seats. Darcy and Dunleavy sat the prisoner in the middle of the back row of seats. Dunleavy sat directly on her right, the gun pointed at her throughout the short walk.

"Okay, Darc," Caleb yelled out, "that's the last of it. Into the car."

Darcy turned, and opened the left rear passenger door, the same position she'd sat on the journey from Phoenix.

"No way, Darcy," Caleb said, opening the front passenger door for her. "You're not leaving my side until this is over. You're in shotgun."

The small action helped Darcy forget her previous trauma, momentarily at least.

The rest of the team entered the vehicle. Casey sat on the other side of the prisoner, with Murphy taking up a seat in the middle of the SUV. Her backpack was next to her. From that, she pulled out her tablet, and a laptop.

"Everybody set?" Caleb asked. Everybody either nodded or replied in the affirmative. Caleb started up the car. The engine was much quieter than he'd anticipated, and the car purred to life. He turned the vehicle around, facing towards the road that led to the abandoned building.

As they headed towards the street, they passed what looked like offices and maintenance hangars. On a typical Sunday morning, there would be many cars and trucks pulling in to start work and make deliveries. This was far from a typical Sunday morning.

As they drove west along the short road, most of the cars and trucks were heading in the same direction, panicked into forcing their way into traffic.

Caleb, a seasoned driver in unusual conditions, weaved in and out of the impending log-jam with ease. The task was made easier due to the Sunday morning traffic, and Caleb appreciated that it would have been worse on a weekday.

"Turn left at the end, sir," Murphy said from behind him, looking at the GPS software on her tablet.

Caleb did as she suggested. The cars were thinning out, leaving the road to let additional emergency service vehicles through.

Darcy turned on the radio, trying to get updates.

Caleb quickly turned it off.

"Babe, not just yet – I'm sure people will be talking about this for a while," he said.

The car approached an intersection. They could choose to either travel west or east. "Where to Murphy?" Caleb asked.

"Depends where you want to go?" Murphy asked. "I recommend west. We need to get to a safe location. Anywhere but Seattle."

Caleb knew she was right. Seattle might as well have been Afghanistan, such was the danger and anarchy present.

Caleb turned west, and headed along 154th St, towards the Pacific Highway. There were fewer cars on the road, as many people had been scared away from the area. As he approached the highway, Caleb veered right. Turning south on the highway, they were on their way.

They sped along the open road, with many of the normal road users absent. There were smatterings of vehicles and people, but not many.

As Caleb looked towards the horizon, he could see the smoke still billowing from the plane's wreckage. He could only imagine the horror of the people still on the scene. People that had no idea it was coming that day. People who had just gone to work, to make enough money to look after their families. While Caleb had prepared himself for the possibility of the attack actually happening, he was still shocked it had occurred.

As they drove past the airport, they all looked out towards the smoke.

"What happened Caleb? Did you find Emmett?" asked Darcy.

"Yes… we found him," replied Caleb, his eyes betraying him.

"So, what happened?"

"It was Matthew."

Darcy was stunned. She'd thought she had built a real rapport with the young man. Ever since she'd stopped Caleb from hurting him in L.A., Darcy had done everything she could to keep him calm, and to keep him safe.

"What? What happened?" she asked again.

Caleb told her how he had tackled Emmett, and the aftermath. He told her that it was Matthew who fired the rocket.

As he told Darcy of the events, the rest of the car listened to the details, and looked at the wreckage. They all had the same forlorn look on their face.

Even Dunleavy.

The only one with a different look was the prisoner, who for some macabre reason, could not hide her smile. For her, the mission had been an unmitigated success. Yes, she had lost some team-members. And yes, Pierre's crew were no more.

But, as instructed by her superior, Robert, *her* primary objective was to ensure the success of the mission. That objective had been achieved and she had done as she was told. She had also been given another set of instructions - instructions that were not given to the rest of her team.

In the case of capture, she was to follow a secondary plan. Now, she was just biding her time, until she was required to act.

Casey noticed the prisoner's smile, and whacked her in the stomach.

While it was indeed more common that enemy combatants were male, the same treatment of women was also practised. After all, just because she was a woman did not mean she was not a threat. Hand-to-hand combat training with Murphy had taught him that.

The body blow sent a jolt through the prisoner's body, and the smile evaporated. The content look in her eyes was replaced by one of hatred, and that hate she directed towards Casey.

It was then Casey's turn to smile. "Before you ask," he said, directing his words towards the prisoner, "yes... I am glad I did it. And yes... it was satisfying. Was it as good for you as it was for me?"

The car continued down the highway for several minutes before Dunleavy spoke up. "Jackson," he said, the gun still pointed at the prisoner, "Where are we headed?"

Caleb looked at Dunleavy through the rear view mirror. "Los Angeles, if we can get there," he replied.

"We won't make it," Dunleavy said, sounding annoyed. "Shit, Jackson, we're in a car that's owned by the enemy. Fuck – they're probably tracking us right now!"

The thought had crossed Caleb's mind.

He knew the Colonials were stepping up their measures to get rid of them. It was evident by the latest batch of people sent to kill them. They were much more technically proficient that Pierre and Matthew, and it was only through luck that Casey and he had survived at the airport.

They were surely being tracked.

"Okay, we'll pull over soon," Caleb said to Dunleavy. "There's something I need to ask our guest."

Chapter Thirty

William knew there was something wrong. It was the first time he found himself sitting in *that* room.

The room had a simple configuration. The floors and walls were atypical of the design of the colony, built for efficiency, not decorative value. There was no thought put into the aesthetic aspects of the colonies design, each room served a purpose, and was built in such a way that it was both easy to build, and easy to take down. While the rooms themselves were all designed in the same way, each had its own subtle variations. Helen's lab had the chairs and the injectors, the quarters had enough beds for the inhabitants, and the engineering labs had the specific equipment. Some of the rooms were quite elaborate with the equipment inside.

This particular room was also unique to the rest of the colony. In the centre of the room was a large, circular table. But any similarities to King Arthur's Round Table ended there.

The table was designed more for ease of discussion rather that to provide a feeling of equality. James had ensured that the table was used only on rare occasions, as there was far too much work to be done. Around the table, there were places for sixteen people. The leaders of the fifteen colonies, plus a scribe. The meetings were only ever recorded on paper, so as to avoid any discussions being leaked.

No person, apart from those directly involved in the discussions, had ever been privy to their goings on.

As William entered the room, he saw James sitting in one of the positions. He did not look happy.

As all the other colony leaders were busy in their various locations, the rest of the positions were filled by digital monitors, displaying the faces of the other fourteen colony leaders.

Zach and John were on monitors, directly on the left and right of James. Robert was one place to the right of Zach. On the other monitors, were other faces he recognised, albeit some of them with much younger features than previously. Albert from Central Europe, Nicholas from Middle Europe, Charles from Northern Africa. They were *all* there.

Some of them had obviously already received the serum, and looked much more alert than their colleagues. They would all receive the serum in due time.

There was one empty chair, the chair the scribe would normally occupy. James pointed towards an empty chair, ordering William to sit.

William made his way around the table, nodding in greeting to the faces on the monitors he could see. They all seemed as unimpressed as James.

When he sat down, the monitors turned to face James. There was no doubting who the leader was.

James cleared his throat. "As I'm sure you are all aware," he began, "the mission in Northwest of Zone Three has met its objective."

A round of applause generated from the rest of the monitors, and William joined them in his ovation.

"Now, let us not get ahead of ourselves," James continued, his young features hiding his maturity. "We have a few issues that need to be resolved. Robert, can you please provide us with an update?"

The monitor two places to James's right moved to face the group, and the other monitors followed.

"Indeed. While the plane went down, we do still have a concern. The reporter who entered Haven a few days ago managed to send an email to his colleague in Zone Three."

Murmurings rumbled through the group. Discontent was palpable.

"The intention was to track the email, so as to identify who else might know about the location of the colony. We attached a tracker to the email." Robert paused as he pressed a few buttons below his monitor, unseen by everyone else. "If you'll turn your attention to your monitors," he instructed.

A picture of Darcy appeared. "The email was sent to this woman, a reporter for the LA Examiner. Fortunately, the email seemed to make no sense, and she has since been trying to discover more details."

"Isn't that a bit dangerous?" Albert said.

Robert continued describing the actions of Darcy, ignoring Albert's question. Robert outlined the details, including Darcy's trip to Dunleavy and her conversation with Chucky. "This, is where it became a problem," Robert said. "Two men were sent to Ms. Chamberlain's apartment, and we haven't heard from them since. The apartment has since become a crime scene, and, as you can imagine, all of our resources are elsewhere."

The rest of the colony leaders began shifting uneasily in their seats, their actions clearly visible in the monitors.

"Now, the last we saw of her, was at her apartment."

"Where did she go?" one of the leaders asked.

"Seattle," replied Robert

"But, the plane. In Seattle. It was shot down."

"Indeed, my thoughts are that they were too late, and our asset completed his mission. Anyway, we sent a team up to Seattle to clean up any mess, and to make sure the mission was completed."

"Were they successful?"

"We don't know. We lost contact with *them* about fifteen minutes ago."

James was getting more and more annoyed. "Enough!" he exclaimed. "We cannot let this situation continue."

"Wait, sir. I have one more thing."

"Are you joking, Robert? What? What is it?"

"The leader of the group, she has been given instructions in the case of her capture."

"And those instructions are?"

"To convince the group to come to the colony."

The rest of the monitors erupted. They were shouting at Roberts's screen, words that the colonists seldom used. The cacophony of noise was rising to a crescendo, when James intervened. "SILENCE!" he shouted.

Within a second, the room grew quiet, the governors waiting with anticipation. James paced the room, and William watched. James was very studious and considerate of all points of view. He was, by far, the fairest man William knew. That's why he had complete faith in him, even when he decided to punish people.

After nearly a minute of waiting, James spoke. "That's brilliant, Robert," he said.

There were murmurings among the governors.

"You've done the right thing. It is pointless looking for them, they could be anywhere by now. But, they are looking for you. Lay out enough breadcrumbs, and they'll come to you."

Robert smiled at the approval to his plan. "Sir," Robert began, "all of our troops are ready to go. There's no way that they'll be able to cope with them."

"How many do you have on standby?"

Robert considered the question. "About one thousand. I could triple that with the serum."

"Okay then," said James, turning to Zach's monitor. "Zach, have your people been treated?"

"We're about half way through," Zach replied

"Good. Send over a sample to Zone Three right away. Send it in the jet." James turned his attention back to Robert. "Robert, it will be there in a few hours."

"Thank you, sir," the Zone Three leader responded.

William had been listening to the conversation, and he saw a flaw in the plan. However, he remembered one of the lessons James had taught him. *Never present a problem without a solution.* And William had a solution. "Sir, if I may?" William said, showing no fear.

"What is it, William?" James snapped. "You are only here to observe"

"Sir, if I may – I see a problem with the plan."

"Indeed, William, I think we all see it."

"Yes, sir. Of course you do. I... I think I have a solution."

"Yes?"

"Well, in the case that Robert's man—"

"Woman," Robert interrupted.

"Woman," William continued, "It may be the case that she hasn't been captured at all, I have a solution."

"And what is it, William?"

"I've been in touch with him, sir. The agent."

"And?"

"He's on his way to meet Dunleavy."

James considered William's words. "Ok..." James looked around at the other monitors. "I think we need to take an extra precaution..." he said.

The others waited, anticipating the final piece of the solution.

"Robert, Zach, John... are your intelligence contacts still in place?" he asked his closest friends.

They nodded in virtual unison.

"Good," James began. "Because I think it's about time New Light had a leader."

Chapter Thirty-One

Darcy returned to the car. "We've got rooms five and six. There's an adjoining door, so we can walk between the two," Darcy said to the waiting group.

"Thanks Darcy," replied Caleb.

It had been twenty minutes since they'd left the airport. After travelling south, they had pulled into the motel, a two storey complex not unlike many others they had passed on the way. They'd travelled more than fifteen miles from the airport, but the repercussions were still being felt.

The motel clerk, distracted by the small television at his desk, needed several prompts before attending to Darcy at the main counter. Darcy had little trouble organising the adjacent rooms, and had paid cash, not-so-generously donated by Dunleavy.

On the lower floor of the complex, the rooms were located near the driveway, as Caleb had requested.

After exiting the vehicles, they walked their prisoner into the first room. Fortunately, the Sunday morning traffic was minimal, and they were able to get her in the room undetected.

The room was reminiscent of several Caleb had been in before. The feel of the room was welcoming, with the beds turned down and the sheets tucked in way too tightly. Not that it mattered; the rooms were just a temporary measure.

Murphy entered the second room, and quickly changed into civilian attire, after which she left the room and began working on the car. While she wasn't the team's designated mechanic, she was by far the best at learning new technology, much more so than Caleb or Casey.

With that knowledge, Murphy would be able to ascertain what the car was capable of. She would also, more importantly, know what parts should *not* be on the car.

Caleb knew there was more than likely some sort of tracking device on the car. He figured if they were able to remotely track an email, they would be more than efficient at tracking their own vehicles. With that in mind, Murphy set to work on the engine of the car, and Caleb turned his attention to the prisoner.

"I'm not sure who sent you," Caleb began, "but considering you and your team tried to kill everyone in this room, I'm gonna assume you know one thing."

The prisoner stared at him, and for the first time since she'd been captured, she spoke. "What would that be?" she asked.

Caleb looked to Casey, knowing that he could sum it up better for the prisoner. "You, sweetheart," Casey said, "are in some deep and stinking shit right now."

"Exactly right, Sergeant," said Caleb.

Caleb grabbed a chair, and sat down opposite the prisoner. She was perched at the end of the queen size bed.

"So," Caleb began talking again, "you have a choice. You can either help us and then you only go to prison… I don't know… probably forever". Caleb paused for a reaction. After seeing none, he continued. "Or you can refuse to help us and… well…" Caleb again paused, "I don't think you want that option."

As she considered her situation, Dunleavy moved to leave the room, to make a phone call.

"Dunleavy?" Caleb turned to the old man. "What are you doing? Who are you calling?"

Dunleavy stopped, and turned to Caleb. "Someone who can help us," he replied.

"Like Carl helped us? Mike, they're tracking your calls."

"Jackson, that's impossible. This phone has so many goddam encryptions on it, that if they do manage to trace it… hell, they deserve to catch us."

"So, how do you explain their team getting to us then?" Casey interrupted.

"I'm guessing that Carl's phone was tapped, and they have someone in the CIA who got intercepted the call. Whatever happened, I don't think Carl can help *anyone* anymore."

It was as Caleb suspected - The Colonials had influence everywhere. It made getting information from the prisoner even more important.

"So, Mike. Who are you calling?"

Dunleavy figured he couldn't lie about it. Caleb was bound to find out soon enough.

"You remember the guy I told you about? The one who did some work for me?" Dunleavy asked.

"You mean, 'when you could only send one guy'?"

"Yeah. I'm calling him in."

"Are you sure we can trust him?" Caleb asked

"Yes, I'm sure," Dunleavy lied. He still had his suspicions about Jacob, but he knew they needed help.

"Fine," Caleb said, and Dunleavy continued on his way to outside the motel room.

As he left, Darcy came into the room. She'd been catching up with the news of the plane incident in the adjoining room. "Caleb, you'd better turn on the television," Darcy exclaimed, a panicked look crossing her face.

Caleb did as he was told.

"Turn to Channel 7."

It was the news channel, and a middle aged, blonde woman sat in the news desk chair. On the graphic next to her was a picture of Dunleavy. "In breaking news..." the moderately-attractive anchor began, "we have just learned that the FBI has released the identity of the suspected leader of New Light. New Light is the terrorist cell which has been identified as being behind the attack on Flight CAL57, and is also strongly suspected of being behind the assassination of former-President Hawkins late last year. The FBI say they have received strong intelligence that the mastermind behind New Light in none other than former Chief-of-Staff Michael Dunleavy. Mr. Dunleavy resigned under a cloud of secrecy in the months preceding the President's death."

"Oh, shit," Caleb said under his breath.

The news anchor continued. "Authorities have noted that Mr Dunleavy was in Seattle this morning, and is accompanied by at least two well-armed persons. If you see Mr. Dunleavy, please do not approach him, as he and his companions are to be treated as armed and dangerous. We will keep you up to date with this story as we can. Repeating the news. Former Chief-of-Staff, Michael Dunleavy, has been identified as the leader of the New Light Terrorist cell."

The prisoner laughed. "Well," she stated, making no attempt to hide her merriment. "Looks like I'm not the only one who's in deep shit!"

Chapter Thirty-Two

The revelation had changed the situation dramatically. It was no longer a case of the authorities looking in the wrong direction. The authorities would now have their sights clearly focused - on Caleb and his companions. Caleb walked out the door, and found an oblivious Dunleavy chatting on his phone.

"I'll call you with a final location in an hour," Dunleavy said, trying to bring the conversation to a close. "...Fine" he said and then he disconnected the call.

"He's on the way?" Caleb asked, not wanting to break the news too quickly.

"Yeah. He got rerouted to Portland. He's there now. I'll call him with our next location when he gets close."

Caleb looked at him, the bad news written all over his face. "What? What is it Jackson?" Dunleavy asked.

Caleb ushered him inside. As he passed the SUV, he asked Murphy for an update. The lieutenant was buried deep in the flooring of the car, her backside facing towards Caleb.

"Yeah, I think I've got it," she replied, referring to the tracking device. "Just wanna make sure."

"Good. Get back in here when you get a chance."

"Yes, sir. Be about five minutes."

Caleb followed Dunleavy into the room. He was standing, watching the television in complete awe. "That... that's..." he struggled to get words out, "that's not me. I didn't do it." He looked around the room, looking for some kind of reassurance.

"We know Mike," said Darcy, her voice soothing to the now-scared former politician. "We all know it's not true."

"Good," Dunleavy said, still lost for words.

"Yeah, that's good and all," Casey interrupted, "but I'm guessing that, rather than a few people chasing us, we've now got about one and a half billion!"

"One and a half billion?" Dunleavy asked.

"Yeah, man. The plane that was shot down. It was a goddamn Chinese plane!"

"Shit."

"Yeah, shit indeed."

Caleb motioned for them all to calm down. "As long as we keep moving, we'll buy ourselves some time."

"Time?" Dunleavy was becoming agitated. "What the fuck is time going to do for us?"

Caleb grabbed hold of his shoulders. "Mike, we really don't need you freaking out right now. The *only* way we can get out of this is to get the truth out there. Now, Darcy's got her connections, and we can get the word out. But, at the moment, all we have is a completely unbelievable story. I mean, it won't take much for them to connect the dots with the stuff at Darcy's apartment. They were probably looking for us, anyway." Caleb made eye contact with each of his people, including Darcy. "We are no worse off now than we have been all day. The Colonials have a plan, and they're ruthless." Caleb paused, and took a deep breath. "And at the moment, we're the only ones trying to stop them."

◆ ◆ ◆

Jacob smiled as he hung up the phone. Once the plane had exploded in Seattle, all flights to and from the city had been rerouted. Jacob had found his way to Portland, Oregon. While it wasn't a major change in direction, it would prove problematic – especially if Dunleavy kept moving. However, all his fears were allayed once he received the call from Dunleavy. After the call, he knew the old man still trusted him, and still needed his help.

Portland International was much busier than usual. Ranked in the high twenties for airline traffic, Portland International was struggling to cope with a sudden influx of travellers to the North West United States. With the incident at Seattle, most of the traffic was being rerouted through to Oregon. Jacob was one of those affected travellers. Not that he really minded, the extra numbers allowed him to walk through the airport with relative ease.

The main problem was the seemingly endless line at the rental car company. The main congestion in the line was caused by the rerouted Seattle passengers, most of them making the assumption that their booking was still valid at a different airport. The rest of the line consisted of people who'd needed to make new travel arrangements.

The FFA had grounded all air travel for the foreseeable future. There was, as yet, no indication as to when travel would resume. It made renting a car problematic.

As Jacob waited in line, he received another call. Not his usual ringtone, Jacob placed his usual phone in his back pocket. He reached into his hooded, faux-leather jacket pocket and retrieved his second cell phone. A familiar name appeared on the display. Jacob answered after a few rings, just so he could make the caller wait. "Yes, William," he said.

"Jacob," William replied, "Where are you?"

Jacob thought about how much information to share. He didn't trust William, but required his support to reach his final objective. "I'm close to Dunleavy," he replied, trying not to give too much away.

"Don't," William said, agitated, "don't toy with me, Jacob. I need to know your exact location."

"Well, since you guys decided to fuck up the travel plans of anyone heading to the North West, I've had to change my plans. I'm in Portland, if you must know."

"Okay, good. We've got the last location on Dunleavy. They are at a motel on the Pacific Highway, between Seattle and Tacoma."

"Is he still there?"

"Unknown. I think that, whoever he's with, they've disabled the tracking device."

"Geez, William. Got yourself in quite a pickle, don't you?" Jacob said, doing a bad imitation of an English accent.

"Don't be obtuse, Jacob. I need your help. Make your way to the motel as soon as possible. There I—"

Jacob cut William off, mid-sentence. "Um, just so you know. Dunleavy will contact me in an hour with their location. Figured I'll just wait for that."

"Really, you're still in touch with him?"

"Yes I am."

"Fine. Meet with him. But, remember our earlier conversation, about taking them out?"

"Indeed I do. Looking forward to doing it, actually."

"Plans have changed. They come from the top, so if you want to take your place in the Colony, you'll need to follow this order to the letter."

That got Jacob's full attention. He always knew that William was not the main decision maker among the Colonials and that he was taking orders from someone else.

He'd known that since the day he was captured on the Bogota mission.

It had been his own fault. He had always worked alone, a choice that had served him well on almost all occasions. The Bogota mission was simple search and destroy, the target being a former DEA agent, suspected to be leaking information to the Colombian Cartels. Back then, Jacob was an assassin for hire. He worked for whoever paid him. Whether that be the United States, China... hell, if the Colombians even knew he existed, he would have worked for them, too.

From the moment he'd arrived in Colombia, he knew something was wrong. It was as though the DEA agent knew he was coming. In the end, he found out that it was, in fact, the DEA agent himself who had hired him. It was a risky plan, as Jacob had a superior reputation in the art of assassination. His specialty was being able to ensure a person died in accordance with the wishes of the people that paid him. He especially enjoyed his job when the target would be inflicted with a painful death.

In the end, the agent turned out to be William. There was a team of seven officers with William in Bogota, and they were well trained.

So well trained that Jacob doubted he would be alive if they didn't wish it. It was the first time he'd genuinely feared for his life. It was that fear that won his allegiance that day.

William had promised much in their dealings thus far, but Jacob had yet to see any real benefits. Over time, William had given Jacob little pieces of information about the Colonials, but had kept the serum a secret.

As far as William knew, Jacob was only aware that there was a *plan* to change the world, and that the plan had been in Phase One for a considerable period of time. After being ordered to kill Hawkins, Jacob knew the plans were starting to progress.

And that's all William thought he knew.

But Jacob knew a lot more than that. Most of this knowledge came from his other contact - Mike Dunleavy.

As a result of his capture in Bogota, Jacob was now officially *on the map*, and a target for many foreign governments. Dunleavy used this as leverage to recruit Jacob into his little group. It was Dunleavy who had told Jacob about the serum, and the fact that it could sustain life indefinitely. And that serum was controlled by the Colonials.

At first, Jacob didn't believe Dunleavy, but after seeing the evidence of the old man's claims thought various missions that he and others carried out, it became obvious that Dunleavy was telling the truth. Or most of it, anyway. Jacob knew that he *had* to have the serum, regardless of the cost.

"Who?" Jacob replied, "Who did the orders come from?"

"They came from my superior. That's all you need to know for now," replied William.

"What does he want me to do?" Jacob replied, embarrassed by the desperation in his voice.

"Good. I can tell by your voice that you know the critical nature of anything we do from now on."

"Just tell me, William."

"You need to bring them to the Zone Three Colony. I don't care how you do it, just get it done."

"I'm guessing that you're doing this to kill them yourselves? Correct?"

"Our intentions are not your concern, Jacob. Do not try to take them out yourself."

"They won't be anything I can't handle," Jacob said, trying to understand why the plan had changed so dramatically.

"Jacob, just listen. They've already killed at least six of our best trained operatives."

"Shit," Jacob's replied, knowing just how hard they were to kill.

"I know, Jacob. Just... call me on this number when you need the location of the colony." William hung up the phone.

Jacob thought back to Bogota. The people who had captured him... William's people, had been the best he'd ever come up against. He'd never been dealt with so easily. Perhaps it was a good idea just to meet Dunleavy, and take them to the Colony as William suggested. Pondering this, Jacob looked at the line stretched out ahead of him. In the ten minutes he'd been standing there, he hadn't moved. So, he decided to make alternative arrangements.

Jacob collected his overnight bag. It contained clothes, and some alternative identification. So proficient was he at killing, he didn't feel the need to carry a weapon. He'd killed plenty of people with his hands alone. Plus, it just added to the risk of him being caught in transit.

He stepped out of the line and moved towards the arrivals gate, where he looked for an opportune target.

It didn't take long, as the passengers from the next flight began streaming through the gate as soon as he took up position. After a couple of minutes, Jacob had spotted several couples, a number of families and long lost travellers. None of these people were what he was looking for. And then, he spotted her in the crowd.

Wearing a light brown business skirt, matching jacket and a light blue blouse, the woman walked fast and with purpose. She was not distracted by the emotions of other travellers around her. Her only concern was getting through the crowd.

As Jacob observed her, her beautiful complexion and features had obviously served her well. She had a Rolex, and Louboutin shoes, not the cheapest stuff money can buy.

Jacob figured that image was very important to her, as she obviously looked after herself. She wouldn't have looked out of place on a modelling runway. She dragged her suitcase behind her and hurried towards the exit. So focused was the woman on reaching her destination, she didn't notice as Jacob followed her out.

The woman crossed the road directly outside the terminal, and made her way across to the multilevel car park. Jacob pulled his hood low over his head and followed, careful not to stand-out. She got in the elevator, and Jacob joined her. The woman pressed the button for the third floor. Having noticed this, Jacob pretended to do the same.

Once he saw the number illuminated, he stopped short, justifying in advance why he would get out of the elevator at the same time.

They were joined by a few others. A young Asian couple and a middle-aged African-American man. Jacob took note of their floors, in case his plan didn't work.

The number three lit up above them, and the elevator stopped. The woman exited the elevator, and Jacob casually followed, leaving space between him and her to ensure she didn't expect anything. She turned left and crossed the parking lot, heading towards a navy-blue Toyota. It wasn't a car befitting her image, but it was practical enough. As she approached, the trunk opened.

Jacob scanned the rest of the lot. There was no-one else in the vicinity. *This was his moment.*

The woman lifted her suitcase. As she did, she felt a pressure on the back of her neck. Jacob had walked up behind her, and cupped the back of her head, almost like a cradle. As she began to turn, Jacob firmly placed his left hand on her chin. The woman tried to kick out, but it was useless. Within a split second, Jacob had twisted his hands, applying a terrifying torque.

The movement created a loud crack, one that would have been heard in the echoes in the parking lot. The crack broke the C3, C4 and C5 joints in the woman's spine. Her lifeless body slumped to the ground, and she was no more.

With the efficiency of a man who had seen much worse, Jacob lifted her slight frame into the trunk of the car, ignoring the fact that her head bumped on the bumper. In the same motion, Jacob grabbed the keys from her limp hand. Her suitcase, which had been tipped over in the brief struggle, lay on the ground behind the car. Jacob picked it up, closed the trunk, and carried it to the driver's door. After getting in the car, he opened the bag and examined the contents. As expected, she had her purse and identification in the bag.

She also had her parking pass.

Using the recently acquired keys, Jacob left the parking spot. As he pulled out, he did one last scan of the area. There was still no-one in sight. He drove around the lot, each left turn bringing him closer to the exit.

As he drove through, he breathed a sigh of relief. He drove the car past the terminal and looked through the windows. The same elderly couple who had taken his place in the line still hadn't moved.

He smiled to himself. *Suckers.*

◆ ◆ ◆

Sensing her moment, the prisoner spoke up. "Looks like you've only got one choice then," she said.

Upon hearing the prisoner talk, Caleb spun around in the motel room. "Oh yeah..." he asked. "What's that?"

"I can help you."

Dunleavy pulled out his gun, and marched up to the prisoner. Barely able to contain his anger, Dunleavy decided to take it out on the prisoner. "You fucking people," he shouted, "you've ruined my life!" The gun was pointing at the prisoner's head, and Dunleavy's arm was shaking.

"Mike," said Darcy. "It's okay. We can get out of this."

"How? How the fuck are we going to get out of this?"

"Mike, we will. You didn't do anything wrong. We can prove it."

"Bullshit," Dunleavy replied.

"Mike," Caleb said, moving towards Dunleavy, "if you shoot her, then we'll be in real trouble. She's our solution."

It was apparent that Dunleavy was slowly listening to reason, and he began to lower the gun. Caleb and Darcy backed away. As they did, Dunleavy returned his look to the prisoner, and noticed the smile on her face. "Fuck you," he said. He raised his gun, about to fire. "Mike. No!" screamed Darcy and Caleb.

As they shouted, Dunleavy swung his arm down, and connected with the prisoner's face. The swinging gun collided with her jaw, causing a fracture and dislodging several teeth. The prisoner fell to her side on the end of the bed. After several seconds, she sat back up, blood teeming from her mouth. She spat out the blood, along with two teeth.

Dunleavy put the gun in his belt, and walked up to the prisoner. He grabbed her under her chin, and brought her face up to make eye contact. "I want you to listen closely, bitch!" he began, a harsh whisper in his tone. "Just because we need you alive, it doesn't mean you get to enjoy it."

Chapter Thirty-Three

After time, the mild concussion she'd received started to subside.

"Mike... what the hell are you doing?" shouted Caleb, pulling Mike away from the woman, surprised he had gone so far.

Dunleavy remained quiet, content for now that his rage had been expressed effectively.

"Who are you?" the prisoner asked, "Are you the good cop? Let me guess, you're gonna tell me that you can protect me from him if I only help you?"

Caleb turned to the prisoner. "Listen," he said as he approached her, "please do not mistake this for a situation where we are weak. We're not the cops. And your *friends* have just put a big target on our backs, so we're kind of at a point where we don't care if we break the law."

Caleb turned to the Sergeant. "Isn't that right, Sergeant Casey?" he said.

"Sir, yes sir. I think you've summed it up nicely. Either way, we're kinda fucked."

"Well said, Sergeant. Well said!" Caleb replied, again turning his focus to the prisoner.

"Now let me ask you a question," he started, his voice filling the prisoner with fear. "Do you think we're more dangerous than we were before?"

The prisoner sat still, not able to move.

"Because, quite frankly, unless you can tell us something – anything – then you're no more than a paperweight with a bad haircut."

The prisoner looked to Darcy, her eyes appealing for help. She knew that Darcy was not military, and would be the one most likely to help her.

Darcy noted the cry for help, able to feel sympathy for pretty much everyone she met. And indeed, she did feel sorry for the woman. But her sympathy was limited. She had wasted too much of it on Matthew, and she remembered the result. "You know what, Caleb?" she asked her boyfriend.

"What's that, babe?"

"I think you're right. If she can't help us…" Darcy's voice tapered off, and she deliberately left the room, completely expecting Caleb to kill the prisoner if required. Even though she had seen death earlier that day, she had no desire to see someone killed again.

The prisoner was surprised. She had expected Darcy to help, or to at least act on her behalf. She quickly realised that there would be no help forthcoming.

Caleb watched Darcy leave. As the interconnecting door closed behind her, Caleb turned his attention back to the prisoner. "You're going to tell me what I want to know," he said. "If you don't, or I suspect you're lying, my colleague over here…" Caleb pointed to Dunleavy. "Mr. Dunleavy will be given permission to shoot you in the head."

"What… no warm-up? No taking my thumbs? No shooting my leg?" the prisoner asked, searching for something to buy her some time.

Caleb ensured he had eye contact with her. "We don't have time for that. As soon as my Lieutenant comes through that door… Casey see how long she needs."

Casey went to the door and stuck his head out, asking Murphy how long she needed before they could leave. Caleb and the prisoner couldn't hear her answer, but Casey came back into the room and signalled that they could go in five minutes.

Caleb again looked at the prisoner. "Five minutes. If I'm not satisfied in five minutes that you're going to help, Mr. Dunleavy will shoot you in the head, and we will leave. Do you understand?"

The prisoner nodded her head.

"Okay, then," Caleb began, sitting back in his chair. "What's your name?"

She was surprised by the question, unsure of why they thought it important. "Natalie."

"Okay then, Natalie. What can you tell me about the people we're up against?"

Confused by the question, Natalie just stared at him blankly. "That would take forever to answer," she replied.

"Let me be more specific. Where are they located?" Caleb asked.

"I could tell you, but it's easier to show you."

"Casey... bring over the map."

"It's not on any map," Natalie said, shaking her head. "You people. You just don't get it. We've been hidden since before you were born, since before Dunleavy was born. We do not appear on any maps."

"So... where is it?"

"It's in the middle. The centre."

"The centre of where?" a confused Caleb asked.

"You know what? FUCK YOU!" Natalie said angrily. Natalie's tone had changed. She knew that if she continued to give out information for free, then they may as well just kill her anyway. That, she couldn't allow. Not because she didn't want to die. She only feared death as it would mean she couldn't complete her mission.

Caleb was surprised by her change in tone. He thought he'd made it apparent that they were willing to kill her.

"No... I'll only show you. If I tell you where it is, you'll kill me. Besides, it will be a long drive if you don't use the plane."

"Plane, what plane?"

"How do you think we got here so fast? We didn't come in a goddamn SUV, did we?" Natalie replied, becoming agitated.

The thought had crossed Caleb's mind. He was surprised that they'd managed to appear in so little time. It had only been an hour and half between Dunleavy making the call to Carl, and the arrival of the pseudo-SWAT team.

"Alright then. Where's the plane?"

"It's close."

As she spoke, Murphy entered the room. "We're good to go, Cap. Trackers all gone. Plus, I discovered some really cool stuff. You're gonna love this thing," Murphy said, unaware of any of the happenings inside the motel. "Geez, everyone. Why the long faces?" she asked.

Casey quickly brought her up to speed about Dunleavy's new status, and Natalie's revelation.

"Oh... that would explain it."

Caleb stood up from the chair, and went into the adjoining room. There he found Darcy, lying on the bed, crouched in the foetal position. She heard him enter, and sat bolt upright. She did not want anyone to see her struggling with the situation. It was important for her to appear strong.

Caleb recognised this, and decided to ignore her obvious anxiety. "We have to go, babe," he said.

Wiping away the beginning of a tear, Darcy nodded, and walked to the door. Before she got there, Caleb closed the door behind him. He pulled her close, and held her. Her head turned and lay on his chest. His bulky arms wrapped around her.

"Babe, I'm okay," she said, not wanting anyone to know how she felt.

"I know you are," Caleb said, "but this is for me."

He looked down and smiled at her. He was also in a dark place, one that he couldn't immediately see a way out of. But, with the information he'd just garnered from Natalie, an idea was starting to form.

Darcy also regained focus, knowing that Caleb needed her too.

"Come on, soldier-boy," Darcy said, "we've gotta go".

Her words provided comfort to him; the familiarity of the good times. The times that seemed they would never end just twenty-four hours ago.

Caleb turned and opened the door and they left the room. In the adjoining room, the others had already made their way out. Caleb left both keys on the bed, and he and Darcy left the motel room.

"Gotta be the shortest stay in motel history... or at least the shortest without payments changing hands," Caleb said, attempting levity.

The joke made Darcy giggle, as they got into the car. When Caleb started the car, he turned toward the back seat.

"Where to?" he asked the prisoner.

"Back the way we came," she said. "Plane's in an airfield off the highway."

Caleb turned out of the motel, and headed back north. A few hundred yards up the highway, Murphy stuck her head between Caleb and Darcy's seats. "Wanna see the cool stuff?" she asked enthusiastically.

"Yeah, sure," Caleb replied.

"Press that red button. The one marked 'Thrust'."

Caleb pressed the button. The car sped forward, going from fifty miles an hour to eighty in less than a second.

"Sweet, right?" an enthusiastic Murphy asked.

"Yeah... very cool. Doesn't really help us trying to stay incognito though," Caleb said.

"Fair enough," said Murphy. "Darcy, why don't you turn on the GPS?"

"What? This?" Darcy pointed at the centre screen on the console.

"Yep. Just go ahead and turn it on."

Darcy did as instructed; and the screen came alive. After a two second boot-up screen, a standard map came up.

"So what, Murph?" asked Caleb. "I've seen this before."

Murphy smiled with glee, enjoying the reveal. "Darcy, press that little blue icon. The one that kinda looks like a London Bobby's hat."

Darcy pressed the button. About fifty blue dots popped up on the screen, the majority in and around SEATAC.

"That, Captain, would be all the police in the area."

"How do you know?"

"Well, one went screaming passed the motel, and this thing tracked it along the highway."

Caleb was impressed, but a little disturbed. "Good work Murphy, should make the drive a bit easier," Caleb said. He turned to Darcy and Murphy. "How do you think they got all this information?" he asked.

"My guess," Darcy replied, "is they have someone inside the Department who has given them the *low-jack* frequency."

"Shit... these guys really do have reach, don't they?"

There was no need for a response, as Darcy and Murphy both understood the implication.

Trying to refocus, Caleb again asked Natalie the location. "Where's this plane of yours?" he asked.

From the back, Natalie responded. "It's at the airport."

The three at the front of the car shared a look. The airport was shut down, and emergency personnel would be covering the entire complex. There was no way they would be able to take-off from there.

"Not that one," Natalie shouted from the back. "The other one... About five miles north of SEATAC."

Darcy typed some details into the GPS.

Sure enough, there was another airport, located exactly where Natalie said – Kings County International, also known as Boeings field. One of the busier non-hub airports in the United States, the airport had over three hundred thousand landings or take-offs each year.

Caleb looked in the rear vision mirror, and directed a question to the prisoner. "Won't we be seen?" he asked her, "I imagine it will be frowned upon if we take off as well."

"Don't worry about that, Captain," Natalie said. "I'll look after the details".

Chapter Thirty-Four

A twenty-minute drive later, and they had arrived at the outskirts of the airport.

The place was almost deserted. Any travel for that day had obviously been cancelled, and any emergency personnel had been sent to SEATAC. They pulled up on the eastern side of the complex. A fence was between the car and the runway.

Caleb exited the vehicle, leaving everything behind except for the binoculars. He moved towards the fence. Darcy exited the vehicle, and walked around its front and joined Caleb at the fence line. Caleb was scanning the area, and could only see smaller jets and passenger planes. No sign of anything that looked out of place.

"What are you looking for?" asked Darcy.

"Couple of things," Caleb replied. "First, we just need to make sure, before we move in, that there are no major threats. From here on, everything we do has some risk. But I just want to make sure we aren't walking into a *no-win*." Caleb again panned across the runways, noting the minimal staff placed mainly around the exterior of the facility. "Looks like we're okay in that regard," Caleb continued, "I can't see anything that could turn into an ambush."

"Isn't that the point of it?" Darcy asked.

"Yeah, you're right. But I've been through enough of these," Caleb answered, and continued, "the next thing we need to look for is the plane. Now, I can't see anything that looks like it doesn't belong."

"What do you mean?"

"I'm guessing that our guest and her friends brought the SUV with them. It's not like anything I've seen before, and I'm thinking they brought it with them from wherever they came from. Plus, they had to have gotten here fast. I mean, there wasn't much time between the call Dunleavy made from the plane and them arriving, so the plane has to be fast. If they've got anything like the boosters the SUV has, they'll stand out."

"And, can you see anything like it?"

"No. No I can't." Caleb turned back to the SUV. "Sergeant. Bring her here!" he ordered.

Casey quickly exited the vehicle, Natalie with him. Natalie had been relieved of her restraints - the sight of a black SUV with four people looking at the airport was suspicious enough, let alone if one of them was visibly restrained.

"I'm sure I don't need to remind you about Mr. Dunleavy's itchy trigger finger, do I?" said Caleb as the prisoner approached the fence line.

She shook her head, still smarting from the blow to the jaw she'd received earlier.

"It's there. It's towards the northern end of the runway"

"I don't see it," replied Caleb.

"Of course you don't," she replied condescendingly. "Do you think we'd hide it in sight?"

Caleb looked into the distance, and tried the different settings on his binoculars. Each view showed nothing.

"Just take us up there, and I'll show you," said Natalie.

Caleb was sceptical. He didn't know how far he could trust her. He knew she was leading them into a trap, but how long would it take for the trap to be activated?

Was it at the airport? Was it at the colony she had mentioned?

At that point, he couldn't be sure, so he decided to play along. After all, he had very little alternative. The only other option was to kill her and run, hoping that the Colonials would tire of chasing them.

That option, however, had too many negative aspects, the main being that the Colonials seemed to have a big plan in motion, and they were the only ones who seemed to be trying to stop it. And if it was as big as everyone had been hinting, it needed to be stopped. "Okay then, everyone back in the SUV. "The four walked back to the car, Casey escorting

Natalie closely. Murphy again stuck her head in the gap between Caleb and Darcy. "Couldn't see it could you?" she said.

"No, Lieutenant. We couldn't."

"I think I know why. I noticed something at the motel, something I think we should test out."

"What do you mean, Murphy?"

Murphy whispered something to Darcy, as though trying to save the surprise. She was revelling in her newfound discovery. "Don't push it until I tell you."

Darcy nodded, and Murphy left the SUV. As she got out, she requested Caleb to join her. "C'mon Cap. You're gonna wanna see this." Caleb exited the vehicle, curious about Murphy's enthusiasm. Murphy stepped about six feet away from the SUV. "Okay, Darc. Hit it."

Darcy pressed the yellow button on the console and as she did, the car vanished.

Caleb was speechless for a minute or two. After composing himself, he finally spoke. "What just happened? Where are they?" he asked.

Murphy picked up a stone, and threw it in the direction of the car. It stopped mid-air in the place the SUV had vanished from.

"It's still there, Cap. We just can't see it," she explained. "Okay, Darcy. Press the button again."

After a second, the car reappeared. Caleb walked up to the car. He looked at Darcy, and she looked back at him with a blank expression.

"What happened?" Darcy asked.

"Darcy. You just vanished into thin air. Or at least, the car did." He turned to Murphy. "So, that's what happened to the plane. It really is there?"

"That's my guess, Cap."

"But that's impossible. There no such thing as a cloaking device. Even in Star Trek, it seemed far-fetched."

"Agreed, sir. But you saw it. I think I know how they do it, too."

The two had returned to their seats, but Caleb had spun around, paying attention to what his Lieutenant was saying. As he looked back, he made eye contact with Natalie. Her secrets were slowly coming out one at a time, and it was plain to see that she didn't want to reveal them. "Go on," Caleb said to Murphy, "Tell me how they do it."

"Yes, please tell us. I'm sure someone with your incredible mind can access the genius of such a design," Natalie interjected, her distain for the female Lieutenant palpable. She could not believe that anyone outside the colony could have figured out how the device worked. It was a closely guarded secret, as were many other things inside the colony.

"Okie dokie, I will" Murphy said, smiling towards the prisoner. "While I was looking for the tracking device... by the way, you really need to hide that a bit better." The last part was directed towards the prisoner.

"Murphy!" Caleb said, trying to keep his excited Lieutenant on task.

Murphy brought her attention back to Caleb. "As I was saying, I found the tracker, and had a closer look at the car. Obviously, I wasn't going to mess with the electronics, so I just studied them. That's how I figured out the GPS and police-tracker. I'm sure it does plenty more, but as we had limited time I decided—"

"Murphy! Tell me how the car vanishes," Caleb said, stopping his Lieutenant mid-sentence. She was prone to rambling when excited.

"How it vanishes?" said Natalie disdainfully. "Idiots."

"I think we should call it a cloak, sir," said Murphy.

"Fine. Murphy, please tell me how the *cloak* works?"

"So, I checked out the panelling on the car, and it didn't feel... right. I mean, the surface was smooth, like a normal SUV, but it felt more... I don't know... so I had a closer look. The car panels are more like segments. Along the side of the segments were heaps of little black dots. I'd never seen anything like it before." Murphy paused, catching herself about to start rambling again. "Anyway, I'd heard about some research that was being done, where tiny micro-cameras would be lined up on one side of an object. Car, building, even a person's body. Those cameras would be directly linked to monitors on the other side of the object. When activated, the monitors would display the image from the other side of the object, thus making the car look invisible. You get me, sir?"

"Kinda," replied Caleb.

"Yeah," Darcy said, "I've heard of that too. But I thought they were years away from perfecting it."

"They are. Or at least, the people we know are."

Caleb smiled. "This will come in very handy."

Natalie appeared distressed that the people in the car had figured it out. "I'm guessing your people don't know that we know about this, right? "Caleb asked. She couldn't even bring herself to look at him.

"Didn't think so," Caleb said, returning his attention to Murphy. "Great work, Lieutenant."

Murphy smiled, content with her work.

Chapter Thirty-Five

Deciding not to use the cloak, Caleb drove the car to the north side of the complex. As the alert level had been heightened in the city, their entry onto the plane had to be precise. He was certain that the sudden appearance of a modified cargo plane at the end of a runway would cause problems. They had to play this right. They had to play this safe. "So, where is it?" he asked Natalie.

"It's at the northern end of the runway," she replied. For so long, Natalie had believed that the people from the Colony were the most advanced people to have existed. If their devices could be worked out by *normal* people, then maybe they weren't as advanced as she'd hoped.

"Murphy," Caleb asked his Lieutenant, "you searched her, right? Did you find anything that looked like a locator, or remote?"

"No, sir. I didn't get a chance to look in her bag, though," Murphy replied.

"Have a look. There must be something in there."

Murphy picked up the prisoner's backpack, which had been resting on the middle seat with her. Among the clothing and smaller weapons, Murphy pulled out the only electronic device she could find; a tablet. She turned it on, but was greeted with a message telling her the tablet required a thumb print to activate.

Murphy turned around, and held the tablet out in front of Natalie.

Natalie looked at the tablet, and placed her hands in her pocket. Her willingness to help had completely subsided. "Surely you can figure that out too, bitch," Natalie said with disdain.

Without warning, Dunleavy reached down and grabbed Natalie's hand. He ripped her thumb out, putting major strain on the metacarpal and trapezium bones. He continued to squeeze, and eventually a small crack was heard. Natalie let out a scream that deafened the people in the car, but due to the soundproof windows, couldn't be heard outside.

Not letting up, Dunleavy pulled her now-broken hand forward, and placed her left thumb on the screen. The tablet opened, and the programs were revealed.

Murphy scanned the program list. There were numerous programs, Threat Analysis, PhoneTrack, Satellite Maintenance, 'Bat Diagnostics... but one caught her eye – Kite Controls. Murphy opened the program, and found a panel similar to what was on the GPS display of the SUV, with a few additional functions. "Cap, I think I have it," Murphy said.

"Good, Lieutenant. Don't touch anything for now. We need to organise this."

Murphy looked through the program, attempting to familiarise herself with the features. She was impressed with the work, but also a bit bemused. Though similar in concept to the most tablets on the market, and the tablet the team used on a regular basis, the Colonials tablet seemed to be purpose built – solely for their use.

While she waited for Caleb, she opened the 'Bat Diagnostics program. It was a display of the SUV. She turned to Natalie. "You named the SUV after something that flies? Are you serious?"

Natalie stared back sullenly.

"Oh well," Murphy continued her mocking, looking at Casey. "Maybe these guys aren't as bright as we thought."

Natalie snapped. The colonies contained the brightest people on the planet, and she would not stand for them being insulted. "It's short for 'wombat', you idiot." She winced, fighting the pain of her broken hand.

Murphy and Casey both laughed. When the humour subsided, Casey asked a question. "Seriously, you called the car a freakin' *Wombat*. You named it after a cute little bear thing. Couldn't think of a better name than that?" he asked scornfully.

Natalie just ignored the statement, not wanting to reveal anything other than what she had to.

"Oh well… let's see if there's anything wrong with the *Wombat* then," Murphy said.

She opened the program and looked at the options.

She pressed the option that indicated "Which 'Bat would you like to diagnose?" The next option was to choose the closest in proximity to the device, which Murphy pressed. The tablet came up with a schematic of the 'Bat, and showed that there were currently six passengers. It also noted that all systems were nominal, apart from the malfunctioning tracking device.

Suddenly, a warning indicator appeared on the main display on the console of the car. Caleb studied the message - a red flashing light saying 'alert'.

After five seconds of flashing, the display changed to show four blue dots converging on their current location. Apparently, they hadn't been as covert as they thought, and someone at the airport had tipped them off.

Dunleavy raised his weapon, as though anticipating a fight. Caleb saw this via the rear view mirror. "Put that gun down, Mike. We're not killing civilians; I don't care how much of a threat they are."

"But Jackson…"

"No 'buts', Mike. That's a line I've never crossed. And I won't be starting now. So again… put that gun down!"

Knowing he couldn't change Caleb's mind, Dunleavy put the gun away, though not before a short pause.

"Besides… they can't shoot or arrest what they can't see," Caleb said, as he pressed the cloak button. Caleb drove the 'Bat a little further up the road, the fence still separating them from the runway.

"Sir, just go about another fifty yards up Perimeter Road, and turn left into the parking lot," said Murphy.

"Are you sure, Lieutenant?" replied Caleb.

"It's okay, sir. Just drive through the lot and park with the 'Bats nose against the fence. That will line us up with the plane."

Trusting his Lieutenants judgement, Caleb followed her instructions. He drove for an additional fifty yards, and turned left. The parking lot was empty, save for one car parked close to the building.

He drove through the lot, coming to a stop as the nose of the 'Bat hit the fence. He turned the engine off, but left the power running.

"What's the plan, boss?" asked Casey from the back.

Caleb heard the question, but chose not to respond. "Mike, how long until your friend gets here?"

"He was in Oregon. Normally takes a few of hours, but I imagine he'll be here soon. I'm not sure he knows how to drive slowly."

"Call him to find out."

Without question, Dunleavy did as requested. He took out his phone, and pressed the green button. This brought up the last number he'd called.

Jacob answered after the first ring.

Before he could talk, Dunleavy spoke.

"We're at Kings County International Airport, Seattle. What's your ETA?"

"I thought you'd go there," replied Jacob, "I've been going about a ninety an hour for the trip, so I'll be there in about twenty."

"Good. Call me when you arrive." Dunleavy hung up, not waiting for a response.

"Twenty minutes," he said to Caleb.

"Good, that gives us some time. Murphy, how is it coming with the controls?" Caleb turned to his Lieutenant.

"All good, sir. I think I've got a plan."

"Good. Let's hear it."

◆ ◆ ◆

Despite averaging close to ninety miles per hour for the trip, Jacob had found time to assess the situation. He'd been requested, by William's superior no less, to ensure that Dunleavy would go to the Zone Three colony. Where that was, Jacob didn't know. All he knew was that Zone Three covered the land that made up North America.

He'd surmised that the group would pick a central location. But, despite his best attempts, he hadn't been able to ascertain the exact coordinates.

As he drove, he was unsure of exactly what awaited him at the airport. He knew that Dunleavy had recruited him to perform individual missions, those that would be bogged down by having too many people involved. Jacob was also the main person to carry out the threat elimination missions. He knew the other team specialised in what was termed by Dunleavy to be aggressive hacking. He knew what that implied. They got the information that allowed Dunleavy to pick the missions and targets that were given Jacob. Once identified, Jacob would go on search and destroy missions.

He remembered his first meeting with Dunleavy. It was directly after the Bogota mission. Directly after he'd made the deal with William. Jacob had been released, in a manner of speaking, anyway. He was led, blindfolded to a location outside the city. On the way, he thought he would just be let go. Instead, when he arrived, he was put on his knees, and told to keep his head down.

It was then he'd heard the shots. His two escorts had been shot, and some more, unidentified people were taking him away. For extra care, they'd put a shroud on his head. To this day, he had no idea who those people were. Only thing he knew, was that they were American, judging by their accents.

For two hours they travelled. First in the back of a truck, and then in a plane. Minutes after it landed, he was sitting in a chair, and his blindfold and shroud were removed.

It was there he'd met Dunleavy. In the following ten-minute conversation, he'd learned more about what the Colonials were up to than in the entire time he knew William.

Dunleavy told him the details of the serum, of how you could constantly regenerate from it. Dunleavy promised that, once he controlled the serum, he would become a billionaire; selling the product to the highest bidders.

Still, it was gaining that control that was the problem, and that was why he needed Jacob's help. He couldn't trust anyone in the government, nor any of his other contacts. He needed Jacob, and Jacob needed him. It was a mutually beneficial relationship.

Jacob also cultivated relationship with William, the representative of the colony.

As he drove, he contemplated which way his allegiance would fall. He knew that this was the time to make the decision, as once a bridge was burnt, it could not be rebuilt.

As he drove towards the airport, now only ten minutes out, the assassin made his decision.

Chapter Thirty-Six

Murphy's plan sounded risky. There were a lot of elements in play. Timing, as always, was crucial. As Caleb thought on the plan, he decided it was the correct way to go, possibly the only way.

He backed the car up, away from the fence. "When will you be ready to go, Lieutenant?" Caleb asked her.

"As soon as you give the word, Cap, I'll lower the ramp," she replied.

Caleb checked the GPS display. The police had hung around for several minutes. When they saw no black SUV lurking in the area, they'd left. They had more important things to deal with than following up on such reports.

Caleb turned to Dunleavy. "Mike… how far out?" he asked, referring to the impending arrival of Jacob.

"He should be here in a couple of minutes," Dunleavy replied. As he spoke, his phone rang. "Just go to the end of the road, I'll meet you at the parking lot entrance," Dunleavy told Jacob. He hung up. Dunleavy checked his surrounds, making sure no one was in the vicinity. When he was certain there was no one, he exited the car, looking strange as he seemed to appear in mid-air.

Caleb did the same, not wanting Dunleavy left alone. He wanted to check out Dunleavy's contact for himself. They walked to the edge of the parking lot, together. As they reached the end, they saw the sedan approaching.

The sedan entered the parking lot, and came to a stop adjacent to where Caleb and Dunleavy were standing, two bays from the 'Bat. A tall, strongly built man exited the car. Apart from his build, the man wasn't extraordinary in any way. No tattoos, and only minor visible scars… just like Caleb.

"Mike," Jacob began, "you're in deep shit. Have you heard the radio?"

"What the fuck do you think, Jacob? Of course I have"

Caleb didn't feel optimistic, as the two clearly didn't like each other.

"Whatever," Jacob said, nonchalantly. "Shall we get out of here?"

"Wait a minute. You two..." Caleb stopped them, "you need to tell me who you are, and what you're doing here. I've heard Mike's version of it all. Now I wanna hear yours."

"Okay then," Jacob replied, "As far as I can tell, whatever we've been up to lately. Your team's missions to god knows where, and my missions to the same... and it's all about to start raining shit on everyone."

"Be more specific," asked an agitated Caleb.

"Yes, sir," Jacob replied, feigning a salute. "We're here to find out where the colony is. And you have a prisoner who is going to take us there."

Dunleavy looked uneasily at Caleb. "Wow, you seem to know a lot," Caleb said, returning Dunleavy's look.

"Look," Jacob said, "I know you're sceptical, I would be too. I mean, shit, I don't know you, you don't know me. But I do know that I wanna hurt those sons of bitches. They blew up a fucking passenger plane. A plane full of innocents."

Jacob had always had a gift for lying and manipulation, and was using his gift to its full ability.

And Caleb almost believed him.

In fact, he may have, had he not noticed the blood on the trunk of the back of the sedan.

Caleb knew Jacob wasn't to be trusted. "Alright then, I guess we can use all the help we can get," Caleb said, acting as though nothing were amiss.

"Good. Let's do this. Where's the plane?"

"That will take some explaining," said Dunleavy, "Follow me to the car?"

"What car?"

Rather than explaining it then and there, Caleb signalled to Darcy, and she turned off the cloak. The 'Bat slowly came into view. Jacob looked on in amazement.

"*That* car," Caleb said.

Jacob was quite taken aback. He had heard rumours of such things, but had never seen it in action. Refocussing, Jacob followed Dunleavy to the car. As they were about to enter, Dunleavy pointed to the middle row of seats.

Jacob got in, and took his place next to Murphy.

Caleb also entered the car. He turned to his team, and introduced Jacob.

"Hi all, this is Jacob. Jacob is going to be helping us get to the colony. Please consider him our amigo."

Casey and Murphy nodded in understanding. In Spanish, Amigo means friend. However, over time, Caleb's team had established a code. The code was simple.

If a person was described in a language other than English, they were not to be trusted, and they were to be treated as though they were a threat. To emphasise their understanding, the Marines repeated the word.

"My amigo," Casey said, extending his hand to Jacob, which he shook.

"Nice to meet you Amigo," said Murphy.

Chapter Thirty-Seven

Caleb turned and faced the runway. "Okay everyone," he began, "So we keep our new passenger in the loop, and so he doesn't completely freak out, let's just run through it again. It's pretty critical that we aren't seen, right? So, when I give the word, the Lieutenant will lower the ramp of the plane, which, as we understand, is right in front of us, correct?"

"Yes sir," replied Murphy, opening the Kite Controls on the tablet she had acquired from Natalie.

"Good," Caleb continued. "Once it starts to open, we'll begin our approach. According to Natalie, the ramp will take about twenty seconds to lower. Correct?"

"Sir, yes sir," Natalie said from the back, mocking the Lieutenant.

Murphy chuckled to herself. Rather than being annoyed that the prisoner was mocking her, she took it as a compliment, a reassurance that she was getting under her skin.

"So, Murphy will lower the ramp, and we'll do a three count. That should allow us to get on the ramp as it hits the ground, allowing for crashing the fence and use of the car's boosters. It's gonna be bumpy, so I suggest you all put your seats in the upright position, buckle up, and hold on."

Caleb turned on the engine, and took a deep breath and focused. Not only would he have to drive the car at speed, but he would need to ensure it was kept straight. But that was the easy part.

The difficult part of the stunt was going to come towards the end. Once he got on the plane, it was difficult to know when to stop. He could start braking before the ramp, but, depending on the angle and traction gained, the braking might be too much, or even worse, not enough.

Caleb knew he would need all his focus, especially as he was risking not only his life, but those of his fellow passengers.

One of those mattered most of all, and she was sitting there next to him. He turned to her, and whispered. "I love you, babe."

She looked back at him. "Just drive straight, babe," she said as she winked.

Caleb smiled; relieved his girlfriend was seemingly relaxed. He looked in the mirror, straight at Murphy. Murphy had her finger poised over the button on the tablet designated 'Lower Cargo Ramp'.

"Okay, Murph," said Caleb. "Whenever you're ready."

"Yes, sir," replied Murphy, "Hopefully lowering the ramp in three... two... one... lowering the ramp."

Murphy pressed the button, and to her relief, it seemed to work. About two hundred yards away, the ramp began to lower in front of them. In the distance, the sliver of a plane cargo bay began to appear. As it opened further, the size of the opening became apparent. The plane was big, if the cargo hold was any kind of guide. The ramp opening could easily hold a truck.

Caleb, marvelling at the image he was gazing upon, remembered the plan. "Okay all, gunning it in three... two... one," he said to the group as he accelerated.

They all braced themselves as Caleb took off. To someone from the outside, the screech of the tires would have been terrifying, especially as the car was currently cloaked. As the car made a brisk speed, and with a burst from the boosters, the fence fractured and fell with ease.

The car continued the journey, and the ramp continued to go down. As the car neared, the ramp touched the ground, the cargo hold on display to anyone standing behind.

The car hurtled towards the entrance, now only a hundred feet from the ramp. Caleb placed his foot on the brake, waiting for the split-second decision he was sure he would need to make. They went up the ramp, and Caleb slammed on brakes, the ABS doing some of the work.

Such was the speed at which the car had accelerated, the brakes had little effect. As the 'Bat screeched up the ramp, there was only minimal reduction in the speed of the car's forward movement. A panicked look appeared on Caleb's face.

It was a look Darcy had not seen previously. For the first time since she'd met him, he looked genuinely concerned.

It was an expression shared by the most of the occupants in the car. They too, were more than concerned about the car's speed.

The only calm face in the car was Natalie's.

The look was fleeting, though.

As the car careened into the cargo bay of the plane, Caleb grabbed Darcy's hand. The car reached the threshold of the plane. Suddenly, the 'Bat jerked to a stop, trapped by a chord that had been activated by the car's approach.

The motion reminded Caleb of the times he'd had to make a trap-landing on an aircraft carrier.

The jolt on the carrier, while a shock to the system, could be coped with. That is, if the passenger knew the shock was coming and was able to mentally prepare for it. *And* physically place themselves in a position so as to absorb the dramatic change of speed.

Only one person in the car had braced themselves – Natalie.

As the car lurched into position, clamps from the floor of the cargo bay snapped into place, holding the 'Bat in position.

Once the car settled, Natalie, sensing a small window to attack, made her move. She swung her elbow into the jerking head of Dunleavy, hoping to break his jaw as he had hers.

She didn't wait to discover the result, repeating the action on Casey, an act which knocked the Sergeant out. Remembering her vow a few hours earlier, Natalie reached over a bleeding Dunleavy, grabbing his gun from his belt. She swung around, and aimed at Casey's head. Her finger poised over the trigger, the hammer clicked back, and struck the back of the gun...

Nothing. Casey's head remained intact.

Dunleavy's gun had jammed.

The lull in action was all that Murphy needed. She quickly unbuckled, having noticed the commotion in the back seat. She turned just in time to see the prisoner lining up the weapon with Casey's face. Fear and anxiety gripped Murphy as the trigger was pulled.

When the gun failed to fire, Murphy's fear transformed into anger, and she half leaped over the seat. She ripped the gun from Natalie's hand, which she then threw to the ground.

The Lieutenant reached into her holster, and grabbed her own gun, a much more trustworthy weapon, and aimed it at Natalie. "Should have shot you back at the airport," Murphy said, anger strewn across her face.

Natalie resigned herself to her imminent fate. As she relaxed, into her seat, defeated, she looked up at Murphy, and smiled. Not the normal happy smile that accompanies a normal person. Natalie's smile was one of smugness, as though she knew something her killer did not.

"See you in the next life," she said, and Murphy began to squeeze the trigger.

Natalie's death was but moments away, when a voice saved her life.

"Stand down, Lieutenant," Caleb's voice boomed from the front.

"Sir?" Murphy replied, easing her finger back off the trigger. The gun was still pointed at the prisoner.

"I said, *stand down,* Murphy," he repeated.

"Sir? She tried to kill Casey! She—" Murphy replied, anger setting the tone for her voice.

"I know... but we still need her."

Murphy kept the gun pointed straight between Natalie's eyes. "Fine sir. I won't shoot..." she said, giving Natalie a dark look, "after all, wouldn't want to get shit all over the back of *our* new car."

Caleb turned to Darcy, who was still breathless from the landing's jolt. "Grab the tablet, and close the door," Caleb instructed. Though struggling with the pain in her chest, Darcy complied.

The large ramp began closing behind them, hiding them once again from the world. Caleb pressed the button on the display, deactivating the cloak. He didn't want to use up any unnecessary power, plus they were in an enclosed space, and the *invisible* car was a trip hazard.

As the car came back into view, Caleb exited the vehicle. The cargo area of the plane was a massive space. As he first observed from the parking lot, the height was enough to carry an entire truck and trailer. Three, possibly four, 'Bats could also have fitted inside the plane's belly.

Though marvelling at the size, it was the aesthetic interior that caught Caleb's attention as well. The plane's creators were obviously perfectionists, clearly spending as much time on the design and look of the plane as they did on the technology.

The interior walls of the plane were shimmering silver, lit up by the lights that had automatically come on when the 'Bat entered the plane.

Darcy also stepped out of the vehicle. She too, was struck by the design. "Geez, how does this thing get off the ground, Caleb?" she asked her boyfriend, not really expecting a response.

"No idea, babe," he replied. "Then again, how do they make a whole car disappear??"

Darcy contemplated his response. In a Caleb-like way, she knew he was saying that, despite everything and the believability of it all, there had to be an explanation.

"They got it here," he continued, "we must be able to get it back."

"Back where though?" Darcy asked.

"Hopefully, we'll find out."

Casey's door opened, and the waking-up Sergeant stumbled out.

"You okay, Sergeant?" Caleb asked.

"I've had worse hangovers, sir," he replied. "They usually come after good times though."

"What, nearly getting your head blown off isn't a good time?" asked Murphy from the car, still intent on making sure Natalie didn't move.

"Not even in my top ten, babe." He winked at his saviour.

Casey made his way to the back of the cargo bay, doing a quick inspection of the area. As he approached the back of the plane, he ran his hand along the side of the cargo hold, as though feeling for any damage that might have occurred. After he completed the right side, he made his way across to the left, easily a fifteen-yard distance, and repeated the action on the left.

"She's still looking good, sir," Casey said as he finished his brief inspection.

Jacob exited the car. "Shit, this'll never fucking fly?"

Caleb looked at Darcy, deciding not to waste his time with the amigo.

"Darcy, can you go find the cockpit? I imagine it's at the top of those stairs. You and Murphy will need to figure this thing out, okay?"

Darcy looked surprised. "I've never flown a plane," she said, half protesting, and half happy that Caleb was entrusting such a task to her.

"I know, but Murphy will be there with you."

As he spoke, Natalie emerged from the 'Bat, in pain from the broken hand and jaw Dunleavy had given her.

"Tie her up," Caleb said to Casey.

"Gladly sir," replied the Sergeant. "Whereabouts? The left or right wing?"

Caleb looked around, ignoring the joke (or at least what he *hoped* was a joke). About three yards in front of the stairs was a door to the emergency hatch. Connected was a handle. The handle that indicated that if it was pulled, the door would open.

"Just over there... that handle should suffice," Caleb said, pointing to a handle on the wall marked 'Emergency'. "That way, if she struggles, well, we won't have to worry about her anymore."

Casey led Natalie to the place, making sure she bumped her head a few times along the way. He secured her to the handle, loosening it slightly so that any movement would ensure she'd be ejected from the plane.

"Now keep an eye on her. She's your responsibility. We will need her, I imagine," Caleb said to Casey.

"Yes sir," Casey replied, raising his gun at Natalie.

Murphy, after making a sweep of the cargo bay, made her way up the stairs, making sure she stayed away from the prisoner. Her rage was still inside, and she knew she would have killed her if the Captain hadn't stepped in. For the meantime, it was probably better if Murphy didn't interact with her in any way.

Caleb walked back to the 'Bat, as Dunleavy had yet to emerge.

He walked to the rear drivers-side door, which was ajar and stuck his head in. "You okay, Mike?" he asked the clearly hurting former Chief of Staff.

Dunleavy moaned.

"Jackson," he started, "I hate to steal a line from someone else, but I really am too old for this shit."

Chapter Thirty-Eight

Finding the cockpit had not proved to be a difficult task. The entryway at the top of the stairs led straight to it. It was an impressive view, to say the least. There were half a dozen seats, each with a different set of controls in front of it. Comfortably the size of her living room, Darcy was able to walk around the area with ease.

She looked at each station. The first was labelled 'Kite Operations'. The next was 'Navigation'. At the front of the cockpit, there were two chairs next to each other, much like one would expect in a standard cockpit. One was labelled 'Control' and the chair to its immediate right was marked '2nd Control'.

As Darcy continued, she studied the other stations. The first one on the left side surprised her – 'Weapons and Defence'. There seemed to be even more to this plane than met the eye.

The last chair was labelled 'Communications'.

In front of each chair was a large black monitor, each about forty inches on the diameter. Until they were activated, it would be impossible to know how they worked.

The exceptions were the two front seats. While they had screens in front of them, they were a bit smaller, closer to twenty inches on the diameter. They did have several buttons and levers, of which some Darcy recognised. There was only one major problem as far as Darcy could see - how did the thing turn on?

As she was contemplating the problem, Murphy appeared in the doorway. Darcy was comforted by her appearance. They had both been through so much over the last few hours, having both saved each other's life. Not bad for a couple of people who had only met early that morning.

"Wow," Murphy said as she entered the cockpit.

"My thoughts exactly," Darcy responded, still trying to figure out how to turn it on.

Murphy walked to the front of the cockpit, looking around the room as she moved. As she was probably going to take responsibility for the plane, she figured she would have to get to know it better than most.

"One question, Darcy," she said as she approached the *Control* chairs, "How do we turn this thing on?"

With a shrug of the shoulder, Darcy gave her a response.

There was no obvious power switch, or sequence. The control that was obvious was used to control the plane - the throttle being the only one Darcy recognised. The rest may as well have been labelled in German.

Murphy continued to scan the console, only pausing to take in the view out the front of the plane. The vista was nice, but not overwhelming. The window spanned from the side of cockpit, near the entry door, around the cockpit to the other side. Standing or sitting anywhere in the room would give a person a view of the outside.

As Darcy looked out the window, she shifted her vision to the south, to where SEATAC was. The billowing smoke had disappeared.

Darcy paused. The view appeared as though the attack had never happened. The sight caused Darcy to briefly ponder the events of the preceding day. Just over twenty-four hours ago she had woken up, next to Caleb, snuggled under his arm. She was so content with the world, and happy. Her career was going well, and Caleb had been home for a few months. Perhaps his lifestyle was about to change. Perhaps it was the end of all the long absences. Perhaps it was the end of the implicit violence he had to endure.

She had never been more wrong.

"Well... I've got no idea," Murphy said, drawing Darcy from her daydreams.

Darcy shook herself back into focus. "No idea?" Darcy asked.

"I've got no idea how to turn this, this thing, on. I was looking for a 'print reader or something, you know, like the tablet. But there's nothing."

Darcy shrugged again. She was following Murphy's lead, and didn't have the slightest idea where to start.

"Hey, Darcy, what's that?" Murphy said, pointing to a slot below the panel.

"It's nothing to do with flying the thing?" Darcy asked. "Don't you recognise it?"

"Nope, it's certainly not standard."

"It looks like, you know, a card reader at an ATM."

"Yeah, that's what I was thinking." Murphy stood up and walked to the door. She stood at the entrance, the stairs bannister visible from Darcy's position.

From her vantage point, she could see Casey, standing across from the prisoner, his gun drawn. Caleb was looking through the 'Bat, talking to Dunleavy. Jacob, their latest addition, was against the side of the 'Bat, casually looking around the cabin. "Cap." Murphy said loudly, trying to get Caleb's attention.

"Yes, Lieutenant," Caleb replied.

Darcy was impressed they still kept up the formalities of rank, even in the most trying situations.

"We're gonna need her up here," Murphy said down the stairs.

"I kinda wanna keep her where she is, Murph," Caleb said. He was content that the emergency exit would provide a good failsafe. "Do you really need her? I don't want her near anything important."

"I guess. I'll do what I can to figure it out. Can't do anything without the power though, and for that… looks like we're gonna need an access card. I'm hoping she has one."

Caleb looked at Casey. "Did you find anything?" Caleb asked.

"Not in the bag," replied Casey.

"Check her person," Caleb said, "I'll cover her."

Caleb lifted his weapon, pointing it at the prisoner. Casey released his gun, and started to pat down the prisoner.

Natalie wanted to struggle, but it had little effect. The combination of the way her hands were tied and the security of the door handle were sufficient to make any fighting impossible. After a token effort, she ceased her resistance.

Casey did a full search of her pockets. She wasn't dressed dissimilarly to the group, her cargo pants complemented by a flak jacket and vest. That meant there were several pockets to check.

After searching her pants, Casey found what he'd been looking for. He pulled out a white card, with a black metallic strip on one side. On the other, there was no identification. There were letters however – Z3 Kite.

"I'm guessing this is it?" Casey stated, directing the comment towards Natalie.

She turned away emphatically.

Casey threw the card to Caleb, who caught it without taking his attention off the prisoner.

Casey again raised his own gun at the prisoner.

"Dunleavy, come with me." Caleb said. "Casey, Jacob. Keep an eye on her."

Jacob was not used to following orders, especially from someone he'd just met. But, in order to keep up his ruse, Jacob obliged. He moved to the front section of the plane, and kept watch on the prisoner.

Or at least that's how he appeared to Caleb, who had begun walking up the stairs. Dunleavy followed close behind.

Murphy waited at the top of the stairs, and as she turned to go into the cockpit, Casey got her attention.

"Lieutenant!" he yelled.

Murphy turned back around to face him. "Yes, Sergeant?" she said with a smile.

"Just get us in the air... I hate the north-west," he replied.

"Will do," she said with a smile.

He winked at her, and she returned the endearment.

Darcy was waiting at the front of the cockpit. She turned to face the trio as they entered. "Have you got it?" she asked.

"Here it is," Murphy said, almost running to the pilot's seat. She was excited, and hoped the card worked. She sat down in the *Control seat.*

Almost ceremoniously, Murphy slid the card into the slot. She only had to insert it half way, and the mechanism took over, bringing the entirety of the card into the slot.

After some whirrs – no doubt the card being scanned - the cockpit lit up. Every screen in the area glowed, each showing a different display.

Darcy looked apprehensive, an expression Caleb caught. "What's wrong, Darc?" he asked, barely able to focus on the question as he was so taken in with the newly lit up cockpit.

"I don't know," Darcy began. "Didn't that all seem a bit too easy? I mean... a swipe card unlocks the plane? Really?"

Caleb shared Darcy apprehension, but he had a theory. "I've been thinking about that myself," he began, pausing to consider his words. "My thinking is that while it was easy, it was deliberately so. I mean, these guys, these Colonials, are pieces of work. They probably never thought anyone would beat their guys, especially the way Natalie's been sounding off. It's almost insulting to them that Murphy figured out the tablet. They're arrogant, narcissistic and have a huge superiority complex. I think they figured no one, except them, would ever see inside this thing, or the 'Bat for that matter. That's why, I think, security is lacking once you get in."

Darcy thought about it, and what Caleb said did make sense. "I guess I'm just uncomfortable with it all," she said.

"Me too, Darc. Me too."

The words helped Darcy, as she needed to feel she wasn't the only one having trouble coming to terms with what was happening.

Caleb gave one last reassuring look to Darcy, and then turned to Murphy. The lieutenant had been poring over the console, scrolling through the various options.

"You think you can figure this out, Murphy?" he asked

"I think so, sir. Some of the equipment has different names, but flying is flying. I'll get us off the ground, sir," Murphy glanced up as she spoke.

"How long?"

"Give me a few minutes. No need to do the checks. I'm guessing they did all that when they left. Where did they come from, anyway?"

"Not sure yet. You just get us in the air, I'll see what I can find out. There's gotta be something on here... somewhere," Caleb said as he scanned the room. He turned to his left, and saw Dunleavy was sitting at the Navigation screen, having anticipated the Captain's next question. He'd pulled up a screen of what looked like the State of Washington. "Jackson, come look at this," he said.

Caleb made his way to where Dunleavy was sitting. He glanced down at the screen, over the old man's shoulder.

"This is clearly us," said Dunleavy, pointing to a red icon with the silhouette of a slender bird, "and this is Seattle." Dunleavy pointed at the mass of grey surrounding the icon.

Caleb studied the image. Indeed, it seemed to show a real life tracking of the plane. "Can you zoom out of that?" he asked.

"Yeah, it all looks pretty simple. I know these guys think they're geniuses, and they may well be, but they've created the easiest user interface that I've ever seen."

"Probably because it wasn't designed to be operated by geniuses, but by grunts. Soldiers." Caleb motioned out the door. "Like our guest."

"And they've done a fucking good job of it too, Jackson."

"I'll pass on your compliments when we meet them," Caleb said, his harsh tone apparent, "but if it's not too much trouble, can you please zoom out, Mr. Dunleavy?"

As they zoomed out, Montana and Oregon came into view. North California, Idaho, Wyoming, North and South Dakota and Nebraska followed. Also coming into view were British Columbia, Alberta and Saskatchewan in Canada.

As Dunleavy continued to zoom out, Caleb noticed another icon on the monitor. It was the same symbol he'd seen on one of his missions. He couldn't remember the specifics, having only seen the symbol in a fleeting moment. When he saw the icon again, he flashed back to the moment, and suddenly realised what it was.

A shield with a knight's helmet on top, the icon was obviously a family crest of some description.

Not being a noted historian, Caleb was unable to distinguish who it belonged to. Instinctively, he pressed the button.

The screen changed immediately. No longer was there just a map of the North West United States. There were about a dozen smaller icons, with pictures of what looked like 'Bats encircled by a blue circle. There was also at least a dozen, if not twenty, icons that were nearly identical to the one that indicated the plane. There were subtle differences, like different kinds of birds. "Oh shit," Caleb said as realization dawned.

Not accustomed to Caleb swearing, Darcy and Murphy hurried from their examination of the piloting console. They stood next to Caleb, and looked at the display, now littered with other icons.

"What are they Caleb?" asked Darcy, fearing she already knew the answer.

Caleb continued to stare at the screen, failing to hear Darcy's question. As he looked, a number of the icons changed position.

They were moving.

"Holy hell, Cap," said Murphy. "Look how many there are…"

Caleb continued to stare. From what he could tell, all the other icons were moving east. "Mike… zoom out some more."

Almost robotically, Dunleavy began to zoom again.

Utah, Colorado, Kansas, Missouri, Iowa, Minnesota all came into view, and all had at least three or four icons each. There were even some coming in from the Pacific Ocean.

The icons in the west were still moving east. The Canadian icons were moving south, while others were moving north.

As Caleb monitored the flight paths, he saw another icon on the screen. At first, he was amused by the simplicity of the icon. A small house, not unlike every operating system, website and GPS he'd ever seen. He pressed it.

A bright yellow circle appeared on the screen.

"Murphy, get this thing going. I think we have a destination."

"Yes sir, where to?" Murphy asked.

Without asking, Dunleavy had zoomed in on the circle.

"Looks like we're following the crowd today," Caleb began.

He doubled checked the screen.

"Head east, Lieutenant. We're going to North Dakota."

Chapter Thirty-Nine

Murphy and Darcy resumed their previous seats. "No problem, sir," said Murphy as she sat down. "North Dakota it is. Anywhere specific?"

Caleb looked closer at the screen in front of Dunleavy. "It's about fifteen miles out of a place called Minot." Caleb turned to Dunleavy. "Why does that sound familiar?" Caleb asked. "Isn't there an air force base or something around there?"

Dunleavy looked at the map. "Yeah, about fifteen or so miles north you can find the base," Dunleavy replied. "Not long ago there were some bombers there, but not much else." He studied the map on his console, but he couldn't find the air force base anywhere on it. "It's not on the map, Jackson. Not surprising though. These guys don't really seem to care too much about the outside world."

Caleb thought about what Dunleavy had said. "I'm not sure that's it. I mean, these guys are obviously very precise with their actions. I'm sure they would note the base on the map. Even if they didn't consider it a threat."

"Possibly. I guess we'll just have to wait to find out."

As Dunleavy spoke, the engines of the plane started up.

Without much waiting, Murphy began moving the plane into position. She steadily taxied the plane towards the start of the runway.

"You got this, Murphy?" asked Caleb.

"Yes sir." Murphy turned to Darcy. "You following so far, Darc?"

"I think so… with these screens, it does make it easier," she replied.

Caleb glanced around the cockpit. In all the time since the attack at SEATAC, there had been very little time to get information out to people. If he could find some way to communicate with the outside world, perhaps, at the very least, they could get some help.

When Caleb looked around the room, the answer was apparent. "Darcy, this'll be right up your alley" he said to his partner.

Darcy spun around in her chair, no longer focused on what Murphy was doing. "What's that Caleb?" she asked.

"Have a look at this one..." Caleb said, pointing towards the Communications console.

Darcy moved immediately. "About time you asked," she said with a smile.

Ever since she'd walked into the cockpit, the Communications station had been the one she was most curious about. Indeed, it was the one area that she recognised out of the five that she could be most useful at.

"Now," Caleb continued as Darcy sat down, "I want you too—"

"See what I can find out about the Colonials, and what else is happening in the world," Darcy interrupted, finishing Caleb's sentence, "But, most importantly, you want me to figure out a way we can get word out to anyone else about our situation."

Caleb stared at her.

"Right?" Darcy asked, with a wink. She knew her boyfriend better than he realised.

"So, why did you—" Caleb started again, and again Darcy interrupted.

"Why did I waste my time in the pilot seat, when I knew what you needed?" she said.

"Yeah."

"Because you asked me to babe, and you were right, too."

"Oh really?" Caleb said, sarcasm oozing from his voice.

"Yeah, really. I do need some practical skills. You know... in case."

Caleb just nodded. He was incredibly proud of her. While he was busy thinking of the next practical step, Darcy was thinking more rationally, despite the fact the he had more of the *formal* training. She was the practical one today.

"Maybe I should follow *your* orders?" Caleb asked, half sincere in his request.

"Oh no, babe. Trust me… when the shit hits the fan and bullets come flying at us…" she said, "We'll all be looking to you." She paused, and made sure she had eye contact. "You're my protector, remember."

Once again, all Caleb could do was smile.

Without saying anymore, Darcy turned to the console and began assessing the panel in front of her.

Caleb turned to the front, and walked over to Murphy. As he looked out at the horizon, he was surprised to see she had already manoeuvred the plane into position to take off.

Something about the view didn't seem right. "Something seem a little off to you, Murph?"

Murphy looked up at the Captain. "Off sir? What do you mean?" she replied.

Caleb surveyed the runway again. There was no-one to be seen. "I knew it was going to be quiet, Murph. But not *this* quiet. I mean, there's no one around."

"I guess. But it is Sunday, and the attack just happened. It probably would have been quiet anyway? Don't you think?"

"Yeah, I guess you're right."

For some reason, Caleb didn't believe what he'd just said. The words didn't resonate at all. He expected to see at least one or two security guards, maybe a technician. But to see absolutely no one on the runway made him uneasy.

He decided to try and allay his concerns, as there were more pressing things to think about.

There was only one way to get to the bottom of what was happening. And, more importantly, they needed to know what was about to happen next. If all that had happened had just been the build-up to something larger, Caleb shuddered to think what the main act might be.

"Take us out Murphy," he said to the Lieutenant.

"Alright… Buckle up, sir," she replied, and motioned for him to take the seat next to her.

Darcy and Dunleavy heard Murphy, and followed suit. "Hold onto something out there!" Caleb shouted out the door.

"Yes Sir!" Casey shouted from the main cargo-hold.

Caleb nodded to Murphy.

"Three... two..."

As she counted down, the thrusters on the back of the plane lit up, causing a roar to generate throughout the plane.

"One..."

The plane began to lurch, as though fighting the urge to spring forward.

"Let's go," Murphy said.

In place of the usual throttle, there was a set of bars on the screen in front of her. At the side of the console, the bars at the bottom were green. As Murphy slid her hand up, the bar turned yellow.

At first, she moved it slowly, as she would with a usual take-off. The screen lit up with a message.

Insufficient Speed.

Murphy pushed it forward more, and the bars turned orange. Still the message appeared on the screen.

"We'll get out of here a lot faster if you just slide it to red straight away," Natalie shouted up from the cargo area.

Murphy followed the suggestion, and slid the bars to the maximum. The plane lurched, its inertia shifting all the people in the plane to move backwards in their chairs.

Within a second, the plane had reached its top speed.

As with the 'Bat entering the plane, Caleb was reminded of taking off from a carrier, the same quick momentum a shock to the system.

The sheer speed of the take-off caught Murphy off-guard. Fortunately, she too had felt the force of a short take-off before, and was able to re-focus. She grabbed the throttle next to the console, and pulled it backwards. The plane began to climb at a rapid rate. Within seconds, they were more than a thousand feet above Seattle.

"Just like a freakin' video game," Murphy said. "North Dakota, here we come".

Chapter Forty

They had been flying for only five minutes. Even after that short amount of time, the advanced nature of the technology was apparent. Murphy had never flown an easier plane. It was often a joke among her and her colleagues that commercial pilots were not actually pilots at all, merely navigators. All they had to do was plug in a destination, and let auto-pilot do the rest.

Essentially, the flying of the Kite was exactly that, but even simpler. When the plane had levelled out at around thirty thousand feet, Murphy's monitor had changed. A map, similar to of the one on the screen in front of Dunleavy, came up. At the top of her screen, Murphy was asked to input her destination. Being a touch screen, Murphy pressed the area that was highlighted in North Dakota – the base they'd seen a few minutes earlier.

As she touched the screen, the plane banked to the left, straightened, and they were on their way.

The screen then changed to display a simple message, indicating the plane was in flight mode. After reporting to Caleb, Murphy returned to the screen. While she was confident everything would be okay, she didn't want to take any chances.

Caleb was standing next to Dunleavy's chair, staring at the screen in front of him. He could barely believe what he was seeing. "Murphy?" Caleb said. "Is this correct?" Are were really going to be there in thirty minutes?"

The Lieutenant checked her screen. According to her information, the Kite was travelling at about two thousand miles per hour – nearly four times the speed of any large plane she had been in before. That meant that Caleb's assumption, though seemingly impossible, was correct.

"Yes sir, in just under twenty-nine minutes, we'll be around Minot."

Caleb and Dunleavy looked at each other, sharing the same thought. They were well out of their league.

◆ ◆ ◆

He walked into the room with renewed vigour. He knew that his superior didn't like to be interrupted, but these were no ordinary circumstances. The game had changed, and Phase Two had begun.

He walked through the door, and entered his superior's quarters. The room was, as always, beautiful in its simplicity. Ever since the original colony had been designed in Zone One, the same form had been instituted across the remaining facilities. The only differentiation was in the styling of the room. Although the styles changed over time, the consistency across the various facilities was always maintained.

It was James who'd insisted that each of the colonies followed the same design. While it had been tried and tested in Zone One, and found to be a suitable design for their purposes, James also believed that having the same design among the group would assist with the focus of the people.

James believed that, if everyone followed the same structure in the same environment they would subconsciously always be aware that they were not alone, and that they were part of something bigger.

It was a simple concept, but an effective one.

Every person who was indoctrinated into the society James had created believed in him, and his work.

Almost everyone.

Isaac was one of the exceptions. He'd been recruited into the organisation by John several years before. He was pulled out of the heart of one of the world's great, recent conflicts.

Back then, he'd been fighting for the cause because he was told he *should*. Since then, he'd been working for a cause he thought he believed in.

Isaac had been told all about Phase One, and most of the details of Phase Two.

The rewards had come at a cost – he hadn't seen his family or friends since he'd been recruited. But he assumed they would have all thought him dead anyway.

Still, he had an opportunity to see the future. And the sacrifices he'd made were well worth the reward, and he'd been happy with his destiny.

All that had changed, when John arrived.

Having been absent from the Berlin colony for the previous twelve months, Isaac had eagerly anticipated his supervisor's return. Soon after his conversation with James, John had arrived via one of the jets.

The following day, as soon as John touched down, Isaac knew his supervisor had concerns. Not the normal, everyday concerns.

These ran much deeper.

After some prodding, John had revealed the issues he was having concerns with. He had told Isaac about the next part of the plan. John had told him about Phase Three – the details of which had changed Isaac's entire perspective.

While he was aware that people were being killed to further the plan, those people had always been a direct threat. They were people who were out to use the serum for their own means.

The next phase changed all that. The next phase was about much more than that. It was about changing the very fabric of the world – and Isaac knew he had to stop it. He was happy to make the sacrifices himself to progress the plan, but Phase Three would affect so many innocent people, people who had no choice in the matter. And that was something Isaac could not live with.

It was then he'd decided that the people he'd been working with all those years had to be stopped.

And a few hours earlier, he'd found his opportunity. John had returned from the conference call with James.

As he walked into the communications room, he knew what he had to do. He couldn't change anything, but he knew the people who could.

He only hoped that when he made the call, the right people would answer.

◆ ◆ ◆

Darcy sat at the communication station, searching through the information on the screen. She was searching through the Kite's 'Information Search Program'. Similar to the internet search engines that are ubiquitous to the lives of everyday people, the key aspect of the Colonials engine was that it was able to combine all the information and extrapolate the data into usable documents. Essentially, it was able to summarise everything with the click of a button and the entry of a search term.

It was an excellent tool for monitoring the mainstream news networks and news websites. What differentiated the Colonials search program, was the fact that it *also* incorporated results from other government databases. Everything from the Pentagon to Mossad.

Darcy wondered how they could have gotten access to such exclusive databases, but given the reach the Colonials had demonstrated so far, she wasn't surprised. They seemed to have people *everywhere*.

Darcy entered the first thing she could think of. She typed in her own name.

After a few seconds, the program sorted through every piece of information that was available to the world, and summarised Darcy's life. Part of her was amazed that they knew so much about her. Another part of her was annoyed that it all was summarised in just a few paragraphs. She started reading the information they had on her.

'Darcy Hannah Chamberlain. Born 8 August, 1979 in San Diego. Graduated from San Diego High school in 1996. Earned Journalism Degree at San Diego State University. Intelligence Quotient of 139. Rated a low-medium risk on the Molyneux Scale. Current whereabouts estimated to be East Coast United States.' LOW RISK???

While she was not surprised the information was there, she was surprised that it went as far as estimating her current location.

She read further down the page. At the bottom, a flashing, bright red sentence drew her attention.

'Update – Apprehend on Site. Eliminate if Necessary.'

Darcy knew then that word was starting to spread among the Colonials. She had been targeted, and would have even more people after her. Not being shocked by any of the information, she tried a new search. She typed in Caleb's name.

As with her, Caleb's sheet read normally.

"Caleb James Jackson. Born 23 September, 1979 in San Diego. Graduated from San Diego High school in 1996. Enlisted with the Marine Corps in March 1997. Intelligence Quotient of 131. Current whereabouts unknown."

Darcy was taken aback by the last line. She reread the small amount of information. She hadn't misread it. Curious about the entry, she spoke up. "Caleb," she said. "Come take a look at this."

Caleb came to join her, alerted by tension in her voice. "What have you found babe?" he asked.

As she was about to speak, the screen changed. *'Incoming Communication – Zone 4'* was flashing across the screen.

Caleb and Darcy watched the screen, not sure what to make of it. "Mike, Murphy…" Caleb began, "need you over here."

As the other two approached, the message continued to flash. With each flash, the tension mounted in Caleb's shoulders. If they answered, and they were not expected, they would give up their element of surprise.

However, Caleb had figured long ago that, as with the 'Bat, there had to be a similar tracker on the plane. He figured the people at the base must also be tracking them. Caleb mentioned his thoughts to the rest of the group.

"Yeah, you're probably right, Jackson," Dunleavy said.

"I'm thinking we need to answer," Caleb announced.

The others just paused and thought for a few seconds.

"I agree, Caleb," said Darcy, "but not you."

Darcy motioned to Dunleavy. "Mike. They already know you, right?"

Dunleavy was surprised by the comment. "What makes you say that?" he asked.

"I'm guessing they think you're involved with us. Why else would it have been leaked out that you were in charge of New Light?"

Caleb was impressed. He hadn't even thought about that, and yet it made perfect sense. "Yeah Mike. You sit in the chair."

Dunleavy was nervous. Not because he doubted Darcy, far from it. He knew she was right in what she'd said. Indeed, they did know of him. It just wasn't for the reasons they thought. Judging by the sounds of it, he reckoned they hadn't even guessed his true motives. "Fair enough," he replied, unable to think of an excuse not to sit in the chair.

Darcy stood up, and Dunleavy took her place. He settled himself, and moved to press the 'Accept' button.

Caleb put his hand on Dunleavy's shoulder, motioning for him to wait.

Caleb motioned for the other two to step to the side to ensure that the only face the caller saw was Dunleavy's. There was no point in putting any of them at risk if they didn't have to.

Once Darcy and Murphy had stepped to the side, Dunleavy pressed the button.

Chapter Forty-One

The face that greeted them was not what they'd expected. Dunleavy had seen several pictures of actual and potential Colonials, but the face he saw on the monitor was foreign to him.

The person on the screen was a young man, no more than thirty years old. He looked upon Dunleavy. Once he saw the face of the former Chief-of-Staff, his face relaxed. It was almost as though he was relieved to see Dunleavy's image in the monitor.

"Good," the young man said. "Obviously you made it, Mr. Dunleavy." Isaac recognised Dunleavy from various briefing notes he had received upon John's arrival in Berlin.

"Okay," Dunleavy replied. "Just who the fuck are you?"

"My name is Isaac," he continued, "And I am from the Berlin Colony. Or Zone Four, as you may know it."

Isaac scanned the area behind Dunleavy, trying to see if he had any accomplices. "Is anyone with you, Mr. Dunleavy?" Isaac asked.

Caleb didn't want to be revealed, nor did he want to further jeopardize Darcy. He could only hope Dunleavy realised this.

"No," Dunleavy replied.

"Okay then, Mr. Dunleavy. I'll have to take that for now," Isaac replied, not believing that Dunleavy could have gotten away with everything without help, not to mention fly the plane as well. "We do not have much time…" Isaac continued.

Dunleavy started to ask a question, but Isaac cut him off. "They are waiting for you in Minot. I imagine that, by now, they have two or three thousand troops ready with the serum. Their only mission right now is stopping you and your group."

Dunleavy looked over at Caleb, aware that Isaac had already guessed he wasn't alone.

"What do you propose?" Dunleavy asked, turning back to the screen.

"I have sent a file. It will give you instructions on how to disable the tracker. Once complete, turn your plane to the south west. I will contact you again in sixty minutes."

A small message note appeared on the screen and Dunleavy opened the file.

It seemed that Isaac was telling the truth. The file contained detailed instructions on how to disable the tracking device.

"Why should we trust you?" asked Dunleavy

Isaac looked directly at the screen, not wanting to appear deceptive.

"Because, Mr. Dunleavy," he replied, "I am the only chance you have. And you are the only chance I have."

With that, the brief conversation ended. Isaac disappeared from the screen.

Dunleavy spun around in the chair. "What do you think, Jackson?" he asked.

Caleb stared at the screen, barely able to believe the conversation. He'd assumed they would be waiting for them at the base. That was why he'd planned to use the air force base to land. Still, even without the element of surprise, they would never be able to get around three thousand troops.

"Caleb," Darcy interrupted her boyfriend's thoughts, "We really don't have a choice do we? The odds are pretty low on getting anywhere in North Dakota."

Caleb knew she was right.

"I agree, sir. Better to listen to that guy," said Murphy. "Worst case scenario, we get a bit more time."

Caleb had been convinced. "You're right," Caleb said, "Let's do it. Murphy, Dunleavy disarm the tracker."

Dunleavy stood up.

"It's located just below the cockpit. Should be a hatch," Dunleavy peered around the room, zoning in on a space near the Control Chairs, "right there"

Murphy went to the spot, and lifted up the hatch door.

She scooted down, and Dunleavy followed.

"What about me, babe?" Darcy asked.

"We're going to use the communications terminal. I want us to find out as much as we can about these… Colonials."

Chapter Forty-Two

"Babe, you still need to look at this." Darcy urged Caleb to refocus on the screen now that Isaac had disappeared. What she had found out prior to Isaac's message had confused her. According to all the databases and searches in the world, her partner's life came down to only three lines, with no real information.

Caleb stared at the screen. "That looks about right." Caleb said, unsurprised that so much information was missing.

Darcy was less convinced. "Caleb. This stuff comes from *everywhere*. No one has any record of you being alive after you were supposedly killed. No tax records. No flight records. No social security, credit cards, rent payment... Nothing."

Caleb thought about what she said. "It's pretty standard, babe. The whole point of sending me, Murphy, and Casey, is so that missions could be completed and not be traced back to the people who gave the orders. It's the nature of Black Ops."

Darcy looked at him, still unconvinced. "But... surely there'd be something... somewhere? These guys have people in the CIA, Washington DC Police. They have secret bases. They have cars and planes that are *literally* invisible. They can track every police car in Seattle. They can take down a commercial airliner and convince people the former Chief-of-Staff was behind it. Surely they'd know if you were dead or not. Especially as, from what you've told me, you've been working against them. Surely they'd know... *something* about you being alive."

Caleb thought it over. He knew she was right. The way she'd put it, it made no sense that these people, as powerful as they were, still had no idea where he was. "I get what you're saying. And there's only one person who can clear that up," Caleb said, moving over to the open hole in the floor of the cockpit. He looked down the opening. "How much longer Murph?" he asked.

"Not long, sir," Murphy's reply echoed up the short shaft. "These instructions seem to be accurate."

"Yeah, should be done in a minute or so," Dunleavy added.

Darcy could hear the pair working away down the bottom, their grunts and groans apparent.

After a few more moments, she heard a large thud.

"Everyone okay?" Caleb asked down the opening.

There was a brief silence, followed by the sound of Dunleavy groaning.

"Yeah, we'll be fine," Murphy said. "I just dropped the thingy."

"Right on my fucking foot," said a clearly unimpressed Dunleavy.

"Is it disabled?" Caleb asked, referring to the tracking device, and paying little heed to Dunleavy's discomfort.

"If it's not dead, sir, it's very unhappy," Murphy jokingly replied.

"Good. Now get up here and change our course."

Caleb stood back from the opening, allowing the others to ascend.

Dunleavy came out first, with Murphy following. In her arm she carried a clump of machinery about the size of a small football.

"That's the tracker?" Caleb asked.

"I think so," Murphy replied, "it's the thing that *whatshisname* pointed at in his instructions."

"Yeah... I think it worked." Dunleavy was looking at his screen. "I can't see us on here anymore."

Caleb walked to the screen, and confirmed the situation. They had vanished off the screen.

"Is there any other way to tell?" he asked Murphy.

Murphy thought. "He told us to turn south west, right?" she asked rhetorically. "If we do that, and we are being watched and tracked, then surely we'll see another plane turning around and following us. I mean, they all have weapons on them."

Caleb thought, and agreed with his Lieutenant. "So, turn us around then," he said.

Murphy again sat down in the control seat. After a few seconds of studying the screen, she pressed a few buttons. The plane once again banked right. After several seconds, they levelled out. "Done," she said. "We're on course for the Pacific. According to the speed of the plane, we should reach the ocean soon."

"Good," replied Caleb, and he turned back to Darcy's console. "Mike, come take a look at this," he said to Dunleavy.

Dunleavy limped over to the console, his foot still sore from the impact of the tracking device.

"Darcy, pull up what you had before." Darcy changed the screen back to the information about Caleb.

Caleb pointed at the last line. "Can you explain this?"

Dunleavy looked at the screen, "Oh. That?" he asked.

"Yes, that."

"It's standard procedure. When any member of the military becomes a part of black-ops, we need to erase them from the system. It's quite simple to put everything back."

Caleb was confused. "But there must be a trail somewhere" he asked.

Dunleavy thought about how to answer the question. "There really is nothing to worry about, Jackson. There is very little information out there about you. Your apartment is owned by the government, and you, apparently, have followed protocol perfectly. No social media, no credit cards. I meant what I said though. Once your career in the military – or at least where our work was concerned was finished – it all would have been restored."

Caleb looked even more concerned. "Mike. I don't mean to be rude. But do you seriously expect me to believe that? As far as I can tell, you are the *only* one who gave orders to me and my team." Caleb was struck by a thought. "Wait a sec. Murphy, Casey and the others?"

"Yes, I'm afraid they will find themselves equally hard to find." Dunleavy answered.

Caleb was getting annoyed. "So... what was going to happen? Say we didn't get the email from Paul, and none of this happened. I'd still be sitting on my ass, waiting for a call and basically not existing, right?"

Dunleavy paused. Perhaps now was the time to reveal a little more. "Actually, Caleb, I wasn't the only one making the decisions and coming up with the missions. There was another person. They would have helped you."

"You mean the President? He can't really help me much now, can he?"

Dunleavy looked at Caleb, ensuring he had his complete attention. "Caleb, I'm not talking about the President..."

◆ ◆ ◆

Robert stormed over to the terminal. "What do you mean?" he began as he approached, "What do you mean they've *disappeared*?"

"I... I... Um..." The nervous technician stuttered.

Robert, annoyed at the worker's fretful disposition, pulled the chair out. With nothing between him and the screen, Robert stared intently.

The technician was correct. The plane that had just left Seattle was nowhere to be seen.

Many thoughts were going through Robert's head, but the critical one needed to be answered. He spun around violently and faced the technician. "How did this happen?" he asked, his attempted calm demeanour betrayed by the anger in his eyes.

"Um..." The technician's nerves got the better of him again.

"I swear, if you say 'um' again, it will be the last stupid thing you say!" Robert said, no longer trying to hide his rage.

"U..." The technician quickly stopped himself. "There's only a couple of ways, sir."

"And they are?" Robert's little remaining patience was swiftly disappearing.

"They might have disabled the tracker."

"And the other way?"

"A malfunction."

Robert knew which answer was correct. After all that had happened in the past few days, he had personally ensured that every bit of equipment was tested, and retested before deployment.

He considered the Seattle mission to be the most important. He had sent his best team to clean it up, and he had ensured they used the flawless machine. It simply had to work. Now, it was just getting worse.

It was apparent that the people who were with Dunleavy were more of a threat than they'd anticipated. Trying to regain his composure, he turned to the screen. "Do we know where they are now?"

"No sir. They *were* coming here though."

Robert considered the situation. He knew there was only one course of action. "Get me Zone One," he ordered.

Without further instruction, a different technician pressed some buttons. "Anyone in particular sir?" she asked.

Robert merely looked at the woman. It was clear from his expression who the technician would be required to call. After some initial typing, she typed in the code 'Z-1-1'.

"On the main screen," Robert ordered, and the technician complied.

On a large screen at the end of the room, the image came to life. The display read that it was in the process of connecting to Z-1-1. It normally took around five seconds to connect, and Robert used the brief interlude to brace himself. He knew that James was not going to be happy. Robert had been given a seemingly simple task, one which he may have failed.

The major issue, as Robert saw it, was that he didn't really know if he *had* failed. As far as he knew, Dunleavy and his people were on the way to Minot as they spoke.

However, he feared the worst, and after all these years, he still remembered one of the mantra's that James had instilled in them all.

Preparing for the best will only make you complacent. Preparing for the worst will make you a survivor.

It was with these words in mind that he knew what he had to do.

James appeared on the screen. While still looking young, the stress of the recent events was starting to take its toll. The serum was effective in that it made a person appear ageless, but it couldn't hide emotion. "What is it Robert?" asked James. "Are they still on course?"

Robert paused, his emotions clearly visible as well.

James frowned. "What is it Robert? What's happened?"

Robert looked at the monitor, "Sir. I wish it was good news, but we really don't know where they are."

"What do you mean?" James asked, his stress increasing.

"Sir. They disappeared from our screens about two minutes ago. They were tracking well. Less than half an hour out. And then, before we knew what was happening, they vanished."

"Vanished?" James pondered the predicament. "We must assume they got to the tracker," James said, arriving at the same conclusion as the technicians had.

Robert had a horrifying thought. "Our thoughts exactly sir. Which obviously means…" Robert paused, the thought he'd just had was inconceivable. He had never even thought of the possibility before.

"Go on Robert." James asked.

"It means that we have a traitor in the ranks."

"What makes you say that, Robert?"

"The more I think on it, sir… The only way they could have turned off the tracker is if they were given instructions. It's well hidden in the bowels of the plane."

"They managed to do it on the 'Bat though… without help."

"Indeed sir. But the 'Bat is, well, less sophisticated. It's easier to control and manipulate, as more people would need to use it. We also made the tracker more accessible as a safety measure. If we were infiltrated, it would be easier to escape in the 'Bats." Robert paused at the thought. Maybe they would need to do just that.

"The planes," he continued, "on the other hand... Let's just say only a few select people knew about where the trackers were, and even fewer people could have got the information to Dunleavy."

James paced the room as Robert spoke. The thought of what he was saying had not crossed his mind for such a long time.

Such was the loyalty of those around him, the thought that someone would betray everything they had worked so hard for made him bubble with rage. "Who? Who did this?" he asked, no longer bothering to hide what he was feeling.

"I'm not sure sir. It was no one from here, sir. I can guarantee you that."

James, calmed slightly, but his rage was still somewhat apparent. "Are you absolutely sure, Robert? How can you guarantee it?"

Robert pondered the question. In reality, the only assurance he had that no one in Zone Three has crossed them was the inherent belief that they wouldn't. Now it was apparent that someone had, he couldn't be so sure. "I'll start an immediate investigation, sir."

"Good. Before you do, contact the other colony leaders. They need to be made aware of the situation. Make sure they begin investigations. This is the number one priority."

"Yes sir. Just one thing, though. What of Dunleavy and his people? They're still out there."

"All we can do is prepare, Robert. Keep your troops in place, and on high alert. Ensure they remain that way until this is over."

"Yes, sir. May I just ask one more question? Why do we care so much about these people? The attack earlier in Seattle... I assume it wasn't to be the only one. Once the others happen, won't the word of these people cease to matter?"

James stared hard at Robert in the monitor. "Robert. If these people find the whole truth, and they can prove it to the world, then we'll have fire reigning down on us from everywhere. No amount of serum, nor distraction, will be able to save us."

"Yes sir. I understand," Robert replied.

"Good. Now get to work."

Chapter Forty-Three

Casey appeared at the entrance of the cockpit, stopping just before the threshold. "You don't write. You don't call. How's a man supposed to know what's going on in your lives?" he asked.

Caleb glanced up at the Sergeant, turning his attention away from Dunleavy.

He was annoyed by the distraction, because he'd been about to hear more about the missions he'd been performing, and, more importantly, who was pulling the strings.

As a consummate professional though, Caleb returned to the mission at hand. "How are our guests, Sergeant?" he asked.

"They're okay, for now, sir," Casey replied. "When you turned the plane around, they both got a bit agitated."

"Both of them?" asked Caleb.

"Yes sir. The *amigo* looked really pissed off. Kinda why I came up. Wanted to find out for myself."

A short scream emanated from in the cargo hold.

Casey turned his attention to the bottom of the stairs. "What the fuck?" Casey shouted as he turned and moved swiftly down the stairs.

Caleb followed him.

As Casey neared the bottom of the stairs he raised his weapon, pointing it at Jacob. The man who had joined them in Seattle was standing over the limp body of the prisoner. Her body was still sitting upright, against the emergency door, her eyes wide open. Her head hung down and to the right, having been disconnected from the rest of her body.

Casey moved off the bottom of the stairs, his focus on the scene.

"What happened?" Caleb demanded.

Jacob, his hands raised, merely shrugged.

Casey moved closer to Jacob. "Answer the question." he said, less than a foot away from the man.

Again, Jacob remained silent.

Caleb went over and checked the woman's pulse, hoping she wasn't dead. Despite the fact that she'd been sent to kill him and his crew, Caleb knew there was no real point in killing her. She'd been no threat, bound to the exit handle.

Again, he asked Jacob the question. "What happened?"

Jacob rolled his eyes. "I did what I knew you wouldn't," he replied, condescension apparent in his tone.

Caleb straightened up, and took a threatening step towards him. "You killed an unarmed and bound prisoner. You killed someone who was no threat to you."

Jacob smiled. It was clear he felt little or no empathy with the others in the group, let alone the woman slumped against the wall. "You military guys. So full of fucking honour. I did what was necessary. The only reason I didn't do it sooner, was that she was a bargaining chip."

"A bargaining chip?" asked Casey.

"We could have used her to either get into where we were going, or to stop the people from shooting at us. As we've now pretty much turned around in the opposite direction, there was no further use for her. She would have slowed us down, and she would have become a threat."

Caleb listened to Jacob.

He was right, and Caleb knew it. It was true that Natalie was the enemy, and that she was waiting for an opportunity to attack.

Just like Matthew.

But that's what separated Caleb from Jacob. Caleb valued each person's life, and would only take it when absolutely necessary.

Jacob, on the other hand, seemed to *look* for opportunities to kill.

Caleb had met Jacob's type before. He'd seen it in the eyes of some of the recruits he trained with, and some of the commanding officers whose orders he'd followed. They were the people who joined the Marines for only one reason – to kill other people.

Caleb stared at Jacob. He realised that rather than being a person who couldn't be trusted, Jacob was actually a clear threat to the group. He also knew that if Jacob felt directly threatened, he would act.

For now, Caleb would need to play along. "Fair enough," Caleb said. "Lower your gun, Sergeant."

Casey turned to Caleb. "Sir?"

Caleb nodded back. "Our amigo is right. She would have killed us if she had the chance."

Casey lowered his gun.

"Glad you see it my way," said Jacob as he lowered his hands.

"Just… don't kill anyone again, without my say-so," Caleb told Jacob.

Jacob shrugged again. "No promises." He replied nonchalantly.

Caleb flicked his head over his shoulder, motioning for Casey to head back to the cockpit. Casey, looked at the Captain, confusion in his eyes.

"Casey," Caleb said as he put his hand on the Sergeant's shoulder. "We have work to do."

Casey inclined his head, and made his way up the stairs. Jacob followed, and Caleb waited for him to pass, and together they headed up the stairs, and back to the cockpit.

Thoughts of how to handle Jacob were flowing through Caleb's mind. His main concern was the safety of Darcy. In Caleb's mind, Darcy was invaluable. She had been his rock throughout the day, and had handled herself better in the situation than he'd ever thought. He was proud of her, and happy she was there, despite the circumstances.

However, one of Jacob's reasons for killing Natalie was that she would 'slow them down'. While Caleb knew that Darcy wouldn't impede them, he wondered how Jacob would view her presence.

"What happened?" Darcy asked, swivelling on her chair as Caleb entered the cockpit.

Casey was about to respond, but Caleb interrupted him. "Natalie is no longer with us," he said.

"What do you mean?" Darcy asked, her eyes widening.

"I took care of her," Jacob said, happy to brag about his work.

Caleb gave Jacob time to justify his actions, but after several seconds, Jacob didn't elaborate on his statement.

Caleb offered up the justification. "Jacob felt the need to take things into his own hands. Natalie is dead."

Darcy looked shocked.

"Now what was the point of that?" Murphy asked, confused by Jacob's thought pattern.

"She tried to kill us before, so Jacob thought it beneficial that we eliminate her as a threat," Caleb said

Darcy looked at Caleb, disgusted that he seemed to allow it so casually.

"I don't agree with what he did," Caleb continued, "But, well, we're *all* stuck in a pretty shitty situation."

Caleb then turned his attention to Jacob, and asserted his authority. "If I think you're going to betray us, or hurt *any* of us," he said, "I will not hesitate to take you out."

Caleb's steely eyes convinced Jacob. It was then Jacob remembered what William had said. The people he was with took out a squad of the very same skilled soldiers who took him down in Bogota.

They were to be feared.

Jacob's confident and brash demeanour disappeared, and was replaced with trepidation. Never had anyone spoken to him like that before and lived to tell the tale. But Caleb was different. Somehow, Jacob knew he couldn't beat him.

Darcy watched Caleb. While watching her partner, she felt almost guilty about her previous feelings. She realised Caleb had no choice but to *tolerate* what Jacob had done. After all, there were only six people in the world who she knew were working against the Colonials. And Darcy now knew that they had to let Jacob help.

Before Jacob could muster a retort, the screen in front of Darcy came to life. Again, it read that there was an incoming message. Again it was from Berlin.

As though asking her opinion, Caleb looked at Darcy.

She nodded back. It was time for a little faith. She remained in her seat, and Caleb stepped up beside her.

As he got into place, he nodded to her. With the nod, she pressed the 'Accept' button, and Isaac appeared on the screen again.

As both parties saw the other, Isaac smiled. "Good. You are alive, Ms. Chamberlain," Isaac began. Darcy was not surprised he knew her name. "I was beginning to worry for a moment."

At this statement, Darcy was taken aback. "Why worry?" she asked.

"We knew you were with him, but we were also unsure if you had survived," Isaac explained. "Besides, if it was only Mr. Dunleavy left..." his voice tapered off.

Caleb stared at the screen intently. "Why do you say that?" he asked, curious as to Isaac's doubts about Dunleavy.

Isaac peered around the screen, as if he was trying to ascertain if Dunleavy was still able to hear. "No reason... but let's just say you are much easier to trust, Ms. Chamberlain."

Caleb didn't want to push the issue, as he feared they may not be able to talk long. "Anyway, you called *us,* Isaac," he said, waiting for Isaac to give away the information.

"I'm sorry," Isaac began, "but who are you?"

Caleb was surprised. He thought they would have worked it out by now.

"Don't get me wrong..." Isaac continued, "We know your face. We've seen you and Ms. Chamberlain on various cameras throughout the day. And to be honest, it's got some of our people confused. They have found numerous video images of you, but cannot work out who you are."

Caleb didn't want to reveal who he was. Not out of fear, but he figured the less they knew, the better it would be for the group. "Who I am is not important," he said.

"Fair enough. But you need to understand that, as far as I can tell... you're the only people who can save them."

Caleb exchanged a look with Darcy. "Save who, exactly?" he asked Isaac.

Isaac paused, as though for some dramatic effect.

Eventually he replied.

"Everyone."

Chapter Forty-Four

The tension in the cockpit was palpable. None of them had expected that answer. For varying reasons, none of them were sure what Isaac was about to say.

Finally, Darcy asked the question on everyone's mind. "What do you mean, everyone?"

Isaac's demeanour changed. "The bad news is that..." he paused. "There are rumours floating around that Phase Three is coming. And—"

Caleb cut him off. "What do you mean *Phase Three?*" he asked.

"Yeah... can you start at the beginning?" asked Darcy.

Isaac shifted his gaze to Darcy. "Unfortunately, I fear I don't have much time. As soon as the tracker was disabled in your plane, they knew they had been betrayed."

"They?"

"The Governor and his deputies. It won't be long until they track this communication and find me, so I'm afraid I must be brief."

Darcy and Caleb held back, realising their questions would have to wait.

"I'll tell you as much as I can," Isaac began.

◆ ◆ ◆

Robert was pacing the room of the main observation chamber. He was still concerned, as he still had no idea where the leak was coming from.

"Sir, we have detected an unauthorised signal."

Robert spun around from the main screen, and faced the female technician. As per James's instructions, Robert had enacted the lockdown protocols. During the lockdown, only the most senior people at each colony would be able to communicate outside their colony. Further, the protocol dictated that the person who instituted the lockdown had to be made aware of any and all communications.

The only exception to this rule was James.

"Where is the signal originating from?"

The technician double checked the information on her screen. "It looks like it's coming from… Zone Four."

"And directed to?"

The technician followed the communication line. "It's somewhere off the west coast, sir. Just over the Pacific. The communication line, it's moving. My guess is at one of the Kites."

"The communication line… Does it show any signs of manipulation?" Robert asked, wanting to be sure before he brought any accusations down.

The technician pressed some icons, and she zoomed in on the communication line. She noticed a pattern that was unlike anything she had ever seen. "I'm not sure what they've done sir, but there's definitely something."

Robert knew they had found the traitor. "Record the conversation," he ordered, and then he turned to another technician. "Get me Berlin. I want to speak with John."

"Sir," the first technician said. "I can't record the conversation."

Robert looked at the screen. His request had been followed, and the main screen was lit up again. Within moments, John's young and portly face came into view on the screen. "Yes Robert. Have you found them?"

Robert looked at the screen, unsure if John was party to the deception. He had known the man for more years than he could remember, and his loyalty to the cause had never shown signs of abating. Robert's instincts told him he could still trust the man. "I have some bad news, John."

John grew cautious. "What is it Robert?"

"We have found a signal going to the plane. It's been tampered with."

"And where does the signal originate?"

Robert paused, taking a breath. "John, it seems you have a rat problem."

◆　◆　◆

"First I'll ask you a question," Isaac continued his explanation to the group. "How old do you think I am?"

The group just looked around at each other. The man in front of them looked to be about thirty years old.

"I was born on 31 March, 1924."

The group, apart from Dunleavy and Jacob, appeared stunned. The man on the screen in front of them was saying he was many years older than he appeared.

Sensing their shock, Isaac continued. "I was pulled out of a battle in 1942. I was badly injured, and barely able to breathe. A man, who called himself John, found me and took me to an underground hospital. Or at least, I thought it was a hospital. Turned out it was a large base. Since that day, I have only ever been outside on rare occasions."

"So… you're a prisoner?" asked Darcy.

"Not at all, Ms. Chamberlain. I stay of my own free will. After all, they are keeping me alive."

"You mean the serum?" asked Caleb.

"Yes. The serum has great, regenerative qualities. So much so, that it makes it nearly impossible to determine anyone's real age. Some of us have been here for more than one hundred years, some even longer. I was one of the last to arrive."

"So, when you talk about Phase 3…"

"I'll get to that," said Isaac, checking over his shoulder. "Phase One was the preparation. We built up our numbers, studied the world, and advanced whatever technology we could."

"But, how did you pay for it all? The materials, the money, the science. That doesn't come cheap," Darcy pointed out.

"To be honest, Ms. Chamberlain, I can't quite answer that. The leaders are very secretive about their actions, and for good reason, as I have recently discovered."

"And what reason is that?"

"Phase Two began yesterday. Before Phase Two, the serum needed to be injected on a regular basis. And, as I understood, the supply may have been running out. But they made a breakthrough, and have perfected a technique which allows for just one injection. Once a person goes through the process, they will never have to be injected again."

"How does it work?"

"I'm not sure. It's a naturally occurring liquid, discovered many years ago. They call it *The Source.*"

"The Source, did you say? Is that what you call the serum?"

"No. The Source is where the serum comes from."

"And where is that?"

Isaac stood up, spun around and walked towards the door. An alarm had begun to sound throughout the colony. They were coming. He hurried back to the monitor. "I'll send you the coordinates. They should appear on the navigation screen."

Dunleavy turned and looked at the navigation monitor. With a nod to Caleb, he acknowledged they were there.

"So, tell us about Phase Three," Caleb said to Isaac.

"Until yesterday, I was happy with the plan. But my leader let something slip yesterday, something that changed my mind."

"What is it?"

"Once everyone has the final serum injection, they will implement Phase Three." He shifted on his feet, looking deeply uncomfortable. "Phase Three – it's the extermination part of the plan. You see, once they all are basically immortal, they don't want to share the world with anyone. So, they are going to eradicate everyone else."

The horror of what the future may hold appeared on Darcy and Caleb's faces. "How much time do we have?" asked Caleb.

"We're okay for now, we've got at least a week."

"A week?"

"It takes time to implement Phase Two. We've got a lot of people to inject, and there is more than one colony. I know we're still working on getting the serum to all of *our* people."

"If it's going to take a week, aren't they taking a risk? With that much activity, someone is bound to —" Caleb stopped himself, mid-sentence. Now he understood the purpose of the attack on the plane. Surely by now, the United States government were looking for New Light, Dunleavy and anyone connected to the attack. And, with the help of the Colonials, the government would be more than occupied. He looked at Darcy. Apparently she had drawn the same conclusion.

"The attack in Seattle – all those people – dead. That was just a *distraction*?" she asked.

"Yes," Isaac replied.

"But that wouldn't be enough," Dunleavy interjected. "Sure, the US and possibly China would be distracted. But you're talking a global enterprise. What about Europe? Africa? The Middle East? Surely someone there would take notice? For fuck's sake, the plan is still going to attract attention. Shit, people are going to find out eventually! You can't deceive governments forever, especially now."

"That is why you must act fast," continued Isaac. "You are correct that their governments would soon turn their attention in the right direction. That is why I fear that Seattle was just the beginning. They will need to ensure distractions are prevalent until Phase Three."

Caleb looked at Dunleavy, who was standing there, shaking his head.

"So, what do you propose?" Caleb asked, returning his gaze to the screen.

"You must destroy The Source."

"How will that help?" asked Darcy.

"They need everyone they have recruited. Without the Source, they cannot create the serum, and the people they recruited will turn on them. They won't have the power to carry out their objectives."

"Do you know how they intend to kill everyone?"

"The only thing that may help is a name. Nightfall."

"What is Nightfall??"

As Darcy spoke, the door behind Isaac flew open. Several people, dressed in a similar style to Natalie, burst through the door. Isaac quickly pressed a button on the screen, and his image vanished.

For a moment, the group was stunned by what had just happened. They needed time to take in the information. They already knew they were part of something important. But the magnitude of that had just begun to sink in.

They lapsed into silence, trying to come to terms with the situation.

Casey was the first to react. "So, where are we goin'?" he asked the rest.

Caleb looked towards the navigation monitor, and saw that Murphy was already in place.

"Wherever it is, Captain, we'll be there in just over nineteen hours," she said.

Caleb straightened up, and moved towards where Murphy was sitting. "Nineteen? I thought this thing was fast?" he asked the Lieutenant.

"Sir, it is," she replied, "but I've been watching the power output compared to fuel consumption. It takes an extraordinary amount of fuel to go at the speed we were travelling to Minot. I've slowed us down to make sure we have enough fuel for the journey. Once I know the destination, I'll work it so we have enough fuel, and we still get there as fast as possible."

"Okay then," Caleb said, once again impressed with his Lieutenant's logic.

He looked at the map, and was disappointed to see their final destination wasn't apparent. He took the seat, and examined the screen. Only Dunleavy had used the console thus far, and he was keen to learn as much as he could. He quickly found the zoom mechanism, and used it to get a better picture of their journey.

The initial image showed an area off the coast of the United States. As the icon of the plane had disappeared, it was difficult to know their exact location.

Murphy looked over Caleb's shoulder, and pointed at the map. "By my reckoning, this is where we are, and this is our course," Murphy said as she tracked her finger towards the bottom left of the screen.

Each time she reached the edge, Caleb scrolled further in the south west direction. The route she was tracking would take them past Hawaii, Samoa, Fiji and New Caledonia.

Eventually, a large island came into view on the screen. Caleb continued to scroll across the page, and there it was. The same yellow circle they seen just outside of Minot appeared again. This time, it had the number "One" inside.

"So," Darcy asked. "Where're we going?"

Caleb looked up. Such had been the events of the day, he'd barely remembered that it was an email from Paul which had set them on this path. It felt like destiny that their path would eventually lead them to the place all this had first started.

"Looks like we're going to find out what happened to Paul," he said to Darcy.

"Paul... geez, I'd almost forgotten," said Darcy. "So I guess we're heading to—"

Caleb interrupted before she could finish. "That's right, babe. We're going to Australia."

Chapter Forty-Five

Isaac slumped back in the chair, a fearful look in his eye as he waited. While the guards had broken in and stopped him, he knew they wouldn't do anything without John's direct orders.

While he waited, he thought of the people on the plane. He thought of all the people that he, through his assistance to the cause, was about to hurt.

Isaac knew it had only been a few minutes, but during those minutes, time seemed to stand still. He knew that even the best outcome would mean his life would change forever. Just the previous day, he'd dreamt of the things he might still accomplish in his long life. He had thought of the places he could see, the people he could meet, and the women he could fall in love with.

None of that would now come to be.

Eventually, his former friend and mentor entered the room. He had an expression on his face that Isaac had never seen before. It wasn't anger, nor hurt.

It was embarrassment.

"How could you do this to me?" John asked, as he strode across to Isaac's chair.

Isaac steeled his eyes. The embarrassment on Johns face made him angry. His mentor obviously spared no thought for all the people whose lives he was about to have a hand in destroying.

"How can you do what you are going to do?" Isaac retorted.

The question seemed to confuse John. "How can I do it?" he asked. "I thought you, of all people, would understand! You fought alongside people who wanted to exterminate a whole race. I was sure you would understand! That's why I told you. Obviously, I was wrong."

"Fought alongside them? John, I did not choose to fight for the Nazis! I was forced to! And, if you'll recall, I didn't fight all that well. Did it ever cross your mind that my heart wasn't in it? After all, I thought that was why you recruited me."

"Don't be so foolish. Where do you think all these people came from? You were just one of the last among many. How dare you think that it is up to you to decide the future of all these people? People you have lived with, for the last seventy years?"

Isaac realised that reasoning with John was fruitless, and decided to bite his tongue. If he was going to die, he was going to do it in a dignified manner.

"Nothing more to say?" asked John.

Isaac just stared at him, his disgust clearly visible. Disgust at John for wanting the deaths of so many people, and disgust at himself for allowing it to get this far.

"I know you probably won't answer this question. But where are they?" John asked.

"Who?" Isaac responded petulantly.

John chuckled. Isaac found the sound deeply disturbing. "It's not going to matter," said John, "I only asked, in the hope that *you* could be saved."

John turned, and indicated to one of the guards to approach. The man quickly came to stand next to John, and held out his pistol. John grabbed the weapon, and pointed it at Isaac. "I had such high hopes for you," he said, his pudgy fingers barely able to fit inside the trigger-guard.

Isaac stared at John, resigned to his fate. "See you in the next life," Isaac said tiredly, using the salutation he'd been taught, and had used for over seven decades.

"No, Isaac... you won't," replied John. He pulled the trigger, and Isaac slumped lifelessly in the chair.

◆ ◆ ◆

Caleb looked at each of the members of his group. Every one of them bore their own scars from the preceding day's events. Some of the scars were visible, like Dunleavy's nose, or Casey's cheek. The others were not so visible.

Caleb could only think of Darcy, and how much she'd had to endure that day. He could hardly imagine how much she had been affected. Less than forty-eight hours earlier, she'd been just a normal woman, an everyday reporter. A person who, like ninety-nine percent of the world's population, had been working towards her life's goals.

In such a short time, Darcy had become absorbed a world that they didn't think could even exist.

Thinking about it, Caleb realised that he too had been irrevocably changed in the past few days. While he knew that *something* was not quite right with the world, he'd never thought it would come to the situation they now faced - the fact that they might be within days of the world as they knew it coming to an end.

To a certain extent though, Caleb realised, it already had.

As the flight progressed, he was getting regular updates from Murphy. She'd done the required calculations, and at the last check, there were just over fifteen hours of travel remaining. He still found it remarkable that a journey that would normally take longer, and require multiple stopovers, would be over so soon.

He contemplated their next move and weighed up the options available to them. They really had no idea of what they would be facing when they got to Australia.

The first step would be for them to all rest and recuperate. There was nothing further they could do at this particular point in time and most of them were running on fumes. "Listen up," Caleb said, "We really don't know what we're getting into, but we do have some time between now and when we arrive. What we all need right now is some rest. Murphy, Casey and Dunleavy; you guys go first. Jacob, Darcy and I will take first watch."

Caleb had split the groups up in this manner purposely. He'd kept Darcy in his group because her presence alongside him was no longer something he merely desired. Over the past day or so, Darcy's presence had become something he *needed*.

Darcy felt the same; she needed to be near Caleb. Not only was he providing protection, but he was essentially, the only part of her previous life that she still recognised. Her previous life no longer existed, and the only lasting remnant of that life she still had, was Caleb.

Caleb had decided to keep Jacob in his group for another reason. He absolutely didn't trust him, and he wanted to keep him in his sights at all times. He couldn't do that effectively if he was asleep while Jacob was awake.

"Yes, sir," Murphy and Casey replied in unison, grateful to be getting some sleep. Dunleavy merely grunted, the previous day sapping his waning energy.

"I saw some bunks in the cargo area," said Casey.

"Good," Caleb replied, "Head off. I'll come down and wake you in six hours." The trio left the cockpit, and headed down the stairs.

Jacob glanced around the room at the others. He was no idiot. He knew exactly why Caleb had kept him in his group. "If you're determined to keep an eye on me, at least let me help." Jacob said.

Caleb thought about it for a few seconds. While he didn't trust Jacob, he suspected the man could still prove useful. Through Caleb's experience, trained, efficient killers were effective, particularly in his line of work. It wasn't Jacob's skills he doubted, but his motivations. Until he understood what they were, he couldn't assess how big a threat Jacob was to the group. "Looks like this thing is pretty much flying itself," Caleb said. "Why don't you and I have a little talk?"

"Talk?" Jacob asked.

"Yeah. I need to figure you out, Jacob," Caleb answered.

Jacob smirked. "Figure me out?" The two men sat down together, Caleb in front of the navigation screen, Jacob in front of Operations. Darcy remained at the Communication screen, offering Caleb a tight smile.

"I'll keep working on this," Darcy said.

"Thanks, Darc. Anything you find that you think is important, let me know."

Darcy nodded, and began tapping away on the screen, while Caleb turned his attention back to Jacob. "How did you meet Dunleavy?"

Jacob took a second or two to think before he responded. While the question in itself was a simple one, the course of action regarding its answer wasn't. He wasn't sure how much information he wanted to give away at this point in time. But he also figured that Caleb, if he was as good as Jacob suspected he was, would be able to ascertain whether or not he was being deceptive with his responses. He needed to tread cautiously.

Jacob came to a realization. The man sitting opposite him was, in fact, the only real hope he had of achieving his goal –immortality. Considering his options, Jacob decided to tell him everything. "It all started in Bogota," he replied.

"Colombia?" Caleb asked.

"No, Bogota, Canada – of course Colombia."

Jacob told the story of how he and Dunleavy had met. How he'd met William, and how Dunleavy had figured out that he could be used to gather more information on the Colonials. He told Caleb about the various missions he carried out for Dunleavy. Mostly, they were along the same lines as the missions Caleb and his team – information gathering. But, every once in a while, Dunleavy had given him other, more specialised missions. These missions had involved the killing of certain people.

"Did Dunleavy ever mention why?" Caleb asked. "Why were those people taken out and not others?"

"He never said. And frankly, I didn't ask," Jacob replied. "As long as the cash was paid, I did what I was asked to do. Now, knowing what we do, it's a fair assumption to believe that they were Colonial operatives."

"What makes you say that?"

"They were all mid to high level intelligence officers. While Dunleavy never gave me too much information, he did find it necessary to share that much. And, from what he and Isaac have said…" Jacob's voice tapered off.

Caleb thought about what Jacob was inferring. Indeed, he had to admit, the guy seemed to have drawn the correct conclusion. "What happened after Dunleavy resigned as Chief-of-staff?"

"Nothing. I just stopped getting the phone calls."

Caleb was satisfied Jacob was telling the truth, but he still had some information he needed, though. "Okay, going back to Bogota," he began, "you said you met with one of the Colonials?"

"Yeah. William," Jacob replied.

"This… William? Have you had much contact with him? What did he ask you to do?"

"I had even less contact with him than I did with Dunleavy. William didn't ask me to go on missions. He just asked me to keep him up to date with how much Dunleavy knew."

"And did you?"

Jacob smirked, crossing his arms. "Of course I did. The guy was offering something more than anyone else ever had. You see, Captain, money I could get easily enough. But to live forever – that was an opportunity I couldn't let go."

Caleb found himself disturbed by Jacob's answer. "So you were playing both sides then?" he asked, annoyance in his voice.

Jacob scoffed. "You still don't get it, do you?"

"Apparently not."

"I'm not on *your* side. I'm not on Dunleavy's side. I'm not on the Colonials side. There's only one person whose side I'm on."

"And that's *you,* I'm guessing."

"Damn straight. I've been fucked over too many times. I won't let it happen again."

Caleb glanced over at Darcy. She'd turned to face the men, their conversation having caught her attention.

"So how do you expect us to trust you?" Caleb asked.

Jacob smiled, and a small chuckle escaped. "I don't need you to *trust* me," he replied. "We don't need to *trust* each other. All you need to understand is that, at the moment, we have a mutually beneficial relationship. You help me, and I'll help you."

"What makes you think we need you?" Darcy asked.

"Well, Ms. Chamberlain. What your partner has undoubtedly figured out by now is that once we get to wherever it is we're going... the people there are not going to be happy to see us. In fact, they might even be waiting for us. Your boyfriend here, he knows that having me with you increases your odds of surviving. Especially considering what I know."

Darcy looked at Caleb. Judging by his expression, he agreed with what Jacob had said.

"But you know what?" Jacob said. "Your partner and I are a lot alike. We think alike. You see, Caleb here is a killer. He could kill me now if he thought it was a good idea, and take his chances without my help."

Caleb shot his gaze back onto Jacob. His eyes were brimming with anger. "Don't you dare think for one second that we're anything alike," Caleb said, his voice menacingly quiet. "I wouldn't kill anyone like you did to the prisoner. She wasn't an immediate threat. And how you got the car you drove to Seattle. Let me guess, you picked a weak target, followed them to their car, snuck up and killed them from behind."

Jacob's face dropped, confirming Caleb's assumption.

"Yeah, I thought so. You're an efficient killer, I'll give you that. But there's something you should never forget – so am I. But there's one main difference between you and me. Do you know what that is?"

"What's that the difference?" Jacob asked, and Caleb detected a tinge of anger colouring his voice.

Caleb leaned closer to him, keeping his voice low and cold. "If I was going to stab you, it would be done from the front."

Jacob seethed at the snide remark. He'd thought they were finally beginning to relate to one another. It had been so long since he had found

anyone he could consider a kindred spirit. He was angry and disappointed to discover Caleb was not that person.

Caleb sat for a moment, letting his last words sink in. "You want to
earn my trust? You want to be part of this team?" he asked.

Jacob scoffed again. "Not really," he replied bluntly.

"Do you want our help?" Caleb asked.

Jacob didn't offer a response. He didn't *want* Caleb's help – he *needed* it.

"In that case," Caleb said, fully aware of what Jacob would be thinking, "You'll have to help us."

"How?"

"I need to know what we're up against. There must be some schematics of the colony. There has to be some record of what the design of
each place is like."

Jacob looked confused. "I wouldn't have a clue. What about the
weapons systems of the plane? I can help there," he replied

"No. You've seen these guys up close, you probably know more
about them than anyone else on this plane. I want you to take a look
and find whatever you can." Caleb continued to push this aspect of
the plan to Jacob, though he had to admit it was difficult to justify. He
knew that Jacob would have been more than proficient working with
the weapons on the plane, but to expose him to them might prove too
risky.

Jacob decided to do as he was told. If, by chance, he happened to
stumble upon any information he could use to his advantage, he would
decide then whether he would share it or not. "Okay. I guess you want a
full report, Captain?"

"I would appreciate one. After all, we're probably going to base an
attack plan on the information you provide, so…"

Jacob was surprised. Caleb really was placing some responsibility on
his shoulders.

"Consider this your opportunity to show us what you can bring to the
table. If we like what we see, then I'll feel a lot better about bringing you
along."

"Okay then," Jacob agreed. Jacob turned his attention to the screen. He began tentatively pushing buttons, trying to find any information about the Colonials that would meet Caleb's requirements.

Leaving Jacob to work, Caleb got up and went over to sit beside Darcy.

She leaned over, and whispered to him. "Are you sure we can trust him?"

Caleb looked across at Jacob, then back at Darcy. "We don't really have a choice right now."

Darcy had seen enough that day to make her believe Caleb knew what he was doing. Caleb could protect them. "While you two were having your little chat, something flashed up on the screen," Darcy said, her eyes filling with sadness.

"What was it, babe?" Caleb was concerned by the unhappiness he saw in her eyes.

She indicated the screen, and Caleb turned his attention to what was written on the monitor.

The reason for Darcy's sadness became apparent.

On the screen, the message continued to flash. "The attack in Zone Five has been completed."

Chapter Forty-Six

Caleb stared at the screen in disbelief. Not long ago, they'd been witness to the attack on the plane in Seattle. Now, there were reports coming through the Colonials system that a second attack had been carried out.

"It came up when I was looking for information about Seattle," Darcy explained.

Caleb was unsure where to start, so many questions were filling his mind. The obvious one came to mind. "Where is Zone Five?" he asked, not really expecting Darcy to know the answer.

She turned off the flashing message, and once again opened the search program, typing in 'Zone 5'.

Within seconds, a map had sprung up on the screen. It featured a picture of the south of Europe. The map began at Italy, and covered countries across the southern part of Europe – Croatia, Albania, Serbia, and Bulgaria. It stretched to the western border of Turkey.

"Where exactly did the attack occur?" Caleb asked.

Darcy pulled up another screen. The title mentioned news stories from Italy. Darcy clicked on the title, and a summary came up. "Reads like an internet search, but it's much more advanced. It looks as if they can get all the information from various websites and news outlets, and cut them down to only the pertinent details." Darcy scanned the page, and found what they were looking for. "Holy shit."

Caleb had been paying close attention to the screen and read the information for himself. *"Multiple explosions have occurred in an area of central Rome. As many as eight separate explosions have been reported. The eighth and largest of the explosions will be heard around the world. As far as we can ascertain, while not nuclear, the blasts held such force they were felt from many miles away."*

There was another link in the bottom of the entry, which Darcy clicked on. It opened up a video.

They saw a reporter, standing in what looked like a warzone.

"Just five hundred yards from me is where the Vatican used to stand. The eighth and final blast was detonated there. No longer are the large buildings, nor the wall that separates the Sovereign nation from the rest of the city. Preliminary reports suggest that there were in excess of five thousand people in the vicinity of the last bomb. At this stage, it is too early to tell, but word from the Ministero della Difesa, the Italian Defence Ministry, suggests that more than one hundred thousand people may have been killed or injured in the attacks. We will bring you more information as it comes to hand."

The video ended and Caleb and Darcy continued to stare at the screen in shock.

Darcy clicked back to the previous screen. There was a new video link, which she opened. The same anchor-woman they'd seen earlier in the Seattle motel appeared on the screen.

"News is coming in confirming that after the attack earlier today in Seattle, there has been a further suspected terror attack in Italy. Once again, the reports are coming through..."

The anchor stopped, put a hand to her ear, and listened to an off-screen producer.

"Word has come through that the terrorist group, New Light, led by former Chief-of-Staff Michael Dunleavy, is claiming responsibility for this attack. In several communications to the Italian Media, the terrorist group has claimed responsibility for both the Seattle and Rome attacks. At this stage, there is no further confirmed information. Stay with us, and we will keep you updated on this... horrific attack."

Caleb switched off the video, disgusted by what he'd seen.

"So many people," Darcy said, a tear flowing down her cheek.

Caleb was equally saddened. Never in his career had he heard of such numbers being killed. Those kind of numbers only really happened during a long-term military engagement. They weren't supposed to happen in a Seattle airport, or the Italian capital. "We need to keep moving, Darc," he said, drawing in a deep breath to centre himself on the task at hand.

"I know," she replied in a little voice.

"Let's turn that off. If we look at the timeline... it may be sometime before the next attack."

"We have to stop it, Caleb. All those people died! We have to stop them." Darcy was visibly trying to fight back her anger.

"There's nothing we can do," he admitted.

"Bullshit. We have to get word out. We have to tell people that 'New Light' is not behind this. We have to tell *someone*."

"Tell them what, babe?" Caleb asked. "Tell them that we're with the most sought after terror suspect in modern history, and we're on our way to stop a group of immortal people from destroying the world?"

Darcy just stared at him. "We have to do... something," she said forlornly, and Caleb's heart ached for her.

"Babe, we *are* doing it," Caleb replied, trying to sound reassuring. "We're the only ones who know the truth. We'll stay the course, and hopefully stop them in Australia."

Darcy remained quiet, but she seemed somehow reassured by what Caleb was saying.

"We need to focus on the task. We need to find out as much as we can."

Darcy straightened up in her chair and turned her attention back to the screen.

"Okay. What do you want me to look for?"

Caleb thought on the question. "Try starting at the top," he said. "Type in 'Zone One' and let's see what we can figure out."

♦ ♦ ♦

William waited patiently by the door thinking about his latest instructions. For many years, William had worked hard to get into the position he was now in. He'd followed his orders with diligence, and performed the tasks in the best way he could.

He was determined that with his latest orders, he wouldn't let his leader down. It was too important, and he would be assuring his permanent place not only in the future, but as possibly the right-hand-man to the leader of the future.

After hearing what James had wanted, William had worked diligently to gather the information he required. He was eager to present the information and impress.

"William, come in," James called from his office.

William entered the room, and found James sitting at his desk, staring intently at the communications monitor. Noticing William's arrival, James waved him over, beckoning him to sit opposite him.

He was pleased to notice James' mood had improved since their last encounter. During their last discussion, James had told William of their problem, and the fact they'd been unable to maintain contact with the plane. As it was an imminent threat, William had shared James' concerns.

While William patiently waited, James completed his conversation with someone on the monitor. "Joseph, that's great news," he said. "You have excelled yourself, once again. Zone Five should be proud of what you have achieved."

"Indeed, my friend," a youthful Russian accent boomed from the screen. "We are very proud. If only we could tell the entire colony, then we could celebrate together. It's a shame about the people we lost, though. They would have made good colonists."

"Ah," said James, "it is a burden we must keep to ourselves, I'm afraid."

"I understand," Joseph said.

William got the impression however, that Joseph was not completely convinced by his own words.

"On a different matter. How are things progressing with the serum? How close are you?"

"Progress is on course. We're about half-way through."

"Good. Keep it up."

"Will do, sir."

James pushed a button on the monitor, and the screen went blank.

"All went well then, I take it?" asked William, inclining his head towards the monitor.

"Indeed," replied James, not wanting to give away too much information. Not out of desire to hide things from his potential protégé, but rather to ensure that he was not lumbered with distractions.

The pause lasted for longer than either man was comfortable with.

To break the silence, William spoke up.

"I've done some thinking about what you asked," William announced.

James raised his eyebrows, silently urging William to continue.

"There must be more than a couple of people on the plane. At the very least, we have Dunleavy and Ms. Chamberlain. The fact that they haven't arrived at the Zone Three colony makes me think anyone *we* have on board is either dead, or incapacitated."

"Go on," James responded.

"We can assume that neither Ms. Chamberlain, nor Dunleavy are capable of taking out one of our Alpha teams. Thus, we have to believe they have help."

"And who do you think that would be?" James asked, hoping to receive the right answer.

"I don't know, sir," William admitted, shifting uncomfortably on his chair.

"You don't know?" James asked, allowing his annoyance to show. "I must say I'm disappointed, William."

William searched for the words which would save his reputation. "That is to say, I don't know *exactly* who they are. What I do know, is that they've appeared in a variety of different locations under our control." William stood, and walked around the desk, leaning over to reactivate James' screen. He pressed a few buttons, and opened up a file entitled 'Infiltrators'.

"Talk me through it, William," said James.

"You've probably heard about the break-in's we've been experiencing for the past few years or so?" William began. "This is all the information we have collected on the perpetrators. There are some pictures, and some video footage. Now, the pictures we have are only fleeting glimpses, as they *usually* wore face masks to disguise their identities. However, we have managed to capture a few images of faces."

William pulled up several shots. They had obviously been taken from a distance, and the faces weren't discernible. "As you can see, they aren't a lot of help, really, and we can only get a basic idea from each."

"How does this help? We already knew they existed? Just the mere fact that computers were being stolen was enough of an insight," James grumbled.

"Agreed. But what we can now do is compare the pictures we have, to those we got from the plane. In the brief window we had, we were able to pick up these five images."

William retrieved a picture file revealing a shot of the hangar in Seattle. In the picture were Caleb, Darcy, Dunleavy, Jacob and Casey.

"Are you saying these are the same people? Are these the people who have been after us?"

"I think so, sir. As you can see, there's our old friend Dunleavy. And Jacob."

"Jacob? The agent?"

"Yes, sir. As we discussed, he's riding along with them, waiting for his opportunity to act. But it seems he may have turned against us."

"What makes you say that?"

"The fact that the others are still alive."

"I knew he would betray us, as soon as he got the chance."

"He did prove useful for a time." William paused. "But, now his fate will be shared with his new comrades."

James nodded in affirmation, happy with William's assessment.

"What of the others? I see Ms. Chamberlain. The other men. Who are they?

"Now, I've done an image search on them, and there is nothing."

James looked bemused. "What do you mean *nothing*?" he asked.

"I mean, sir, it is as though they don't exist. There is nothing from the military, Homeland Security, FBI, Pentagon, Mi6, Mossad... or any other agency we have someone in. There is no trace of them. They're ghosts."

"What about this one?" James asked, referring to a sixth figure.

"Not sure, sir. They didn't even raise their head while they made their way toward the back. I figured they were the one who accessed the camera control and switched it off?"

"On purpose?"

"Hard to say, sir. It would take some pretty amazing luck to accidently find the panel that controls the manual override."

James looked at the image in front of him, happy with William's work. Unfortunately, it was only partially complete. "Have you had the serum yet?" James asked William.

"Yes sir. About an hour ago."

"Feeling okay? I know I was a bit groggy after I received mine."

William was feeling the aftermath of the serum. "I'll be fine sir. I just need to focus on something."

"Very well. I need your help, now more than ever, William."

William was encouraged by the statement. The fact that he was contributing to the plan was reward enough, but to have James ask him again for personal assistance was a big step towards where William wanted to be. "Anything for the cause, sir," he replied, hardly able to contain his pride.

James got up from his chair. "I'm not sure what you know. God knows, this kind of thing could easily find its way down the grapevine," James said as he walked around the desk.

"Not sure what you're referring to, sir," William replied.

"What do you know about the events out of Berlin?"

William lifted an eyebrow. "Nothing, sir."

"Good. What I'm about to tell you is of the utmost secrecy. Even more so than the less... *attractive* parts of Phase Three."

William knew what that meant. He'd been aware of the details of Phase Three for some time. At first, he had been taken aback by the prospect of such a huge loss of life, but in the end, he'd come to believe it was the right decision. William had always suspected that the world was travelling a path that could only be disastrous in the long term, and it needed to be stopped. "I understand, sir."

James began to tell William about Isaac's apparent betrayal, and the harsh nature with which John had dealt with the situation.

William took it all in. He wasn't surprised that someone would betray them. Someone he considered weak. "It's for the best, sir. I think we need to weed out those who may come up against us. Better that it happens now, rather than during or after Phase Three. You need people around you who you can trust completely."

"I couldn't agree more," James said with a smile, "and the fact that you can see a positive is why I've always kept a close eye on you, William."

"Thank you, sir."

"I am also a man who sees the positives in any situation. While the traitor did give away our position to Dunleavy and his people, he also made the mistake of giving us *their* position. From where they were when we lost them, compared to where they were when the traitor contacted them, we've been able to identify where they are going."

William looked at his leader, glad they could find their targets. "And, where is that sir?" William asked.

"William. Prepare for company. We're going to have some guests."

Chapter Forty-Seven

"Wakey up, Lieutenant," Caleb said to his team member.

The time had come for a changeover, much to Darcy's relief. For the majority of the time, Caleb and Darcy had painstakingly searched the Kites system for more information regarding their enemy.

Unfortunately, most of the information was unavailable, requiring something referred to as *Endeavour Access Only*. There was no indication as to what *that* even meant. Although it had revealed something very important to Caleb, and he was able to verify some of the things Isaac had referred to earlier.

To Caleb, it confirmed that the Colonials had a very strict hierarchy, and that those at the top knew a lot more than they were willing to share with the people who followed them. This gave Caleb an idea on how to attack them, and how he could expose them.

He'd walked towards the end of the cargo bay, and approached the pods on the side of the area. Two of the pods had been opened. Upon closer inspection, each pod revealed a sleeping area. The available room was akin to that on a submarine for the enlisted. While it wasn't spacious, a person could easily get a few hours' sleep. Or even two people could, as Murphy and Casey had apparently elected to share a pod.

"Yes, sir, just five more minutes", Murphy muttered; clearly not ready to get up.

"Up and at 'em Marine," ordered Caleb.

"C'mon Dad, just five more minutes. I don't wanna go to school today," Casey joked.

Caleb walked away, knowing they would be up by the time he returned.

Darcy was standing at the third pod, opening the door. She was exhausted, and understandably so. It had been nearly a day and a half since they had last slept. Even Caleb was feeling the pressure.

Dunleavy was in the adjacent pod. Before Caleb reached him, he saw two legs swinging over the side. "What did you find out?" he asked, his voice raspy.

"Not much," Caleb replied. "We've found out some thing's that will help us out, but not much about the Colonials. All that stuff is buried pretty deep."

Dunleavy exited his pod, his clothes dishevelled. "Let's see if we have better luck, Captain," said Murphy as she appeared from her pod, yawning.

"My thoughts exactly," replied Caleb.

Without missing a beat, his team headed up to the cockpit, ready to take over.

"Anything in particular, sir?" Murphy asked from the top of the stairs.

"Find out what you can. Anything at all will help at this stage," he said, the acoustics of the cargo bay proving useful to carry his voice.

Stepping into the pod Darcy had reserved, he turned and shouted up to the cockpit. "Oh... and one more thing, Murph."

"What's that, sir?" she shouted back.

"Try not to let us fall out of the sky today."

"No promises, sir," she retorted.

Jacob moved towards the pod Dunleavy had just exited.

As he was about to enter, Caleb caught his gaze. Caleb still didn't trust him, and he was hoping that the earlier conversation they'd had was still ringing in his ears.

"Don't you worry your pretty little head, Captain." Jacob said, "I'm too fucking tired to hurt anyone." He entered the pod, and shut the door.

"Casey..." Caleb yelled from the bay.

"Sir?" Casey replied as he stood at the entry to the cockpit.

"Keep an eye down here." Caleb ordered, wanting an extra layer of protection from Jacob.

"Read my mind sir." Casey replied.

Caleb entered the pod, and Darcy stood to one side. Better he get in first, considering they will be facing out into the cargo bay.

It was a cosy fit, his large frame barely able to move. It was the first item in the seemingly vast list of technological marvels of the Colonials that he'd been less-than-impressed with.

On the other hand, at least they thought to make the pods. In a normal cargo plane, it was somewhat difficult to get any kind of effective sleep. It was a case of sleep where you sat. Combined with the bumpy ride, the pod looked very appealing.

Caleb turned in the pod, giving Darcy room to get in. Turning his frame was hard work, and he got wedged in.

"Shall we use the car, babe?" she suggested with a knowing smile.

Caleb felt a bit foolish for not thinking of it himself. While not purpose built, the 'Bat would be easier for them to share.

As he rolled back over and shunted out of the pod, Darcy had already opened the door of the SUV. After a short examination, she found a switch.

As indicated, the chairs lowered in the back section, allowing plenty of room for both of them to lie down. She got in the car, and moved over to the far side. Caleb, adjusting for the strain it took exiting to pod, moved in alongside her.

Darcy was lying facing the right side of the car, her legs curled into the foetal position. Caleb moved behind her, his body moulding to hers. He put his right arm under her, and she elevated her body to allow him to do so. He wrapped his left arm around her, and embraced her.

Despite it all, Darcy finally felt safe. When Caleb wrapped his arms around her, she let out a soft moan, remembering how nice and content her life had been only two days ago.

Still, she couldn't completely forget where they were, and how worried she was. She couldn't help but think of the hundreds, potentially thousands, of people who had lost their lives.

"Caleb," she asked over her shoulder. "Tell me we're going to be okay."

Caleb held his partner tightly. He shared her emotions. He too was feeling the loss of so many people. He was especially burdened, as it was the first time all day that he'd been able to lie quietly, and think about the events which had led them to this point.

"Of course we are, babe," he replied. "I've been in trickier situations than this."

Darcy knew he was lying, but appreciated what he was trying to do.

"Time to go to sleep," Caleb continued, "Something tells me we've got a big day ahead of us."

"I love you," she said, a quiver of emotion in her voice.

"I love you, too."

Darcy closed her eyes, fatigue finally catching up to her.

Caleb was left alone with his thoughts. The events of the day kept repeating through his mind. The main thing which bothered him was the events at the airport. The whole time they'd been with Matthew, Caleb had been convinced that Matthew was not a threat.

Never in Caleb's career had he been so blind-sided. He'd felt sympathy for Matthew. He'd felt sorry for the young man. He thought he was just a kid who had made some bad choices.

In the past, Caleb had met several undesirable people. From members of the Taliban, to Somali gangsters, to Nazi sympathisers in London, Caleb had seen his fair share.

Every once in a while, he would need to take prisoners. They would range from those who were zealots, people committed to their cause, to those who were only there for fear of death. Over time, Caleb figured he had learned the difference between the people. He also felt he knew how to detect when people were deceiving him.

Matthew had proved an enigma. Caleb had thought he had worked him out, and in a bizarre way, even trusted him not to betray them. He cursed himself for how arrogant he'd been.

His overconfidence had contributed to the plane being brought down. It had caused the deaths of so many people.

The more he thought on it, one thing became painfully obvious – the Colonials were unlike any enemy he'd encountered before. Lying there with Darcy, Caleb made a vow to himself. The vow was a simple one, but he would need it in order to continue his mission. He vowed to make good on his failure. He vowed to make them pay for what they'd done.

The vow brought a quiet serenity to Caleb. He now had an emotive purpose to stop the Colonials. The serenity combined with his fatigue, and Caleb drifted off to sleep, Darcy tucked tightly in his arms.

Chapter Forty-Eight

William had grown frustrated with his task. After more than five hours of searching, he couldn't find anything.

After his conversation with James, William had contacted the Minot colony. Fearing that Pierre had been killed, William no longer knew who Robert's Head of Security was, and William respected the chain of authority and spoke to the leader.

To save time, William had asked Robert for his help. Robert had freely offered it. Now that Caleb and his colleagues were heading to Zone One, Robert was in a much more amenable mood. William had one simple request. He wanted to find out as much as they could about Darcy Chamberlain.

It was that information that William was now waiting. He paced the room, trying to push his mind to think of an alternate solution, another path down which he could walk to retrieve information. He checked his watch. By his reckoning, they didn't have much time. He knew Dunleavy, Darcy and their companions were on the way.

The colony was little more than a series of tunnels and rooms. If Dunleavy and his team got past the town above, the numbers of the Colonial troops would be nullified by the closed space. As protected as they were, William still felt as though there was work to be done. He currently knew little, if anything, about the people Dunleavy and Darcy were with. The less he knew, the harder they would be to anticipate.

As he continued to pace the room, his phone rang. Pierre's code flashed on the screen.

"Pierre?" he snapped when he answered the phone.

"Afraid not," said a husky female voice. "Pierre didn't make it."

"What happened?" William asked.

"He was killed. At the reporter's apartment. An asset in LA relayed the information when she flew in."

"What? How?" William asked.

Pierre was his equal in almost every way. He had never seen anyone fight so well, with such tactical knowledge. The only person who had ever beaten Pierre in hand-to-hand combat was William, and even that had been a struggle.

"Our best guess? He was taken out by the one of Dunleavy's people. Your man was in the apartment, too."

"*My* man? You mean Leon?" William asked.

"Yeah. He was dead, too."

William grew more concerned. He'd trained Leon himself. Despite the fact that Leon lacked the upbringing needed to endear him to the colony, he was a substantial fighter. He could hold his own with the best of William's men. He'd had confidence that he could take on any outsiders.

Now he'd been proven wrong, and his nerves increased. "Okay then." William paused, calming himself. "What do the LA police know?"

"They dusted for prints, but couldn't find anything. The guy – he's a ghost. It's like he's one of ours," the woman replied.

William saw the irony. The same tactics they'd been using for years were the same tactics that might prove problematic. "I guess our friend Dunleavy has been training them, based on what he learned from us."

"Agreed," the female voice replied. "Anyway, I have some news for you."

"Good news?" William asked.

"It's news. You can view it how you like."

William liked the woman on the other end of the phone. She sounded a practical, no-nonsense type of person. He could see why Robert had handed Pierre's duties to her. "What is it?" he asked.

"I have an identity of your mystery man. The one we suspect killed Pierre, and is responsible for the near miss in Seattle."

Williams's eyes lit up. "That's great," he said, barely able to hide his enthusiasm.

"Don't get ahead of yourself, William. I said we have a name. When we did a search on him, it was as if he didn't exist. Much like the work he's carried out so far."

"How did you get the information, then?"

"The old-fashioned way. We paid Ms. Chamberlain's editor a visit. His name is—" the woman paused, referring to her notes, "Freeman. Marcus Freeman. Anyway, he told us many details about Ms. Chamberlain. And about the reporter who got into the Zone One colony."

"Paul Jenkins?" asked William.

"That's right. We also found out about Ms. Chamberlain, particularly her private life. Seems she is involved with a Marine Captain - a man by the name of Caleb Jackson. The name sound familiar?"

"Not at all. What information could you find on him? Was the editor more helpful?"

"Unfortunately, Mr. Freeman was unable to deal with the stress of our agent's questions. Apparently his pain threshold was quite low..."

"So, all we have is his name."

"And the fact that he's involved with Ms. Chamberlain. I told you it was *news*."

William was silent for a moment or two. Almost immediately, he'd started to form a plan. William knew Caleb was a Marine, who had been trained in the same way as the Colonial troops. Fighting him could prove more problematic than it was worth.

However, Darcy had *not* been trained in such a way. She was the key. If Jackson's men were proving a problem, she might be the key to bringing them down.

"I think we can work with that. Well done." William stopped. He didn't even know the woman's name. "What should I call you?"

"My name is fine. Catherine."

"Well, Catherine. Thank you for your help."

"You're welcome, William. Though I'd love to chat about your plan, unfortunately, we need to make preparations. The attack in Seattle is not having the effect we had hoped for, and we need to activate the back-up plan."

"Very well. Can I ask what the target is?" William asked.

"I'm afraid I cannot say. It is a bigger target than Seattle, though."

"Fair enough. Well, Catherine, though I'm hoping it may be sooner, 'See you in the next life'."

"See you in the next life, William."

◆ ◆ ◆

Caleb was woken by his alarm. He rolled away from Darcy, not having let her go for the entire duration of their nap. As he rolled away, Darcy started to move. "Not yet, babe," he whispered in her ear. "You stay here."

"But I..." she started to reply, fighting her drowsiness.

Caleb rubbed her back as he sat up. "Take your time, babe. We've got some time ahead of us."

Darcy didn't need any more convincing, and she fell back into a coma-like sleep.

Caleb gently moved his arm from underneath her and left the car. He made his way towards Jacob's pod. There was no way he was going to leave him alone in the cargo bay with Darcy. With a whack, Caleb roused the sleeping man.

"Fuck off," Jacob muttered with his usual charm.

"Get up," Caleb said. "We've had our six."

Without a further word, Jacob rolled out of his pad, and found his feet. They headed up the stairs to the cockpit.

"Sleep well?" Caleb asked.

Jacob grunted.

Out of all the people on the plane, Jacob had slept the soundest; such was his ambivalence to what had occurred that day. The number of deaths didn't faze him in the slightest, whether they were the people on the plane, those in Rome, or the lives he had taken personally. It was as though the previous day was like any other to him.

"Good morning, sir," Casey said from the Communications chair.

Murphy spun around from the control chair. "Technically, it's more like 'Good Afternoon' Sir. Australia's about twelve hours ahead of the states."

"Are we there already?" Caleb asked.

"Not quite in Australian airspace. I cranked up the speed a bit. We'll be there in a couple of hours."

Dunleavy was in his standard Navigation seat. "Where is Darcy?" he asked, looking towards the door.

"Sleeping. She's earned it today."

Dunleavy smiled in agreement.

"We should wake her in an hour or so though, sir." Murphy said.

Caleb walked in her direction, leaving Jacob at the door. "Why's that, Lieutenant?"

Murphy glanced over at Casey, and he nodded, as though approving whatever she was about to say.

"I have a plan sir. A plan that will get us inside the colony."

Chapter Forty-Nine

"How far out are we, pilot?" the man asked. The flight had thus far been uneventful. In fact, the whole time he'd spent away from the colony had been similar. He was, after all, purely an observer.

He didn't have any special training. He did not go through any of the vigorous programs that many of his level were put through. And for that, he was more than grateful.

Francis had never been a fighter. He was much more of a *manipulator* of people, and a keen observer of human nature. Though many would think him a coward, he always saw himself as more practical. *Why fight if you can convince someone to do it for you?* It was a lesson his father had taught him in his youth, and had thus far served him well.

As per James' instruction, Francis had been based in New Zealand for the better part of the last two decades. It had been a long time since his last visit to Haven.

The only contact he had with the rest of the Colonials had been intermittent, to say the least. That was the way James had requested it. It was the way things were done. Each member of the leadership had a task, and it was important that each task was not sullied with information that might distract.

Francis' main task was to report on activities within New Zealand's Intelligence Services.

And, he felt he had done his job admirably. Over the past two decades, he had slowly worked his way into the country's Ministry of Defence. He ensured he was only ever the third or fourth person in the chain of command, never higher. In this role, he was never in a position where he could be fired through political whim, but he was still high enough that he had the ear and trust of those who could.

Over the years, apart from a few minor infiltrations, there had been nothing that Francis considered a violation. And now, after all the time away, Francis was finally receiving his reward. He was going home. He was about to fulfil his destiny in Phase Two.

The only concern Francis carried with him was the notion of what he would be doing in the next phase of the plan.

James, as was his nature, was very secretive about the next Phase. Despite Francis' standing among the colony, he was not privy to the discussions.

He knew that they would announce themselves to the world soon. The fact they were all being recalled was evidence of that. It was finally coming to the moment where he would receive his final injection of the serum, and he looking forward to that.

However, there was another thought that made him smile - the thought of no longer living the lie.

The flight back to the colony from Wellington had only taken forty-five minutes so far, but such was his anticipation he was keen to be updated on their progress.

"Almost there, sir…" the pilot replied, checking the instruments on the small plane. "I'd say we'll be there in about ten minutes."

The cockpit was much smaller than the majority of planes in the fleet. There were Kites, the huge planes that were primarily mass transport vehicles. The Hawks were the fastest planes in the fleet, usually reserved for top level passengers. And then there were the Darts – the type of plane Francis and his pilot currently occupied. It was, essentially, a two-person transport vehicle. The only space was available was for the passengers, and some light luggage. Since the range of the plane was less than three thousand miles, and the journey would only take an hour or so, the lack of room wasn't an issue.

Francis admired the view from the plane. The wingspan was small, but it was more than sufficient. As he looked at the wing, Francis realised something. "Pilot," he began, "why can I see the wing? Why are we not invisible?"

The pilot looked over at Francis. "No need for it yet, sir. We're over the Pacific, no one around. We're flying low enough that no radar's going to pick us up."

"Don't we have Stealth... stuff?" asked Francis, demonstrating his lack of understanding of technology.

"We do sir. But, as we've been instructed, we need to take precautions," the pilot responded.

Francis sat in silent thought for a while. Being so close to the end of his task, he wanted to be certain they were safe. "Just to make sure, Pilot," he began, considering his words. "Just to be sure... can no-one see us?"

Without hesitation the pilot responded. "Correct sir," he replied. "That is, not quite no-one. Except the colony..."

"How?"

"The transponder, sir. Still showing our course. On track for Zone One base as we speak."

The words spoken by the pilot relaxed Francis. As long as the colony could see them as they approached, they would be protected. Unfortunately, Francis' conclusions were about to be disproven.

◆ ◆ ◆

The smaller plane Murphy had been monitoring came into view.

"Easy, Lieutenant, we don't want to make them crash."

Caleb was watching the instruments with care. Murphy had switched to manual controls, as the manoeuvre she was about to perform was not in the plane's prelisted movement patterns.

"No problem, sir," she said, her confidence apparent. "Piece of cake." Murphy continued to focus on the screen.

They had changed course approximately half an hour ago, and headed south. The small icon on the screen had attracted Murphy's attention. As they bore down on the small plane, Murphy had needed to switch to manual flight. She had to muster all of her knowledge and focus to complete the task.

Caleb walked over to Casey, who had been sitting at the Operations control. "How does it all look Sergeant?" he asked, "Are we going to make it?"

Casey smiled back. "You worry too much, sir. Murphy's got this. She'll get us there."

Caleb turned back to the pilot, and then to Darcy. The look in his eyes almost beckoned Darcy to reassure him. And with a wink, she did just that. Not that she entirely believed it herself.

Sometime earlier, she'd been woken by a raucous discussion from the cockpit.

She'd hurriedly made her way upstairs to see what the fuss was about. There she'd found the five other group members, feverishly working away on their monitors. She'd asked Caleb what was happening.

His response had caused her some trepidation. But the fact that Murphy had suggested it, and that Casey had backed her up, gave her and Caleb cause to show a bit of faith.

Dunleavy and Jacob were not as convinced.

"You must be out of your fucking mind!" Was a verbatim account of Jacob's opinion.

Despite the protests, the plan was adopted, and they were in the process of making it happen.

As the time passed, it had become apparent that Casey and Murphy had been able to crack the computer system on the plane, and they were able to find out much more information about their upcoming destination. Some of what they found out was good for the plan, and there were other aspects that were not.

After using the plane's systems to download the information into their tablets, Caleb had relayed the information to Darcy. The place they were travelling too was referred to as *Haven*. It was earmarked as the Zone One base of operations, and indeed held the 'Source' that Isaac had discussed.

None of this was really helpful to formulating a plan though. The important information was on the base itself.

Caleb showed Darcy a schematic of the area on his tablet. While the town above, Haven, seemed to be a normal, albeit small, town, what was underground was far from ordinary.

Under the town was a network of tunnels. Along the tunnels were several pods.

As they studied further, they found that not all the rooms were earmarked as living areas (quarters, entertainment suites, refectories and the like), but there were many rooms that had been given specific names. The one that drew the attention of the group was called "Hangar". The room was much larger than all but two of the rooms.

One of the other rooms was designated for storage, and the other was for something called "Control".

Darcy continued to listen to what they had found out, and particularly about the Hangar area.

Murphy had recognised some of the components that made up the cargo hold of the plane they were currently flying in, only on a much larger scale. It was then deduced that planes would be 'caught' by the hangar as they flew in, similar to the way the Kite had caught the 'Bat in Seattle.

Or at least, that was what they hoped as they flew behind the small plane.

"Lieutenant," Caleb began, "Just walk me through the plan one more time. Just so I'm clear."

Murphy was used to Caleb's thoroughness.

It was not uncommon for the team to come up with an outrageous plan – one that may or may not work. Despite the apparent improbabilities for success, Caleb had always made sure he gave all plans due consideration. He also made sure that any risks were minimised, at least, as much as they could be.

And so far, the strategy had worked, and any plans they had made had worked out just fine, for the most part.

As such, Murphy was happy to cover everything again. "Yes sir," she began. "See that little plane there?" She motioned with her eyes towards the object they were tracking. "We are gonna follow that little thing all the way to Haven. Once we get in range, they will, presumably, send a message into the base that they're going to land. Kind of like *Open Sesame*. Once the hangar door is opened, we'll cut-in the line. That is, we'll make our move in front of them, and take their place. The door will be open, we'll fly in and be caught by the hangar."

"I still don't get why we have to take this much of a risk?" Jacob exclaimed, "Surely we just need to land outside of the town, high-tail it in there in the 'Bat, and shoot our way through. They surely couldn't have enough troops to take us all out."

Caleb looked over at Jacob. He didn't like his orders being questioned, especially by Jacob. "Jacob, we've been over this," he began, trying to contain his frustration. "Looking at the base's structure, and the schematics of the place, they've obviously prepared for a ground assault. My best guess…"

"See… you're guessing. This whole plan is a fucking guess!" Jacob angrily intervened.

Caleb kept his cool. "My best *guess* is… that the majority of their defence will be on the surface, waiting for us there."

Jacob was about to speak, but Casey stood up, and stomped towards him. "Look, Pal," Casey said, his anger not as easily controlled as Caleb's. "You do not get a say here today. You are a fucking murderer, and if it were up to me, we would have thrown you off the plane the second you took out the prisoner."

Jacob stood up in an attempt to prevent Casey from standing over him. It didn't work, as Casey pushed him back into his seat. Casey leant down, his voice reducing to a menacing whisper. "If you dare question what we're doing, I *will* put a bullet in you."

Jacob had never been so intimidated. There was something about the way Casey spoke, as though he commanded fear from the assassin.

Murphy was impressed, smiling as Casey delivered his words.

Caleb continued to explain his decision to Jacob. "One thing we do know about these guys is that they're arrogant. They probably assume that the only rational course of action, the only rational attack we can make is from the surface. And you know what? They're right. No-one in their right minds would dare attempt what we're about to."

Before Caleb could finish, Darcy spoke. "That's why we need to go with the plan. It's the only way we can surprise them."

Dunleavy had remained purposely quiet during the entire exchange. He had faith in the team, and therefore the plan. All that he'd needed to say had been said.

Jacob turned to the old man, as though looking for absolution in his perceived ally.

When it didn't come, Jacob resigned himself to following instructions. The only way he would reach his goal was to do so. Even if it meant, as he believed it would, that they would be killed in the process. From what he knew, if they didn't get the serum, death would be a near certainty anyway.

Feeling the situation had resolved itself, Caleb moved to the seat next to Murphy. Before he sat down, he turned to Darcy, and gave her a wink. "Light in my dark, babe."

"You too," she replied.

Caleb sat down to the right of the Lieutenant. "How long?"

Throughout the previous conversation, Murphy had kept speed with the plane in front. "I'm glad you kids have finished, because, by my reckoning, we should be on approach as we speak," she answered.

The plane in front began to lose altitude, as though coming in for a landing.

There was no runway in site, only trees and roads.

"You're sure this'll work?" Caleb said to Murphy.

"Like I said… piece of cake."

Chapter Fifty

The plane cruised for a few more minutes, the crew silent. None of them wanted to disturb Murphy. As accomplished a pilot as she was, she had never attempted a move like she was about to, and certainly not in the size of plane she was currently in.

After a few more seconds, they saw it. In the distance, a hill became apparent. Not because it was identifiable in anyway. On the contrary, it looked almost exactly like the hundreds of hills they'd passed and on the horizon. The only reason it was apparent was that the plane in front seemed to be heading straight for it.

That must be it, Caleb thought. His thoughts were soon proven correct.

An opening began to appear in the side of the hill. The image was reminiscent of the plane opening as they drove in back in the states. Caleb turned to the rest of the crew. "Okay. You know what you have to do. When we stop, we have to move fast. Has everyone got their gear?"

"Yes," was the near-unanimous reply.

Darcy had taken equipment from Natalie, whose body was still sitting in the cargo bay.

"Okay then. Get ready, it's gonna be bumpy."

As the opening got larger, Murphy pushed forward, increasing their speed. It was imperative they beat the smaller plane into the hangar. The plane drew in line with the other plane, but couldn't accelerate any harder.

"Sir, we need more power," Murphy said. "We're going to have to shut off the cloak!"

Caleb figured the Colonials would find out they were there soon, anyway. "Do it." Caleb said, turning to Casey, sitting at Operations.

Without question, Casey did as he was told. "Done" he said, the buttons pressed.

The plane came into view. Everyone looking in their direction could now see them. There was no hiding from that. Murphy was correct though. The cloak had been draining significant power. As soon as the plane became completely visible, it was able to gain some extra speed, and overtake the smaller plane.

With less than a thousand yards between the plane and the hangar, Murphy quickly lost altitude, and dropped down in front of the smaller plane. Their continued higher speed was helping them pull further in front, providing a buffer to minimise the risk of a collision. She angled the nose of the plane down, and lined up with the gradient of the hangars ramp. The plane now headed straight towards the hangar.

"Ten seconds!" Dunleavy shouted from his navigation seat.

The plane hadn't slowed. Based on Murphy's interpretation of how the hangar worked, she figured they wouldn't have to.

"Five... four... three..."

The plane passed the threshold of the hangar bay doors. Suddenly, the plane reduced speed. As with the 'Bat entering the cargo bay, the force of the rapid change of speed caused the group to lurch forward. This time however, they were prepared, and allowed their bodies to flow in their natural form, thus escaping injury.

And, within the space of a minute, the plane had gone from soaring through the sky to come to a complete stop, right in the heart of the Haven Colony.

♦ ♦ ♦

Francis could barely believe what he'd just seen. The plane had appeared out of nowhere. His first reaction was that of annoyance. How dare they land on his time?

His annoyance quickly morphed into fear.

His fear became prevalent when he looked at the pilot, who'd turned a ghostly white.

"Won't the runway still catch us?" Francis asked, more through hope than confidence.

The pilot turned, and just shook his head.

Unfortunately for the Francis and the pilot, the landing mechanism could only be deployed for one plane per occasion, as all the power in the magnetic field had to be focused on one specific moving object.

This meant that any other vehicle would slide across the surface, not slowing down at all.

Francis realised this, as the rear of the Kite approached their screen at great speed.

◆ ◆ ◆

"What happened to the other plane?" Dunleavy asked. As he spoke, Francis' plane careened into the back of the Kite, the explosion enough to shake the entirety of the Kite. "Never mind." he said.

Caleb, focusing on the moment, unbuckled his seatbelt and stood. "Okay team, let's move," he ordered. "We have to get off this plane. It won't be too long until they realise we're here."

Though it took some longer than others, they all headed out of the cockpit. Jacob was the last to stand.

"Come on then," Caleb ordered.

Jacob remained seated, a look of sheer surprise on his face. He had expected to be dead.

"If you don't move, I'll kill you myself." Casey had returned to the cockpit, not wanting to let Jacob out of his sight.

With that, Jacob stood, gathered his thoughts, and made his way out of the cockpit.

Caleb quickly followed behind. The first element of the plan had been successful.

Now came the hard part.

Chapter Fifty-One

The good news was that they now had the element of surprise on their side. But, if the Colonials were half as well trained as Caleb suspected, they would not be shaken by the surprise attack for long. Caleb knew they had to move fast.

They had all moved quickly to the cargo bay. Once they'd all arrived, Murphy popped open the emergency hatch, the same one Natalie had been tied to. The door blew away from the side of the plane, and was jettisoned across the hangar bay.

They exited the plane, one by one. Murphy was the first to exit. As she did, she ran straight towards the control room. Closing in, it was apparent the operator inside was suffering from a state of shock.

She just stood in the middle of the control room, and watched as Murphy came through the door. Almost instinctively, the woman suddenly realized the danger she was in, and tried to reach for the emergency call button. Her reflexes weren't quick enough, and before she realised what was happening, Murphy had neutralised her.

While Jacob would have preferred the operator's *death*, the rest of the team didn't. After all, the people they were attacking were not necessarily the enemy. Isaac was proof of that.

Remembering this, Murphy elected to hit the woman with the butt of her gun, after which she dragged her to a seat, and bound her to it. All this happened in less than ten seconds.

Realising that Murphy would not need any assistance, Caleb and the rest moved to the exit of the hangar. By this point, the noise of the explosion would surely have been heard by other guards and potential combatants. Caleb knew they had to move out of the hangar as fast as possible.

Once Murphy was satisfied the controller would no longer be a threat, she joined the others.

"Nice work, Murph," said Caleb. He ran through the instructions with the rest of the team, glossing over the details they'd discussed in the latter part of their flight.

Caleb was sure they would be more effective in smaller groups. That way, if one of them was killed or captured, it would not adversely affect the rest of the group in a significant way. With any luck, the plan would allow at least one of them to escape.

"Okay," he began, "Darcy, Casey. Your job is intel. Do what you can to download whatever information you find. Use the tablet. Once you have something... anything... that is definitive, head back here. With any luck, we can open the hangar bay doors and get out that way. Whatever happens, be back here in thirty minutes. If you're not back in thirty minutes—"

"What, you're gonna leave?" Casey asked smugly.

"No!" Caleb said tersely. "If you're not back in thirty minutes, I'll have to come and get you – got it?"

Darcy and Casey nodded.

While Darcy would have liked to accompany Caleb, she knew that her expertise was best served gathering the intelligence. She would further be able to prove herself useful, especially as she knew better than anyone how to dig for information in places people didn't want her to find it.

"I love you, baby," she said. She moved over to Caleb and embraced him, perhaps knowing this might be their final kiss goodbye.

Caleb felt the intensity in her touch. He couldn't deny that he too felt as though it could be the last time they saw or touched each other. He wanted the moment to last forever. Unfortunately, the moment passed much sooner than either of them would have preferred.

As he pulled away from her, he stared down into her eyes, then brought her forehead to his. They briefly touched, just long enough for him to repeat the words he had said too often for one day. "You are the light in my dark."

She pressed her forehead against his for an instant, then pulled away. They both fought against the tears now lightly welling in their eyes, hoping it would not be their last shared moment.

"Okay. Go," Caleb said reluctantly.

Darcy turned, and she and Casey ran out the door, making their way to the left.

"Murphy," Caleb continued, "you think you know where the 'Source' is?"

Murphy nodded in reply.

"Good. I'll leave it to you to locate it. On the way, go to the main power room. Try to find some way to shut this place down."

"You mean blow it up?" asked Jacob.

Caleb looked over at Jacob. He was about to argue the point with him, but then he realised Jacob was right. If there was no way to safely shut down the colony, Murphy would need to ensure they were stopped. Permanently. He turned his attention back to his Lieutenant. "Just do what you have to do, Murph. We need to cut off their supply. If that means—"

"Yes sir," Murphy said.

She gave an understanding nod to Caleb before she left.

"You two... come with me." Caleb said to the remaining pair` – Dunleavy and Jacob.

Dunleavy looked tense. "And what exactly is our job?" he asked. "You didn't specify on the plane."

Caleb began to move, and the other two followed. "Our job is simple. Find out who is running this place, and get some real answers."

"Sooo... We have to track down the most protected person here, capture them, and find out information from them?" Jacob asked, seemingly angry he wasn't making the decisions.

Caleb just nodded, and kept walking. He knew it was a tough mission, especially given the potential of the Colonials. It was probably the hardest mission he had ever tried to accomplish. But if they were to have any chance of stopping the Colonials, they would need to find out more about their plan, more about their next move. And, if his instincts were correct, there was only one place he could find answers.

Chapter Fifty-Two

As they walked through the tunnels, it became apparent the plan had, so far, worked as he wanted. They hadn't run into any resistance for the three or so minutes they'd walked. While this did provide an element of comfort, it was also disturbing. The Colonials were surely aware of their presence in the facility, and yet no resistance had been encountered.

Caleb tried to not let it cloud his judgement, and continued with their task.

Indeed, every time they tried to enter a room, they were allowed to move unfettered. However, there was still a feeling they were walking into a trap.

They continued down the corridor, Caleb with his gun raised, Dunleavy directly behind, and Jacob bringing up the rear. Caleb had his gun drawn to stave off any attacks from the front, Jacob doing the same to cover their trodden path.

Caleb looked around the corridor, observing the stagnant nature of the place. Had he not know better, he could have sworn he was in a science-fiction film. Each room they passed was nearly identical. There were no signs of any individuality at all. Each room was equipped with a bed or two, a hand basin, mirror and a set of controls on the wall. What these controls did, Caleb couldn't be sure, but he doubted their intent was malicious.

To him, they looked like nothing more than living quarters, places for people to sleep and prepare for their work. Whatever *that* was.

They continued down the corridor, towards the room that had caught Caleb's attention. After several metres, they reached an elevator.

Caleb motioned for Dunleavy to press the buttons outside the door. As the older man moved forward, Caleb swung around and pointed his gun in the direction they had come, protecting their position while the elevator reached their level.

As they waited, Dunleavy asked the question that Caleb had been considering. "Let's assume they know we're here," he began. "What's to stop them from trapping us in the elevator?"

Caleb thought about the question. It was a valid point to make. There were seemingly endless opportunities for the colonials to lay a trap, especially considering the fact they had the home-field advantage.

Still, Caleb had to remain positive. They had probably travelled further into the colony that any outsider had in the past. He was hoping they wouldn't be prepared for it. "Let's try to remain positive, okay?" Caleb said. "After all, the alternative is to run and hide. Frankly, that's just not in my nature."

The other two knew it was pointless to argue. Besides, despite differing agendas, they all had *something* to gain by moving forward. Running and hiding would not have suited any of them. After about ten seconds, the elevator arrived. The metal doors pulled apart, and the trio stepped inside. As the doors closed behind them, Dunleavy looked for a control panel inside the elevator. None was apparent.

"Well shit, Jackson. What the fuck do we do now?" he said, his anger slowly surfacing.

Caleb glanced around the elevator. There was nothing apparent in the way of controls. Then, as though reading their minds, a voice came over the intercom.

"Please select your destination." The friendly female, English-accented voice said, offering its services of transport.

Caleb looked at the other two. He didn't know if it was a case of asking for a floor, or asking for a specific room.

Almost as a joke, Jacob spoke to the voice. "Take us to the Governor," he said with a smirk.

Caleb rolled his eyes. It was hardly the time for jokes. Besides, an off-the-cuff remark like that could alert the rest of the colony to their presence. Just as he was thinking of ways to assert his views, the elevator began to move.

"You've got to be fucking kidding me," said Dunleavy, equally surprised that Jacob's idea had worked.

The elevator started moving downwards. As it moved, locations began appearing on a black panel above the door. It was as though they were riding on a public train. Names like 'Engineering', 'Science', and 'Education', flashed across the screen. At that point, Caleb really did begin to feel as though he was in a movie.

After several seconds and destinations, the elevator slowed down and stopped. As the trio waited for the doors to open, the elevator quickly began to move, this time heading parallel to the ground, towards what Caleb felt would be the middle of the colony.

Again, several different names of the various areas' they were passing flashed across the blackened panel. 'Refectory', 'Communications', and 'Medical bay' were all bypassed.

Eventually the elevator came to a stop. Caleb waited for several seconds before reading the panel one more time.

As he read the screen, it appeared they had reached their destination. It read 'Command Accommodations'.

"This is it," Caleb said emphatically. "Get ready. I don't think they'll be too happy to see us in here."

◆ ◆ ◆

"Have they arrived yet?" James asked down the phone. He was becoming agitated. The plane was due into the vicinity of Zone One more than an hour ago.

His nerves were shared by William. The head of security had laid the troops out in the best possible way. Whether or not the plane was cloaked, William had employed a seemingly impenetrable web of troops, both throughout the town and the surrounding bushland.

As an extra precaution, he'd ordered all the remaining civilians to their alert positions. The many women and children had moved to quarters and bays in the middle of the colony, and they were accompanied by plenty of troops. After all, they were the people that William was there to protect. They had to make it through to the end, otherwise all James' work would have been for nothing. The remaining support staff were in their operational positions, ordered to be especially vigilant.

"Trust me. If they're here, they will not get through us," William said, masking his nerves.

"Okay," James said. "Just keep me updated on your progress." James paused, considering the questions he wanted to ask. "Are the people protected? And the serum? And the source?"

William was a little annoyed by the interrogation. "Of course sir. Trust me, the situation will be neutralised."

As he finished, the phone call ended abruptly. Though the end came not by James, nor by William.

James sat in his chair, inside the office he'd once considered to be the safest room in the world. As he considered his current situation, he realised just how wrong his assumption had been. This was further compounded by the two guards, lying motionless at the brace of the door, and the other two guards by his side, who now appeared in an equally motionless state.

As he'd been speaking to William, the man and his associates had burst through the door. Before he knew what was happening, James had a gun pointed directly at his temple.

Part of him was in awe of the tall, strongly built man who held his life in his hands. The rest of him was gripped by fear. Never did he think anyone would threaten him this closely.

After what seemed like an eternity of terror, the man spoke. "I have absolutely no idea who you are, but I think you've been looking for me," said Caleb. The man looked over at one of his group. The other man nodded, and raised his weapon towards James. "We have some questions for you," he said, his American accent providing James with his first clue regarding his identity.

"Who are you?" James asked.

"You tell me," Caleb replied, "I mean, you seem to have control of virtually every piece of information… you tell me who I am."

James was surprised by the response. Normally, the people who followed him would answer questions without delay. He was not used to being spoken to in such a manner. Gathering his composure, James looked around the room.

He studied the other two men. The first man was older, and instantly recognisable. "You are Michael Dunleavy," James said to the man who had his gun pointed at him, "I hear some people are *very* interested in finding you." James cracked a smile, enjoying the fact that Dunleavy was a wanted man. He had proved to be a source of irritation for the past several years.

When James smiled, Dunleavy had to use all his strength of will not to retaliate. He was angry with the man he had a gun pointed at. He knew he could kill him in an instant. But Dunleavy also realised it wouldn't solve the problem, and used this as motivation to control himself.

James continued to scan the room, and turned his attention to the other man. The third man was stationed at the entrance of the room, covering the door to ensure they were not bothered by any other guards. "You are Jacob," James said, "I've heard all about *you*."

A smile appeared on Jacob's face, seemingly satisfied his reputation preceded him.

James turned back to the man who had spoken, the man he didn't recognise. "You? I don't know who *you* are. Who might you be?" James asked Caleb.

Caleb considered his options. Indeed, not revealing who he was had certain advantages, but they were irrelevant. At that point, he and the other man were at a stalemate. He needed the man alive, and he was sure he knew it. Caleb needed the information the man held in his head. He was certain he'd found the one man who could reveal the entire truth. In order for that to happen though, the man needed to be alive. "How about we make a deal?" Caleb said, trying to remain as relaxed as possible.

James was intrigued. In the space of a few moments, he had been shocked, surprised and confronted. Now, the man who'd perpetrated all these circumstances was trying to make a deal?

The prospect made James smile. He now knew the man hadn't infiltrated the colony on a mission to kill him. On the contrary, the man needed to keep him alive. James thought about how to spin it to his advantage.

The first thing James realised he needed to do was buy some time. It wouldn't be too long until William figured out what was happening. Or at least, that is what James hoped. "Okay," James replied. "What kind of deal?"

"I'll tell you my name, if you tell me yours," Caleb said

James considered his options. The more he thought about it, the more he realised the position he was in. No matter how well trained the man was, he was never going to make it out of the colony alive. James considered this, and made his decision.

"Okay. You first," James said, not wanting to give something without receiving first.

"My name is Caleb. Captain Caleb Jackson, USMC."

James was surprised. He'd assumed the man was military trained, but he had also assumed he worked for an agency. He didn't ever consider the person capable of breaching his facility would be a mere soldier.

Caleb nodded towards the man, indicating it was his turn to speak.

"Very well. You want to know my name?" James asked.

"Yes. Yes, I do," replied Caleb.

James paused, knowing that what he was about to reveal would provide more of a shock than anything they had heard for a while. As he was about to reveal his identity, he was struck with a plan. A plan to buy him some more time.

"My name," James began, "will take some time to explain…"

◆ ◆ ◆

Darcy and Casey had made their way through the colony. As they moved, Darcy found herself getting distracted. She couldn't help but marvel at the design and innovation in the structure. There was elegance to the design, and she was nothing if not impressed.

Had she had more time, she would have ensured they stopped in each room, examining the similarities and differences. This would allow them, in her mind, to better understand their opponents. Unfortunately for Darcy's ambitions, the time was not right for such thoughts.

They had left Caleb and the rest about ten minutes earlier. As they made their way through the facility, they'd tried various avenues to what they thought would be the colony main frame. Even if it wasn't the source of all information, it would hopefully at least provide a guide as to where they could find it.

The room, identified as Communications, had a different basic design to the rest of the rooms. It had more Ethernet wiring, both flowing to and away from the room. Darcy only hoped they were walking in the right direction. After all, the rooms looked so similar, she could have sworn they were travelling in circles.

Fortunately, Casey didn't share her trepidation. He moved forward with the same confidence Darcy had observed so many times in Caleb. It was a walk of confidence and consideration. Casey moved purposefully, as though prepared for anything that might be lurking around the corner.

Darcy did what she could to ensure their rear was protected. As such, she tried to mimic Casey's movements. She wasn't helped by the equipment she was wearing. The equipment was not cumbersome, but nor was it light. Just the weight of the various equipment, communicators, utility belts, knives and the rest was enough to remind Darcy that she really should have used the gym membership she had purchased months ago.

Her non-physical strength had always been one of her best qualities, and she would need to draw on all its power just to navigate the colony.

After a time, Casey stopped. He held up his fist, which signalled to Darcy to hold her position. Casey turned to Darcy, and whispered, "We have contact. I can see a line-up of people around the corner."

"Line up?" asked Darcy. "What for?"

"Not sure. I don't think they're waiting for the communications room though."

Darcy was compelled to agree. "We need to find out what's in that room. Are they guarded?"

"Not that I can see, but I can only see about three people. Who knows how long this line extends for? Plus, I imagine the place is on some kind of lock-down. That would explain why we haven't seen anyone yet."

"Why's that?"

"All non-essentials would have been sent to some kind of muster point. Only the people who *need* to be away from the main population would be wandering the base." Casey looked up from the tablet, towards the line of people. "Which makes me think that, whatever they are lining up for has to be important."

Darcy could only agree. There was no argument against it. "What's the plan?" she asked.

Casey couldn't answer, he did not have enough information. While there was no indication of guards, there was certainly the possibility they would be there. After all, the room was important enough that people were still using it during the lock-down, and therefore it was important enough to protect. "We're going to have to get closer." Casey said.

As he took his first step, an alarm began to sound in the colony. Similar to an air raid siren, the speakers whirred with the sound. The noise was so loud, and so unexpected that it caused Darcy and Casey to cover their ears. Casey, however, continued to observe the line. They too, it seemed, were surprised by the alarm. The people Casey could see also held their hands over their ears.

Several loud bursts emanated from the intercom. After the initial bursts, the noise was interrupted by a voice. It was a voice neither Casey nor Darcy had heard before, and yet it sounded eerily familiar.

"Attention, Haven Colonists. Due to an incursion by outsiders, the colony is now required to shut down. Haven will implode in thirty minutes. Please make your way to your emergency departure zones. Supervisors, make necessary preparations for departure. This is not a drill. Repeat. Please make your way to your emergency departure zones. More information will be provided upon your arrival."

Darcy and Casey looked at each other.

"Murphy!" Darcy said with a smile.

Casey also smiled. "I knew she would come through. She always does." Casey returned his attention to the people waiting in the line. Most of them had started to disperse. A few remained behind, and seemed to be remonstrating with a woman. The woman was dressed neatly, in a similar motif to the rest of the colonists. The main difference was her white coat.

Darcy crept closer to Casey, so she too, had a good view of the woman. The argument was turning aggressive, but from their vantage point, neither Darcy nor Casey could hear what was being said. Without formal acknowledgement, they moved closer to try and hear the discussion.

It was clear that the woman was being pressured by the remaining people. "It will only take a minute! Why will you not let us in, Helen?"

The woman, Helen, was trying to calm the people down. "Look. The alarm has sounded; we don't have time for this," she said. It was obvious she had had enough of the insubordination. "If you do not move to your departure zone now, I will make sure you are left behind."

The remaining people looked at each other. Darcy could see the moment they resigned themselves to the situation. It was even more important they get in the room now. Whatever it was, must be important, and that was even clearer now.

The remaining people moved away, leaving only Helen and a guard in view. After a few seconds of quieter discussion, a conversation neither Casey nor Darcy could make out, they moved back into the room. Casey then used the moment to attack.

Moving swiftly, Casey launched himself towards the door. There was a heartbeat between Casey's movement, and Darcy's reaction. She followed as fast as she could. Casey moved to the door, and he quickly disappeared inside, weapon raised. Darcy did what she could to keep up, but by the time she entered the room, Casey had done his work.

The guard was slumped on the ground, having received three bullets to his chest from close proximity. Casey stood a few yards into the room, his weapon firmly fixed on the other woman.

Darcy entered the room, not surprised by the precision of Casey's work. As she entered she looked around the room. The room was similar to the many rooms they'd passed on their way. The major difference being the medical stations that were set-up around the room. Each bed had a contraption adjacent - a contraption that had needles attached.

From as little information as Darcy had gathered on the Kite, she knew this was the room where the serum was administered, and it became apparent just who the woman in front of them was.

The woman had her arms raised.

"Now what?" she asked Casey.

Casey spoke to her, without taking his eyes off the woman. "Now... we get some information," he said.

Chapter Fifty-Three

The sound of the alarm was almost predictable. William had been outside the motel. The same motel Paul had hidden in, only a few days earlier. He'd been waiting patiently, hoping the rogue group of outsiders – Dunleavy and his people – would try to make their way through.

All throughout the small town, William had positioned his men. Some were hidden, like the dozen inside the convenience store, and others were hiding in plain sight. Most occupied the main street of the town, posing as outsiders. In actual fact, William had planned the situation very well. He had accounted for virtually every entry point into the town. He had planned the perfect strangle. He and his people would lie in wait, allowing the outsiders to enter the town. Once inside, they would be cut off from all angles, no escape possible. It was almost perfect.

Almost.

When the alarm had sounded, William realised just how imperfect his plan had been. At that stage, he didn't know for certain who had set off the alarm.

Had James set it off? That was the only option as far as William could concede. The only person with access and the correct codes to set off the alarm was James. William had been briefed on the nature of the alarm, but the final input of the code had and always would fall to Haven's leader.

All William knew for sure, was that whatever was happening inside the colony, it had caused the alarm to sound, and that he was not where he was most needed.

As the alarm continued to sound, William considered his options. He had a couple of hundred troops scattered throughout the town and its surrounds. While others would think the numbers overkill, William considered them essential. While Haven was by no means the largest

Colony – designed specifically to be the most inconspicuous – the security detail was essential to protect its secrets.

The question he was asking himself now, was what to do with them all. If the alarm had been set off by James, then they all needed to get to their evacuation points. James would not have set the alarm if it were not the case.

However, if it had indeed been set off by the outsiders, and was a ruse to evacuate the building, then William would need to act to prevent the outsiders from continuing. It was not an easy set of circumstances, and it was not a situation William had ever contemplated, let alone planned for. He would need to call on his instincts, for those were all the training he had for this situation. After contemplation, he made his decision and lifted the communicator to his mouth. "Squad One," he began, referring to his best team, "make your way to the Entry Point One." William referred to the convenience store back room, "the rest of you, move to your evacuation areas."

With those words, the town came to life. Hundreds of people emerged from the buildings, all moving towards their departure areas. As protocol dictated, the hangar bay was off-limits. This was largely due to safety. As the implosion would eminate from within, all colonists were to make their way to the surface, and make their way from the colony in 'Bats, or via the nearby airfield.

Once at their designated evacuation points, the colonists would make their way across the country, their destinations varying. Some would head to the closeness of Sydney, no more than a few hours away. Others would face a long journey across the country, taking them to Perth, the Western Australian capital. That journey would take upwards of forty hours in the 'Bats. Other destinations included Melbourne, Adelaide, Brisbane, Townsville and Darwin.

From there, each group would again have varying instructions. Some would fly out on commercial airlines, others on private planes. The lucky ones would be taken away from the country in Kites.

Some would leave immediately, whereas others would wait weeks. The very fact that there was so much time from that moment to all the

Haven colonists being safe further alerted William to the seriousness of the situation. Such action would slow their plans, and Phase Three and beyond would be put on hold.

As the troops moved to their various locations, William waited at the entry for Squad One to arrive. He felt it his duty to return to the colony, to James' side. Not only to ensure his leader's safety, but also to ensure James knew he could be relied upon.

As the members of Squad One arrived, William motioned for them to follow him. They were, without a doubt, William's best people. They had all been taken from their previous lives at the height of a conflict. They had all died fighting.

Fighting for a cause they believed in. Some were Nazis, some were Viet Cong, and some were Green Berets. And regardless of their ideology from their previous life, all of them had adopted Haven's way of life, and Haven's ideals.

William had promised them glory, and so far he had kept his promise. They followed him with the fervour of zealots, such was their devotion to the cause. "Follow me" William said, his tone implying a sense of urgency.

As he took a step toward the door, one of his men spoke. "Where are we going? Why do we not go to the 'evac'?"

William paused at the entry of the petrol station, the façade that protected the surface entry of the colony. "We are going to James. I have a feeling he needs our help."

As the words left his mouth, the Squad reached a new level of readiness. They had, after all, been lying in wait in the town, hoping the outsiders would arrive. Now, they were required to focus even more. They were being asked by their commander to potentially save the leader of the colony.

For many of them, it had been many years since they had seen any *real* combat. For the weeks after they were pulled out of their various conflicts, they were recovering. Recovering from their near-death experiences.

William found it was the most effective way of recruitment. Explore the world's conflict zones and find the soldiers who were near to death.

Such was the power of the Source. There was no ailment, short of complete bodily disfigurement, that it could not cure. Bullets to the body were not a problem, provided they were removed with speed and did not immediately shut down any vital organs.

The Source had worked miracles, sometimes right before William's eyes.

And he used those miracles to recruit the people who were now following him. They were already trained killers, and bringing them all back from the brink of death always turned them into loyal followers. It was this loyalty that William used on this occasion. He knew they had all been trained well. Hell, he did it himself. One of the most important lessons that any of the Colonial's learned was the alarm. Once heard, it meant immediate evacuation. The alarm would not be sounded unless absolutely critical.

William realised he was asking his team to go against their instincts, but he knew it was the right thing to do. As he saw the Squad tighten their focus, he moved into the convenience store.

He briskly rounded the aisles, ignoring any and all of the products on the shelves, and moved to the counter. As he approached, he activated a trapdoor. As it opened, it revealed a staircase that led down to the basement. He paused at the top of the revealed staircase. Drawing his weapon, William decided to take no chances. He slowly moved down the steps, and entered the colony.

◆ ◆ ◆

Caleb was unnerved by what James had just told him. The story he'd recounted for the three of them had been, to say the least, unbelievable. Or at least it would have been, had Caleb not heard what he had over the past few days. In fact, his words did not shock him as much as he would have presumed.

James had begun by talking about the founding of the colony.

According to James it went right back to before the country they were in was founded. He told the story of how he brought his ship to the coast.

The Dutch has been the first to step foot in Australia, though they landed on the West Coast. Fortunately the Dutch had left, abandoning the country for enough time that he and his men could claim the land.

When they arrived, there was little of anything around. That was for the first few days. After some further exploration, they met some of the natural inhabitants, the original occupiers of the nation. After befriending one of the members of the mob, as they called themselves, they were led to a cave.

And in that cave, James made a discovery.

"We knew when we arrived that we were bound to find something we'd never seen before. Little did I know just what that would be," James said. "When we reached the centre of the caves, after what seemed like days of travel, we found it. We were shown what would change our world."

"The Source?" asked Caleb.

"Yes," James said.

"So wait a second," Caleb interrupted. "You're telling me that you were part of the crew that colonised this country. Wasn't that two hundred years ago?" Caleb had very limited knowledge of Australian history, only what he'd partially learned from the Discovery Channel. For some reason, he remembered the name of the man who is generally credited with the founding of Australia. "Are you telling me you're Captain Cook? James Cook?" he asked, once again taken aback by the inordinate amount of time the man in front of him claimed to have been alive.

James nodded smugly.

The revelation took a few moments to sink in

"Wait one goddamn minute," Dunleavy interjected, "Didn't you die? In Hawaii?"

James again nodded, but this time followed up his affirmation. "Indeed, that is what history has told you all."

Caleb and Dunleavy stared at each other. Once again, what James was saying was hard to believe, but they couldn't help themselves but think he was telling the truth.

James continued. "I knew that once we found the Source, we would need to control it. Knowing what I did, I knew that people would become suspicious of what we'd found, especially if I stopped growing older, let alone became younger. So, my men and I came up with a plan. We would *live* out our lives, and once our deaths could be seen as a natural end, we returned, and began the next part of our journey."

"Some journey," Caleb scoffed. "You've been responsible for so many deaths. So many people have died so you can complete your *journey*." Caleb could feel his anger taking hold. While he appreciated the epic story he was being told, the result had been catastrophic so far.

"What is it you mean to achieve?" asked Dunleavy.

James turned to the older man. "That... is not for you to know."

Caleb again pulled out his gun, and pressed it against James' temple. "I bet your Source doesn't stop fucking bullets!!!" Caleb said, anger taking hold.

James, for the first time in the conversation, looked tense.

"You are killing so many people, and you plan to kill more!" Caleb continued.

"Your point?" James asked, his voice filled with disdain.

"I need to know why? At least help me understand," Caleb pleaded.

James considered the request. Again, he realised it would do no harm to his plan to speak the truth. "Take the gun away, and I will explain." James said, glad that he had an opening to buy some more time.

With some reluctance, Caleb removed his gun from James' temple, comforted by the fact Dunleavy still had James in his sights.

"You ask why?" James began. "Surely you can see it? The world has become infected. We have sat back and observed the so-called evolution of the planet. We have seen wars fought over everything. Oil, food, land. The world is at a point where it cannot be saved. People cannot be saved."

Caleb listened to the James, disturbed by what he was hearing.

James continued. "Politicians are sending men and women to their deaths by the thousands... and why? So they can win another election.

So they can justify how much money they are spending. And then, when they have reached their goal, they change their minds and say the war wasn't worth it to begin with. That is why we are doing what we are doing. The world is broken, and we need to restart it. We need to begin afresh. It is time the world had a rebirth."

"So," Caleb retorted, "let me guess this straight. You're killing people because of what politicians do?"

"People are complicit in their actions."

"Complicit?"

"Yes. People let their leaders do whatever they like. They allow them to kill. They allow them to make the poor poorer and the rich richer. They allow oppression of religion, sexual differences, skin colour, gender. People have not done enough to help. Most of them just ignore what happens in the world. For goodness sake, countries with a widely documented, public history of human rights abuses have been allowed to showcase themselves to the world, to put themselves on pedestals. And what do people do? They clap. They cheer. They applaud the façade and ignore the reality."

"So, why don't you try and change it? I mean, you have all these followers. All this technology. Why use it to kill? Why not use it for the betterment of the human race?"

James smiled. "That is exactly what I *am* doing. I am changing the world for the better. The human race will go on. The human race will prosper. All the problems we have today will be gone. No longer will bankers be able to send others broke while they laugh about it on their jets. No longer will clothing manufacturers be able to live in mansions while the people working for them can't even afford to eat. No longer will the few have more than the many."

"And you get to decide this, do you?" Caleb asked, astonished by James' conviction. "What gives you the right?"

After consideration, James spoke. "Are you a god-fearing man, Captain?"

Caleb was unsure how to answer. He'd never really given the thought of *God* a second thought. "Not really," he replied.

"Well, I am," James said. "Not in the traditional sense. While once considered I myself to be Christian, I have seen too much to make me doubt that. I do believe, however, that there is... something... something that controls who we are and what our destiny will be. Some call it God, some Allah, and some Muhammad. Me, I don't like to name such things. What I know is this..." James paused, catching his breath. "What I know, is that I, and the people with me, were given the gift. We were given the gift of immortality. No one else has been given such a gift. Therefore, we have been ordained. Ordained by a higher power to make a difference. It is not our choice to do what we are doing. It is our *responsibility* to do it."

Caleb had seen zealots before, but James was different. James not only believed in God, but he believed he *was* a God. He knew James had to be stopped. The *Colonials* had to be stopped. "This... this *rebirth,*" Caleb asked, his voice shaking. "The goal is to wipe us all out."

James didn't answer. He didn't need to. Caleb knew the answer. He knew the endgame.

The Colonials were planning to wipe out the human population so they could take over, and begin the world again, in their own image.

Once again, Caleb raised his weapon to James' temple. "I cannot allow that to happen," he said, a strange calmness appearing in his voice.

James began to shake. He knew that, as powerful as the Source and subsequent serum was, a bullet to the head meant death. "Now don't be so rash," James said, trying to maintain his composure. "I can help you all."

Caleb kept the gun firmly focused on James' temple. "We don't want your help," he said. "In fact, I think that if we blow this place up, you won't have your Source, and your plans will be gone."

James turned his head as much as he could in an attempt to face his possible assassin. "You know how many colonies we have. You know how powerful we are. One colony does not make a difference. Everyone has the serum now. It is only a matter of time until everyone has had their injection, then the time will come."

Caleb almost had the information he was after. It was true; his anger was getting the better of him. But he also knew that the only way he could get anything further from James was to apply pressure. "The time will come for what?" he shouted, pressing the gun further into James's head.

As he did, he felt a familiar feeling against the back of his head. He had not felt it for some time, but it was a feeling that sent a quick shiver down his spine. "Drop your fucking gun," Jacob said, holding his pistol to the back of Caleb's skull, "Captain."

Caleb realized he'd made the wrong decision with Jacob. It was not the first mistake he had made these past few days, but it could be the most vital. Upon walking into the room, Caleb already knew he may have to kill James.

It was a logical move. At the very least, the Colonials would lose their leader, and it would buy them some more time.

Now, the opportunity may be lost.

Caleb lowered his weapon. He would have to wait for another opportunity. Wait for a moment where Jacob would drop his guard.

After several long seconds, the alarm sounded again.

Caleb felt the gun move slightly. It was enough for Caleb to determine that Jacob was momentarily distracted. Without delay, Caleb sprang into action. He began to wheel around, when a sharp pain began in the back of his head.

Jacob was no rookie. He knew what Caleb was planning. As soon as he heard the alarm, Jacob's instincts kicked in. He knew Caleb would use that opportunity to attack, and he was ready. No sooner had Caleb moved than Jacob struck him with the butt of his gun, knocking him unconscious. As Caleb slumped to the floor, Jacob grinned at James.

He felt he had proven his worth. He had shown his hand, and he was comfortable with his decision. His grin turned into a smile, a smile that James did not return. "So..." Jacob asked, "What now? Should I kill him?"

James looked at Caleb's still body, and back at Jacob. He saw the look of pure evil in Jacob's eyes, a look he had not seen in Caleb. "No." he replied, "Not yet. We may need him."

Chapter Fifty-Four

Darcy looked down at the tablet. The Colonials were nothing, if not efficient. She scrolled through the Levels of the virtual complex. Apart from a few people in a room several levels down, the colony looked virtually empty. All the movement was heading away from the centre of the colony.

"Please," Helen said, "Please don't kill me."

Casey scoffed. "Don't give me a reason to."

Darcy moved towards the blonde woman. "What is it you do here?" she asked. She'd already figured out the answer. She was using an old reporter's trick, asking a question she knew the answer to. That way, she would be able to tell if the interviewee lied to her. Normally, if she was lied to, she would use the information against the interviewee. She decided against that tactic on this occasion. Darcy figured it would be more useful to let them think they had the upper hand.

"It's just an infirmary," Helen replied, lying.

Darcy nodded, feigning belief. "Okay then." She walked around the room, evaluating the beds.

Each bed had an injector next to it. It looked, as with the other rooms, to be efficient in design. It was clear the beds only had one purpose – to deliver injections quickly to a large number of people. "What's the move?" Darcy asked Casey.

"Well, if it's just an infirmary," Casey replied, also not believing what the blonde had told them.

Darcy glanced again at the tablet. It was then she saw them. There were several colonists moving in on the room she assumed Caleb was in. After all, every other room was being evacuated, and it was the only room that showed little or no movement, just a single dot. "Casey, we have to move."

"Why?" he asked, his gun still fixed on the blonde.

"Just trust me," Darcy replied, her instincts telling her not to share information with the woman. "I'll tell you on the way."

"Okay then. What should we do with her?" Casey asked.

Darcy was surprised he was asking her opinion. As a Sergeant, surely he had ordered people before?

"Um, I guess she's not a threat. We'll just have to take her with us."

Casey nodded, and motioned for Helen to move.

Helen stood fast. "Where? Where are we going?" she asked.

"Just move," said Casey, his voice forceful.

As Helen began to move, Darcy stepped towards one of the beds. Next to the injector was a medical box with several epipen-type devices.

Darcy reasoned that they must contain the serum. It was the only explanation for them being in the room. She surmised that, while it was better to inject in the room, the colonials wouldn't be so foolish that they couldn't do it on the run. Sensing the serum would be her proof, Darcy grabbed a handful of the devices.

As she began to put them in one of her pants pockets, Helen screamed out. "Noooo!"

In an instant, the slight blonde woman had grabbed Darcy, swinging her around by the throat. Darcy now faced Casey, acting as a human shield.

"They are not for you!" Helen said, furious they'd dared take the serum.

Darcy struggled against the woman. While they were both of a similar height and weight, Helen had the advantage. With her arm around Darcy's neck, Helen began to squeeze. Darcy could barely breathe.

Casey continued to aim his gun at the blonde, hoping for a clean shot. However, despite being an excellent shot, he wouldn't take the risk, not with Darcy.

Darcy continued to struggle against Helen's arm. Then, as though her destiny was at stake, Darcy remembered what she had learned in the plane. The thought brought a calm focus to her. As she struggled, she reached for her pocket, and pulled out the knife Murphy had given her.

Casey saw what she was doing, and realised her intent. He distracted the blonde. "Okay. I'll put it down," Casey said, as he slowly lowered his gun.

Helen saw this, and momentarily loosened her grip. It was all the help Darcy needed, as she swung the knife into Helen's right flank. The knife plunged deep, imbedding itself in Helen's liver. As instructed, Darcy twisted the knife, exacerbating the injury.

Helen doubled back, her breath forcing out a scream, a scream of such volume it almost burst Darcy's eardrum.

Darcy sprang free, pulling the knife from Helen's gaping wound. Darcy turned and faced the dying woman.

Helen fell back, blood pouring out of her wound. For the first time in her life, Helen felt mortal. She fell to the ground, knocking over one of the injectors. She tried to scream again, but the feeling of dread was over-riding. She continued to writhe in pain, the blood spilling onto the once pristine white floor.

Darcy stared in horror. Helen's wound had started to heal itself. The Source, flowing through Helen's blood, had started to take effect.

Darcy, sensing that Helen would attack once fully healed, did the only thing she could. She took her gun out of its holster, raised it towards the still-writhing doctor, and fired. Only one shot was required, as the bullet shattered the back of Helen's skull into the floor.

Casey grabbed Darcy by the arm, trying to usher her out of the room.

"No, wait," Darcy said, regaining some composure. In the struggle, she had dropped the serum. She went over to the box again, and collected half a dozen more. She put them in her pocket and turned to Casey. "Okay, let's go," she said, a tear welling in her eye.

◆ ◆ ◆

The room slowly came back into focus. Caleb had no idea how long he had been unconscious, but he figured it couldn't have been a long period of time. As he woke, it became clear the advantage he'd had, had dissipated. At first, the image was a mess of blacks and greys, with the occasional white. As the seconds ticked by, he was able to make out shapes. Some were large and wide, others thin and tall. It was a feeling he'd experienced before.

The blow he'd received from Jacob was substantial, and there was a severe pain in his head and neck. It would take a lot of concentration to not be distracted by it. Fortunately, that was not a problem. Quickly, Caleb was reminded of the nature of his situation. Seemingly moments ago, he was about to find out what James' *endgame* would be, but then Jacob betrayed him. While Caleb wasn't surprised, he was angry. He had thought he had convinced Jacob of the right thing to do.

Apparently, he was wrong.

Again.

As he came around, Caleb could see the positions had almost completely reversed. He was now sitting down, his hands behind his back. With a quick motion, he realised he was bound to the chair James had been sitting in. Dunleavy was in a chair next to him, his hands bound in the same fashion as Caleb's. Dunleavy seemed to be more alert, meaning he had chosen to sit, rather than being forced to as Caleb had.

Immediately in front of Caleb stood James, a smug smile spread across his face. He was obviously enjoying their role reversal.

Jacob seemed equally jovial about the situation. He was basking in his betrayal. So far, he'd achieved everything he wanted. He had made it to the Zone One base, or Haven as he now knew it, and saved the life of the leader.

Not that James' life mattered to him, he was just interested in the reward he would receive for his work. Now, all he needed was the serum. Once he had it, the rest of them could go to hell for all he cared.

Caleb looked at Jacob, seemingly asking *Why?*

Jacob saw this, and answered the unasked question. "C'mon Captain. You didn't really expect me to be on *your* side, did you?" he asked. "You're fighting the strongest group of people in the world. They'll win. I've merely chosen the winning side."

Caleb looked at Jacob in disgust. It was then he realised just how different they were. "You... are the worst or the worst Jacob. These people would be fools to help you."

Caleb turned his attention to James, and saw a look he wasn't expecting. He saw a look of agreement. It was then Caleb saw more of James' true intentions. "...and it looks like you're not too sure about him either?"

James wasn't surprised by Caleb's statement. He wasn't a man who hid his emotions very easily, and even less so based on the ordeal he'd just experienced. He'd spent much of the past in Haven - primarily by choice. He had seen a lot of the outside world, and what he saw, he didn't like. In Haven, and the other colonies, James had created a small society free of the encumbrances of the outside world. Free of the corruption of money. Free of the need to stand on the shoulders of others.

The people he had chosen to work with him and to lead the other colonies - they thought like he did. All the colonists had their own skills. Some were accomplished scientists; others were of the arts. Some were dangerous killers, and trained soldiers. Together, they formed the perfect society. No one wanted to use, abuse or corrupt their brothers and sisters. None of them wanted to hurt the plan.

James didn't have that same level of confidence in Jacob. In fact, he knew he didn't trust him in the slightest. Those thoughts of mistrust were coupled with the fact that Jacob was such a ruthless killer.

James had always been reluctant to use the man. His techniques were questionable, and his complete lack of empathy was disturbing.

For that reason, Jacob couldn't be allowed to be part of the future. But, that was not a problem that needed to be solved right at that moment.

"Jacob will be rewarded as appropriate," James said, choosing his words carefully.

Caleb struggled, trying to free the hand ties that held him. They wouldn't budge, and Caleb started contemplating alternatives. His eyes panned the room. It was the first time he cursed their design. Such was the practicality of the design, the only unique aspects were in no way designed, or able to be used, for escape. He would need to divert James' and Jacob's attention, unwittingly taking the same tactic James had used minutes earlier. "I'm curious," Caleb began, trying to sound calm, "if you're so prepared, and your followers are so devoted, where are they? You'd think they'd do whatever they could, to ensure your safety."

James scoffed. "I know what you're trying to do, Captain, and it won't work. My people are not mindless drones. But they are disciplined enough not to listen to their emotions. I specifically ordered them not to return. When your cohorts set off the alarm, I imagine they thought there would be panic. I imagine you thought there would be chaos."

Caleb was silent, and it betrayed him, giving James the answer he wanted.

"The people here have doubtlessly begun moving to their safe zones, and are well away from the colony."

"Answer the question, Cook. Stop fucking around," Dunleavy said, finally finding his backbone.

"Very well," James responded, put off by Dunleavy's uncouth language. "As I was saying before Mr Dunleavy's... input... my people have been trained to get to their locations. What kind of leader would I be, if I told any of them that my safety over-rode theirs?"

The door behind Jacob swung open violently. Several men entered the room, led by a tall, dark-haired man. The dark-haired man ran up towards James, his weapon focused on Caleb.

"Is everything okay, sir?" the man asked.

"Yes it is," James replied. "Is everyone safely away?"

"Mostly, sir. I've ordered everyone to their evacuation points. Even if we aren't as fast as the practice drills, the colony should be evacuated soon.

"Good. Well done."

William looked at Caleb.

Caleb was busy scanning the room. He counted a dozen other people. The way they moved, they were obviously highly trained soldiers. He imagined there were a couple more outside the room.

Upon realising Dunleavy was one of the prisoners, William understood his plan to keep the colony safe had failed. "I guess it wasn't you who started the evacuation."

"No, William, it was not," James said, seemingly blaming William, "But the situation can be rectified."

"And... how is that?" William asked.

"You must stop the colony from imploding."

"Imploding, sir?"

"Yes, William. Once the countdown ends, the colony will implode. A further measure to ensure the Source could not be exploited by others."

"Very well. How do I stop it?"

"Go to the Control Room. Enter my security code."

"Word or numbers, sir."

"A word... *Endeavour*"

"I won't let you down, sir," William said enthusiastically.

"Make sure you don't," James said firmly.

William nodded, and turned to leave the room. As he began made his way to the door, James called him back. "Wait. Give me your sidearm."

William handed over his pistol, unsure of what James intended. James walked over and took possession of the weapon. He then made his way back over to where Caleb and Dunleavy were sitting. "There comes a time in every man's life, trust me, I've seen it," James began pontificating, looking at William's weapon and providing no eye contact to either Caleb or Dunleavy, "There comes a time when a man realises that he has outlived his usefulness. He realises that he is no longer as powerful or suitable or necessary as he once was. That time can stretch out for a decade, or happen in a fleeting second. Now, the time has come for you."

Caleb and Dunleavy looked at each other, wondering who James was talking to.

James continued, still not making eye-contact. "Now, you are no longer required or wanted." James raised the weapon at Caleb.

Then, without warning, he quickly spun around, and pointed the gun at Jacob. "You will not live forever. We will *not* see you in the next life."

Jacob reacted. Still holding his gun, he lifted his arm. All his efforts were in vain.

As Jacob's arm reached his hip, the bullet flew from the barrel of William's gun. It sped through the air, headed towards Jacob's eye. With an explosion, Jacob's eye popped, a mixture of blood, aqueous humour and skull fragments flying out from the back of his head. The once strong, arrogant and devious sociopath's body slumped to the floor, never to kill again.

The room remained silent, the only noise the echo of the gunshot.

James, the only relaxed person in the room, turned and walked over to William. He handed him the weapon. "Now... go." James said calmly.

Without a word, William ran out the door. He didn't want to be on the receiving end of James' wrath.

Chapter Fifty-Five

William ran out of the room, turning right down the corridor. Had he turned the other way, he would have seen Darcy and Casey, waiting around the corner.

They were watching the tablet closely, unsure of what was happening in the room. When there was three previously, there was now more than a half dozen people in the room, and two outside.

While watching the screen, they heard a gunshot. Darcy's heart sank, her thoughts of Caleb. If he was in the room, with that many opposition soldiers, he had no chance of survival.

Casey refocused her. "Look, I know the Cap. He'll be fine," Casey said. "We've still got *surprise* working for us."

Casey's words didn't improve Darcy's mood. Still, she tried to maintain her focus.

Casey turned to Darcy. "Are you ready?"

She took in a deep breath, trying to push the thought of Caleb from her mind. She knew he might be dead, but she had to try control her emotions.

She nodded to Casey, readying herself.

Casey turned back to the screen. While pointing at the screen, Casey laid out his plan to Darcy. It involved Casey doing most of the work, taking out the two guards outside the room. Once that was done, it was a case of each of them taking out one half of the room.

That would mean Darcy would have to shoot at *least* two more people that day. But, with Caleb's life possibly in danger, she knew she had no real alternative.

Casey moved quickly, and Darcy followed. As he moved, Casey raised his weapon. He fired only two bullets. For two targets, his ammunition use was more than sufficient.

The door was left unguarded, but Casey knew that the sound of the men hitting the floor would be more than enough to gain the attention of those inside. Again, Casey moved forward quickly. As he was the better trained, he ran to the opposite side of the open door. Darcy approached the closer side.

"What's going on out there?" a voice emanated from the room.

Neither Casey nor Darcy thought to respond. Darcy had her weapon ready, as did Casey. They were both standing on opposite sides of the door, their backs to the wall. Darcy's left side was next to the opening, and Casey's right. Casey looked at Darcy, and raised his hand; his middle, ring and pinkie fingers extended. He started to count down. The middle finger went down, then the ring. As soon as the pinkie finger fell, Casey spun to his right. As he turned, Darcy followed suit. She swung to her left.

The room was much smaller than she'd anticipated. Without close inspection, she saw two men in her line of sight. As they turned in her direction, they lifted their weapons. Without hesitation, Darcy fired. Without the same precision training, she didn't hit her target on the first try. After several shots, the first armed soldier was struck, and fell to the ground. From her vantage point, Darcy was not sure if the wound was mortal. And she didn't have time to think.

As she moved her aim to the second target, they moved.

Unfortunately, they had moved into Casey's line of sight. With his primary targets taken down with a flurry of bullets, Casey was able to take care of Darcy's without a problem. The bullets flew from his weapon, shredding the soldier's clothes, turning the black façade red, such was the impact of the shots. With the immediate dangers nullified, Casey walked into the room.

Darcy was close behind.

As they entered, Darcy's attention immediately focused on the men in the chairs. While a little battered, both men looked to be alive. She saw

Caleb, and her relief was palpable. She had feared the worst, and her fears had been allayed. She smiled at her partner, and he returned her gaze.

Behind Caleb's chair, a man was crouched down. A man she didn't recognise.

"And who is this?" Casey asked, breaking the silence.

James was standing behind Caleb's chair. When the bullets started flying, James had swiftly dived behind the two imprisoned men, hoping he wouldn't be hit.

When Casey spoke, James realised he was in trouble. He analysed his options, of which there weren't many. He relented, placed his gun on the ground, and stood up with his hands raised.

"Are you okay, Cap?" Casey asked.

"I'm fine, Sergeant. Nice work," Caleb replied, "It would be good to be able to stand up though."

"You," Casey said, referring to James. "Untie them."

Darcy looked around the room and the bodies on the floor. All of the men were unrecognisable. Either they had masks covering their faces, or their faces had been shot away. "Where's Jacob? Wasn't he with you?" Darcy asked.

Caleb looked over to the right of the room, and motioned to the body closest to the wall.

As James continued to untie Caleb, Casey walked over to the Jacob's body. Showing the disdain he felt for the fallen assassin, Casey kicked the boot of the man, as though testing the tyres on a new car. "Yep, he's gone."

Darcy couldn't help herself. She was relieved. Jacob had always seemed like a threat, and now that threat was gone.

Chapter Fifty-Six

James finished untying Caleb, and had moved to Dunleavy. The huff coming from him was a result of the situation. Once again, he had found himself alone in his own colony.

His only hope was William, whom he had just sent away.

Caleb stood up, and turned toward the now-defenceless man. He had seen him kill Jacob without remorse, so not only was the man untying Dunleavy suffering a God-complex, but he was ruthless as well. Caleb knew that, left alive, James would be one of the biggest threats to humanity he had ever seen.

And he had to be stopped.

The main problem that Caleb was facing, was the dilemma of whether or not to keep him alive.

Caleb thought about his options as James finished untying Dunleavy.

"Cap," Casey spoke up, "Have we heard from the Lieutenant?"

"Not yet, Sergeant. No doubt she's fine, though," Caleb replied with confidence.

The conversation concerned James. He was sure that one of the four people with him had been the one to set off the alarm. Now it was apparent they were being assisted by someone else... this 'Lieutenant'.

"What's the plan, Caleb?" Darcy asked.

Caleb had been considering that very question. For the meantime, he figured it would be better to keep James alive. Being alive, Caleb knew James could be useful. Dead, and James would be nothing but a memory.

He also had the William problem to deal with.

"Darcy," Caleb said, turning his attention to Darcy. "You take Dunleavy and Casey. Find us a way to get out of here."

Darcy, who had become accustomed to Caleb sending her away, reluctantly nodded. "What about you?" she asked, "Where will you be?"

Caleb looked at her, trying to sound confident. "Just before you got here, this guy," he said, referring to James, "sent one of his men to stop the self-destruct that Murphy set off."

Darcy already knew what he was going to say.

"I'm going to stop him," Caleb continued.

"But," Darcy said. "What if you can't? You'll be stuck down here."

Caleb looked into her eyes. The love that emanated was combined with fear. Caleb did the only thing he could to quell that thought. He placed his arms around her, and pulled her tight. "I will come back" he said, unsure if he believed it.

Darcy knew that what he'd said was a promise he might not be able to keep, but she tried to be strong. Not for herself, but for Caleb. She knew her show of strength might help him focus. "You're damn right you will be…" she said, as she pulled tighter on what she thought may be her last hug from Caleb.

"Okay lovers, let's go" Casey said, trying to lighten the mood.

Darcy moved her head away from Caleb's chest and looked up at him. "You come back to me, okay?"

"Okay," Caleb said, smiling as he let her go.

Darcy took a few steps back, towards the door where Casey and Dunleavy were waiting. For the last few steps, she turned to face her companions.

"Babe…" Caleb called out.

Darcy turned around.

Caleb pointed at her, "You're the light in my dark".

Darcy smiled, then turned and jogged out of the room.

Caleb watched his partner leave. Not knowing if it would be the last time he saw her, he wanted to take in every last image. He watched her disappear behind the wall, followed by Dunleavy and Casey. Knowing Casey was there would make it easier for Caleb to cope.

He looked around the carnage of the room. It was only he and James left. He raised his weapon at James.

"Lead the way."

◆ ◆ ◆

William entered the room. His gun was drawn, although he was hoping he would not need to use it. He had no real reason to believe he would be confronted by a group, though he did anticipate *some* resistance.

As he entered the room, William realised that any movement may be difficult to track, due to the red lighting in the room, a result of the activated countdown. Apart from the lights, the room was, as always, strikingly similar to the others in the complex - the exception being its size. The room was easily the largest in the facility. Given he was only two hundred or so feet underground, the scale of the room was impressive.

The room housed the computer main-frame. Any and all commands that ran to and from Haven were routed through this large piece of machinery. Once designed, the builders knew it would not be easily concealed under the town. Therefore, they had to adjust the surrounding landscape. Over time, a hill was built around the room. Little by little, layers of dirt, soil and rock were brought in. Luckily, most of the people in the surrounding area were too occupied with their own lives, and the hill was built with little to no distraction or suspicion. As the Colonials were a patient people, the ten year wait just for the camouflage was insignificant.

William knew all of this, as he had heard similar stories many times. The patience of the Colonials was their greatest asset. It was also, as William saw it, a weakness. While patience was indeed a virtue, it had also led them to the point they were at now.

It seemed so long ago that James had told William, and a few select others, the true nature of the plan, and of his vision for the world. William had always believed in the plan, so much so that he believed their lack of earlier action had been folly. Had it been his decision, William would have set things in motion much sooner, thus helping move the plan forward in two distinct ways – the outsiders would be fewer in number, and their technology would be less of a threat.

As it was now being demonstrated, William may well have been correct.

Looking at the mainframe, which towered up into the centre of the artificial hill, William tried to make sense of it.

It was as he expected. A tall congregation of wires, metal supports and plastic cases, the machine stood a hundred feet tall and thirty feet wide. While there were bigger mainframes at the other colonies, this one had been the first - the prototype.

The machine's sleek and smooth façade hid the microchips and Ethernet cables with precision. This only assisted in ensuring the room have the same look as the others. Towards the base of the mainframe, about five feet from the floor, was a monitor. Not unlike others William had seen in the colony's other rooms, this monitor was displaying an ominous message.

More than fifteen minutes had passed since the countdown had begun.

While the number displayed was still counting down, William was relieved he still seemed to have plenty of time. He approached the base of the machine, his gun still drawn. There was only one entry point to the room, and no obvious places to hide.

Stepping forward, he continued to scan the room, turning to face the door at least once for each yard he walked.

Arriving at the screen, William noted the display. Along one side of the screen was a series of icons, not dissimilar to the ones found on a normal working PC.

Taking up the majority of the forty-two-inch screen was the countdown. Broken down to the millisecond, the numbers showed there was fourteen minutes and forty-three seconds until the complex would implode.

Implosion was James' preferred method of destruction of the colonies. He had felt that, should the need arise, the implosion would attract the least attention. The town situated above the complex, simplistic in its own design as a truck-stop for travelling people, was reinforced at its base with fifteen feet of high-density steel alloy. This would allow the colony to implode, and the surface town to remain untouched. To those on the surface it would feel like a small earthquake.

The town itself was relatively isolated, being at least thirty miles from the next civilised area. Apart from the low-level seismic activity, the force of the complex's destruction would go relatively unnoticed.

Unless you were standing inside it.

William appreciated the irony in his situation. For so long, he had wanted to be close enough to James to have him confide the secrets of the plan and the colony with him. Now that he knew, William found himself in arguably the most dangerous position he could possibly be in. Here he was, about to type in the code James had provided him.

Additionally, Willian was troubled by the knowledge that someone else might have tampered with the countdown. As far as William knew, there was only one person alive who could have set the countdown into motion – James. If one of Dunleavy's outsiders had managed to set it off themselves, there was no telling what impact the new code would have.

Regardless, William knew what he needed to do. The code had to be put in, as, frankly, it was the only option. William pressed one of the icons on the side of the screen.

The main interface changed, and requested a code be entered. Below the message, an alpha-numeric keyboard appeared. William carefully entered the code. Completely aware of James' history, and of his initial journey to Australia, William knew *Endeavour* was the name of the ship James had commanded.

It amused William that the name had turned out to mean so much more than was intended. He finished typing in the word, and pressed the *confirmation* button.

William gasped at the result. He normally didn't have any kind of penchant for overreaction, but on this occasion, the situation more than merited it.

The result of his attempt to stop the countdown had proved futile. In fact, as William had feared, the situation became even harder to resolve. The screen had gone black, seemingly switched off.

The only indication William had that the countdown was continuing came from the overhead lights in the room which were still flashing red.

Unfortunately for him, now that the screen had turned off, there was no way to track the remaining time of the countdown.

After pondering the futility of his situation, William made the decision to leave and make a dash for his evacuation point. With any luck, the countdown would continue on its previous time scale meaning he had ample time to escape the facility.

He had little choice other than to trust in this possibility. After all, the only other option was to remain, and risk being stuck in the implosion.

With his new-found immortality, it wasn't something he was willing to do. For too long, he had waited for the serum. He wouldn't waste the gift he'd been given.

Turning to run, his motion was interrupted by the sight of a man at the entry doors.

Though he was yet to learn the man's name, William knew he was someone to be feared. Not only was he an outsider, but he was also the man who had figured out a way to get into the base without detection.

It was apparent that James was there under duress. In the time since he'd been sent away, the man behind his master had not only broken free, but also made James bend to his will

William realised the man had a gun pointed at the back of James' head.

"Sir?" William said, cautiously.

"William," James replied, seeming to be quite relaxed, given the circumstances. "How did it go?" The tone of James' voice was hopeful rather than optimistic.

William wasn't sure how much to reveal.

If the man knew the system had locked him out, then he would have no need to keep either himself or James alive. He decided it best to conceal the information, given the circumstances. "All went well sir. The shut-down has been averted."

Caleb sensed the man was being less than truthful. Combined with the fact that the red lights were still flashing, Caleb was certain William was lying. "Bullshit," he announced, moving out from behind James.

William's facial expression gave away the truth.

"I'm betting you put in the code, and the system shut itself down," said Caleb, after glancing at the monitor.

James wrestled free, and turned to the man behind him.

"Right," James said loudly, fed up with being kept in the dark. He still couldn't understand how they had been so effective in their incursion. They'd been able to manipulate their plan so well, it was as though they had received inside information, "How the hell do you know *anything* about this place? I understand that you might have found out *some* information regarding the Colonials. And I realise that we were perhaps not as… efficient… in hiding ourselves as we could have been. But, I must say Captain, I'm at a loss to understand how you could possibly have done what you have. I am the only one who could have possibly set the timer to count down until this place implodes. There is no-one else who could have done this."

James' words resonated with Caleb. Indeed, he had always been impressed with Murphy's abilities. She always seemed to have a knack for understanding technology before he did.

While Caleb was a better strategist and leader, Murphy was simply better with technology. But, this was different. If what Cook was saying was true, then Murphy had performed above and beyond even *her* standards.

James was visibly angry. "Tell me, Captain! How did you know?" he shouted.

"Oh, James." A voice spoke from the corridor. "How quickly you have forgotten me."

A figure appeared from around the doorway, leading with the nose of a gun.

The figure had a feminine voice, the accent English – much in the same vein as James'. There was a certain plum to her voice when she spoke.

"Murphy?" Caleb said in disbelief.

" "Yes… and no," Murphy replied.

James was dumfounded. He couldn't seem to understand how the person in front of him could actually be there. His face grew visibly paler, as if he'd seen a ghost. "It— It can't be," he stammered.

"But indeed," Murphy continued, her English accent growing more pronounced, "it is me, James."

Caleb and William looked at each other briefly. Neither of them had the slightest idea of what was happening.

Caleb spoke up. "Murph? What's with the accent?"

Murphy continued to stare at James, revelling in the shock and surprise in his eyes. "Why don't you tell him?" she asked.

James shook his head in disbelief. "It can't be you."

Murphy raised the gun, aiming at James.

"Just tell them. Tell them who I am." She was desperate for James to reveal her identity – just the way she had planned it.

"If you are who I think you are," James began, "You are Charlotte. Charlotte Cook."

"Cook?" Caleb asked, his confusion increasing with each passing second.

"Yes, Captain," *Charlotte* said. "That is I." She turned her attention back to James. "Tell them *who* I am."

James, still trying to realise the implications of Charlotte's return took a minutes to respond.

"This… this is my daughter."

Chapter Fifty-Seven

Caleb was stunned into complete silence. Though taken aback, he was unsure if what he had heard was true. He looked over at Charlotte, trying to gain some kind of assurance that she hadn't been deceiving him.

Unfortunately for Caleb, such an assurance didn't come. When he looked into the eyes of his Lieutenant, he saw nothing but steely determination. It was a look he had seen in her eyes on many occasions, and usually it would serve as a source of comfort. On this occasion, it was anything but.

Time seemed to slow, as the events that had led them to that point took on a different meaning. While he had always though her intelligent, it was now clear how Charlotte had managed to understand the Colonial technology so quickly. While she was intelligent, she had prior knowledge of what they were up against.

She was one of them.

Caleb couldn't help but feel betrayed. His mind was a muddle of anger and disbelief. After all that had happened, particularly in the past few days, he was unsure of how he would ever be able to recover.

First, Matthew had deceived him, shooting down the plane at Seattle after convincing Caleb he was not a threat.

Then, Jacob had betrayed him. Though not unexpected, it had once again shown Caleb that his judgement was a little... *off.*

Now, with Charlotte revealing her true identity, Caleb found himself asking questions of himself that he'd never thought would need answering. It was a question of judgement, and three times in the past forty-eight hours, Caleb had been found wanting.

Fortunately for him, the thoughts were quickly replaced by more urgent matters.

"I... I..." James stuttered; his formerly calm, almost cocky demeanour replaced with sheer bewilderment. "It's impossible. You died. I saw you fall."

Charlotte scoffed. "Come now, James," she said, her weapon pointed towards James, "You always said that life and death had no meaning for us."

Charlotte began to chuckle, as though the weight of secretly being alive had been lifted, "And of course, when you pushed me, what was it you said?"

James was silent. He remembered the exact moment he had thought he killed her. And, he knew what he'd said.

Charlotte waited patiently, as though baiting him to say it again. When no response came, she spoke for him, "*See you in the next life*. That was it, right?"

James still remained silent.

Caleb was watching them, trying to ascertain what was happening. Despite her deception, it was clear that Charlotte was fighting the same cause as Caleb. However, her final plan was, as yet, unclear.

Charlotte, her weapon still aimed towards James, reached into her pocket. She pulled out what looked like a small box. Black and basic, the box resembled a garage door remote, with only one button.

"Can you guess what this is?" Charlotte asked James.

James stared at the box, but remained mute.

Caleb looked at the device. While he had no way of knowing what it was, he could hazard a guess. After all, if it had been Charlotte's goal to destroy the base and her father the whole time, the device was obviously something that would assist with that outcome.

Charlotte spoke, impatient at her father's refusal to answer. "I think you can guess. After all, I'm sure you remember that I helped you in the beginning. That I helped you design and build this god forsaken place..."

Charlotte was about to continue, when James interrupted, clearly rattled by her last statement. "*God forsaken?*" he said, fury filling his voice, "How dare you? You were with me, almost from the beginning. You know what we're doing is what the almighty would have wanted. How dare you stand there, about to destroy everything we have worked for? How dare you stand there and say that *God* has forsaken us?"

Charlotte moved towards her father, emotion urging her forward. As she stepped closer, her anger was replaced by sadness, and tears welled in her once confident eyes. "How dare *you*?" she responded. "So many people. You have killed so many people... all for your *cause*. All for your *'New Era'*."

"They were necessary. The world, Charlotte," James tried to calm his daughter and distract her. "The world has got to a point where we should... no... where we *must* intervene."

Charlotte stood no more than two yards from her father. She could hear the sincerity in his voice. "You're lying to us all," Charlotte said, her voice calming. "Don't try to tell me you're doing this for anyone but yourself." Charlotte exclaimed.

James considered his words carefully. "I *am* doing this for the betterment of the human race - for the betterment of the world."

Caleb could see where Charlotte's statements were heading, and he decided to remind them of his presence. "I hate to interrupt, Captain, or whatever title you've given yourself, but I'm guessing that you would be the leader in this *New Era*?"

James didn't need to respond.

Charlotte turned to Caleb when he spoke. After hearing his question, she nodded and smiled. She knew Caleb was a man of honour who could be trusted.

"You've decided that because we don't fit in with what *you* want, you're going to kill us," Caleb said. "And once we're all gone, then you take your place as de-facto leader of the world?" Caleb waited for a response, though he didn't really expect one.

He knew James was too canny to admit to his ultimate goal. "Not such a noble cause after all," Caleb remarked.

Charlotte turned to her father. "As you and I know, James. Once Haven is gone, there will be no more 'Source', which means you cannot create the serum. And, I'm guessing that not all the people you need have received the serum yet... probably the African and South American colonies. I'm guessing you need them, to instigate your plan."

James smiled, as though he knew something Caleb and Charlotte did not. "You two. You're such fools," James said.

Charlotte was surprised. It wasn't a response she'd expected.

"Do you really think that, after all this time, we haven't figured out a way to *synthesise* the serum? Do you really think that I would let my plan be threatened so... so *easily*? My dear daughter, you have grown foolish in your time away from us."

Charlotte responded with more than a little apprehension in her voice. "You're bluffing." she said.

"Trust me. All of your *success* here is for naught. Well may you kill me. Well may you destroy Haven and the colony that you so fervently worked on for so many years. But trust me, my dear... the New Era will begin."

Up to that point, William hadn't moved, such had been the shock of the revelation that Charlotte was still alive. It had been more than two decades since the accident which had taken her life.

Death, as was the nature of the Colonials, was not a common occurrence. Sure, they had had to deal with the death of outsiders, but to lose someone from the inside was so uncommon, it was almost unthinkable. Coupled with the fact that the person meeting their end was the daughter of the Governor himself, William could hardly believe it possible.

The fact that Charlotte Cook's death was an apparent accident had softened the delivery of the news, and allowed the colony to move on. But, in light of this information – and understanding that James had apparently been the cause of her death –William was questioning his dedication to his role model.

As Charlotte spoke, and the outsider assisted, William waited for the right moment to attack. The moment would be difficult to ascertain, as William feared that the man assisting Charlotte may prove to be the toughest opponent he'd ever faced. When he couldn't see an opening for his attack, William decided to create one.

He took a few steps forward, away from the large central computer. The movement had its intended effect, and distracted the man who'd been pointing his gun at James.

"Where do you think you're going?" he asked, turning the gun on William.

William looked straight back at him. "I would like to leave," he replied. It was a risk, as he was unsure how volatile the man was.

"Don't move, William," Charlotte said. "You're just as guilty of the atrocities James has perpetuated, as he is. You both deserve the same fate."

"If you press that button, we will all share the same fate," William replied coldly. He hid his fear behind a brash exterior.

"Oh, William. You've been hanging out with James for too long," Charlotte replied. "You both think that I care about my life. You're both so obsessed with immortality, with power. But you need to understand something," Charlotte said, ensuring she had their complete attention.

"What's that?" James asked, defiantly.

"Some of us don't want to live forever. In fact, some of us would rather die for a cause than live a long life for ourselves."

Caleb could see that Charlotte had no intention of leaving the base. Her final mission was to destroy the work of her father. A noble cause, but one that would leave the mission only partially complete.

Charlotte turned to Caleb, as though sensing his thoughts. "You'd better get going," she said.

Caleb didn't want to leave her behind. Despite what he'd just learned, a part of him still felt as if he needed to protect her. He wanted to help his lieutenant.

"Don't worry about me, Captain," she said. "We'll be fine." Charlotte did have the advantage. The gap between her and the others was sufficient for her to press the button without interruption.

"Why don't you come with me?" Caleb asked. "We could stop the rest of them together. God knows I could use your help."

Charlotte took a step back, her gun pointed at James, the control in the other hand.

"My place is here," she said defiantly.

Caleb realised he couldn't change her mind. He had to go, find Darcy and the others, and do whatever he could to stop the rest of the Colonials. After all, there was no telling what the news of the loss of their leader would cause them to do.

"Okay then," Caleb said, the moment catching up with him. "I guess this is goodbye."

Charlotte rolled her eyes. "Come on, Captain. Don't get soft on me now."

She briefly turned to wink at Caleb, her fondness for their friendship apparent.

It was all the time William needed. As he saw her head turn, and her body ever so slightly relax, William made his move. With the skill and speed he had learned from the years he had served the Colonials, William leapt towards Charlotte.

Before Caleb or Charlotte could react, William closed the gap, enough that he was able to strike her. The force of his quick punch had two effects. One, she immediately lost consciousness, the concussive blow shaking her brain enough to make her black-out. The second result was that the remote that Charlotte was carrying spilled from her left hand and fell to the floor. As the control fell, William grabbed Charlotte before she could do the same.

Caleb, who had partially turned to leave, moved as swiftly as he could. It was not enough, and by the time he had redrawn his weapon and aimed, William had a firm hold of Charlotte. He held the unconscious Lieutenant between himself and Caleb.

Caleb wasn't surprised by the tactic. From what he had learned of the Colonials, they would stop at nothing to get what they wanted. He now knew this meant using the prodigal daughter as a barrier.

This knowledge didn't deter Caleb from targeting William. It was more out of instinct than any real desire to shoot.

They were both seasoned soldiers, and they understood the situation immediately. In silence, they sized each other up.

William struggled with Charlotte's body, dealing with the awkward nature in which she fell into his arms. With some effort, he was able to thrust his left arm under her shoulder. From there, he reached across her chest, holding her full weight with one arm. While this caused him some discomfort, it also allowed him to free his right arm, the arm holding his gun. Under strain, William raised the weapon towards Caleb. He now had the advantage.

Caleb knew it.

It was only a matter of time before William fired. Caleb had to make a split-second decision. Did he fire at William, and risk hitting Charlotte? Did he shoot through her shoulder, hoping to take William out and leave her alive?

He found his mind cluttered with second-guesses and doubt. For the better part of the last few days, Caleb had misjudged situations.

Then, unexpectedly, a third option popped into his head. Initially, the thought merely complicated his thought process. But then he remembered what Darcy had said to him earlier in the diner, seemingly so long ago. *"You've been through some tough times, and you're still alive. I think your instincts are good enough."*

Without giving any indication of his actions, Caleb swung his weapon away from William, towards his right. Panning the room, he stopped on his new target – James.

William saw Caleb move. Caleb's arc towards his leader didn't come as a surprise, but it was enough to distract him.

So distracted, in fact, that he didn't notice Charlotte regaining consciousness. William loosened his grip on his captive as Charlotte began to struggle.

Not wanting to lose his advantage, William took it. While fighting off Charlotte, he tried to focus on his target. He needed to be quick, faster than the man could pull the trigger. With barely enough time to think, William lined up his weapon, and pulled the trigger.

The shot was loud enough to stun the four occupants of the room.

Being stunned wasn't Caleb's only problem. As he was about to fire on James, he realised Charlotte and William were struggling. He knew William would be forced to act. As the pair struggled, Caleb attempted to significantly shift his position, hoping to get out of the way of the bullet that would be heading in his direction. He didn't make it.

To Caleb's dismay, William's gun was loaded with armour piercing bullets. Not enough to shoot through a room, but more than enough to get through his vest.

The bullet pierced his skin, sending searing pain through his body. He'd been shot before, but no more than a graze.

This time was different. Caleb had moved to his right and away from the bullet causing his body to turn side-on to William – not enough to avoid the bullet, but far enough that, once the bullet entered his arm, and left on the other side, the only course it could follow was through his ribs.

Once there, the bullet had slowed sufficiently, and taken up place in his thorax.

As he hit the ground, he knew he was done for.

He was going to die.

As the images around him turned from light into a blurry-grey mess, Caleb heard Charlotte's voice.

He then heard a scream, and then a few thuds on the floor. Caleb was so blinded by the pain, he couldn't determine the location of the noises and their meaning.

Lying on the ground, his thoughts turned to Darcy. The thought he would never see her again was almost too much to bear.

Time seemingly stood still, and he tried to refocus his thoughts.

He tried to remember the happier times.

Unfortunately, the happier thoughts did not enter his mind, and he continued to lament the loss.

While pain overtook his body, and he felt his blood flow out, he was glad for the fact that he could see her face, and that she would be his last thought.

For the final few seconds, he held onto her image, his *light in the dark.*

The room turned from grey to black, and all thought left his body.

Caleb's limp and lifeless body lay motionless on the floor.

Chapter Fifty-Eight

"You've got to be kidding me?"

The words resonated from Casey's mouth. They were all thinking essentially the same thing. Only moments earlier, they had been in what was seemingly a technologically advanced base, aesthetically and practically well designed.

Now, the contrast between the locations couldn't have been more severe. The network of underground tunnels, each lined with its perfectly smooth walls, bore little resemblance to the town they were currently standing in.

Using one of the tablets found on the Kite, Darcy, Casey and Dunleavy had found a way out. After exiting the base, they'd found their way into a store. It wasn't what they'd expected as they climbed the steps.

With Casey taking 'point', they tentatively made their way up the steps, and out the hole in the store's back-room. The silence surrounding them was the most apparent thing. Darcy knew they couldn't linger, they were there for a specific purpose. They needed to find a way out of the Colony, and out of the town.

Walking out of the storeroom, with Casey in front, they began to realise they were, indeed, alone. The walk out of the store seemed to take a long time, such was the trepidation of their steps. Eventually, however, the trio made their way out, only to find even more emptiness. It was as though the entire town had been built, and no one had moved in.

"What the fuck is this?" said Dunleavy, struggling to catch his breath.

It was a question they were all asking themselves. The town was best described as a hamlet. From their vantage point, they felt they could see every aspect. Across the road was a motel, and further down what had to be the main road, was a few specialty stores. The only other physical buildings appeared to be houses.

"Where are all the people?" asked Casey. "Surely, someone lives here?"

Darcy suddenly realised what the town was. "Ahhh" she began. "This is no town. This is a façade."

"Façade?" asked Dunleavy, still puffing heavily. For an older man, he had done quite well, but the rigours of the last day were beginning to catch up with him.

"Yeah," Darcy responded. "That's what it is. Just something to throw people off. You can't have people going in and out of here without giving them somewhere to go. That would raise suspicions. No, this is a town that is protecting what's below. Plus, it doubles as a living area."

Casey, still attentive on what was going on around them, began to fidget. "Well, whatever this place is," he said, "we're exposed. Let's just do what we came to do."

Darcy concurred, and pulled out the tablet. She pressed a few buttons revealing a detailed outline of the town they were currently standing in.

Studying the map, she realised her first impressions had been slightly... off. The town actually stretched quite a bit further than she'd originally thought. There were several roads operating off the main road, and each had several buildings along them.

What she noticed most was the dots. As she zoomed out on the map, she saw all the red dots that indicated the colonials and their whereabouts. To her relief, every single one of them was moving away from the town. Some were headed north, some south – roughly half in each direction.

"Casey, check this out." She motioned the Sergeant to come closer.

Casey looked at the screen, and breathed a soft sigh of relief. "Where do you think they're headed?"

"Don't know," Darcy replied, "but whatever Murphy did, it scared them away from here."

Dunleavy approached them, taking the tablet from Darcy. After looking at the screen, he turned to them. "You know what this tells me? This tells me that whatever your girlfriend did, is really going to fuck this area up. Now, I don't know about you, but I'd rather not be here when that happens."

Darcy and Casey agreed.

They were in a precarious position.

Darcy, taking the tablet back from Dunleavy, examined the screen. Pressing a button on the screen, the red dots changed to the previous blue, indicating the vehicles on site. What Darcy saw significantly reduced her levels of stress. While there were several blue dots moving away from the town, there were still a few left behind.

"Remind me what those are again?" Dunleavy asked, peering over Darcy's shoulder.

Darcy smiled. "Those are our way out. They're the SUV's."

Dunleavy, reassured by Darcy's smile, shifted position. "Well, what are we waiting for? Let's get out of here."

Darcy and Casey both looked at Dunleavy, shocked by what he'd just said. Dunleavy felt he understood their predicament better. "You guys seriously think Caleb and Murphy are gonna make it out of there alive. One – we have no fucking idea of how long we have before this whole goddam place blows. Second – we don't know how much farther into the facility they are. Third—"

Before he could continue, Darcy broke into his rant. "Dunleavy! Shut up!" Her tone caught the older man off-guard. "We're staying. This is not a debate. If you like, we can go get one of the 'Bats, but that's it. We stay until Caleb and Murphy join us."

Dunleavy's posture communicated his disagreement. He scoffed.

"I imagine you can't walk to a city from here. By my reckoning, Sydney's about two hundred miles," Casey said. "If you start going now, I reckon you'll make it in about a week."

Dunleavy threw his hands in the air. "Fuck you guys! Seriously, this place could go up at any minute! Did you see how those little red dots were scattering?"

Darcy turned away from Dunleavy, not wishing to continue the conversation further. Her mind was made up, and there was nothing he could say to change her mind. She looked at the screen again. It seemed as if there were a group of the 'Bats, located about a hundred yards north, along the main road.

"Follow me," she said, giving her first order.

Without hesitation, Casey followed. With much hesitation – more out of anger and dissent than anything else, Dunleavy eventually plodded behind in formation.

"Up ahead, there should be a 'Bat or two."

Casey moved to the front, the position he considered his duty. While it did serve the purpose of him fulfilling the orders of his Captain, it also gave him focus. If he didn't have such focus, he knew his thoughts would begin to dwell on Murphy.

Darcy had no objection to this. Despite the fact that she'd killed a few people in the last couple of days, she had no desire to kill any more. Added to the fact that she still had limited ability to fight, she was happy to lead from behind.

"Which building, Darc?" Casey asked, observing the town along the top of his gun, raising the sights at any potential target.

Darcy closely examined the screen to ascertain their target building.

"There," she said, pointing to a house-like building, approximately seventy yards ahead.

Casey looked in the direction she pointed.

The trio, led by the Sergeant, took several more steps towards the building. As they approached, Casey kept watch. As far as he could tell, there was no movement in the town. Not wanting to take any chances, Casey stopped them short.

"What is it?" Darcy asked, seeing Casey's hand extend towards her.

"Let's just have a look at that." Casey reached for the tablet. He pressed the previous button, to show how many people were still in the vicinity.

After a second, the screen changed. Where the blue dots had been, had now been replaced by half a dozen red dots. There were people inside the building.

"Well, shit," he exclaimed. "Looks like this will be a bit trickier than we'd hoped."

Chapter Fifty-Nine

Without missing a beat, Casey darted towards the wall of the building, and Darcy and Dunleavy followed suit. Darcy ended up next to Casey, directly to his left. Dunleavy waddled up to Darcy's left as well.

The garage was no more interesting than a typical mechanic's workshop. Blue in colour, the one story facility had enough height to facilitate two car hoists, and enough width to fit three SUV's through the large, open garage door.

Casey stood silently, looking down the wall to the open garage bay doors. He handed the tablet back to Darcy, having justified his previous caution. There were three Colonials waiting inside the garage.

"What are they waiting for?" whispered Dunleavy. "I thought they'd all left?"

Darcy pondered the question. "I imagine they're waiting for the guy that Caleb's with. He's their leader, after all."

Dunleavy shrugged his annoyance.

Darcy, not interested in the old man's emotional state, turned to Casey. "What now?"

Casey smiled. "No problem," he said. "Piece of cake." Darcy noticed in his voice a reluctance to relay the true nature of what he was feeling. She decided not to press him on it. So far that day, he had been reliable, and there was no reason for her to change her belief in his abilities.

From the tablet, Darcy could see that there were at least three Colonials in the garage. What she couldn't see was exactly how they were positioned in relation to the fixtures of the room. All the screen showed was the dimensions of the room, the fact there was several 'Bats and the aforementioned Colonials.

Casey, much more adept at combat, began to brief the other two. "Okay, so we're gonna hope they aren't expecting us…"

Dunleavy obviously felt compelled to interrupt. "Wait… we're actually going in there? Are you fucking crazy?" he whispered angrily.

Casey looked at him, steel in his eyes. "What do you suggest? There are no other vehicles that we can see, and we need to have transport. If we don't, there's nothing stopping them coming after us in those vehicles, and on foot. To use your vernacular, we would be fucked."

"Doesn't mean we have to go in there and try to take them down."

"What do you suggest then?" Darcy interjected.

Dunleavy tried to think, but an alternative was not readily apparent. He confirmed his lack of ideas with silence.

"Fine then," Darcy said, and turned her attention back to Casey.

He needed no further coaxing. "As I was saying, they're probably not expecting us. There's only one place we can attack them from. Well… at least to keep the surprise up." Casey motioned to the large open door on the left of the building before he continued. "We're going to take it slowly. Stay close. When we get to the door, I'm going to get to the other side. You two stay on this side of the opening. Dunleavy, you take the tablet." Darcy handed it to Dunleavy. "You're our spotter. You need to tell us which direction to shoot. Darcy, just fire where Dunleavy says. With any luck, we'll hit them early. As I said, I don't think they're expecting us, so we can take them by surprise."

Darcy nodded her head, and Dunleavy shook his.

Casey ignored the pessimism, and stepped towards the door. His gun raised, Casey took himself to his usual alert state. Only fifteen feet away from the door at the start, the trio made their way to the opening in little time. Casey turned back, "Ready?"

Darcy nodded, and breathed deeply.

Casey turned, and sprung forward, rolling three times across the precipice of the garage. In less than a second, he had made it across.

He stood up opposite Darcy, pointing his gun inside the garage. He stood for a moment, regaining his composure. "NOW!" he shouted.

He fired his weapon at the only target he could see, taking him down with a headshot.

Darcy swung around the corner. There were three 'Bats towards the back of the garage, two occupied by Colonials soldiers. The one Casey had taken down was slumped on the floor near the edge of the room.

Darcy raised her pistol, lining up one of the soldiers in the car. She fired, the resulting projectile bouncing off the window as though propelled by a force-field. Darcy tried again, with the same result. Fortunately, the startled soldier made the worst decision he could.

Instead of appreciating the protection the 'Bat provided, the soldier leapt from the vehicle, propelled by his own arrogance. As they had come to learn, the Colonials were not modest. They had a sense of bravado and superiority only shared by the likes of the Harlem Globetrotters. Only this situation wasn't rigged in their favour.

As soon as the soldier exited the vehicle, Casey snatched the opportunity. A hastily fired bullet split the frontal lobe of the soldier's skull, rendering his last action irrelevant.

By that time, the element of surprise had been lost. Dunleavy, focused on the tablet screen, began to panic. While he could see the red dots on the screen disappearing one at a time, there were still four soldiers remaining, and they were beginning to scatter. "Fuck," he exclaimed.

"Where are they, Mike?" Casey demanded, unable to see any of them.

"They're splitting off... towards the right."

Casey looked towards where Dunleavy had indicated. "I can't see them."

The soldiers had run for the main office of the garage, and they were making rapid progress. As soon as Dunleavy realised what was happening, he turned to his right. "They're coming out the other door." Dunleavy shouted.

The door to Dunleavy's right burst open, and three Colonials came out.

The blood drained from Dunleavy's face, the lead Colonial raising his weapon to the old man.

"Mike, get down" yelled Darcy.

Dunleavy did as he was told, barely ducking under the bullet as it whizzed past his head. To his surprise however, it was the Colonial that fell, shot down by Darcy.

The other two kept running towards the other side of the street. Darcy, having just taken out the lead gunman, was in no mood to chase them. She aimed her weapon as they fled, and fired an array of bullets. As she fired the men hit the floor, falling back towards her.

Perhaps I've hit them low, Darcy thought, as the gunmen's falls did not match their previous running momentum.

Dunleavy, still shaken from yet another near death experience, hunched on the ground over the tablet, hoping to see the remaining four dots vanish.

His wish was mostly answered, with three of the four disappearing. But, there was still one remaining.

Dunleavy turned to Darcy and signalled as such.

"Casey," Darcy yelled, no longer concerned by the possibility of alerting the Colonials, "One to go".

After a brief pause, a different voice replied. "I'm sure he's aware of that," the low baritone voice declared.

Darcy moved inside the garage, her gun drawn. She stepped slowly through the room, careful not to avert her eyes from any potential target.

As she rounded one of the 'Bats, it became apparent why Casey hadn't answered. He stood with his weapon still drawn, but his shoulders were slouched.

Behind Casey was a masked man, the last Colonial left in the garage. His weapon was pointed straight at the back of the Sergeant's head.

"Put your weapon down, or your comrade will die" he said, the slightest remnants of a Russian accent in his voice.

"Don't you dare, Darcy" ordered Casey, "Shoot the fucker."

The Russian held his weapon firmer, attempting to accentuate the power of his position.

Darcy, knowing that a bullet wouldn't be fast enough to stop the gunman from taking out Casey, paused.

The gunman repeated his threat. "I will shoot him if you do not drop your weapon."

Darcy figured there was no other option, and she began to lower her gun.

"Don't Darcy, he'll shoot you, then me, and then plug one into Dunleavy. Shoot him!" Casey urged.

The gunman saw his opportunity, and swung around to face Darcy, his gun bearing down her.

Then, something happened that none of them were expecting.

The ground began to shake violently…

Chapter Sixty

Such was the force of the ground moving, Darcy and the gunmen lost their balance. More importantly however, the surprise also broke their concentration.

It was more opportunity than Casey needed. Using the focus he'd learned through his years of experience, Casey swung around, faced his attacker, and fired. The hail of bullets was more than enough to shred the Russian's vital organs. As he lost his balance, he also lost his life, hitting the ground in a bloody mess.

Darcy, fell to the ground. She'd experienced earthquakes before, but this was different. The ground only shook momentarily, and it was over before she'd realised what was happening. As she regained her composure, the reality of what happened had sunk in. "Was that the implosion?" she asked Casey tentatively.

Casey feared the same thing, but knew they needed to move on. "Hard to tell right now," he said. "Let's keep going."

Following their original mission, Casey surveyed the room. As a result of the impact, the garage structure now seemed a lot more unstable, with some of the windows cracked. This was a good indication they needed to move.

"Get in that one," Casey ordered Dunleavy and Darcy. Casey pointed towards the 'Bat that was closest to the doors – a logical choice.

As Darcy attempted to open the door, there was no resistance. It appeared that the Colonials' arrogance was still reliable - the keys were still in the ignition.

"Everyone in?" Casey asked, confirming Dunleavy was in the back seat.

Not waiting for an answer, Casey drove through the open door.

The journey back to the store was a quick one, and less than ten seconds later, they were at the entry.

As they approached, Casey stopped the car.

"Are you insane?" said Dunleavy from the back. "We have to get the fuck out of here! Who knows if there'll be another earthquake, or implosion, or whatever the fuck that was."

Once again, Dunleavy's lack of testicular fortitude had become apparent. Casey turned to Darcy, as though to gauge her reaction. Darcy's face said everything he needed, and without her saying a word, Casey said, "We're gonna wait right here."

"For fuck's sake," a clearly annoyed Dunleavy retorted from the back seat.

"You're free to get to Sydney on your own," said Casey, "it's only about 200 miles that way." Casey pointed towards the front of the car. In truth, he had no idea where they were in relation to the nearest city, but he felt he needed to make a point.

Darcy assisted. "Mike. We're staying. Caleb and Murphy may still be—"

"Alive?" Dunleavy interrupted. "May still be alive? Are you fucking kidding me? They said they were going to destroy the base. An implosion, if I'm correct. Now, I'm sure that fucking tremor wasn't an earthquake, so it's pretty safe to say they succeeded. And since they're not here, I'm pretty sure they—"

"Don't you dare say it," It was Darcy's turn to interrupt. "We're not leaving. This is not an argument. This is not a debate."

Dunleavy, knowing his argument was falling on deaf ears, held his face in his palms.

◆ ◆ ◆

"What is going on, John?" Robert was clearly flustered as he stared at the image on the large screen in the Minot base, "We've received notification from Haven that they're evacuating. Now, I've just discovered that the lock-down protocol has been enforced. The god-damn place has imploded".

John was visibly upset. He too, had been monitoring the situation in Australia. "I'm not sure," John responded. "All was okay when I last spoke with James."

"Well, it's sure as hell *not* okay now!" Robert said. "I've tried to contact them, but haven't heard anything."

"Leave it with me," John responded, trying to make it appear as though he was in control.

"Jesus!" Robert exclaimed, as John's image left the screen.

The technicians around Robert shared his look of trepidation. None of them had any idea what was happening on the other side of the world.

As the Colonials normally compartmentalised their situation, this would generally not be a problem. Though, the implosion of the original colony was obviously enough to cause some concern.

"What are we going to do?" one of them asked Robert.

Robert turned to the technician, his exasperation clear. "We wait."

◆ ◆ ◆

Several minutes had passed since the ground shook, and Darcy feared the worst.

She thought back to the shooting at the garage. Something didn't feel right.

"Casey," she began, "Back at the garage, two of them were running away, but they didn't…"

"Didn't what?" asked Casey.

"I'm not sure, but they didn't *fall* right. I shot at them, and they doubled over backwards."

Casey pondered the question.

"Hard to say. Sometimes people just fall differently. What are you thinking?"

"Not sure. But if I had shot them, wouldn't they have fallen forwards?"

"Probably. Try not to overthink it though. You can see strange stuff in a fight."

Darcy was not convinced, but she turned her attention back to the store, hoping to see Caleb and Murphy emerge.

"Seriously, how long are we going to wait?" Dunleavy demanded.

Darcy didn't respond. Her thoughts dwelled on Caleb, and any exterior noise was easily muffled.

Casey had left the vehicle, his weapon raised. His training had taught him to be alert, even though the fighting seemed to be over. Suddenly, Casey was alerted to attention – a noise emanated from the store. Without hesitation, Casey moved into the building, motioning with a hand gesture for Darcy to remain in the vehicle.

Darcy did as she was told - Casey had earned her trust.

Casey moved smoothly – slow enough to not make a noise, but fast enough that he would quickly discover the source of the disturbance.

Darcy sat and waited, her hope fluctuating. *Maybe it was Caleb? Maybe he's has made it?* Darcy thought. It wasn't long before her questions were answered.

Though the dusty cloud of the doorway, Darcy could only make out fleeting images. As the figures made their way through the dust, Caleb's circumstances became more apparent.

Three figures exited the building, one at a time. Casey emerged first, and it was clear he was burdened with carrying someone. As he left the building, he swung around. Darcy's blood turned to ice.

Cradled between Casey and an as-yet-unknown third person, was Caleb. His body was flaccid, as though devoid of life. Darcy also noticed the large blood stain on his side.

Her worst fears had been realised, and all she could do was stare.

She didn't even realise whom the third person was, she was so transfixed on her dead love.

"Darcy!" Casey yelled, "we're going to leave!"

Darcy couldn't hear the Sergeant's screams. Her world, the world she had physically and mentally fought for over the past few days, the world she had lived in since high-school, had seemingly irrevocably changed.

Casey opened the back door, and slid Caleb's body into the vehicle. Buckling him up, Casey rounded the car to the driver's seat. Upon Casey taking his seat, Darcy came out of her trance. She realised Casey was there, and immediately turned to the back seat.

There she saw several things she hadn't been expecting.

First, *he* was there - the other man from the room with James.

Second, she saw Charlotte. The woman she knew as Murphy had her weapon firmly trained on the man. As Darcy turned to look at Caleb, Charlotte began to talk.

"Casey," she said. "Drive."

Without hesitation, Casey started the vehicle and drove away.

It suddenly struck Darcy why Casey was so calm. This situation, while it still had plenty of new technology and a whole new enemy, couldn't have been much worse than anything he'd seen before. The whole time they were trying to get the vehicle, shooting the Colonials, Darcy had been worried about Caleb. She was sure Casey had felt the same, though he'd never shown it. The training these people went through had served them well.

"Darcy," Charlotte barked from the back, "don't worry."

Darcy was surprised, and slightly angered by the comment. While she understood Charlotte and Casey had training and they could compartmentalise their emotions, Darcy had assumed Charlotte understood that she hadn't. "Jesus Christ," Darcy began, not known for her blasphemy, "I can get a little emotional can't I? Caleb's dead, after all."

Charlotte stared back at her. "No he's not. Not *yet*."

Chapter Sixty-One

Darcy didn't understand. It was only moments earlier when she'd seen Caleb's lifeless body. How could Charlotte suggest otherwise.

Now, the reality she was confronted with had changed, and hope began to return.

"What?" It was the only word she could muster.

Charlotte, her weapon and eyes still focused on William, spoke in a reassuring tone. "Trust me Darcy, he's gonna be okay."

Casey glanced at them through the mirror. Darcy could see he shared her confusion.

Charlotte, divulged her idea.

"Darcy..." she began, "you were in the lab, right? The one with the doctor?"

"How did you know that?" asked Darcy. As soon as she said it, she realised how irrelevant the question was. After all, there was a more pressing issue confronting them.

"Never mind that now," continued Charlotte. "Did you grab any of the vials?"

"A couple... Why?" Darcy had grabbed several, but until she knew exactly what was going on, she didn't wish to give too much information to anyone.

"Trust me," Charlotte said, her tone as comforting as she could make it. "Use one on the Captain."

Still uncertain, Darcy looked at Casey, probably the person she trusted second most next to Caleb. They'd been through a lot together since their arrival in Australia, so she looked to him for guidance.

Casey, in no mood for his usual jokes, turned to Darcy. "What choice do we have?"

Darcy could hear it in his voice. The *doubt*. It was clear he had the same questions that she did - the same questions about Charlotte.

They both knew this wasn't the time to address those thoughts. Darcy hunched forward and reached down into her pants pocket. She pulled out one of the vials and showed it to Charlotte.

"Excellent", said the Lieutenant from the back seat. "Give it to Mike."

"What the fuck do you want me to do with it?" Dunleavy responded, after being handed a vial by Darcy.

"Simple really," Charlotte said, "just jab it into Caleb's leg."

Darcy was still unsure. "Are you positive this will work?" she asked.

"I'm pretty sure," Charlotte replied. "One thing I do know – he'll definitely die if we don't. Do it, Mike!"

Dunleavy looked at Darcy, as though seeking permission. Darcy, after a short pause, nodded her approval.

Without further hesitation, Dunleavy thrust the contents of the vial into Caleb's leg. As it made contact, a slight hiss emanated from the device, a sign that it had opened, and the air was thrusting the fluid out.

After several seconds, Dunleavy withdrew the device.

"Now what?" asked Darcy.

"Now, we wait," replied Charlotte.

"Wait? Wait for what?" Dunleavy asked.

Charlotte had a quiet air of confidence about her. She knew what was supposed to happen.

"How long does it take?" Darcy asked.

Charlotte sat still, her gun still focused on William. "It depends on how far gone he is," she explained.

"C'mon Murphy," Darcy implored, still unaware of Charlottes true identity, "you're gonna have to give me more than that. What's going to happen? Is Caleb dead?"

Charlotte smiled. "Trust me, Darcy. It will all be okay."

"I'd like to trust you, Murphy. I really would. But, damn it, you have some explaining to do," said Darcy, her anger becoming apparent.

Charlotte, keeping her gun trained on William, responded. "Fine. What's bothering you?"

Darcy hardly knew where to begin. So she paused, turned away from the back seat and took in the view of the country side the 'Bat was now travelling through.

Casey was driving the 'Bat through the winding country roads. On any other day, Darcy would have been taken in by the beautiful surrounds she was witnessing. Australia was not like she'd expected. Far from being the 'driest country in the world', the lush surrounds reminded her of a trip she had taken to Oregon when she was a child. While the tree species were different, the green, natural environment was something to behold. Had it been in different circumstances, the passing trees would have provided Darcy with some respite. Regrettably for Darcy and her cohorts, this was not the case. Despite her surrounds, Darcy still was flooded with emotion. She took a deep breath. "Okay then," Darcy began, "Why is *he* with us?" She motioned towards William.

"Simple," Charlotte replied. "I needed help with Caleb, and William here will be able to help us." Charlotte pushed the gun into the back of William's head, causing obvious discomfort to the Englishman.

"What about the other one? The one in charge?" asked Darcy.

"He's still inside the colony," Charlotte replied, emotionless.

"So... he's dead?" asked Dunleavy.

"Must be," said Charlotte. "The building imploded.. Can't see how anyone could make it out of there."

Casey looked back in the mirror. Something about what Murphy had said disturbed him. Darcy was about to question the Sergeant, when Dunleavy spoke again. "So, why don't we just waste this fucker?" he said, referring to William.

Charlotte looked agitated. "We don't just *'waste fuckers'* Mike. He could be useful. From what I can tell, he's closer to Cook than most."

It was Dunleavy's turn to look agitated, but before he could speak, Darcy asked the obvious.

"Murphy, I gotta know… How do you know any of this? I mean, you seem to know everything about the place."

Casey divided his attention between the road ahead and the mirror. It was clear Darcy had asked a question that he wanted answered.

Charlotte's response wasn't what he wanted to hear. "I will explain everything, but not now. Right now, we have more pressing concerns."

"Like what?" Casey asked, his annoyance apparent.

"Babe, please," Charlotte pleaded sensing Casey's frustration. "I promise I will explain it all. Right now, we need to figure out our next move…"

Still believing they should trust Charlotte, Casey and Darcy fell momentarily silent. After a brief time, Casey spoke up. "So, have we won?" he asked no one in particular.

"Far from it," replied Charlotte, "We've got a lot of work to do."

"In that case," Darcy began, "Where do we start?"

"Sydney," replied Charlotte. "We make our way to Sydney."

Darcy turned around and faced the lieutenant. "Why Sydney?" she asked.

"Because that's where *they* are going."

Chapter Sixty-Two

"Well?" Robert asked. It had been some time since he'd spoken with John. He had feared the worst; that James, and the plan along with him, had passed.

John's face appeared on the monitor, as morose as Robert had ever seen it. "No further news, I'm afraid," said the portly Englishman.

Robert was less than satisfied with the report. But before he could speak, John continued. "I'm bringing in Zach," said John.

After a few moments, Zach's face appeared on the screen, the three colony leaders now able to collectively discuss their next move.

"Robert..." John began, with a confidence that had been missing from their last conversation. "Zach and I have spoken. We feel Haven may be lost."

"Lost?" enquired a nervous Robert, sharing none of the confidence his superior had.

"Yes..." said Zach. "Now, don't interrupt."

John looked satisfied with his friend's remark, and continued. "The colony has been lost. In these circumstances, James made it clear that we were to follow protocol."

Robert grew even more concerned. He hadn't heard of *any* protocol that would follow the loss of Haven.

"Robert, I believe the doctor is with you now?" Zach asked.

Robert, gaining a clearer understanding of what was expected, simply nodded in response.

"Good." Zach replied. "Send him here immediately."

Robert couldn't help himself, and interrupted. "Immediately?" he asked. "Can I assume it's time, then?"

Zach took a moment to respond. Realising he had no other option, he informed Robert about the protocol.

"Indeed it is," he replied. "James told us that, once we were enhanced by the serum, if anything happened to him—"

John interrupted. "Even if we *think* something has happened to him, we were to accelerate the plan."

Robert took a noticeable breath. He knew exactly what that meant. "In that case, I'll have him on the next flight," Robert said, referring to the doctor.

Zach took a moment before he continued. "Excellent. Tell him it's time."

Again Zach paused, as though to add some drama to the moment. He took a deep breath before he added, "It's time to release Nightfall."

Made in the USA
Charleston, SC
29 October 2016